Patient 002

A Novel

Floyd Skloot

All inquiries and permission requests should be addressed to the Publisher,
Rager Media, 1016 West Abbey, Medina, Ohio 44265.
First edition 2007

11   10   09   08   07   5   4   3   2   1

ISBN 978-0-9792091-6-1

Manufactured in the United States of America.
The paper used in this publication meets the minimum requirements of
American National Standard for Information Sciences—Permanence of
Paper for Printed Library Materials, ANSI z39.48—1984.∞

Cover image: Shutterstock # 371909
Design: Amy Freels

A version of this novel's first chapter appeared in *Shenandoah*.

I would like to thank the Oregon Arts Commission for a Literary Fellowship
during the composition of this novel. The support, encouragement and
inspiration I received from my wife Beverly Hallberg and from my daughter
Rebecca Skloot made the long process of writing *Patient 002* possible.

None of the characters or institutions appearing in this novel exist outside its
pages. *Patient 002* is entirely a work of fiction.

Patient 002

Other Books by Floyd Skloot

Novels

Pilgrim's Harbor
Summer Blue
The Open Door

Memoirs

The Night-Side
In the Shadow of Memory
A World of Light

Poetry

Music Appreciation
The Evening Light
The Fiddler's Trance
Approximately Paradise
The End of Dreams

For Beverly

Human experimentation for whatever purpose is always *also* a responsible, nonexperimental, definitive dealing with the subject himself. And not even the noblest purpose abrogates the obligations this involves.
—Hans Jonas, "Philosophical Reflections on Experimenting with Human Subjects"

Only in the breaking does life make sense.
—Leonard Kriegel, *Falling Into Life*

One

1.

There was a droning behind everything, a faint throb as if the autumn morning had a small engine inside it. None of the subjects noticed the sound.

They noticed the rain, bordering on sleet, and a peculiar smell in the Research Department's long hallway. Something fungal, or maybe an unappetizing but healthful dish being prepared in the gleaming kitchen. Cabbage and oat bran soup? They noticed full sheets of flip chart paper covering the glass in the room's doors. Later, patients with Parkinson's disease would be filmed as they tried to walk the hallway, so daylight needed to be blocked. They noticed the air was billowy warm but sliced through by a shaft of autumn chill. And they certainly noticed one another, everyone the subject of some medical experiment, a randomized drug study, an innovative therapy or treatment protocol.

Some had volunteered out of desperation, after all treatments for their illnesses were exhausted. A few had signed up out of boredom, thankful for a place they had to be and a time when they had to be there. Others were present because of simple benevolence, actually choosing to participate as subjects of medical research for the good of humanity; or out of faith in science; or to pay off an old family debt, the heroic efforts of a mild-mannered physician on that snowy night sixty-six years ago, back in 1924, when a grandfather's life was saved.

A young man clacked away at his laptop computer, suit jacket draped over the back of his chair, fluid dripping into his arm. He'd been coming to the Department for gamma globulin infusions once a month since he was fourteen, and the head nurse had watched him grow up as closely as any aunt. A teenaged girl in a wheelchair sat by the far windows gazing at the parking structure, her toes where they jutted from braces wriggling to some inner music. An emaciated man with eyeglasses the size of a physician's mirror was reading a newspaper he held against his nose.

None of them noticed the noise yet.

"I'm radioactive," said an old man in overalls. He backed away from the doors, arm extended like a traffic cop's, and shuffled around the card table. "I'm probably glowing right now, Vi, so don't come too close."

His wife gazed up from a jigsaw puzzle. The left lens of her eyeglasses was darkened, making her seem to wink at him. "You *are* glowing, Homer. Yes, indeed you are. Always glow when you act out." She looked back at Matisse's *Harmony in Red* half-finished on her card table, fitting a piece in place and then shaking her head slowly. "I'd say your face is about the color of this picture here. You ought to sit down, Fool."

Homer turned away from her, his smile bright enough to illuminate the edges of the room. He smoothed out the bib of his overalls, then rubbed a hand over his grayed burr, which was the same shade and length as his wife's hair. To the room at large he announced, "My cholesterol was 557 and her's was 594. Bad numbers, folks, serious numbers. A miracle we're still around."

He poked at the catheter in his right forearm, lifted it to look into the small opening, let it go again, and smoothed the tape that held it in place. Then he noticed a man in his forties curled and shifting position in a beige leather recliner near the steam radiator. Homer rotated to address him.

"Some doctor fresh out of school sent us up the hill here for all these free tests. Not a bad deal for a retired couple. Isn't that right young man?" When there was no answer from the man in the recliner, Homer took a few steps toward him and cocked his head. "So this morning they give us some nuclear active stuff, supposed to let them follow the food right on through our bodies or something."

"Leave it be, Homer. Come over to the table and help me with this top section."

He stared at the man in the recliner for a moment, willing him to open his eyes and respond. Maybe he was really asleep. Homer squinted. Little fella, too skinny, too much curly hair, and lookit: a little black stone in the lobe of his left ear. Wonder what that's all about, earring on a fella his age.

He started to turn away. "Vi don't glow, though. Just me." Homer stuck a finger into his ear and worked it around vigorously, as though trying to clean out some wax. He frowned. "We're both down under three hundred already."

"Homer."

He dropped his hand to his side. "I'm coming." But he didn't move. "What the hell's that racket, Vi?"

By now the sound was becoming annoying. It was still in the background, like a neighbor's chain saw at dawn on Saturday morning, but getting louder.

2.

Sam Kiehl stirred again in the recliner. Voices poured over him, painful as ice water over a body with fever. When the place was this crowded, they always put him over by the radiator. Down to a tee-shirt in November and he was burning up anyway. The hotter he got, the more he stuck to the recliner, which had been built at the state penitentiary in Salem and was about as comfortable as a bare gurney.

Sam dozed off, but held his elbow stiff along the armrest. That was no longer something he had to think about. He'd only had to bend it once with the needle embedded in his arm to master the art of keeping his elbow straight.

The sound continued to intensify, draping itself over the beeping of volumetric pumps and the chattering of Vi and Homer. A pair of women were watching *The Galloping Gourmet* as they ate low-fat breakfasts and waited for their blood draws. A bearded man with hearing aids in both ears hummed by the sink, where he was stacking and restacking alcohol preps and rolled-up rubber finger guards that looked like condoms for a toy poodle. An enormously obese man was squeezed into an armchair and talking to a researcher, loudly asserting that his daily diet for the last decade had consisted only of granola, turkey sandwiches without mayo, carrots, and unsalted pretzels.

Tracy Marsh, upright in the recliner next to Sam's, was talking about her husband again. Tracy was Sam's partner in the double-blind, placebo-controlled study of a drug called Zomalovir, his fellow guinea pig for the year the experiment was scheduled to last. She was slightly more than half his age, had slightly less than half his hair, and ate exactly what would keep her weight at one hundred pounds. Like Sam, Tracy might be receiving the drug that had shown promise in controlling the herpes virus that was ravaging their central nervous systems. Or receiving nothing more than salt water. But she responded to her infusions as though they contained a compound that forced her to talk nonstop.

Her husband was a dunderhead, she said over and over. Still doesn't believe she's really sick, and yet here she is in the clinical trials of the world-famous Zomalovir at the world-famous Cascade-Kennedy School of Medicine, for God's sake. The same trial Sam was in, and Wally certainly believed Sam was sick. What did he think, they let her into this thing because she was pretty?

Sam was fully awake now. He smiled at Tracy, then rolled his head toward the west windows. Two large sweet gum trees filled a horseshoe of space between wings that housed the Research Department on this side and the Emergency Department across the way. No longer cone-shaped, spreading out a little as most aging things around here did, these sweet gums still had it in them to turn brilliant every autumn. Sam had to admire them.

He knew the sound that was no longer in the background. Nearly every man Sam's age did, those who'd served in Vietnam, those who hadn't served but felt guilty or curious enough to see every movie and television show about it, those who continued to read about it more than two decades later, or dreamed about it whether they'd been there or not. Helicopter. The discordant thwapping music of his generation's war, *Concerto for Chopper and Downpour.*

Certain sounds never failed to trigger Sam's automatic, decades-old reactions: head down, eyes wide, voice raised, full-alert. He thought of Fourth of July fireworks, the music of The Doors, the noise of heavy drenching rains as his Southeast Asian soundtrack. Even birds gone suddenly quiet, a perilous non-noise. And, of course, helicopters.

The noise this morning made Sam remember a project he had done for the state police a few years ago. It was one of the last things he'd finished before getting sick, so this must have been two-and-a-half years ago. It was amazing to Sam how quickly the time had passed, especially since time moved so slowly for him now. The state police had wanted to know if rural taxpayers were offended by the cops buying a fleet of fancy helicopters. They also wanted to develop a positive publicity campaign about how the new equipment helped them investigate the sparsely populated miles between Portland and the rest of the state. Sell the country folks on how the new fleet helped them out, helped them even more than those Liberals up in Portland. Sam had done an extensive phone survey, then met with the superintendent at state police headquarters in Salem to discuss his final report. It had been early summer and hot in the Willamette Valley since April. Superintendent Clem Garnett's allergies were acting up.

"Forgive me, Sam," Garnett wheezed. He pointed to a chair. "Goddamn pollen count's in triple figures."

The man's nose was vermilion. He balled up a Kleenex, turned away from Sam and chucked it through the basketball hoop affixed to his trash can. "That's two."

"Keep working on that shot. The Trailblazers might be able to use you next season."

Garnett snorted. Then he had to reach for another Kleenex. "You know, the average pro basketball player makes more money in one season than I'll make in my entire career?" He turned back and put his elbows on the desk, leaning closer to Sam. "Can you imagine that?"

"Sure, but they work out twice a day and watch their diets."

"If I was their size, I'd make a million bucks too."

"Speaking of earnings: time is money, right Superintendent? You brought me down here to discuss my report."

"Call me Clem." He rubbed his nose. "Yeah, that's what I did, all right. You turned up some interesting things." He began thumbing through a copy of the report. "Here, now what's this, page eleven, about Vietnam?"

"People still connect copters with Nam, Clem. Especially when they hear the things. Whap-whap-whap. They inspire a visceral response. Fear."

"Great. So you're telling me I buy a bunch of new helicopters to give my citizens a sense of security, make them feel the cops are on the job, and I end up scaring the shit out of them?"

Sam nodded. "But I think you could play on that fear. Page thirteen. Like do a promotion on war themes: Oregon State Police declare war on drug traffic. War on illegal aliens, war on weirdos in the hills and desert, speeders, whatever."

Garnett smiled. He balled up the Kleenex and tried a hook shot. "That's two. OK, on page nineteen, what's this about cost? Explain to me how I say it's gonna keep our costs down if I buy nine million dollars worth of helicopters?"

"My guess is that people like the idea of cops in helicopters, gut-level. So they try to see it as improving efficiency. Or maybe they think you won't have to hire as many highway cops. I don't know for sure. Important thing is, you can play that up also. Talk about all the man-hours you save avoiding the traditional investigations, all the cops you don't have to hire because of the helicopters. How they intimidate bad guys. Serve as deterrents."

"Jesus."

"And here, Clem. Recommendation number four. Have an officer go into a couple elementary schools and talk to the kids. You land a helicopter on the baseball field, they all go home and tell their parents how great it was."

Garnett had taken Sam's ideas and put together a popular ad campaign. He'd invited Sam to test out the new helicopters by riding along for a day and was impressed to learn that Sam knew how to fly them. He'd hired Sam for another survey, after the election, to investigate what the typical taxpayer thought the differences were between state and local police, and to suggest ways to enhance their image. Sam never got to finish that project.

Now the helicopter's backwash bent the sweet gums, stripping their few remaining red and gold leaves, tossing rain. Sam had enough advance warning to stifle a typical flashback. Instead, he was ten-years old again, and back thirty-two years looking out the window of his home as a hurricane swept across the barrier island where he grew up. Can't win. He'd had no idea something alive could bend as far as those trees bent without snapping, could withstand such force and such damage. But a few had. He'd always wondered why them? Why not the others?

Everyone not hooked up to a machine walked over to the window, even the guy from the study on sleep deprivation with electrodes all over his scalp. They looked up at the medical evacuation helicopter drifting into view.

"Life flight," somebody hollered.

The helicopter hovered above the landing pad on the roof directly opposite them. There was a right way to listen to one of these things, Sam thought. Sort out rotor and motor sounds, air from exhaust and spray, so it was more than just this tsunami of noise.

"Wonder what happened," Homer said. When no one responded, he raised his voice. "What do you think happened?"

"Probably it was a drive-by shooting," answered one of the women who had left her breakfast and was now returning to it. On her way, she reached to turn up the television's volume and then had to holler in order to be heard. "You read about another one of those shootings every couple days. What's this world coming to?"

"Nah, I bet it was some hung over driver," said the man with Parkinson's. He took his left hand from his pants pocket and it cut figure-eights in the air as he tried to point toward the helicopter. "Some idiot jabbering on his cell phone, doing seventy-five, eighty on the Interstate trying to get to work three minutes early. Head halfway up his ass already, the accident just finished the job."

Homer ignored him. "Look, there's the doc. Tall guy in the white coat running like hell. Better keep his head down. That's what I call service."

"Sure. The doctor comes right out to greet you when there's almost nothing can be done to save your life. Costs the loved ones five thousand bucks a heartbeat. Meanwhile in this place, you could be dying slowly on the floor, poisoned by some crap they just shot into your veins, and there wouldn't be a doctor to be seen anywhere."

Homer looked at him, then back out the window and shook his head. "What's eating you anyway?"

"Nothing that wasn't eating me before I signed up for this experiment. My brain's turning to rock, just the same. Thought I was going to get a little help out of this business, but what I get instead are questions and needles and twenty billion maxigrams of aggravation. A nurse half my daughter's age sits there telling me I look great and don't hardly shake at all now. Who needs that?"

"They're doing wonders for me and Vi, I'll tell you the truth."

"Maybe so. But that's probably by sheer accident. What happens in here's about the drugs, some rich company's goddamn new product. It's not about people."

3.

With the helicopter shut down, and the patients all drifting away from the window, the lessened level of noise made Sam feel as though he'd fallen into a hole. He took off his glasses and closed his eyes again.

After about the halfway point of an infusion, Tracy Marsh no longer needed his attention in order to keep talking. He'd told her that he liked listening to her this way, and often he would rouse himself from a semi-sleep and find that he knew exactly what she was saying.

But sometimes he conked out. Here in the uncomfortable chair and tropical heat, with the murmur of voices and clatter of equipment, was one of the few places he seemed to have dreams, and somewhere he could occasionally find his way back to lost memories.

Now he was running through the parking lot of a suburban high school and down into the stadium. There was scattered cheering. Unintelligible words were coming from the loudspeaker. He entered the track and immediately felt hot summer wind gusting in his face. *Give me a break,* he thought. *How about a little wind at my back instead.*

There was just under a quarter mile to go. If he looked to the right, he would see the finish line banner, but long ago he'd disciplined himself not to do that. It was amazing how the finish line never seemed to get any closer if you watched it.

He felt strong and solidly connected from head to sole, as if he were dancing to an inner music. His breathing was under control, and his left hamstring hadn't knotted up this time. The image of Jessica Foster, his massage therapist, came into his mind. Jessica was a wonder worker, though her deep probing into that hamstring had made Sam flop around on her table like a trout on the floor of a rowboat. Not only had she eased the hamstring, she'd also explained to him about seeking help from outside himself before a race.

"From who?" he'd asked, lying face down on her massage table. "The Great God Nike?"

As usual, Jessica didn't answer at once. He lay there listening to her breathe, the air whistling as she inhaled through her nose for what seemed like a half-hour. His question floated above the massage table.

"Whom," Sam said, now that he'd had a moment to rehear his phrasing.

"The world is full of spirit-helpers, Sam" she'd said. "All you have to do is ask."

"I still don't get *whom* I'm supposed to ask."

She pressed deep into the knot behind his left thigh and he groaned. Such hand strength in a woman so slender. Her power never failed to amaze him. "You will," she whispered.

Sam didn't think any of the dozen runners ahead of him were in his age group. At least there wasn't anybody he recognized at the starting line, and among the strangers he saw no sinewy bald guys or obviously old hippies with their graying hair in long pony tails. No competition for a trophy as far as he could tell. So he did what he always did at times like this, turned wholly inward. Found his Inner Spirit-Helper.

Don't ease up. Less than a minute and the dance would be done.

"That's Sam Kiehl coming on the track," the announcer said, his words now clear. "Our first masters runner this morning."

Sam fought to stay calm. First masters! This was one of the hidden benefits of turning forty. All of a sudden, you got to be the youngest again, the spriest among the oldest. And sometimes the fastest.

"And that's Andrew Kiehl right behind him, folks. Looks like Sam's son is going to give the old man a run for his money. This could get interesting."

Suddenly the whole world seemed hushed. Maybe it was the effect of the wind in his ears as he ran through it. Sam could hear nothing except his own breathing and Andy's coming up steadily on his left shoulder. Normally, Andy would be a minute or so in front of him, but the young man had drifted away from running after high school and gained fifteen pounds. Andy had only been running again for six weeks. He wasn't in race shape yet. Sam knew this would probably be his last chance to beat his son.

As they moved into the final turn, Sam forced his mind forward, leaving everything that was behind him to Andy. The wind disappeared. He began reaching, trying to extend his stride, trying not to tighten up, and everything he wanted was there for him. He passed under the banner, still accelerating, and was amazed to find his arms raised overhead in joy, his exhausted legs stuttering in a quick victory jig.

In a moment, he felt Andy jogging beside him. At thirteen, his son had outgrown him, that high waist eventually coming nearly up to Sam's heart. They walked together onto the infield of the track and stopped, turning to face each other, heads bowed together, foreheads touching.

"Nice kick, Dad."

Sam couldn't speak. He reached out to touch his son's arm.

4.

Tracy Marsh loved spending these mornings in the hospital. Hated to admit it, even to herself, but it was so nice to be away from Wally. From the kids too, God forgive her. Who cares if it's sizzling hot in here, and she's drenched? She felt like she was on a mini-vacation to England or somewhere. Was it hot in England? Sitting here drinking her cup of tea with all these interesting people.

Sam Kiehl had introduced her to this cup-of-tea business. Urbal, not Herb-al. She didn't know tea could taste so soft. Sam thought the tea would help calm her down. Ha! Also thought it would be a good way for them to hydrate their systems and help the medicine run through their kidneys. The Zomalovir. Accent on the MAL, Sam says, and always winks. Because it sounds like a marshmallow cookie, Tracy thought.

But who knew if she was really getting the medicine? If either of them was getting it? Jeepers, that would be awful, coming up here all the time, going through all this, and neither one getting the real McDonald.

Random, they'd told her. Like dice or something. Luck of the draw.

She'd only gotten into the study in the first place because of Sam, and she felt she owed him her life. Nothing she wouldn't do for this man, though she'd only known him for a few months, tops. Look at him over there, half asleep, getting worse instead of better as this thing goes along.

When Tracy had first met Sam, she was so sick she couldn't get up from the couch after seeing the kids off to preschool or their aunt's house. She spent all day lying there, crying her eyes out, and Wally would come home and she'd be like some kind of grandma in the living room with a kitchen towel over her eyes, snoring. Wally was the one who came up with the idea of going to a self-help group, one of those clubs where everybody is as sick as you are and they go around the room complaining in turn. He actually took a Sunday off from watching football and drove her to the meeting in a hospital basement. Made her promise to stand up in front of everyone and tell them her story. Complete strangers! She nearly died. But then, she was already nearly dead anyway, so what the heck. Sam was there that day in the basement. Everybody lying on the floor or slouched in chairs, mumbling and coughing. Sam was easy to spot because he was quiet as all get-up. No, wait, all get-out, she remembered Wally telling her to say it correctly. Where was she? Right, the meeting, Sam sitting in the back, couldn't wait to leave, you could tell just by looking at him that it was his first and was going to be his last time at a group like this. She looked at him and smiled, then cleared her throat and launched into her story, trying not to whine like everyone else had. When she was done and checked her watch, holy heck, she'd been talking for almost fifty minutes and everyone except Sam seemed to be asleep.

She walked right up to him after the meeting and introduced herself. Didn't know where she got the nerve, never did stuff like that, guys were always thinking the wrong thing if you did, and then Sam said the words Tracy knew she would never forget. *I don't know if it'll help, but there's this Zomalovir study getting organized up at the medical school . . . .*

Now here they both were, fat needles stuck way up their arms, a liquid the color of baby's pee going into their veins, drinking tea out of ratty mugs, tea that was only one or two shades darker than what was going into their arms, and Tracy knew something that she couldn't even say out loud. The way her insides tingled. The way she didn't have to be on the couch anymore. Tracy knew it. She was getting the drug, sure thing, Bingo, lights out. Either that or she was nuts. It was the Pluto Effect or whatever, placebo, and she was nuts, never had been sick in the first place, and that would be enough to make her sick all over again. Well, at least she could take some Zomalovir then.

She couldn't help sneaking a look at Sam. Nothing, zero, zilch. Just sitting there, eyes closed, cute as a carnival ducky. She saw no sign of the tingle on him, which she was sure anyone could see on her if they looked closely enough. An aurora. Her whole self was throbbing, that's what it was. She could see it in herself every time she looked at the window, which was dark because of the clouds and the rain and gave back her face hovering out there like a ghost in the cold. A flickering ghost, jazzed-up by the tingle in its veins.

5.

Katrina McCabe came into the room just as Sam's infusion was finishing. She knew he hated when the alarm on his volumetric pump went off. The high-pitched, frenzied sound jacked his blood pressure up twenty points. Scattered and busy as she was, Kate always managed to reach him before the beeping started.

"How're my little rats this morning?" she said. Her smile took in both Sam and Tracy, enfolding them in a way that, for a few minutes, clearly separated them from all the other subjects in the room and their disparate research studies. She made them feel like patients again, people with names and faces.

Kate pulled up a ladder-backed chair and sat in front of him, taking Sam's hand in hers. He struggled to sit up straight.

"Doing OK, Patient 002?" she asked.

He nodded. "Got a little dozy there for a while, and I had this dream that wasn't really a dream, more like the video of a memory about running. Is it a dream if it's exactly what happened?"

"Technically, no. We call them *Fantasiae Testosteronicus* because it's only guys that have them and they're always about sports."

As she wrote his pulse and blood pressure numbers on her palm with a ballpoint pen, Sam looked up at the bottle that had just been emptied into his arm. It hung from its stand, the tube dangling into a lock at his elbow, the mysterious liquid reduced now to a few drops of mist against the plastic, all its secrets intact.

Kate removed the tube and then began on the lock. If staring could tell him whether this bottle contained Zomalovir or a placebo, Sam would certainly know by now. All he had to go on were hunches, strange sensations and changes in symptoms which might or might not be caused by whatever was in the bottle twice a week. He wasn't getting any better. It was still too soon to tell for sure, but he was always tired during the infusion, so maybe that meant something.

"I really don't know, Sam." As usual, Kate seemed able to read his mind. "The drug company doesn't tell us who's getting the drug because they know someone like me would reveal it in a flash." She stuck a thermometer in his mouth. "One look at those sad eyes of yours and the secret would just fly right out of me. It hurts to see you drift off like this into the Valley of Sam."

Kate's no-nonsense cap of short blond hair framed a smooth, elegant face that was round some days, oblong other days. She was large-boned but thin and had to work hard to disguise her beauty. Green eyes, which had seen more than you would ever show her, were set far apart and edged by a matched troika of laugh lines sharp enough to seem etched. Her pouting mouth burst into its joyously wide smile so suddenly that it made Sam blink whenever it happened. She wore long, flowing skirts that let her sit in her two favorite positions, knees flexed outward or legs drawn up under her, without worrying about feeling exposed. A simple wedding band and a name tag pinned cockeyed above a breast were her only ornamentations.

Conducting a clinical field trial was supposed to be easy duty for Kate after five years as a surgical nurse and three years in Infectious Diseases. It wasn't working out that way. She was uncomfortable with the routine and the impersonality. The fat black notebooks she lugged around with her, one for each of her fifteen subjects, made Kate feel like a harassed student again. Worst of all, the printed forms provided by PER, the drug company sponsoring the study, didn't allow her to ask the questions she knew needed asking, and they had no space to record the answers she was getting. Elements of the protocol weren't happening the way PER's training said they would: small glitches, reactions that hadn't been anticipated. No one thing so significant that it seemed disastrous, but together they made her uneasy. It was the same at the other three sites around the country, where the remainder of the study was being conducted. Dealing with PER was like dealing with the Internal Revenue Service, an impenetrable bureaucracy with rigid rules covering every human contingency. Kate couldn't wait for the study to be over.

The first time Sam had met her, Kate was seven months pregnant and smiling at him over a syringe of gamma globulin. That was nearly two years ago, after Doctor Martin Fong had finally diagnosed Sam's mysterious symptoms as relating to a viral attack, identified Human Herpes Virus VI as the probable agent and begun trying the few standard, mostly ineffective therapies.

It had taken Sam half a year to find out what was turning him into a shredded husk of himself, with a brain that seemed crosswired by Gracie Allen, six frustrating months of shuttling among specialists and undergoing endless diagnostic procedures and being told it was nothing, it was all in his head, it was maybe some kind of reactivation from a childhood vaccination, it was maybe an autoimmune thing, it was going around, a little rest and he'd be fine. Meanwhile, Sam couldn't work. He couldn't find his way back from the coffee shop to his office, couldn't operate the computer properly anymore, couldn't spell or do math. He couldn't run, couldn't climb, could barely lift the bedcovers off his body.

Then Fong, nodding, had hummed a vaguely familiar Brahms melody and flipped through the file while Sam rattled off his symptoms. At the end of the litany, Fong had said he'd seen several cases like this. Wasn't sure what to call it, but in every instance a previously healthy person had gone from flu-like symptoms to total collapse with deep neurological dysfunction in a matter of weeks. And in every instance, the patient had teemed with Herpes Six.

Fong promised to try everything in the puny arsenal of treatments that had been reported in the literature. But he was careful to make sure Sam knew that nothing had yet been proven to work.

"Look, at least you won't die from this. There hasn't been one fatality reported in the literature. Discounting suicides, of course."

Then he turned Sam over to Kate. She rubbed the syringe between her hands, like a child molding clay, and gestured toward the table.

"Warms the stuff up, Mr. Kiehl," she said. "Otherwise it feels like a shot of toothpaste in your ass. Speaking of which."

Sam pulled down his sweatpants and bent over the table. But he was smiling for the first time in a long time. Finally he was not only believed by a doctor, but he was also being treated with kindness by a nurse. Even if they weren't going to cure him, he began to understand that they might help him heal.

Seated before her now, Sam looked in Kate's eyes as she waited for his answer. He smiled. "I haven't gone into the Valley of Sam, Kate. You make it sound like I'm on the moon."

"Precisely."

"I'm just tired."

"Don't talk with that thing in your mouth. Don't smile, either."

Sam removed the thermometer and handed it to her. "I'm fine."

"Hey, this is me. I know what I know and it doesn't take a genius to detect you're not fine. Now tell me what you're feeling."

"This is the part I hate," said Tracy from beside them. "Sam's sure he's getting the placebo and here I am, breaking out in rashes, tingling like somebody's jabbing me everywhere with pins, and my joints have all stopped hurting. I'm a walking side-effect. Plus I'm getting better and he's not. My symptoms are almost all gone and it's just awful. I mean, I'm glad I'm feeling better, don't get me wrong, but I wouldn't even be in this study if it wasn't for Sam. I feel like I stole his cure, and that makes me feel bad. Even if I feel good. Does that make any sense?"

Tracy Marsh was twenty-three and looked twelve. She'd had two children by the time she was twenty and, till getting sick last year, had been an unbeatable racquetball player. She did nothing slowly. Her eyes were constantly moving, her hands were always working; every word zinged after the previous one and every gesture was quick as a kill shot. Sam had imagined she always tingled.

"That's how these field trials work, Trace," Kate said. She handed Sam a cup of orange juice. "Half the people get the drug and half the people get salt water. He had the same chance going in, and you all signed the same form saying you'd get the drug in the end if the stuff works. So you didn't steal anything from Sam. Besides, we don't know for sure that he's getting the placebo. Or that you're getting the drug."

"We do too." Tracy nearly dislodged her needle as she jerked herself upright. "Oh, Kate, I'm sorry to contradict you. But I know it like I knew when I was pregnant. And I don't need any tests to tell me."

Kate shook her head. She put an alcohol swab in the crook of Sam's elbow and gently bent his arm up. "Hold that tight so you don't keep bruising. And answer my question. What are you feeling?"

"Who the hell knows anymore?" He heard the tone in his voice and consciously calmed himself, taking a deep breath, closing his eyes. "When my throat hurts, I can't decide if that's a reaction to the drug, which I don't even know if I'm getting, or a flare-up of my symptoms, or nothing. Maybe it's a reaction to all the tests you're putting me through, the treadmills and the blood draws. Maybe it's all in my head. I mean, I get overjoyed when my muscles start twitching and my bones ache. It's crazy. I see Tracy itch and I start to itch." He stopped to calm himself again and was surprised to find that he was on the verge of tears. "I don't know what I'm feeling, Kate."

"Inside, Sam. What's going on inside?"

"That's what scares me the most. I'm hopeful. Just what I need. If being sick for two-and-a-half years has taught me anything, it's taught me to beware of hopefulness. I'm starting to sound like one of those twelve-steppers saying *one-day-at-a-time* to myself like a mantra. Ol' Even Kiehl. But here I am thinking I'm going to be cured, whether I'm getting the drug now or later. I can see what's happening to Tracy. The stuff works."

"Damn it, Sam, you don't know that. She could be getting better spontaneously. It could have nothing to do with what's dripping into her arm."

"Give me a break."

Kate put a strip of adhesive tape over the cotton ball in Sam's elbow and patted his forearm. "I keep telling you to shave that arm, my friend. All right, let's say she is getting the drug and it is helping her. Let me get this straight: you're worried because you're going to get the drug and get well too?"

"No, I'm worried because I feel hip. Hope, I mean; I feel hope. Too much can still go wrong." He struggled to rise from his chair. "Now get out of my way, I've always got to go pee after these things." Using his cane for leverage, he tottered upright and headed for the doors.

"How do you know you have to pee because of the infusion?" she called after him. "Frequency of urination is a common symptom of your illness."

The doors swooshed shut behind him, and Sam didn't know whether to laugh or be angry. He banged his elbow against the edge of the nurses' desk as he walked by. Oh hell, he thought, confusion is both a common symptom of the illness and a reaction to the drug, too.

Two

1.

The rain had stopped. Sam walked out of the Research Department and paused to rest under the sweet gum trees.

There was almost an hour before he and Tracy had to be in Fong's office for their monthly physical exams. Sam understood why Fong, expecting delays in the Research Department, wanted to keep the schedule loose, and it wasn't that Sam had anyplace else to go or any other appointments to keep. But it was still difficult to cope with killing time.

Before getting sick, Sam had several foolproof ways to handle a blank spot in his schedule. Since he usually ran at dawn, running was not an option during the workday. But if he had enough time he would go to his climbing club downtown, near the river. It had a great set of fake walls, sheer and slick like a nightmare of the worst ice-storm, with a few dandy tweakers and chicken heads on the advanced wall if you wanted to test yourself, and there were always a few other rock jocks to talk to. No mountain air, and the only running water was in the pipes overhead, but it was the best he could do with thirty free minutes. If time were even tighter, there was always the large finger-board Sam had mounted on his office wall in the spot where clients might have expected to see a Hopper print or a set of diplomas. Perfect for strengthening the hands and practicing his hangs. With its small wooden holds and rounded nothings shaped to resemble those on a real climb, the board could easily have been mistaken for a piece of post modern art. Or performance art, if Sam were caught hanging from it before a meeting got started. *Climbing the Walls, 1989.*

He'd given up flying, though. Hadn't sat in a helicopter cockpit since about 1980. Well, since January 14, 1980, to be exact, when it occurred to him that he might sleep better, might alter the composition of his dreams, if he didn't keep bathing his senses in helicopterness. So he went cold turkey, and started climbing the wall.

During the years when his consulting business was peaking, Sam's worst time was that gap between his clients' close-of-business at 5:00 and an evening meeting at 7:00 or 8:00. He had too much energy to sit in the office, didn't want alcohol before a meeting, and was never hungry that early. Andy was busy with his music and girlfriends, and Sam had no desire to go home. At first, he solved the problem of killing evening time by taking a class in jazz dance, something he'd always wanted to try, at a little studio near the river. Nice light workout, great to be moving, but the teacher seemed distracted, recalling better days. Then Sam tried modern dance, followed by a three-month experiment with ballet, which his body hated, and a six-month trial in ballroom dancing. He finally stopped the dancing, after Andy commented that it seemed a good way to meet women and Sam realized that it was, instead, just making him feel lonely. He began yoga lessons, but before he'd gone very far with it, had gotten sick.

Now, if he were home Sam would probably just be sitting in his recliner with a mystery novel face down on his lap, gazing at the cobwebs where the ceiling met the walls. So it made no sense for him to be this impatient. For a year now he had been patiently working on his patience, learning to accept rest as an aggressive form of treatment, learning to listen to classical music. Last week he'd gotten all the way through Schumann's *Cello Concerto in A-Minor,* the quintessential music of illness, without having to leaf through a magazine at the same time. He'd actually heard the cello's opening theme come back in the woodwinds near the end of the second movement, a feat that made him squirm with pleasure like a little boy.

Maybe Tracy would like to grab a snack with him in the hospital cafeteria. It was always fun to watch the physicians in their turquoise uniforms gobbling down midday meals of bacon and eggs. He squatted with his back against the tree and tried to forget he was getting impatient.

Sam didn't need any fancy biochemical analysis or Fong's examination to figure out that he was not getting better. Tracy was right. They were five months into the study, and if he had been getting the drug, he would be showing some side effects. He would be able to walk five blocks without having to rest and he'd have less pain by now. He would remember Andy's birthday, or his own phone number, and stop putting the newspaper in the oven instead of the recycling sack. He'd be able to sleep, balance the checkbook, avoid walking into walls.

What did he need this for? Come up here to the medical school two or three times a week, get poked and prodded, and end up feeling worse than ever, just for the privilege of having salt water dripped into his veins.

2.

"Research is not treatment," Fong had said, more than half a year ago at the pre-study meeting. All those enrolled had been gathered to hear the same presentation at the same time, to make sure everyone had a similar sense of what they were getting into. "For purposes of the study, you won't be patients anymore, you'll be subjects. And I'll be a scientist, not a doctor." He had smiled, but no one smiled back.

Sam recalled Fong's spiel clearly, though he couldn't remember the title or plot of that Robert De Niro movie he'd watched last night, about a Vietnam vet. The meeting had taken place just past noon on a day that was altogether too cool for early June. Fong had scheduled ninety minutes to explain the research study's rules. Sam could see that he could hardly endure it. Few eyes were lifted to meet Fong's as he scanned the room.

"Research is something you do for the product. Treatment is something you do for the patient."

Sitting in the front row, Sam tried to write down what Fong was saying, but it came out *Starch no treats.* He stared at the page. That can't be right. He took a deep breath, capped his pen, and bent over to check the microcassette recorder on the floor between his feet. It was a voice-activated model, so he didn't have to worry about whether he'd remembered to turn it on. But had he really put it down there at all? *At least I'll have the meeting Xeroxed,* he thought. *I mean recorded. I'll have it recorded. If I can remember to turn the damn tape over.*

Fong sat on a battered desk, legs dangling, rubber-soled shoes hammering the metal front when he got lost in what he was saying. He was short and lean, with hair cut so close it stuck up all around his head and gave him the appearance of perpetual alarm. Yet he always behaved calmly, with a soft, milky voice and a taut face that would, on rare occasions, shatter in vectors of laughter as though sudden humor destroyed him. If Sam looked closely, he could always detect the twitching in Fong's long fingers. Kate McCabe had told Sam that Fong relaxed by playing piano. *Someday,* he thought, *I'll have to ask him what piece he's playing when his fingers twitch.* The doctor's audience of two dozen slouched in their seats or leaned forward, heads supported by their palms. A few were still trying to take notes, a few others were doodling, but most looked comatose.

"The first studies in treating any disease have to be done against a placebo. I think you understand that. You're going to help us answer the question *is something better than nothing?* And to do that, half of you are going to get nothing."

No one laughed. No one grumbled. They just sat there like people watching a twelfth straight hour of television. Fong smiled at the exhausted faces. There was Alice Hardy, a gifted cellist he'd performed with a few times. Laurel Blackburn was married to a medical administrator who once tried to recruit Fong to his HMO. Hannah Lee Price taught at Reed College and wrote occasional opinion pieces on feminism and racism for the Portland newspaper. He knew these people as patients, had known several of them and their spouses for years. It would be hard for him to think of them as subjects. Of course, he knew it would be harder for them to think of him as a researcher. No matter what he said today, they were all expecting to be cured, it was that simple, though the most likely outcome was that a few of them might improve slightly over the course of the study and a few might get worse.

"Now we're hoping that those of you who receive what we call *active agent* will benefit from it, but that's almost considered a side-effect of the study. We're simply out to see what the benefits and risks of this agent are."

"What *are* the risks?" said a voice from the back.

Sam couldn't see who'd spoken, and it was clear that Fong couldn't either. "I'll get to that in a minute, all right? I want to go over the background stuff first."

"Can't hear you," the voice shouted.

Now Sam recognized Molly Carroll's distinct sound. She must be lying on the floor behind the chairs. Too exhausted to sit, but not too exhausted to boom out her questions. Sam had gotten to know Molly a year ago, when they both participated in a pilot program of occupational therapy at the medical school. He remembered her wearing the same hooded sweatshirt to every session, freshly cleaned but as frayed at the edges as Molly herself. She never smiled, and hated every moment. Molly somehow managed to complain in amplified surround-sound, and the group discussions at the end of each therapy session were enough to make Sam weep. God, he hoped Fong could talk her out of participating in the Zomalovir study. The doctor reached out as though adjusting a volume knob and raised his voice a little.

"How about now? All right? It's going to be nice if some people get better, and obviously we're hoping that's the case. But half of you are going to be receiving nothing more than salt water and you may not be better off than you are now."

Next to Fong, like a stack of test papers, were clean copies of Patient Consent Forms for Participation in Medical Research, which the sick people in his audience would sign before leaving. He knew and they knew that what got said today was a mere formality. There was little choice. No treatment existed for the illness that had left lesions on their brains and fired up their immune systems so that they kept churning out poisons like factories polluting their own bloodstreams. The subjects had read the forms at home and already made up their minds to participate. The meeting was being held because it was required by the research protocol. And it gave them a chance to ask questions they were too shy or too befuddled to ask in Fong's office.

He picked up a form. "Let me read the key parts to you. First: You are eligible to participate in this study because you are suffering from significant brain dysfunction, which has produced impairment in your ability to perform all but the least strenuous of daily activities. I guess you know that, huh?"

At least that got a couple of chuckles. The room they were in was so hidden among Cascade-Kennedy's labyrinthine corridors that Sam had gotten lost trying to find it. In the process, he appeared to have stumble through some kind of time warp because Fong's prepared remarks seemed to go on for hours, but were finished before Sam had heard what he'd come to hear. *Exactly when am I going to be better?* Finally, Fong opened the meeting to questions, and Sam forced his attention back to the present.

"Doctor Fong, I don't understand," said a woman holding a sleeping child in her lap. Sam knew it was Tracy Marsh by her high, squeaky voice. "I mean, if I don't feel something in a few weeks, I'm going to know I'm not on the drug. So why should I stay in the study if I think I'm just getting salt water?

"That's a very good question, Mrs. Marsh." Fong held up his right hand as though swearing a vow. With each point in response, he folded down one finger until he was left with just his pinky in the air like someone testing the direction of the wind. "One: there's the very positive effect of just being involved in one of these studies, coming in regularly to be checked over and cared for. And two: there's the placebo effect, sometimes as much as a 30 percent improvement that we can't account for. Three: you should stay in the study because it means you're actively involved in doing something about your disease. You're fighting back. Besides, you really can't be absolutely sure from what you're feeling whether you're on the drug or not. Four: you'll get the drug in the end, if the study shows that it's effective. But if you drop out, you won't."

"So what really happens at the end of the study, Marty?" There was a slow straightening of bodies as people looked around to identify the questioner. It had come too quickly, and a few people looked toward the ceiling as though the question might have been piped in. Besides, who would call him Marty? "Is the drug–excuse me, the agent–going to continue to be available or what?"

"Yeah," Fong said. "A second study is going to be backed up onto this one where everybody gets Zomalovir."

"So it won't just stop?" It was Molly Carroll again. Sam knew that patients like Molly drove Fong to consider giving up his clinical practice altogether and devoting himself entirely to research. He'd told Sam so during their last office visit, the closest Fong had ever come to making a joke.

"No, that's unethical. We can't do that."

He was asked for further clarification. How long would they get the drug? Would it continue to be provided for free? He was growing impatient. He picked up his sandwich, turned it over in his hands and put it back down.

"Because it's unethical to stop an effective drug prior to marketing, the open label phases of these tests go until the drug is licensed. That's the ethical thing to do. All I can tell you is we're advocating as researchers that those people receiving benefit from this drug should be continued on it and have the cost paid for by the company until it becomes licensed and available. I can't tell you that's what will happen, but it's what we're assuming."

"I find that real risky," Molly said. "Say I get the placebo for six months. The study's successful and everybody gets the drug for another six months, and then the study's over. . . ."

"No no no. That second study's open-ended. There is no determined end point on that."

"So who determines when it ends?"

"It ends when the FDA approves the drug and it becomes licensed."

"And there won't be any charge during that time?"

"Right."

He looked at his watch. It wasn't difficult to read his mind. *How can it not be 1:00?*

3.

Above all else, Doctor Martin Fong hated ambiguity. That's why jazz never appealed to him and classical music did. Why Bach and not, say, Debussy. He wouldn't call himself rigid, certainly not compulsive, but he did appreciate clarity, and elegance of structure, and what's wrong with that?

Now he sat at his desk, fingering an imaginary keyboard, refusing to think about seeing Sam Kiehl and Tracy Marsh. Their appointment was still an hour away. If there was one thing that drove Fong crazy about clinical practice, it was patients he couldn't help. Help? He couldn't even give their illness an official name. Yet here he was, directing a research project that made him examine and listen to them anyway. Remain neutral about their progress or lack of progress, and help them maintain their faith in him, their faith in this Zomalovir, and, more troubling as the study went on, their faith in PER.

Their illness was just a catalogue of signs and symptoms. So technically it was not even an illness, it was a syndrome. But Fong had seen enough to know it was real, it was viral, and was devastating. It was also spreading fast, based on the cases that kept showing up in his clinic.

Hepatitis Fong could work with, even Hep C. HIV he could work with. More and more that was a chronic condition now, no longer routinely fatal. He never really minded working with the early AIDS patients anyway, even when the outcome was clear, because he could do things for them, could treat their infections and predict their course and ease their way.

Not this crowd, though. He had nothing for them, and they all came to see him with their desperate eyes and their terror. Then along came PER and Zomalovir, and Fong realized it was time for him to leave clinical practice for a while. Now he was coming to believe it was time to leave research too, at least research on patients. Take a break. Leave limbo land for those colleagues who had more tolerance for it. He could write a book. Certainly he'd seen enough for that. What about administration? Or a run for political office? The current Governor started out as an emergency room doc.

Now Fong heard a few notes, the hint of a tune, floating just out of reach. He grew still, welcoming it, letting everything else go, until he heard the way the notes began to connect, a fragment of something. Was this what it was like for Vivaldi? For his beloved Bach? Was this how it worked? He liked to think of himself as being at his most Martin when he was following the logic of melody. Maybe he could quit medicine altogether and join the symphony orchestra, or get the chamber group he played with to be more serious about performing again. Compose.

That's right. And the first task he had before him was to compose himself.

4.

Tracy emerged from the Research Department and came toward Sam. He liked to watch Tracy walk. Arms pumping furiously, her lithe little body fully committed to speed, eyes riveted ahead as though sizing up the forecourt, she hurtled headlong and had a lot of trouble changing direction. She drove the same way. Since Sam couldn't drive, he appreciated Tracy chauffeuring him through the study, but he couldn't bear to watch the road while she was behind the wheel.

Before she reached Sam's tree, she began talking, continuing out loud a conversation she had been having with herself. She'd put on fresh eye shadow but was unconsciously wiping it off as she walked. The sockets were blackening as though her thoughts were bruising them. "Should I get a divorce?" she asked.

"What are you talking about?"

Tracy walked past the tree without pausing and headed toward the building that housed Fong's office. She went on talking, barely noticing that Sam wasn't beside her. "I mean it. Maybe the time has come. If Wally doesn't believe in me, he can't really love me, right? If a couple isn't in love and they stay together, it poisons the kids. Everybody knows that. Sam, you're the poll-taker, you know how people think, tell me what to do."

Sam pushed away from the tree and moved after her. "What I did was opinion research, Trace. Conducting polls was only part of how we collected our data. And I don't remember ever doing a project on the factors that influenced divorce. Would you slow down?"

Tracy spun around and glared at him. "Well, maybe you should have. Maybe you could've written a book about it and gone on *Oprah.* Then I would know a famous person."

"How about some tea?" Sam said, finally catching up to her. "Doesn't tea sound nice? You had licorice spice last time, I think, so you're up to mellow mint for today. We've got almost an hour to kill."

"Tea. Who drinks tea? Tell me that."

"We do. After every infusion, because we decided it helps your body metabolize the drug."

"I'm talking about divorce! Will your tea help me metabolize that?" Tracy looked away. She hated talking like this to Sam, but she couldn't help herself. She was remembering the last time Wally had volunteered to take care of the kids while she had her infusion. Two months ago, her birthday, and this favor of Wally's was supposed to be her big gift. So she called her sister and called the preschool, wrote down what everybody liked to eat for lunch, who napped where and when. She made the kids put away their toys so they could find something to play with while their Daddy was in charge, and she made them pick out the clothes they would wear, and she took her pager, and she was so nervous throughout the entire infusion that she had heart palpitations and was afraid Kate would tell Doctor Fong and they would throw her out of the study.

Of course, Wally was available to take care of the kids because he was out of work again, and had been for a month though he hadn't once volunteered to help cut expenses by being a real damn father, pardon me, and watching his own kids during the few hours Tracy had to be away. Trying to get better so she could watch the kids all the time instead of only ninety-nine percent of the time.

So Tracy drove off and picked Sam up, and swore she could hear the screaming and crying all the way across the river at the hospital. When she got home, the kids were lying on the living room floor watching television, their faces unrecognizable under a coating of lunch and dirt and something that looked to Tracy exactly like tar. Wally was nowhere to be seen.

"Where's Daddy?" she asked her older boy, Georgie.

Georgie rolled over and looked up at Tracy by arching his neck, his upside-down grin turning into a huge frown. He pointed upstairs and rolled back to face the screen. "Taking a nap."

Tracy put her things down, picked up some of the mess in the kitchen, and went upstairs. The bathroom floor and toilet looked like a shooting gallery where the weapon of choice was urine. There were hand prints all over the mirror and whoever showered hadn't closed the curtain all the way. She washed her hands and face, then went to the bedroom, where the door was shut.

Inside, she found Wally lying under the covers with a silly grin, pretending to be asleep. She saw the pile of his clothes and underwear on the floor, so she could guess what he was grinning about. This was his idea of being romantic. She shut the door behind her and walked toward him.

He asked no questions about how she felt. Nothing about how the infusion went. Wally simply flipped back the covers, pointed at his erection and said "Payback time."

5.

"Popcorn headaches?" Doctor Martin Fong asked. He stopped probing Sam's neck and moved down around his abdomen, looking out the window while he worked.

"That's what it feels like," Sam said. "Little explosions, like pop-corn going off inside my head, and it can last for hours at a time."

"Interesting." Fong returned to his chair and made a few notes in the file. "What are you taking for them, aspirin?"

"Nice try. You know I can't make any dedications during the course of the study. Goddamn it, I mean I can't take any medications."

Fong looked down and smiled. "Notice any change in your balance?"

"I was going to mention that. When I squat down in a book-store to look at the bottom shelves, or bend to get a frying pan out from under the oven, then stand up, I feel like I'm going to faint."

"Happens to me all the time," Fong said, continuing to write. "Squat, it reduces blood flow to the brain. Stand and the blood rushes back. We'll keep an eye on it, see if it has anything to do with neurally mediated hypotension, but I wouldn't worry about it, Sam. A headache isn't one of the side effects we've seen from the drug, but we'll send you to a neurologist if this persists."

"What's that?"

Fong looked at Sam, then looked down at his own hands on the desk. "What's what? This is called a pen."

"Neurologically meditated hypo something."

"Neurally mediated hypotension means your brain isn't regulat-ing blood pressure in the normal way."

"You think that's what's going on with me?"

Fong shrugged. "We'll watch it, OK?"

Sam closed his eyes, listening to Fong scribble away. How does he pay attention to all the complaints he must hear from each of the fifteen subjects? Molly Carroll alone must fill up an entire yel-low pad. Sam shifted on the table, and the loud wrinkling of its sanitary paper made his head feel worse. "Plus my eyes burn."

"You've had dry eyes since you first got sick. Just keep using the artificial tears. Now come on, stand up."

"In a minute."

Fong came over to the table and grabbed Sam's arms, easing him to a sitting position. Then he helped him stand, holding on till he was sure of Sam's balance.

"Arms out," Fong said.

Sam extended his arms. He hated this part of the exam because it focused so clearly on actions he could no longer perform properly. Sam remembered what it was like to be running by the river's edge in early morning light, coming around a bend to startle a great blue heron into taking flight. He had felt so buoyant that it seemed he was skimming over the riverbank like a bird in the air, and he spread his arms like wings, like Fong was asking him to do now, leaping for joy, squawking as he passed the place where the river spread itself out over the falls. Try that now and he'd fall in.

"Copy my movements," Fong said. He smiled at Sam. Sam smiled back. He also mimicked Fong's next move, straightening his right arm and bringing his left index finger to his nose. Then he was able to straighten that arm and bring his left index finger back again, but not as quickly as the doctor. Fong reached out, palm up, and Sam's palm met his.

"OK," Fong said, spreading his arms again, "now this." He shut his eyes and arched his neck back until his nose was pointing at the ceiling. So did Sam. Fong was there to catch him as he lost his balance and fell to the left.

They clung to each other for a moment like clumsy dancers until Fong eased Sam back against the table and helped him sit.

"You OK?"

"I hate that," Sam mumbled.

"Just a few more things and you can go home." Fong stayed close to him, resting a hand on Sam's shoulder. "All right?"

Sam nodded. Without being asked, he raised his arms so Fong could check his lymph glands.

"Got your bloodwork back this morning, finally. The lab forgets to send them back here. Your lymphocyte profile looks the same. Suppressor cells still low and memory cells high for all the activation markers. No surprises."

"Which means?"

"Which means nothing, Sam. It doesn't mean a thing that it didn't mean before the study."

"Yes it does. It means I'm not getting the drug."

"We've been over this dozens of times. Some people respond at different rates, so repeat after me: *it doesn't mean a thing.*"

"*Samuel Kiehl is getting the placebo.*"

Fong sighed. "Did you fill out your forms?"

"Over there, beside your blood pressure gauge."

Fong turned around to pick up the set of forms Sam had turned in. He shuffled through them with his back to Sam, ignoring the Activities of Daily Living Form and the Self-Assessment Matrix, stopping at the Monthly Psychological Questionnaire, the SCL-90-R. "Oh, man," he moaned, "is it time for this one again?"

The form asked one question, *How much were you disturbed by?*, then listed ninety different psychological problems, from *nervousness or shakiness inside* and *loss of sexual interest or pleasure*, to *feelings of guilt* and *the idea that something is wrong with your mind.* Sam had to circle one of five possible responses ranging from *not at all* to *extremely.* The form took him two hours to complete.

"What's this?" Fong asked after scanning the two pages. "Number eighty-seven. You circled *extremely,* what's that one? Oh, *The idea that something serious is wrong with your body.* My Lord."

6.

When he got home that afternoon, Sam was too exhausted to think about dinner. He was almost too exhausted to make it up the fifteen steps into his row house without stopping halfway for a nap. He threw his keys in the dish he kept on top of a stereo speaker by the door so he wouldn't forget where he put them. Then he plopped down in the recliner, which was about two strides away from the door, thinking *at least this one has padding.* He cranked up its hassock.

Too bad Andy was coming tomorrow night instead of tonight. Sam looked forward to his son's visits, even if they ended up saying very little to each other because Sam was too worn out. Andy would bring the Vietnamese rice paper rolls and noodle soup that Sam liked. They would sit together on the living room sofa and eat at the coffee table, watching the Trailblazers game as they used to when Andy was young.

Andy had shuttled back and forth between his parents every few days from the time he was four until his mother remarried when he was twelve. Then she moved to Knoxville, Tennessee, and Andy moved in with Sam for the remaining half-dozen years of his official adolescence, flying to visit her a few times in the first two years, then stopping by mutual agreement. At eighteen, Andy had taken his drum kit and found an apartment just across the river from Sam. He started a band he named Glissade, then re-named Freefall, then Slick. Finally, at the insistence of Kayla, his lead singer and girlfriend, the band became Navel Lint and was now popular in the northwest music scene. Instead of going to college, Andy practiced his drumming, made money by giving occasional lessons or working in a sheet music shop or playing back-up in recording studios. He cut demos, taught himself to manage Navel Lint's schedule and finances, and soon was traveling through Oregon, Washington, and northern California playing gigs. They'd even been booked for a week in Boise, Idaho. Then two months ago, Navel Lint had signed a recording contract with a company in Los Angeles. Their first CD, *Grotty Hands*, would be out soon. Andy would be touring southern California, the Southwest, the South, and, if things went according to plan, would end up in Tennessee early next year, where he would see his mother for the first time since he was fourteen.

Sam treasured each visit from his son these days because he believed there would be few more once Navel Lint hit the road. It was time to face letting Andy go. He just hoped his son wouldn't be disappointed when he got to Tennessee. If he didn't stay long, if Victoria wasn't in rehearsals or in the run of a production, it should be all right. Warm and beautiful as she looked—her cheekbones and jaw mesmerizing as a cubist portrait while she whispered in some vaguely French accent, those hazel eyes and the lush auburn hair cascading down her back—over time Victoria Louise Valadon Kiehl Anthony could be utterly chilling. Vic. How she hated when Sam called her that.

A model and dancer when they met, Vic had quit work to study acting as soon as they got married. He should be glad, she said, because it would teach her to lose herself in someone else, an idea that seemed so strange to Sam that he forgot about it entirely until her accent began shifting toward the French. She appeared in a few plays in Portland, refusing to be in musicals, refusing to dance, concentrating exclusively on high drama. Then Mandy Welch, the famous film director, had shot a World War II era love story in Portland and Vic landed a small role as a dancehall girl. She was convinced it was the start of her Hollywood career, but then she turned up pregnant with Andy. It seemed as though she never forgave either of them. For three years, she hardly ever left the house, which she wallpapered three times and then repainted six times as though it were a stage set. When she suddenly left them, her note pinned to the refrigerator said *Exit, stage right.*

She was acting again now, and her husband managed the regional theater in Knoxville. Vic had put Andy on their mailing list, his only regular contact with her.

Sam had had relationships with a few women after his divorce, but he'd been alone since shortly after getting sick. At that time Nell Nichols, a political editor for the *Portland Oregonian,* was living with him. They'd met at an election night party downtown. Sam had left the KPOR-TV studios, where he had his own desk next to the anchors for election broadcasts. He'd brazenly declared the winners ten minutes after polling places closed, and as the night progressed it turned out that he was correct down to the precise percentages. He was feeling jubilant when Nell Nichols strolled up to him at the bar.

She could certainly knock back her manhattans. All they did was shade her freckles a deeper red and straighten her otherwise lopsided smile. It seemed impossible to make her eyes any narrower than they were normally, but the drinks gave them higher sheen, like well-polished steel. She was famous on the local political scene for the toothy tone of her political analysis and for her scathing wit, those terse punch lines at the end of her paragraphs that left a reader shocked by their rightness. The people Sam did business with would memorize them for use at parties.

"You sure have balls," she had said to Sam by way of a greeting. "Calling the winners before the ballots even got shaken out of their boxes. I'm Nell Nichols, by the way."

"I recognized you from that little drawing in the paper beside your editorials. Doesn't do you justice, though." They both smiled. "The trick is exit interviews, Nell. I knew most of the winners by lunchtime."

Even now, Sam could hear her wheezy laugh, which reminded him of how she'd looked sitting up in bed naked and alternating asthma inhalers after they made love. For someone with such fire, she was actually a very pale, frail woman. But she had a voice, especially late at night, that was a couple turns below smoky, down where her breathing was still fine, which Sam liked almost enough to forget about her periodic withdrawals or endless hours of work, even at night after they had made love, and her passion for speechwriters. It didn't really surprise him when she left two months after he got sick. He returned from a fruitless visit to a gastroenterologist and saw before he had shut the door that her Cassatt and Kahlo prints were no longer on the living room wall. She'd even taken the pottery they'd bought to replace his grandmother's dishes, which Nell loathed and packed away in boxes that she'd stacked for him on the kitchen table. Later, she left a message on his answering machine. Didn't give her name, just that unmistakable voice saying "Call me when you find out what's wrong."

He hated the way these skeins of memory would wrap themselves around his thoughts and crush them, taking advantage of his body's weakness, his mind's least stillness. That's why he was unwilling to try meditation.

It was always like this when Sam got home from a long day at Cascade-Kennedy, as though the fatigue and the infusions stimulated his lousy memories instead of his weakened natural killer cells. Another side effect. Maybe he should report it to Kate.

Sam cranked the hassock down and stood. Clearly, this was not a good time to be thinking. He was supposed to relax, regenerate, regroup, restore, not get himself agitated. Might as well eat if he wasn't going to let himself rest.

Sam opened the pantry, reached in and removed the broom. Then he put it back and quickly shut the pantry door, having forgotten what he'd been looking for. He filled the kettle with water for tea, then remembered that he intended to eat. In the refrigerator, he found a leftover half of tamale pie from earlier in the week. Or was it last week? He couldn't remember when he'd eaten the first half, but the leftovers looked like an oil painter's old palette, mostly earth tones, and now he was pretty sure he'd bought the thing a week ago Friday. He dumped it down the disposal, then went back to peer in refrigerator. Nell's voice returned to him from that first time she had looked in there herself, calling over her shoulder to tell him *You don't have any food, Sam. All you've got in here is ingredients.*

Nothing appealed. As the water heated, Sam sat at the kitchen table and decided that a Macintosh apple might be the perfect dinner after a hard day of clinical research. A Macintosh apple and maybe some sweatpants. Wait a minute, that wasn't right. Some Swiss cheese. Apple, cheese and blood. No, bread. Hell with it, he'd eat a big breakfast in the morning.

Sam knew he should simply go upstairs to bed and stay there for most of the next sixty hours. He only had two days to recover before going back for his monthly treadmill test, after which he was always bedridden for at least five days. Sometimes it seemed as though the drug company was actually trying to kill him rather than to see if their drug worked.

The only thing keeping him in the study was the fact that Tracy was improving, and that he'd been promised the drug at the end. He figured he'd need massive doses just to catch up to where he was at the study's beginning.

When the phone rang, Sam almost didn't answer it. After all, that's what he'd bought the machine for. But he couldn't help himself. Since starting his opinion research firm a decade ago, Sam had never been able to ignore a ringing phone, and on the third ring, he grabbed it. Could be Andy, after all.

But it was Kate McCabe, chopping and munching on vegetables as she spoke. "There you are," she said. "I've been calling for hours."

"I just got home. This was my day to see Fong."

"Oh, yeah, that's right. Hey, don't you have an answering machine?"

"Forgot to turn it on." Sam pulled a stool over so he could sit while he talked. "What're you eating?"

"Celery. Which, slathered with peanut butter and studded with raisins, is my kids' dinner for tonight. Want to know why?"

"Because it's high in fiber? No, I've got it, high in Vitamin A and protein, and you're a mother devoted to her children's wellbeing."

"Try this. Because I've been on the phone for the last two-and-a-half-hours, except when I was trying to call you and Tracy, my favorite guinea pigs. And do you know who I was talking to? My counterparts in this mad experiment of ours at the other sites."

"Really?" Kate had his full attention now. "Is something wrong?"

"I don't think so, Sam. But I'll tell you this, and don't ever say you heard it from me: there are changes coming. This is one creepy drug company we're working with."

"What kind of changes?"

"Don't know, exactly. Chicago says they've heard PER is thinking of stopping the study at the six months point, because initial results look so promising. At the Rhode Island site, four people quit and the company says they may have to drop the rest. Albuquerque says they were asked about starting a new group on a different dosage, and three times a week instead of two. It's all very strange, Sam."

"I don't get it. How can PER already know the results are promising? How can they start people on a different protocol? Won't that hem the results? I mean harm, you know, skew the results?"

"Good question. Be quiet." Kate's children were screaming in the background. "I gotta go. Look, I'll see you at your next infusion and we can talk about this some more. Don't worry. I just wanted you to be prepared in case things change. Maybe you'll be getting the drug sooner than you thought, eh?"

"Gotcha! I thought we didn't know that I'm not getting the drug now, remember?"

"Wise-ass. Oh. The real reason I called is to tell you that PER wants to do a skin test on everybody this week. Something to do with seeing how your immune systems react to common allergens. This won't be a big deal. Anyway, you have to go up to the Research Department after you finish your treadmill test, all right? Shouldn't take more than another half-hour."

"Sure. Just have an ambulance outside the Sports Medicine Clinic to take me up there when I'm done, because they make us walk the treadmill till we collapse."

Three

1.

Andy Kiehl was worried about his father. Sometimes he thought Sam might have cancer and wouldn't admit it because he didn't want Andy to worry. Didn't want him to cancel the Navel Lint tour. Sometimes Andy thought his father was just a hypochondriac, and that there was nothing seriously wrong with him. He was tired, that's all, and making a dune from a grain of sand.

Andy didn't like to visit his father anymore. The old man looked so pitiful sitting there in his recliner like a robot with the batteries all corroded, like a snowman in a heat wave, like a man sinking into the quicksand of air. Play with those a bit, Andy thought, and they could work in a song. "Sick man!/Just a snowman/in a heat wave/Just a lone man/sinking in the quicksand/of his grave." That's even better.

Andy knew he should visit more, not less, but there was always something going on in his life. There was always a reason to reschedule. Rehearsal. Fixing the bus. Finishing the song he was working on. Outfits for Kayla, for the band. The sound of his father's voice on the phone every time Andy called to cancel. His father's face whenever Andy left for the night after a visit, no matter how long he'd stayed. The meals unfinished on Sam's plate, his skin a funny color, his eyes so dry you could hear them blink. He was brave, Andy realized; he was handling this business of suddenly being sick. He was being stoic. But Andy knew it was all an act. Inside, he knew, his father was devastated.

Unless he wasn't, in which case Andy didn't know what to make of it at all. He would just as soon go out on the road and come back to a father healed and climbing rocks again, running races, even doing those strange dances. As long as Sam didn't dance them at a Navel Lint gig.

He did that once. Andy would never forget it. Back when his father was seeing that woman from the newspaper, the one with all the freckles and the great voice. Andy had looked up from his kit at the end of a song and there they were, drenched in sweat, right in front of the band, out of breath and laughing. Everyone was sneaking looks at the old couple, then looking up at Andy, matching faces, and Andy thought he would die.

If he was being completely honest, Andy truly wanted to disappear for a while and then show up to find his father back the way he was before. Just a fold in the fabric of time. Hey, that's not a bad line either. I want to climb/through a fold in the fabric of time/with you. Work on it.

Kayla, Andy's girlfriend, said there's another, truer reason Andy didn't like to visit his father. It wasn't about how bad Sam looked, or how confused Sam made him feel, or how much Andy thought his father needed him. No, it was about failure. Andy believed he should be able to protect his father. Should have protected him before, when he was working too hard and wearing himself out, and should be protecting him now that the virus had hold of him, or whatever it was, even if it was cancer, even if it was something no one could protect Sam from. That was Kayla's take, and as usual Kayla was right on top of the truth.

She said Andy felt like he'd let his father down. She said he was tormenting himself, and his father, and her, and the band, over guilt, which she said was very Freud of him, and he should just let it go.

2.

Tracy was supposed to pick Sam up at 9:30 for their 10:00 appointments at the Sports Medicine Clinic. It was now 9:44. He was trying to stay calm.

He closed the blinds and forced himself to sit on the sofa. Picking up the morning paper, he folded the Metro section in the middle and stared down at the sketched face of Nell smiling back at him. *And a good morning to you too, Ms. Nichols.* He laid the paper aside.

The idea behind these exercise tests was simple enough. Each subject mounted the treadmill–torso peppered with electrodes, mouth stuffed with a breathing tube, nostrils clipped shut–and walked until collapsing from exhaustion. The duration was noted, as were various measures of cardiac and lung function, and blood was drawn. Last month, Tracy had marched along for forty-eight minutes before signaling that she was ready to stop; more, it seemed, out of impatience than fatigue. However, after eight minutes Sam had ended up dangling from the treadmill's bars by his forearms as the technician struggled to get him unhooked from the machinery.

During the years he had been running and racing, Sam had wanted to have himself tested at the Sports Medicine Clinic. He wanted solid measures of exactly how strong he'd made himself, wondered if he might be one of those people who outlasted the machines, running until the astonished physicians stopped him because they couldn't spare any more time, it was obvious that he was in such phenomenal condition that he could not be exhausted, could take anything they threw at him, any pace, any incline, for any length of time. He'd put off doing it, worried about the cost because his health insurance wouldn't cover such an elective procedure, and now when he went up there every month the best he could do was walk for eight minutes before collapsing.

Tracy pulled her van into his driveway and honked, jerking Sam out of his reverie. He checked his watch as he walked outside to join her: 9:49. Well, the way she drove, they still might get there in time.

"Sorry I'm late again. Just could not get the kids up for school and of course Wally wouldn't help. Oh, no. Not that I blame the man. Buckle up, Sam."

"I understand, Tracy. And I really devastate your picking me up all the time. I mean appreciate. Don't know what I'd do without you."

"After all you've done for me? I'm just thankful to God that I can drive, you know? And then what do I do? Just talk talk talk, I'm always late, your poor blood pressure's probably exploding while you wait for me. You're fed up hearing about Wally and the kids, I know that, but I don't know where else to turn. My pastor doesn't have a clue. Forget my brothers and sisters. According to them, the whole thing's my own fault and I should just get my act together. Listen, Sam, you're a guy, what do you think Wally thinks? Oh here, see, I brought a thermos of hot water for our tea."

Sam nodded, then looked at his watch. "You know, maybe we ought to back out of the driveway and get going."

3.

The Sports Medicine Clinic was located on the south slope of Seacrest Hill, in one of the oldest buildings on the Cascade-Kennedy campus. At 9:56, Tracy's van roared past the entrance, heading for the indoor parking facility. She snatched a ticket from the attendant, screaming her thanks over the revving engine, and as usual found an empty spot immediately, right by the entrance, even though the lot was teeming with vehicles.

"Amazing," Sam said.

"Let's go." Tracy slammed her door before Sam could unbuckle his seat belt. She swung her purse over her shoulder and charged toward the lab.

"Go on ahead, Tracy. Maybe you could check us in. I'll be right there."

"Sorry," she said, and took off at a run.

The lab shared the second floor of the Student Activities Building with a gymnasium. Sam hated coming there, where medical students, interns, physicians, nurses, faculty, and staff all went to work out. Gym apparatus was scattered near snack machines and televisions were mounted high on the wall. Bright blue and yellow LifeCycle machines, LifeRowers, and StairMasters were arrayed throughout the lobby like futuristic furniture, each with a sweaty person mounted on it, each angled toward televisions where *CNN News* flickered. To use the restroom, Sam walked past a fully equipped strength center and into the locker room. Wire baskets stuffed with clothes, long rows of combination locks like a vast Warhol panel, and the intense odor of sweat swamped him with waves of nostalgia. Jesus, Sam thought, I get weepy from the smell of old jockstraps.

Upstairs, perched outside the lab like sentinels, were three more LifeCycle machines. As he got off the elevator, Sam was greeted by the familiar sound of basketballs being dribbled on waxed hardwood, and the screak of sneakers as someone cut for the hoop.

"Hi Sam."

He could not remember her name. Sally? Lily? Phyllis? The first time he had arrived at the lab for a test, the elevator door opened to reveal this young woman bent over backwards in her spandex shorts, her smiling face peering at him from between her legs while she worked on her flexibility. It had made quite an impression on him, but her name hadn't stuck.

"Today is Shelly's birthday," Tracy said, coming to Sam's rescue.

"Today?" Sam said. "That's incredible, Shelly. Today was also my grandfather's birthday. Do you think that means we might be related?"

Shelly, uncertain what to make of that, smiled with more strain than when she'd been twisting herself inside-out. She slid her hands along the sides of her spandex shorts as though searching for a pocket, and Sam could tell she was trying to decide whether she'd been teased or insulted, but was too sweet to make anything of it either way. She gave them forms to fill out instead, dug two pens out of her desk and motioned toward the couch beside the gym door. Then she disappeared into the lab. Everybody here was so damn healthy. Sam gazed at the space Shelly had vacated, shook his head, and looked down at the form.

Did he, the undersigned, accept that this test could kill him? Would he waive the Cascade-Kennedy School of Medicine from any responsibility if it did? How old was he, and approximately how many miles had he run that week?

He looked to see if Tracy found the forms as unsettling as he did, but she was bent over them as though taking a midterm for which she'd fully prepared.

"Who goes first?" he asked.

"It's your turn, Sam."

He stood. "Don't get too comfortable out here, Trace. This won't take long." The doors closed behind him with a gasp, as though he'd walked into a vacuum chamber.

Inside the lab, Sam nodded to the technician and a young man he assumed was a new resident. They were huddled together at a computer screen, quite amused about something. Sam wondered if they were studying the results of his previous test and were tickled by his pitiful performance.

He went behind a screen at the far end of the room to remove his shirt and wait for them to be ready. There was a gurney to lie on, and Sam had just begun to doze when a strange face edged around the screen, revealing in slow sequence its forehead, eyebrows, eyes, nose, mouth and chin. Sam figured he was dreaming as the perfectly oval, utterly hairless head began appearing, and he just stared at her without acknowledgment.

"Ready, Mr. Kiehl?"

He nodded, still not sure he was awake, and said, "Sam." The rest of her came out from behind the screen, a short, thin body draped in an enormous white lab coat that hung down to her knees, where a pair of black and orange tights took over. She was next to his gurney in a flash, moving with the precision of an assassin. Placing a cold hand on his chest, she frowned and then produced a razor from the pocket of her lab coat.

Patient 002

"The hair grew back already, I see."

Sam looked down at his chest, where four sparse rings of stubble were nestled in his otherwise thick hair, then back at the woman's hairless head, and down to the razor in her hand. He closed his eyes and waited for her to slit his throat. When he opened his eyes, she was smiling gently down at him.

"Yes," he said. "I guess it did."

"OK, just relax. I can tell you don't remember me." She started to shave him deftly within the previous circles—no soap, no warm water—and now he began to remember her.

"You're Bella, right?"

"I'm Willa Ballinger, but I had my wig on last time because the docs from that drug company of yours were here. Remember? The very tall man in that awful brown suit, the bald guy, he kept mispronouncing your name. Called you Mr. Kile the whole time. And he kept looking at me as though he knew me, but I think it was just that he knew I was wearing a wig and he wanted to ask me to do something kinky with him. There, Sam, you're all done. Let me hook up these electrodes and get a quick EKG. Then we'll get the belt on you, and go over and wind you up."

"Could we turn off the windshield wipers?"

"Huh?"

"I mean could we close the blinds? I'm real sensitive to light."

"No problem."

In a few minutes, Willa led Sam over to the treadmill, where a chair had been placed for him on the machine's belt. This ought to be quite a challenge, he thought. Maybe they want to measure how far the chair will fling me when they turn on the machine. Then Willa explained that he was just supposed to sit there while they took various measurements of his respiration. The chair was a gesture of kindness. She remembered how tired he would get.

Like a snorkler, Sam breathed through a tube in his mouth for the next six minutes. Drooling into his beard, he watched the resident and technician as they watched their screen, studying his oxygen uptake and carbon dioxide production.

Soon Willa was back, helping him up, removing the chair,

steadying him. She patted his hand as he gripped the treadmill's rails and told him to spread his feet so that they were not in contact with the belt as it began to turn. He waited a few moments, looking at the belt but not really watching it, the way a platform diver gazes at the water far below, then stepped on while simultaneously tightening his grip on the rails.

"Easy," Willa said. "Keep loose."

Sam nodded, but he felt distress almost immediately. Willa could see it in his eyes, so she slowed the machine even further and smiled encouragingly. Sam barely noticed. A minute later, she tightened the blood pressure cuff on his right arm and took a quick reading. He was already up to 132/95.

The machine's pattern of noise seemed to Sam to be a raspy wind, as though the gods were needing to clear their throats, and he wished the technician would turn down the radio blaring golden oldies, although normally he loved hearing the Edsels sing "Rama Lama Ding Dong." But it wasn't good treadmill music, at least not for a sick man, and then Willa tightened the blood pressure cuff again, and when she was finished with that she tapped his hand to get him to loosen his death-grip and suddenly it felt as though the machine's pace had been quickened or the incline steepened and suddenly he lost the rhythm or something, he stumbled a bit, and Willa was right there to grab his arm above the cuff but it was no use, he couldn't breathe and his shoulders ached and his knees buckled and there he was, Sam Kiehl, once the fastest forty-year-old 5K runner in Portland, Oregon, dangling again from the treadmill's rails while Willa and the technician tried to untangle him from all the wires and help him over to the chair.

Soon his breathing calmed and he could do more than just nod in answer to all their questions. He'd stopped walking, he said, because his legs fell apart. Yes, his muscles hurt, all the way up through the hips, down through the shoulders, meeting nauseatingly at his belly, that was a dumb question. Sorry, sorry, he knew they were just asking the questions the drug company wanted them to ask. Yes, he thought he could walk out to the reception area and lie down on the couch till Tracy was done.

"Look," Sam said, "could I just wear these electrodes home? I think it's going to hurt too much when you take them off."

4.

Kate had left word that before the skin test they needed to have blood drawn. When Sam got to the laboratory, they told him the drug company needed seven vials this time.

"No," Sam said. He slumped into a chair in the waiting room. "I don't have that much today."

He was cold. He folded his arms across his chest.

"Let's do it together!" Tracy said. She turned to the phlebotomist, whose button identified her as Noreen C., and smiled. "Is that all right? We could both go into your office and Sam could sit on one side of the table and I could sit on the other. Because Sam's right-handed and I'm left, so you can draw it out of my right arm and his left, which means you could do us both at the same time. Or almost at the same time, I mean, since you need to use both hands. Wouldn't that be all right?"

Noreen C. shuffled through some papers and responded, "You two from Doctor Fong's study?"

Tracy took that for a Yes. She reached over to pat Sam's hand and said, "Uh-huh, we are, and it's been a long day already and it's only noon. It would've been eleven except I just kept going. On the treadmill? I could've walked forever. And just a few months ago I couldn't get upstairs to bed at night. And we still have to go up to the clinic and have some kind of allergy tests and I'm afraid my friend Sam here won't make it."

"Well," Noreen C. said, "my notes indicate you also have to give urine samples for pregnancy tests." She looked up at Sam, then back down to her papers and shook her head. "Can I assume you don't need to take that test together too?"

This would be Sam's third pregnancy test since the study had begun. He no longer felt the need to comment, but he hoped he could control the shaking of his fatigued arms long enough to get some urine into the test tube.

After turning in their specimens, they went into Noreen C.'s office and rolled up their sleeves. She took Sam's blood first and was, he had to admit, efficient. He hardly felt a thing and there was no need to distract himself because Tracy narrated her entire treadmill test from the moment the machine was turned on until Willa stopped it at one hour.

"Can you imagine? I mean, look what's happening to me and soon it'll happen to you too!"

Tracy even continued talking throughout her own blood draw. As the vials were labeled and stacked in segmented wire holders, Tracy rolled down her right sleeve. Then Noreen C. got up to put the specimens in their shipping rack, bumped her right arm against the phone and dropped the holder containing Tracy's vials. All seven shattered on the floor, leaving a gorgeous Jackson Pollock splatter of blood that almost matched a poster hanging near the phone.

For a moment, Tracy was actually silent. Sam looked from the floor to Noreen C. and then to Tracy, who had a peculiar smile forming on her face. She turned to Sam and shrugged, then began rolling up her left sleeve.

5.

When Sam and Tracy walked into Doctor Fong's clinic, it was like slipping into a replay of the pre-study meeting from last summer. All the subjects were there, slumped in chairs or on the floor around the reception area, and they all had one sleeve rolled up as they waited their turn for the skin test.

Seen as a group, Sam thought, we must look comical, like tranquilized animals ready to be shipped back to their natural habitat. He knew everybody in the study now, and he was the only male.

It was unusual for them to gather in one place. Tests were scheduled two-by-two, as the infusions were, to avoid logjams and stress, to keep things manageable. Except for Tracy, Sam seldom saw his fellow subjects, though they sometimes spoke by phone to compare symptoms and reactions. He waved in the general direction of the reception room and walked to the registration desk.

As soon as they had checked in, Sam heard Molly Carroll calling to him from where she lay underneath a row of chairs by the wall. Her arm curled up from behind the last chair, twisted a few times in the air, and thumped back to the carpet.

"Over here, you two. I've got some questions for you."

Tracy excused herself to go to the bathroom, but Sam stepped over Molly's body and plopped into one of the orange plastic chairs.

"Skin tests," Sam said.

"Yeah, I know what you mean." She sounded as though she'd been crying. But then, Molly always sounded as though she'd been crying.

Near the end of the pilot program he'd been in with her, Sam could hear her shrilly raging voice in his sleep, almost as though it had taken over his own quieter voice of anger at being incurably ill. When he'd heard himself thinking *Now we're really off our pickle*, using language that was Molly's own, he stopped talking to her outside the clinic. This was the first time he'd seen or spoken with her since the start of the drug study.

"Listen, Sam," Molly whispered, "I don't want the others to hear, but there's something going on."

"What're you talking about?"

Molly moaned as she shifted onto her left hip and looked up at him. "Which word didn't you understand? There's. Something. Going. On."

He closed his eyes and took a deep breath. "I guess *Something*, Molly. That was the word I didn't understand."

"All these changes, that's the Something that's going on. I talked to people in Albuquerque who say there are so many different protocols that it's like every third person is in a different study. Different dosages, different timetables, different tests. And one of the patients in Rhode Island tried to kill herself, did you know that? Took like fifty Tylenol. Melted her kidneys, I think. We're not even allowed to look at painkillers, remember. We're supposed to lie around in agony because a couple of Tylenol might skew the test results. A girl in Chicago says PER is in financial trouble and on the verge of bankruptcy. I'm a very intuitive person, Sam, and I know Something's going on."

Tracy came around the corner with Kate McCabe, both carrying trays filled with syringes, small bottles, and alcohol preps. All smiles, they seemed like parents carrying birthday cake and milk into a party room.

"Remember," Kate was saying, "try not to touch the injection sites after we do this. If you have any reactions to the allergens, and PER thinks most of you won't, they will occur in forty-eight hours and you just phone me with the results, OK?"

"Half of us," Molly mumbled. "The ones on the drug ought to react like crazy."

6.

Sam and Tracy stayed after the other members of the study left, talking with Kate about the treadmill test and blood draw, enjoying the relative calm. For a moment, they were all silent, and Sam remembered that his son had canceled dinner plans with him each of the last three nights. He would have to find out what was going on with Andy.

When Doctor Fong came out of his inner office to pick up a chart, he saw them sprawled out on the chairs and walked over. His smooth face was crinkled with delight when Sam looked up at him.

"I have good news," he said, sitting down between Sam and Tracy, rubbing his palms together. "Was in Seattle this weekend to meet with the other study leaders. This drug is very interesting stuff, and not just with what you've got either. It slows down HIV, shrinks some tumors, gooses up the immune system. Abby Lewis, in Chicago, says she sees people with rheumatoid arthritis regaining some movement and having less pain on Zomalovir."

Fong stopped, looking first at Tracy, then at Sam, but barely registering their presence. Neither of them breathed.

"Let me tell you something," Fong continued. "We're all seeing the same thing. Subjects get better. I don't know when they'll unblind, because the study has to go on long enough for statistically valid numbers. But they see improvement in killer cell numbers, in lesions on the brain and cerebellum. It looks like a point's reached where you can go off the drug and hold your own for four or five months, then go back on from time to time for a boost. I tell you, this stuff looks very interesting."

When he was sure Fong had finished, Sam leaned forward and asked, "How do they know? I mean, I thought you guys weren't allowed to look at individual results."

"Right," Fong said. "PER can't either. But we see things. We talk."

Sam nodded. He didn't want to press Fong too hard, but he was having trouble understanding. "Bribe me, if you don't mind," he said.

Kate giggled. Fong looked at him as though Sam had just arrived. He blinked once slowly and said, "Huh?"

Sam played it back. "What did I say?"

"Never mind, Sam. What did you want to say?"

He looked to Tracy for an explanation, but she was staring at the reception desk and concentrating hard on something. Sam knew she hadn't heard him.

"I only said bear with me, because I'm a little confused. I mean, it's good news and all, but I guess I don't understand how this thing works. Does PER know who gets the drug and who gets the placebo? Do they know how it's working? Because if they do, and it works like you just said, why can't we stop the blind part and get on with it. If the drug works, let me have it."

Fong nodded. "You know how it is, Sam, I told you before. They have to collect enough data for the FDA to approve the results, then we go on to Phase Two. That's how drug research operates. It's slow, but that makes it safe."

"Yeah, I know. But I'm getting worse. There ought to be another way to test certain drugs, you know what I mean? Rather than let a patient keep getting sicker when they know the stuff works."

Fong sat back and frowned. He took his stethoscope from around his neck, held it in his lap and clacked the tips together. "It really is safer this way, Sam. There could still be side effects, liver toxicity, whatever, that don't show up right away. I know it's tough."

"Doctor Fong," Tracy said as though waking from a dream. "You know what I want to do when this is over? I'm thinking of studying for the test to become a mail carrier. Walk all day outside, bringing people news. You think I could do that? And could I learn enough to pass the test and everything?"

"I don't know, Tracy. But I don't see why not."

Sam ran his fingers through his hair, ending up with his palms on either side of his neck, their sides supporting his jaws. He took a deep breath.

"And in the evenings, Trace, you'll play in racquetball tournaments. I'll be there to cheer for you."

"Cheer hell, you can be my doubles partner."

7.

Four months ago, Sam had finally done something he'd planned to do ever since meeting Martin Fong. He went to see him outside the clinic, outside the structured medical setting, where he might glimpse another side of him and learn to better understand the man in whom he'd been asked to place such trust. He went to hear him play music.

Fong was a pianist who sometimes accompanied Portland's best chamber players in summer concerts at Reed College. Fong never mentioned this sideline of his; Sam had found out from Kate, after she learned that Sam was listening to classical music.

"Go sometime," she had said. "You should see Marty let go in the third movement of Beethoven's *E Flat Major*. The man's an animal."

Sam had ordered a ticket and spent the three days before the concert in bed, hoarding his strength. He had to plan excursions with care, though he'd only be out of the house for two-and-a-half hours. The centerpiece of the program would be Ravel's *Piano Trio in A Minor*, so as he lay in bed Sam listened to a recording and read an essay about the composer in a book he'd borrowed from the library. Ravel, it turned out, had been desperately ill in his late fifties, victim of a strange neurological disorder called aphasia, which left him unable to communicate speech, writing, or music. He could hear music in his head but couldn't write it on paper, could read notes but no longer find them on his piano. He recognized when a composition of his was being played incorrectly, but could not say or show how to play it right. Over and over, knowing the sound was wrong, he'd play the mi-mi instead of the do-do arpeggio until someone placed his fingers on the proper keys. Sam laid the book aside, thinking that from this one essay he now knew more about the man who wrote *Boléro* than he could have learned from reading a thousand-page biography.

Traveling to the campus by taxi was an extravagance, but Sam wanted to be alone at the concert. He'd secured an aisle seat in the front row and brought along two small pillows, one to sit on, the other to support his neck as he stretched out and leaned back. He rested his cane against his thigh and looked around. The theater was full. Sam could feel his energy oozing away in the presence of so many people.

When the three musicians appeared from the wings, what struck Sam was Fong's animation. He strode smiling onto the stage, acknowledged the applause, and perched himself on the piano bench, radiating energy. With a look of glee on his face, he adjusted the score, smoothed his tuxedo jacket, flexed his fingers, nodded. He whipped a handkerchief from his pocket and mopped his sweating face. It was an energy born of assurance, not nervousness. Sam was glad to see it, but glad also that Fong didn't approach his patients this way. It made him tired just being ten yards away from the man.

When the Ravel began, Sam realized he could barely keep Fong's hands in focus. The initial folk dance melody turned around on itself through an array of variations, and Fong's eyes seemed to find Sam for an instant as they swept erratically across the audience. Sam could swear he felt their heat pass over him. Fong's entire visage was transformed as theme progressed into theme. He looked as though he were being manipulated by a wizard of special computer effects, his smile becoming a grimace which became a leer and then a pout, brows lurching, eyes narrowed to oblivion before flying open in astonishment. It was almost too much for Sam to watch.

The music sparkled and dazzled like a vibrant Impressionist seascape. As time passed, Sam had no trouble distinguishing Fong's soaring sound as he both established his unique presence and blended with the violin and cello. The variations seemed endless, dense and rich, and Fong's playing was expansive. But it was in the final movement that Sam saw what he'd come for. Fong grew suddenly very still, closing his eyes, and out of this withdrawal came a sound more lyrically haunting than anything Sam had heard before. Fong looked exactly the way he looked when laying his hands on Sam's abdomen: distracted, his mind surely elsewhere. But his hands were filled with magic.

8.

Sam's massage appointment was for 5:30 and he could hardly wait. Things were changing between them. It was not her touch but her tone of voice that told him she too sensed the change. He'd been talking more; Jessica was asking him questions, not just listening, and she was telling him about herself, not just about what she was doing.

She had been coming to work on him every other Thursday, arriving tired but somehow cheerful even after a full day at *Foster's Plants,* her family's nursery. She managed the place alone, since her brother spent most of his time with the landscape design operation. She also dealt with wholesale and retail clients, had installed a wall of aquariums in the nursery to begin selling tropical fish because, after all, she had a degree in zoology with a minor in ichthyology, and had two parrots sitting among the houseplants to entertain customers' children. She was restructuring the company's accounts, too, making use of her passion for computers. Sometimes as she lugged her portable table up his front steps, Jessica looked like the one who needed an hour of massage.

She was four or five inches taller than Sam, with long arms and hands, and a swimmer's broad back. She wore her dark blond hair in a short shag, but had retained the childhood habit of twitching her head back as though to shake phantom strands from her eyes. Those eyes seemed to shift from gray to green, much as the moon moved through its phases, and she swore that they had actually been blue all her life, until she lived for a year in eastern Finland, where she believed they became leached of their true color. Her voice had a vast range; some days it was high and sweet as a child's, some days it was so husky that Sam thought she might be sick.

He had his massage-day routine carefully planned. He wrote the check in the morning, before leaving for Cascade-Kennedy, so he didn't have to bother with it after the day's activities or, worse, after the massage, when he was either relaxed or in pain and likely to make mistakes with numbers. And now, the way they would extend Jessica's visits by talking afterwards, he was even more likely to mess up the check. He tucked it into his calendar book, along with a pencil to note the next appointment, and left them on the stereo speaker in the living room, near where Jessica set up her table.

Jessica had been his massage therapist for nearly five years, since the heyday of his racing and climbing, long before he got sick, long before she consented to join her family's business. At that time, she had a massage practice downtown, not far from Sam's office. He had met her after running the Portland Marathon, when she was one among dozens of licensed massage therapists to volunteer their services at the finishers' tent. As soon as he felt Jessica's hands touch his cramping calf muscles he knew he wanted to become her client. Her touch seemed unerring in its ability to find the places where it was most needed. He would walk to her office bimonthly after work, and had come to depend on her familiarity with the knots in his hamstrings, the peculiar imbalance between deltoids, her way with occasional injuries. He also depended on her friendly, open presence, her stories of life in Finland and her tapes of New Age music.

When she closed her practice to begin working in the nursery, Sam was miserable. He went from therapist to therapist, unable to find someone whose touch seemed so sure and right for his body. But more than missing her touch, he missed her friendship. After he got sick, Sam called her at the nursery. They talked for an hour. At the end, he described the pain he was in. The next week, Jessica called back and offered to take him on as her only massage client. She had been coming to his house ever since.

Today she seemed perkier than usual as she set up the table and covered its padded top with sheets. It had been a good day at the nursery; her father was opening a new facility in Tigard, and Jessica was going to design and operate it. She paused as she rummaged through her purse for the oil and looked at him.

"Don't worry, Sam. I'll still come to work on you."

Jessica went into the bathroom to change into a tee-shirt, then went into the kitchen to warm the oil in the microwave. He liked hearing her move out there, liked her small cry of surprise when she found the tea he had brewed for her. Sam chose a CD, a soft assortment of John Field nocturnes, and turned the volume low, then stripped and climbed face down onto the table, covering himself with the sheets. When Jessica returned and pulled the sheet down to his waist, she gasped.

"What's all this?" She rubbed her fingertips across a series of purple pinhead spots on his back.

"Bruises," Sam said. "Or petechiae, to be precise. I almost died when I saw them in the mirror last week. Thought they might be something like those Kaposi's sarcoma that AIDS patients get. Fong says they're caused by small hemorrhages. I get them just from leaning back against a wooden chair sometimes. He says not to worry about them yet. It's the *yet* that I don't like."

"You think it's all right for me to massage here? I don't want to trigger more bleeding."

"Let's go ahead since he says there's nothing to worry about."

"Yet."

"Right. Yet."

Sam heard her squeeze some oil into her palms and rub her hands together. He inhaled deeply, in part to relax his muscles, in part to take in the familiar smell of these sheets, saturated with years of almond scent. Her first touch was always cold, no matter how long she'd zapped the oil or how much she'd warmed her hands with tap water. As she worked to ease the pain in his back and shoulder muscles, Sam could hear her finger joints clicking, and her soft humming. Then he began to lose himself in the delicate notes of a nocturne and the thoughtless blank state of deep relaxation Jessica brought to him.

9.

When the massage ended, and Jessica had gone into the bathroom to wash her oily hands, Sam sat up but didn't get off the table and didn't get dressed. Instead, without having planned it or thought about what he would say, and with the sheet draped across his body like a toga, he called her name.

"What is it, Sam? You all right?"

"Thanks to you, yes. Listen, maybe you could stay for dinner."

Jessica appeared in the doorway, her head turned toward him, her hands still wet and hanging limply in front of her chest. "Dinner?"

He could hear the fatigue in her voice. "So you won't have to wait till you get all the way home to eat."

She nodded. "Why not. Let me get cleaned up here." She disappeared, then popped back into the doorway. Sam hadn't moved. He seemed to be stunned. "Are you planning to wear your sheet to dinner?"

After he got dressed and looked in his refrigerator, Sam suggested they go out to eat. Stroll along the riverbank where there were a half-dozen restaurants within walking distance.

She walked slowly, though her legs were much longer than his, and kept her hands thrust into the pockets of her coat as the evening chill came on. Sam felt comfortable walking with her. He breathed in the cool evening air and thought it would be possible just to keep walking, to follow the river all the way to Willamette Falls and back without feeling the need to speak. The idea made him smile. He'd be lucky to make it to where the river bent west a quarter mile ahead.

At the water's edge, they stopped to watch a great blue heron as it took off. The bird lumbered up, rickety as an old outfielder circling under a fly ball, and settled fifty yards downriver.

"One of the things I loved the most about living in Finland," Jessica said, "was all the water. It seemed like I was never far away from it. That, and the saunas. Instant peace, Sam. A few whacks across your shoulders with a damp *vihta*, everything loosens up and you know you can deal with whatever comes your way. You ought to put a sauna in your basement."

"Since I got sick, I can't manage heat at all. Sometimes a warm shower is enough to keep me in bed for three days. It's as though my inner thermostat is busted."

"Who knows, maybe a sauna would push you through to the other side of that."

She's right, he thought. Maybe anything is possible after all. Screw science. "What's a *vihta*?" he said. "Sounds to me like an implement of torture."

Jessica laughed. "It can be surprising, what feels right under the right conditions." She paused, then turned away from him to look across the river. "It's a bunch of fresh birch twigs tied together like a whisk. Soft as velvet when it gets dipped in hot water."

He nodded slowly, trying to picture it, to picture moving a *vihta* like velvet across Jessica's naked back. "What brought you to Finland? You never told me."

"A boat."

They began walking north toward the lights of downtown Portland. Instead of walking on Sam's left to avoid his cane, Jessica stayed on his right side and offered her arm for support. He took it, crooked the cane under his left arm, adjusting to her pace, and they moved together in silence for a while.

"How far can you go?" she asked as they reached the dock.

"I have no idea."

"OK, we'll take it slow." She squeezed his arm lightly and said, "I came to Finland to get away from everything I later came back home to find. Isn't that strange, Sam? I wanted to get away from my family, away from the business of trees and plants and flowers and herbs. I wanted to find a strange land. A place with lots of water. Finland qualifies, far more than I imagined when I chose it. And then there was my Esko."

"Esko? What's that, some kind of condition?"

"Sort of," she laughed. "Esko was my boyfriend. We met in graduate school at Portland State."

"Oh." Sam liked having her beside him for balance instead of a cane. "And was he the one who killed himself? I remember you mentioning that a long time ago."

"Hardly. Though at one point it looked like he might try to kill me. No, that was someone else, a roommate's cousin."

Sam could sense that she was trying to decide how much to tell him. Her face seemed to hide nothing; he felt that he could see exactly what she was thinking. She looked over at him for the time it took to walk a few steps.

"You probably think you can tell exactly what I'm thinking, don't you, Sam?"

It was such a penetration of his thoughts that it brought Sam to a sudden stop, which threw Jessica off balance. "How did you do that?"

She smiled. "I always thought you were pretty transparent when I worked on you. But this is very funny. You're even more transparent when I can see your eyes."

All he could do was smile back at her. "Transparent."

"And yet more solid than I thought. In some ways, you changed almost overnight, when you first got sick. Even before your body and your mind slowed down. That whippet in a three-piece suit was nobody I could imagine knowing. This clear, delicate man is somebody I want to know very much."

They turned back toward Sam's house. He suggested that they eat in the little café on the corner of his street, the place closest to his home.

"I knew you were going to say that," Jessica said.

He was surprised and delighted at her appetite. She ate most of the complementary antipasto, her eggplant lasagna, salad, two servings of bread, the leftover portion of Sam's chicken, and then ordered cheesecake for dessert. They walked home afterwards, trying to decide exactly how long they had known each other—four years and about ten months—and Sam was astonished to find that it was already 8:15.

Jessica declined to have a cup of coffee. She began packing away the massage sheets and folding the portable table. Sam walked toward her from the kitchen, where he'd gone to heat some water for himself, and she stopped what she was doing, watching him approach. When they embraced, Sam had to arch his neck in order to rest his chin on her shoulder, and when they kissed he felt as though he might topple over backwards because of his balance problems. They looked at each other, Jessica laughed, and they kissed again, leaning back against the wall.

"I really enjoyed this tonight," Jessica whispered in his ear. "And don't worry about making me late."

"Jesus. Stop reading my thoughts." He had never breathed in her full scent before, only the scent of oil that came with her sheets or her hands when they massaged his chest and face. "Me too," he said.

"I think you should start looking for another massage therapist, Sam."

He moved his head back to look at her. "Why? Is something wrong?"

"No. I think we may be starting down another path, though. One that's going to be good for us both. And on that path, I can't take money to be your massage therapist anymore. It wouldn't be ethical."

"What will you be?"

"We'll have to see."

10.

Sam drew a bath. Though most of the massage oil had been absorbed into his skin by now, he still sensed a surface slickness. He had the feeling of being clogged up, and he was tired, but exhilarated. Jessica had touched his face after their last kiss, and that touch was something altogether new between them, another kind of kiss. He knew he'd been more and more drawn to her over the last year, but had refused to look at that for what it was, and had never thought she might be drawn to him. Tonight left him in a confusing jumble, and he liked it. But his muscles were sore after Jessica's probing, and he hadn't taken the time to soothe them afterward. A man in need of a bath.

He was sitting on the closed lid of the toilet, cursing himself for drawing a bath hot enough to poach a salmon and waiting for it to cool when he heard the front door open. Andy had a key, as did Nell, who'd never returned hers but had surely lost it by now, so Sam knew who must be there. Yet he suddenly felt adrift in time. What day was it? What time? How long had he been sitting there watching the bath oils swirl? If it was dinner time, why wasn't he hungry? How many times this week had Andy backed out of dinner? He watched the steam rising off the bathwater and thought it was a nice morning for a swim.

Once when Andy was about three, Sam had taken him for an early morning swim in the ocean. They'd spent the night in a motel just outside Cannon Beach. Spent the night, but didn't sleep much because Andy was frightened by the noise of the surf, which seemed to envelope the entire motel. *Someone's breathing outside, Dad!* At the first sign of dawn, they'd gotten up, put on swimming trunks and sweat suits because the August morning at the coast was cold. Andy looked so tiny, a twig bent by the least wind. His long straight hair, a gift from Vic, riffled in the wind as they walked across the sand. If Andy thought the night surf was someone's breathing, he must have thought this morning's version was sheer rage. The air was filled with spray. Sam thought *this is not a good idea* but Andy was so excited, so eager for the ocean water. They took off their sweatpants. Sam held his son's hand and they walked to the foam line, Andy squealing when the icy water touched his shins, Sam silent but feeling a scream trapped somewhere below his heart. They stood there, then tiptoed out a few feet, until the water was up to Andy's chest. While Sam felt himself shrink down to the boy's size, Andy did the strangest thing. He ducked under for an instant, came up smiling, and patted his father's hand, saying *It's OK, Dad, we can go back to the room now.* Then he slept till noon while Sam lay beside him fighting back tears.

In the last year, Andy had learned not to call out to his father when he came in the house because Sam might be asleep. He would just turn on the television and sit in the recliner to wait until he heard stirring upstairs, or might sneak up to peek in the bedroom.

If Sam got in the tub, he knew he might stay there for an hour, might even fall asleep, and Andy would leave. So he walked down the steps and met Andy and Kayla tiptoeing up.

"Hey," Sam said. "If it isn't Navel Lint in the flesh."

Kayla actually giggled before looking down. Andy, pointing toward Sam's crotch, said "Speaking of in the flesh."

"Oh, man." Sam spun around and hustled back into the bathroom for his robe.

"If the show's over, Dad, we'll go back downstairs. Brought some dinner from the Saigon Kitchen and it's getting cold."

When Sam came down again, Andy and Kayla had the dining room table set, a bottle of Chardonnay open, and three coconut-scented candles flickering in the place where a fourth person would normally sit. The hand-thrown soup bowls they'd bought at a fair when Andy was ten sat on placemats instead of bare table. The plastic chopsticks were even mounted on little holders that Sam had bought years ago on a trip to Vancouver, British Columbia. He checked the clock, saw it was almost 9:00. Then he remembered how his evening had been spent, and why he didn't feel particularly hungry. Well, he could always eat a little more.

"Uh-oh," Sam said, spreading his arms as though to bless the table. "The royal treatment. This can only mean one thing: I'm about to learn something that would shock me too much if I heard it in the living room eating off paper plates at a normal dinner hour." He looked into Andy's eyes, then at Kayla and down to where their clasped hands disappeared under the table. "No, don't tell me."

"It's nothing, Dad. I just thought it would be nice to sit in here again and eat without the television on. There's no game tonight, anyway."

"Besides," Kayla added, "since we're leaving tomorrow for L.A., we thought we'd come over and celebrate."

"Jesus, Kayla," Andy sighed.

"Tomorrow?"

"Listen, Dad, we got a call on Tuesday saying they wanted us down there to do some publicity for *Grotty Hands*. Turns out it's already been released and it's just taking off. So they want us down there a couple weeks early."

"L.A.?" Sam said. "You leave tomorrow?"

"Yeah, and then we figured it didn't make a whole lot of sense to come back up to Portland again before the tour, so we'll just head out early." Andy poured everyone a glass of wine as he spoke, avoiding his father's eyes. "We'll be back in a few months."

Sam wanted to tell Andy it was all right, he was glad for him, glad for Kayla too, but just then he knew his voice wouldn't work. Maybe that was a side-effect of the drug? He smiled and lifted his wine glass, thinking how much of the little boy was still there in his son's downturned face. Andy certainly didn't look like a typical rock drummer. With his short hair neatly parted just right of center, his tuft of moustache, and his penchant for pale blue shirts with button-down collars, he looked like a young high school history teacher, or maybe a law clerk, an accountant. He had given up running again when Sam got sick and so had lost that lean edge which always seemed to keep his face in shadows, like his mother's. He looked sweet and safe, the prototype of a 1940s crooner. On the other hand, Kayla, the singer, looked exactly like a drummer should look. A dedicated weightlifter, she was densely muscled in her sleeveless tee-shirts, which she wore regardless of the weather. A tattooed vine crawled down one exposed shoulder, its leaves caressing her biceps. She was always tapping something: the floor with her feet, the table with her chopsticks, her teeth with her fingernail. Kayla radiated efficiency, a steadiness born of strength rather than timidity. She wore her black hair short and spiky, and stayed away from jewelry, anything that might clutter her hands or arms. She seldom smiled. But she laughed and laughed large, leaning back and roaring her pleasure when something did finally amuse her. Which Andy seemed to do, almost constantly. They were a strange couple, but devoted, and Sam was growing to love the young woman.

"To Navel Lint," Sam said, raising his glass for a toast. "I'm really very pleased for you, Andy." He knew he would not be able to get another sentence out, and so did Andy, so they reached across the table to clink glasses, shut their eyes, and drank.

Four

1.

Kate McCabe was playing solitaire on her computer. She dragged a run of cards beneath her king, then sat back watching the clock run up and the score run down.

Her fat notebooks spread out over three tables against the wall were calling to her. They actually had voices, dreamy, slowed-down versions of the patients' voices, and underneath the cacophony she could hear Sam's baritone saying her name over and over, patiently, clearly. Kate. Kate. Kate.

Before this study began, nobody but her husband called her Kate. It was always Katrina, or maybe Nurse McCabe, even Mrs. McCabe, though her husband's last name was Davis, but never Kate. She liked the way Sam said it, though, fast and with a very hard "t," like bold type. Her name was pulsing through the room's air, precise and calm, the same note repeating until she could no longer stay seated.

This was not the first time the notebooks had spoken to her. Whenever that happened, Kate knew something was wrong, someone was having a crisis, there was a problem at the drug company, there was cause for concern. She wished she could interpret it sooner, or better, but she always found out a few days later, after she'd seen a full round of patients. The first time, Daphne Warren had a spiking fever from the flu, nothing to do with the study. Another time, Alice Hardy had been in a car accident, no injuries, but was frantic for a Xanax, which of course was not permitted under the Zomalovir protocol. Recently, Hannah Lee Price complained of gut pain and malaise, and lately had begun favoring her right leg when she walked, problems that weren't anticipated side effects of Zomalovir.

So Kate knew she was right to worry now. This was awful, she was not supposed to get involved like this with her subjects, she was a professional, experienced in clinical research now. But from the start this study had bothered her. Maybe it had to do with the illness itself, so strange and frightening, so ambiguous, a cluster of symptoms she'd never seen before, people simply falling out of their lives as though through trapdoors. Or maybe it had to do with the pharmaceutical company PER, which struck Kate as even more sinister than the average firm she dealt with, doctors who loathed patients, who could not make money fast enough, who cornered the market on a lifesaving drug and inflated its price as subjects—no, victims—died. Or maybe it had to do with the drug itself, Zomalovir, which she knew in her soul was as toxic as mercury. She could see the curve already, a few patients improving quickly but hitting a plateau now, their systems going haywire. Last time, Tracy Marsh could barely sit still, as though each drop of the stuff were a pin pricking her veins from the inside.

Kate picked up the notebooks, flipped one open to a few random pages, thought about covering them with her sweater so they'd shut up. It was getting dark now, an early winter night, and she knew she should be heading home, starting dinner, working on her first glass of wine.

She walked to the window. On the computer screen, the game's timer kept going and her score approached zero.

2.

Every once in a while, when he'd first gotten sick and none of the specialists could diagnose what was wrong, Sam would get out of bed and solemnly dress in his running gear. He could no longer double-knot his laces or tolerate his contact lenses, and he often ended up with his hooded sweatshirt on backwards and his face buried in its hood, but he'd eventually put himself together and head out onto the trails anyway, patting his hip in a panic to locate the house key that he'd zipped into a nylon band on his wrist. As he ran he considered the various diseases his doctors had suspected. Perhaps he really was harboring some rare cancer that was as yet impossible for their computers and sensors to find, or dying of some degenerative muscle disease that by next year would find him wheelchair-bound and unable to communicate except by electrical impulses coming from his eyelids, or developing a new syndrome triggered by exposure to an unknown toxin which would shortly cause his hair to fall out and his bodily fluids to turn the consistency of spreadable fruit. Soon he'd imagine blood oozing from his eyeballs and toenails. Something had to be causing all the zany symptoms. Maybe whatever was making his liver function abnormally would soon manifest itself, and the uncertainty, at least, would be over. Those days Sam believed he just had to test his body in the only manner that ever made sense to him. In a deeply nonrational way, he thought he might actually be able to feel the spot where things were going wrong if he got his blood and organs pumping at their maximum, a kind of whole-body stress test. If something was going to burst, if a body part was going to fail, let's get on with it.

Inevitably, Sam would find himself at a standstill in the middle of the trail, unable to continue moving forward or figure out how to get back. He'd sit on the soft dirt beside the trail, resting and dreaming, palpating himself here and there, drifting off to sleep sometimes, unaware of runners zipping by, or responding to their calls of greeting by squawking back something like *garlic* or *leuke-*

mia or, on one occasion when a woman and her huge malamute streaked by, *George Gershwin*. After sitting for a while, Sam might feel capable of walking back down to the car, but when he got there he often found himself unable to drive reliably. He would put the car in gear before turning on the ignition, or turn around to look out the back window and lurch forward when he pressed the accelerator, or fiddle endlessly with the radio dial in hopes of clearing rain off the windshield. He got lost driving home, though he'd come this way hundreds of times. He failed to see pedestrians or notice what other cars were doing, lost the ability to downshift and turn the car at the same time. Or he fell asleep sitting behind the wheel, only to awaken three hours later with his forehead deeply indented by the steering wheel.

Even though he'd seemed to reach his maximum heart-rate in a fraction of the time it used to take him to work up a sweat, and his body erupted with exotic aches in places he didn't know could even feel pain, during these runs Sam never did discover for himself what was wrong. Doctor Enid Emerson finally did that. He had been referred to her by Clem Garnett, the State Police Superintendent, who was worried when Sam could not complete his project on enhancing the force's public image. They'd worked together often enough that Garnett knew something serious had to be going on. He called Sam at home one evening. At first it seemed as though he just wanted to talk about the Trailblazers and their losing streak, or complain about his allergies. Anything but the project. But then he got down to business.

"Jesus, Sam, forgive me for saying this but you sound terrible," Garnett had said. "I'm worried about you."

"It's probably nothing. At least, that's what the doctors are finding."

"It's not nothing, my friend. You've been looking like shit for months. Time to find out what's going on."

"I'm not sure what else I can do."

"Well get yourself over to see Enid Emerson, you hear me? The Miss Jane Marple of Internists. I'd trust her with my life. Once did, in fact, and my late wife's too, but there was nothing Enid could do about Sophia."

"Enid Emerson? Didn't she save those folks who ate the poison mushrooms a couple Easters ago? The family from Thailand, I think it was."

"She's the one. Three or four of them had to have liver transplants and she performed those too. Woman's a genius, trust me. Say, you didn't eat any funny mushrooms, did you?"

"No, Clem. At least not since 1974."

"Go see Enid. She'll know what to do with you."

After examining him and after looking at the various laboratory, ultra-sound, X-ray and MRI results that Sam had brought along in a thick portfolio, after going for a solo stroll around the perimeter of the building in which her office was located so that she could think about it all, Doctor Enid Emerson did know what to do with him. She returned to the examining room, folded her arms and said that the various things going wrong with him—his liver, spleen, immune system, brain—weren't what was wrong with him. They were caused by whatever was really wrong with him, and while she didn't know what that was, she knew who would. She sent him to Martin Fong up at Cascade-Kennedy.

But Fong didn't have an appointment available until six weeks later, and Sam felt he had to do something while he waited. There was no point in seeing other specialists; he'd seen nearly all the ones covered by his health insurance, and besides, he felt convinced by what Doctor Emerson had said. It seemed that Fong was the proper next step as well as his best hope among traditional medical practitioners. So Sam made an appointment to see Doctor Eli Moskowitz, Portland's best-known acupuncturist, herbalist and naturopath, whose advertisements appeared every week in the alternative newspaper that Sam picked up when he did his shopping at the health food store.

Moskowitz had three offices in the greater metropolitan area, including one in a building next to the postal substation where Sam went to buy stamps. He was available for appointments there on Wednesday mornings and every third Friday afternoon, and Sam was able to get in to see him within a week. He had never tried acupuncture or taken herbs, but Sam couldn't imagine just sitting in his recliner for the next fifty-six days till Fong could see him. Besides, Jessica knew Moskowitz and liked his work.

When he walked into Moskowitz's office, a woman was standing at the receptionist's window with her arms spread wide, belting out an aria of her latest symptoms in a shattering coloratura soprano. She could not turn her head to the left, she could not bend from the waist, she could neither sit nor lie on her back for longer than twelve seconds at a time. She now ate nothing but corn and tapioca pudding, heard the sound of a glockenspiel constantly in her right ear, had ferocious bouts of sweating while remaining chilled to the core, to the very core, and found herself sometimes living in 1931, which was four years before she was born. The receptionist was nodding and thrusting a clipboard full of forms at the woman.

"Doctor will be with you in a moment," she kept saying, in a kind of recitative counterpoint to the patient's presentation. "In a moment."

Sam didn't know what to do. Sitting down during the performance seemed rude, as unthinkable as nudging his way to the window in order to announce his presence. He considered leaving, but the receptionist caught his eye and blinked knowingly, then crooked a finger at him.

The other patient simply took a step to the right, timed perfectly with a deep inhalation, and pressed onward in her description of symptoms. She had blurred vision and gas, her hair had lost its curl, there were growths the size and shape of espresso cups all over her abdomen. The receptionist handed Sam the clipboard of forms that she'd been proffering earlier and pointed toward the seats behind him. There was a selection of herbal teas and a thermos of hot water on an endtable, so he made himself a cup of Mint Magic and sat in the corner, with the clipboard on his thighs.

The forms were so complex that as he flipped through them Sam felt he might begin to weep. That would be just what the receptionist needed. He'd had enough practice by now to get the insurance information and medical history down easily. But after a brief series of questions about his current problem, there were pages exploring his family background and the nature of his personality, his likes and dislikes, his sleep and dreams, his ability to tolerate heat or spices or certain kinds of cloth. He did the best he could, then thought about going home for a nap before actually seeing Moskowitz. He laid his head back against the wall and closed his eyes.

When he opened them again, perhaps a half-hour later, he found a tall, thin man of about forty-five, who looked shockingly like Mr. Rogers, standing five feet away and gazing down at him, studying him. Sam thought that if the man started singing *It's a beautiful day in the neighborhood,* he would add hallucinations to his list of symptoms. He sensed that the man had been there for some time, rocking back on his heels, flexing his knees, rubbing his hands together, smiling with grave comprehension.

"Eli Moskowitz," he said, taking two steps closer and reaching a huge hand down toward Sam. "I know you from somewhere."

"Sam Kiehl."

"It'll come to me." Moskowitz continued holding Sam's hand and gazing down at him. "I knew you better when you were sitting down, why is that?"

"Beats me."

"Television? Did you used to be on TV? Wait a minute, Sam Kiehl, of course, the election guru. Now wait a minute. You sat at a desk under this map of Oregon and you always looked like you wanted to pop out of the thing and skip around the studio. So much energy, I used to think, don't make the poor man sit." Moskowitz finally released Sam's hand and took a step backwards. "Sam Kiehl, I'll be damned. I don't know how many hours you've saved me from sitting in front of the tube listening to election night returns. Polls close and five minutes later we got all the results. I'm glad to meet you."

"Likewise. I've read all about you in the filters."

"I beg your pardon?"

"The newspapers. Sorry. I see your ads all the time in the newspaper."

"Yeah, in the filters, I see what you mean. So come inside."

Moskowitz led him to a dimly lit room and told him to get comfortable, then went into the office to read what Sam had written. The door to the treatment room rattled shut and Sam was immediately aware of a strange, familiar smell, something that made him want to sleep and cough at the same time. It seemed to be made of equal parts sage, cedar, and marijuana, and was not at all unpleasant, though he wouldn't like it to be any stronger. He looked around the small room, whose only furnishings were a small table on wheels, a high stool and a narrow table covered in thick mauve leather, and couldn't see where the smell was coming from. Maybe Moskowitz piped it in through the HVAC system.

The room's back wall was covered with two gray and maroon charts labeled *The Points and Meridians of Acupuncture.* One showed the female anatomy, the other showed the male, each in three distinct poses. Normally his gaze would have lingered on the female, but as soon as he understood what the charts were about, Sam froze and could not take his eyes off the three male figures. In the middle, a man stood facing away from the room as though unwilling to look at what was about to happen, arms at his sides, fingers spread wide, toes pointed east and west, his entire body speckled with black or red circles and triangles, the whole connected by a network of solid or broken lines. A cartography of potential needle points. To the left of this figure was another man, sensibly striding out of the poster as quickly as he could, a swarm of shapes buzzing around his head like flies. To his right was a third man who, at first glance, seemed to be signaling to Sam via semaphore. His left arm was crooked at the elbow and his right arm was reaching as though for a tasty canapé while he stood on his right foot and had his left poised in the air. Maybe this wasn't a signal, maybe this was what happened if Moskowitz hit the wrong acupuncture point. What troubled Sam the most was an inset near the bottom of the chart, beckoning him closer to the wall so he could verify that he was seeing what he thought he was seeing. Sure enough, the inset revealed the close-up detail of a man lying on his back, legs spread to reveal the area between his raised scrotum and gaping anus, with three dots to illustrate precisely where needles must be stuck to address certain symptoms, none of which Sam was prepared to admit he had, regardless of what they were.

Sam thought alternative medicine was supposed to be about comfort and relaxation, not horror. Now he could hear soft music, Chopin, he thought, which was at least a step in the right direction. The gorgeous *Nocturne in E Flat Major*. Except that if this was the same album Sam had, and he thought he recognized the Ashkenazy touch, then in about a half-hour the *Funeral March* would start. That should be right about the time he had a dozen pins sticking out of his toes, ears, shoulders, and forehead.

He turned toward the side wall, where he found a chart illustrating the five symbolic elements of wood, fire, earth, metal, and water, which are the basis of ancient Chinese medical practice. Safe enough. On the opposite wall hung a poster of Monet's hazy, soothing *Grain Stacks at Sunset*. Sam wondered if a few tongue points might have helped clear up old Claude's eyesight.

Sam lay on the table. He didn't know what he had expected, perhaps jars of strange herbs, lacquered bowls filled with scented oils, Chinese and Hebrew prayer books, delicate paintings that captured all the complex beauty of a mountainside in three brisk strokes. It sure wasn't this, nor the gaunt man in an unbuttoned sweater and slicked-down thinning hair who strode into the room barefooted and seemed ready to talk about Mister Needle.

"I read your forms, Sam. Today you need help with the headaches first, am I right? Next with the mind-fog and fatigue, then the muscle and joint pain? Don't say anything, I understand."

Moskowitz examined Sam's tongue, then took his wrist and began to feel his pulse. Smiling faintly, Moskowitz pressed firmly and didn't let go, holding on for at least three minutes, eyes closed, adjusting the pressure now and then, barely breathing. Then he took hold of the other wrist. When he opened his eyes again, and looked intently into Sam's, there was such a burst of kindness and compassion on his face that Sam could not look away.

"Your deep pulses are very strange, Sam. May I call you Sam? Clearly, you're dealing with layers upon layers of imbalance."

"That's about what I've been saying for months, Dr. Moskowitz."

"Eli, please. And I suppose you've had some difficulty being heard by your physicians, am I right?"

Sam shut his eyes in a slow blink. Was this guy trying to get him to cry? Maybe that's part of the therapy, making the patient expel chi-choked tears. "So what does it mean in terms of treatment? Can you help me?"

"Yeah, I think so. But it'll take some time." He put his vast hands out and brought his palms together as though in prayer. "We have to work through these layers. Today I think we'll just try some basic points and see if we can ease your pain."

"Look, Eli, I have to admit there's some anxiety about this."

"That's a good sign. You're new to Chinese medicine, especially to acupuncture. Most westerners focus on pain, on the needles. I would be worried if you didn't feel anxious. Now lie back, I really don't think you'll feel any pain."

Moskowitz dimmed the lights further. In the last few minutes, without Sam noticing, Chopin had been transformed into Asian-sounding synthesizer music and a pillow had materialized on the mauve table. As long as he didn't look at the chart on the wall, Sam thought he'd be all right.

"Eli, what's that odor?"

Moskowitz appeared beside him, dragging his table and carrying his stool. He sniffed. "Oh, that? Moxa. In a couple weeks or so, we'll be burning some just below your navel. Now relax."

"Dear God."

Sam could feel Moskowitz's warm hands moving across his torso, along his neck and face. There was a tap above the bridge of his nose, and a quick sting, then Moskowitz whispered "There, that wasn't too bad, am I right?"

"It's in?"

"Shah!"

Moskowitz inserted several more needles, some of which he twisted till Sam winced. The stool creaked as Moskowitz leaned back and Sam knew the man was looking at him carefully. That gentle, penetrating gaze was almost like another needle.

"I'll leave you now, Sam. Be back in twenty minutes or so to check how you're doing."

When the door closed, Sam let out a huge breath he didn't realize he'd been holding in, then opened his eyes. There was a shadow above his vision, as though a bird were perched on his head, beak poised to strike Sam's own. Then he glimpsed the shape of a long needle protruding from the place Moskowitz had called his Third Eye, and decided it was best to keep his eyes closed. After a few minutes, something happened inside Sam's head that almost made him gasp. He could feel his headache crack into shards, literally become fragments within his cranium, which then seemed to be absorbed into the unfeeling matter of his brain. The headache was gone.

Sam slept. He hadn't heard Moskowitz return, but became aware of the man's presence above him as the needles were being withdrawn.

"So?" Moskowitz asked. "Tell me what happened."

Sam found himself too tired to speak. He opened his eyes and tried to get his mouth to work, tried moving his hands to rub his forehead, considered sitting, but he was immobilized by fatigue.

Moskowitz saw the look of concern in Sam's eyes and said, "I know, sometimes acupuncture does that. Worsens a symptom before clearing it away. It's a good sign, this fatigue. How's your pain?"

"Headache's gone," Sam managed to whisper. He flexed his legs. "Hips are still there."

"I should hope so."

"The pain, I mean."

Moskowitz nodded vigorously. "That's a good sign. Each pain will declare its presence more forcefully before it begins to abate."

"And I have to go to the bathroom."

"Of course you do. It's the tea."

Sam continued coming to Moskowitz's office after he'd been diagnosed by Doctor Fong and begun the battery of treatments Fong recommended. Taking herbal supplements and a shifting array of naturopathic remedies, receiving weekly acupuncture and an occasional spinal adjustment, Sam felt he was embracing everything that medicine could throw at him. But Moskowitz's work never managed to do anything but alleviate the headaches for a day or two. If anything, Sam felt more exhausted than ever. He stopped thinking it was a good sign.

Then came the drug study. Sam never really questioned whether to participate. It dangled there before him like a string from the attic door, offering him a wisp of hope he could not ignore. Something might be up there, even if all other attempts by the medical profession to solve the mysteries of his disease had so far failed. Part of the agreement Sam had to make with Doctor Fong and PER Pharmaceuticals was to give up all other treatments during the period of the study. At the time, feeling that he reached a plateau in the work he was doing with Moskowitz, Sam had been ready to stop the treatments. But as the study progressed, Sam realized he missed the relief Eli's needles could bring to his headaches. Also the pleasure of his company and the sound of his voice saying *Yes, that's a good sign* whenever Sam complained about the needles' side effects, and the hope that someday they might achieve a breakthrough.

3.

The morning after he'd eaten dinner with Jessica and then with Andy and Kayla, Sam woke feeling the familiar desire to test his body again. He rolled over in bed and looked out at the wintry drizzle. Well, maybe go climb some walls. That way, he thought, he could surely figure out if he was getting the drug or the placebo. His taxed body would say so. Right. Dream on. He still hadn't recovered from his last time on the treadmill.

Before there was any further testing of his body, he remembered, he had to have his head tested by the brilliant Doctor Henry Ferrier of Santa Barbara and San Luis Obispo, who had written papers about the impact of this syndrome on bloodflow to the brain, and been hired by PER as the consultant for their study. This meant Sam had to spend the next hour figuring out how to get out of bed, dress himself, and venture downstairs so that he would be ready when his friend Gary Maxwell arrived to take him for the bimonthly neuropsychological exam. He rolled onto his back again, and realized that Max was the reason he was thinking about working out again.

Max had called Thursday to ask if there was anything Sam needed help with over the weekend. He cheerfully agreed to give up his Saturday morning so that he could drive Sam to the exam. Located off I-5 at the exit for the new Mormon Temple, the motel where the exam was to be administered could not have been less convenient for disabled patients to get to while still being within the Portland city limits. He hated to ask it of Max, but there was no other way. Tracy had been scheduled for her neuropsychological exam yesterday, so Sam was on his own. It seemed as though all the tests were coming due at the same time. Typical PER scheduling.

Sam fumbled with the appointment slip on his bedside table. He had to be in room 112 of the motel at 10:00, which gave him about two hours to get ready. That could be pushing things, especially if he wanted to eat anything for breakfast besides Special K. Sam folded back the sheets and turned to dangle his legs over the bed's edge. So far so good.

According to Kate McCabe, Doctor Ferrier had promised that today's test would last only an hour. The first exam, when Ferrier was collecting baseline data on each subject, took three-and-a-half hours of steady concentration and nearly killed them all. The neuropsychological testing consisted of a stream of monotonous questions, a bunch of puzzles to assemble, shapes to draw from memory after studying them for thirty seconds, cartoon panels to decode and arrange chronologically, stories to recount after Ferrier had recited them in his breathy voice, details from pictures to recall with precision when the same picture reappeared with components missing, and several other tasks designed to pinpoint deficits caused by organic damage to the brain. If the subjects could have done half the things on the test, they wouldn't have qualified for the drug study in the first place. Even after taking the same test three times now, or hearing Ferrier recite the same stories and seeing him toss the same shapes onto the table between them, even knowing when he was blindfolded that the circle went in the slot next to the tall triangle, Sam still struggled with most of the material. He wondered if Ferrier considered the familiarity factor so that he would not falsely attribute a slight improvement in the scores to an improvement in Sam's health. Ferrier's brain-teasers were the kinds Sam used to love doing with his son when Andy was young. They would spend hours together at the kitchen table, working on a complicated jigsaw puzzle or playing a game in which various oddly shaped pieces had to be fitted into slots that exactly matched their form. Now these activities felt like torment, reminding him of all he'd lost.

Gary Maxwell was the kind of friend Sam hadn't had since childhood. He'd had colleagues and clients, neighbors, acquaintances who came into his life through Andy, but no close male friend until he met Max inside the finishers' chute at a 10K race. They sat together under a giant oak tree gulping water and eating sections of orange, talking about their training methods and best races. Then they went to breakfast at a nearby restaurant and talked about politics and urban planning, since Max was a freelance writer whose passion was liberal politics and economic policy, and Sam was always tracking changes to the political scene. The next morning they arranged to meet at the mouth of the trails where Sam liked to run. They had trained together for years, once spending most of a fifteen-mile run along the wooded trails of Forest Park on an April morning trying to calculate how many miles they'd covered together in the years they'd been friends.

After he got sick, Sam couldn't reliably compute anything, even with a calculator. Without having to be asked, Max had started helping him do his income taxes. He'd computerized Sam's finances, helped with the bills, and filled out the IRS forms each year. He'd also showed up at Sam's apartment two or three mornings a week, talking about basketball or music or politics as if nothing had changed between them except the location of their conversations. Now as Sam got out of bed and shuffled toward the bathroom, he wondered whether he would have had the moxie to stay as loyal to Max if the situation were reversed.

When Max pulled into the driveway, Sam was just finishing his cereal and gazing absently at the sports section of the *Oregonian*. He'd lost track of time and didn't hear the car. Max let himself in, a half-eaten Egg McMuffin in his hand, and came over to sit at the kitchen table.

In all the years Sam had known him, Max never seemed to change. He still looked thirty-two, was still as lean and unlined as he'd been a decade ago and wore his brown hair and moustache with the same careless disarray. He also still ate his high-cholesterol, high-fat diet without seeming to gain an ounce.

"What time is it?" Sam asked.

"About 9:15. Thought I'd get here early and make sure you were up."

"Been up for hours. It's being in motion that's the issue."

"Can I say something?"

Sam put down his spoon and leaned back. "I know, I know. But it just frustrates the hell out of me that getting out of bed, taking a shower, and eating breakfast is enough to put me back in bed for the day."

"That wasn't what I meant. It's just, I don't know, you seem to be getting a lot worse since this drug thing began. Those are haversacks under your eyes, Sam, and your color reminds me of fish spawn. Maybe you should think about dropping out if you're not getting the drug. I would. Before they go ahead and kill you outright."

"No way. You remember when I couldn't get up that hill during the Cascade Run-Off and every grandmother in the race passed me by? Even the belly-dancers were finished shaking by the time I passed their corner. But I still had to finish."

"Right, with this disease corroding your gizzards and a frayed hamstring pulling at you. I remember it well. You finished something like eight thousandth out of seven thousand runners."

"So there you go. I have to stay with this thing. Besides, the damn drug works, I can see it does. Tracy is just about fully recovered already."

"Well, think about it, all right? It might make sense to be alive at the end of this process."

Sam nodded, then took a spoonful of cereal. "Maxwell, why don't you throw that shit you're eating away and let me Xerox you some oatmeal. It'll only take two minutes."

"How many copies?"

"What?"

"Never mind. Oatmeal sounds good, but I'll eat this sandwich too."

Sam looked at Max closely for a moment, taking in the freshly showered look, the faraway eyes, the slump of his shoulders. "How far did you run this morning, twenty miles?"

"Nah, just a fast ten, but I didn't eat much last night." He got up and moved toward the pantry. "I'll make the oatmeal myself. You should see the political cartoon in the paper."

When they arrived at the motel, Doctor Henry Ferrier was not waiting in the lobby as he'd said he would. Sam rang room 112 and got no answer.

"Could this be the wrong day?" Max asked.

"You've been around me too long." Sam took an appointment slip out of his pocket and checked. "Right day, right time. Maybe he's eating breakfast, I'll check in the library."

"Do that. And see if they have the new le Carré novel."

As Sam turned toward the dining room, he saw Ferrier walking down the hall. The plump, gray-haired psychologist was wearing a pair of bikini swim trunks, or at least that's what Sam thought he saw glimmering turquoise underneath the man's shining belly, and was working on cleaning water out of his ears with a towel as he approached the front desk. He walked right past Sam and smiled, then turned toward the clerk and said, "Has my ten o'clock arrived yet?"

"Right here," Sam said.

Ferrier spun around like a gunfighter, even crouching slightly, glaring at Sam and Max as though he'd been challenged. Then he smiled, draped the towel around his shoulders, walked over to them and reached for Max's hand. "Good to see you again," he said

Max shook hands, then pointed at Sam. "This is your man right here. One Samuel E. Kiehl. But you don't have to run any tests, if you want my opinion, because everyone knows he's an idiot."

Ferrier nodded as though in complete agreement. Then he smacked his forehead and exclaimed, "Ha ha ha, Mr. Kiehl, I'm so forgetful myself, you see. Maybe you should give the tests to me, eh?"

Sam hated it when people tried to reassure him by saying that they, too, had trouble remembering things, or were often tired, or had stumbled just the other day while crossing the street. He wished he could think of something snappy to say to Ferrier, but he just nodded and followed the doctor back toward his room. Ferrier resumed the cleaning of his ear, singing as he walked, something that sounded like a jazzed-up rendition of "Harbor Lights." Sam fell into step behind Ferrier's left shoulder. Nice voice, a sweet tenor. The old fellow may have missed his calling. When Ferrier stopped suddenly, Sam walked right past him, just managing to avoid a collision.

"Damn it, Mr. Samuels, you see what I mean? Now I forgot to pick up my room key."

"Kiehl."

Ferrier looked at him as though making a mental note that Sam did not any longer understand the meaning of the word 'key.' "No, I forgot my key, you know, the thing that opens doors. K-e-y. Not keel. Now why don't you wait here," he ordered.

After unlocking the door, Ferrier motioned for Sam to wait again, and disappeared inside. Hearing the shower start, Sam sat on the hallway floor with his back against the wall and fell asleep.

When he ushered Sam in a few minutes later, Ferrier had obviously checked the files because he now had the name right. They sat at a small round table by the bathroom, which was expelling a warm, moist fog into the room despite the raucous labors of its ventilation fan.

"You fell asleep out there."

"I know. I was there when it happened."

Ferrier smiled. He had either heard everything before or heard nothing, ever. Adjusting imaginary knickknacks on the table, he said, "Mr. Kiehl, can you name the last seven presidents in reverse order, please?"

When Ferrier got to the storytelling part of the test a half-hour later, Sam asked if he could possibly lie on the sofa until it was time to do the puzzles. Ferrier paused before answering, as though trying to decide if this anomaly might somehow skew the results, but ultimately gave his permission. With shirttails hanging out in back, shirtsleeves rolled to the elbows and bow tie shifting toward the vertical, the man already looked as though he needed another long swim.

After Sam got settled on the sofa, Ferrier smiled and said, "All right, then, tell me as much as you can remember."

"About what?"

"The story, of course. Remember: *Mrs. Ferguson was worried about her daughter's birthday party. . . .*"

"You haven't told me the story yet, Doctor Ferrier."

Ferrier looked at Sam with deep compassion. He crossed his hands over his belly, looked down, noticed that a button needed rebuttoning. "Surely," he said, then stopped. He turned around to the table and picked up his notes. "Ah, of course. You see, I do these tests with a certain rhythm and you broke that rhythm when you asked about the sofa. So. Please listen to this story carefully and then tell me as much of it as you can remember, eh?"

After the test ended, Sam asked if he could use the bathroom. Ferrier checked his watch and nodded. Sam splashed cold water on his face and, gazing into the mirror, was struck by the redness of his eyes, which were so dry he was afraid to blink in case the cornea cracked. He felt as though he could sleep for a month. A day and a half would have to do; he had another infusion on Monday.

"Oh, man," Max said when Sam walked into the lobby.

"You should see the other guy," Sam said. "He looks much worse."

"Let me go get the car, all right? I'll pick you up in front of the door."

"No need."

Max put his hand against Sam's chest and pushed him gently

backwards. Sam collapsed into a soft leather chair. He closed his eyes and nodded.

4.

It was Saturday afternoon, but Kate McCabe was up at the medical school campus to give Molly Carroll her infusion. Molly didn't have a partner in the study because no one was willing to be with her that often. She scrounged rides from the others when she could, sometimes harassed her seventy-nine-year-old mother into driving the family's seldom-used Rambler, sometimes took public transportation. It was always dicey. This week, Molly couldn't make her Friday appointment because snow had closed bus routes up the hill to the hospital, and her mother refused to drive in such conditions, and no one else admitted to being free.

Kate was actually glad to be there. She'd arrived just after lunch and luxuriated in the quiet. No patients, no nurses or staff or docs, no announcements blaring from the ceiling speakers, no bells dinging, no phone calls. Just the hum of the heating system and rattle of window panes, and her own breathing. She got some paperwork done, collating subjects' reports on their week's activities, noting any abnormal physical responses to the infusions, accounting for each bottle in the week's shipment.

She sensed Molly's presence before hearing her, before Molly even passed through the double doors of the Research Department. Kate closed the notebook she'd been evaluating and made sure Molly's was nowhere near the top of any piles, then faced the door.

"Can we do my right arm today?" Molly said, skipping any greeting as usual.

"My dear Ms. Carroll, we can do anywhere you like. Right arm, back of either hand, upper chest. If you have a vein, I can infuse you."

Molly shrugged and headed toward the infusion room. Kate continued looking through the doorway. *Maybe irritability is a little known side-effect of Zomalovir, applicable only when the subject's initials are M.C.*

The weekly supply of drug was kept in a basement freezer. Kate had to request her day's bottles the night before so a technician could thaw it properly and a messenger could bring it in a timely manner, before the stuff began breaking down. It was an intricate procedure that, to Kate's astonishment, had not once failed to work during the study. Yet.

She was sure that if there would ever be a breakdown, it would happen during one of Molly's appointments. She could just hear the ruckus. Phone calls to the Ethics Committee, Congress, the ACLU. But there it was, the solemn yellow bottle in the little refrigerator, with a great red X drawn across the blank label.

Kate put the bottle on a cart along with all the infusion equipment, thermometer, sterile pads, preps, and the blood pressure gauge. Molly was waiting for her in the corner recliner, as far away from the windows as she could get, with her back to the door.

"You know what I was thinking?" she asked.

"I don't even know what *I* was thinking Molly. It's been that kind of week."

"I was thinking, why don't we have a little taste, eh?"

"What are you talking about?"

Molly pointed at the bottle. "A Zomalovir cocktail for a wintry Saturday morning, know what I mean? Squirt a few drops out into a cup, let's see if it's salty, like a placebo, or maybe vinegary, like a drug."

Why didn't I think of that? "You don't think PER considered this? I'm sure the Zomalovir is suspended in saline. Looks the same, tastes the same. Nice try."

Kate began fiddling with Molly's elbow, poking at the vein to make it stand up. She reached for a catheter.

"I bet you'd do it for Sam if he asked you."

"What's that supposed to mean?" *Don't let her get to you.* Kate continued working on Molly's arm. "I don't have any favorites, you know that. You're all numbers to me, just numbers."

"Come off it, Kate."

It took all her self-control not to jab the tender crook of Molly's arm, or miss the vein on purpose. Kate concentrated, as always, on getting the line in gently. Even the best nurses had trouble with arms like these, the veins all corroded by constant pricking.

"There. Now crank back and relax for an hour. Can I get you anything?"

Molly just looked at her. Didn't smile, didn't blink, didn't frown. It was as though she were gone. Only just before she started picking up the packaging for disposal, Kate noticed that Molly's normally dry eyes were filling with tears.

Five

1.

"Hi there," Jessica said.

Sam could hear the parrots squawking in the background, so he knew she was calling from the nursery even though it was past dinner time. "I was just thinking about you."

"You were?"

"Well technically, at the moment the phone rang, I was thinking of Finland. I was trying to imagine you swimming in a fjord."

"Fjords are a little cold for swimming, Sam. And they're mostly in Norway."

"This was a warm fjord in southern Finland. Admittedly rare."

Jessica chuckled. Sam could imagine the little shake of the head that accompanied that chuckle. Then her voice deepened. "Listen, I called because something's come up, and I'm really sorry about it."

"Uh-oh, this sounds ominous."

"No, no, it's nothing like you're imagining. But the timing could be better."

"Your old boyfriend called?"

"There's no old boyfriend, Sam. It's just I'm going to be out of town for a while.

"Oh."

"With my father. We're going to take a look at some bigger nurseries. Oregon, Washington, Idaho, and maybe up into Canada. He wants me to see how they operate. And I think he's considering an expansion here. Wants to talk to some people he knows. Anyway, I'll be gone maybe a week."

"When do you leave?"

"Probably tomorrow. I know, Sam, I'd love to see you too, before I go." So she could read his mind over the phone, too.

"I could stay up late. I had a long, long nap."

"It's just not possible."

They agreed that she'd come for dinner as soon as she got back. Take another walk. Who knows, maybe go see a movie, drive into the Columbia Gorge. She would try to call him during the week.

"OK. Enjoy the time with your father. Meanwhile, I'll read up on fjords."

2.

Molly Carroll dreamed of flight. She had lustrous wings, pale green and ebony, and her long nose had sharpened and curved even further into a beak. But otherwise she looked and felt like herself, only airborne and light. If she were not careful, she could be happy.

Then she realized she was part of a flock. This added to her happiness, though if she knew anything about herself she knew she hated being part of a group. Yet here she was, feeling full of hope, not alone at all but deep down one side of a long Vee, and she had no idea where she was going. Well, south, because she could already feel the air growing warmer and see more color coming into the land below, but that was as much as she knew.

When Molly woke up, she was furious because the dream hadn't resolved. She hated dreams anyway, the surreal jumble of images, the confusion of memory and imagination, if that's what it was, the feeling of utter chaos. She hated it most when something short-circuited the process. The least They could do was let a dream resolve, give a person a fighting chance to make sense of things.

She got up and heard the one sound in all the world she loathed more than any other. More than winter wind coming straight down from Alaska to swirl around her particular house, more than the petty snick of snowflakes against the windows, or that awful furnace yakking and screaming over the wind. It was her mother snoring away on the other side of the wall. Since Molly had been a child she'd had to sleep with that racket going on, endure it polluting her dreams, wake up to it, hear it before she could even collect her thoughts of a morning. Molly suspected that her mother worked on the snoring the way a singer worked on a voice, practicing, studying, exercising the muscles. It drove Molly's father out of the bed and out of the bedroom, which was probably her mother's goal, then it drove him downstairs and eventually out of the house and into the arms of that harridan he was living with, Moira, perfectly named since she always wanted more-a of everything.

It didn't matter where you were in the house, you could still hear the snoring. You could also smell the mold that had been taking over the place since 1962. Molly headed downstairs, lusting for coffee, which of course she couldn't have now that she was sick and had to stay away from caffeine. Or for the stickiest sweetest donut the world had ever seen, which of course she couldn't have either, stay away from sugar, or her favorite breakfast dish of Canadian bacon and American cheese slices, her famous North American omelette, which of course she couldn't have either, stay away from processed foods and preservatives. What's left, taste-free cereal? Been there, done that.

Molly decided to skip breakfast altogether, as she had been skipping breakfast for months now, ever since the goddamned Zomalovir study got going. Talk about false hope! She gave up all her painkillers and her sleep medications and her antidepressants because that was the rules, that was the PROTOCOL, and in return she got what? Stuck like a pig, used, poked and prodded and studied, and run into the ground, and she couldn't tell but finally in the last week or two she thought maybe, just perhaps maybe, she might be getting the drug because she wasn't getting any sicker and she should have been getting sicker from all the shit they were putting her through. OK, she may even have been feeling slightly, just a teeny slight bit better. A scad. An oodle.

But there was such a long way to go yet, and she was not really sure, and it would be stupid to hope, even for a moment, that this was really where she was headed, that she might get her life back. Been there, done that too.

It was strange that Mr. Sam Kiehl, Fong's favorite, McCabe's pet, wasn't getting better. Molly would have bet her entire fortune, all twelve dollars of it, that Fong and McCabe would've rigged the study to be sure Mr. Sam Kiehl got the drug. It gave her a feeling she recognized as pleasure to see him slumping around the clinic, to see the darkness under his eyes. Just as it once gave her pleasure, when they'd first met, to imagine him inviting her over to his home.

Molly sat on the back steps looking out toward Mount Tabor and took a deep breath. She closed her eyes, opened them wide, stood up. What the hell was she doing out here in her nightgown, for Christ's sake, it was twenty-five degrees! She tried to stand but found herself almost unable to budge, as though she were stuck to the steps, as though she'd sat bare-assed on ice. No, that's not it.

She was rooted to the spot, she knew, by exhaustion. Infinitesimally less than before, maybe fatigue to the seventh instead of tenth degree. And by the absence of joy, which every fool knew was the very thing that gave us buoyancy.

3.

Sam lay on his back in bed staring across the room at the wall. It was covered by an enormous landscape in oils, a blue hillside in upstate New York capped with boiling clouds that seemed to reach down after the trees. It had been done by his boyhood friend, the famous painter Barry Callendar, and captured a place they had walked together dozens of times. Barry had sent it after Sam got sick, inscribed on the back with a terse message in charcoal ordering him to look at the hillside every morning when he woke up and every night before he went to sleep because they were going to walk there again some day.

But today was not the day. Today there was a hole where the barn should be, a ragged black aureole just to the right of the painting's center. Around the inner edge of the hole, toothed shapes rotated like gears, flashing brilliantly, changing directions, growing and shrinking, bursting into blinding yellows, then disappearing for an instant. Sam blinked, but the shapes remained.

Sitting up, Sam looked at the bedspread, a solid moss-green field across his lap, and the dazzling hole was there too, right about at his kneecap. It was on the doorframe as well, and the ceiling, and he lay back down thinking it was not a good sign.

He closed both eyes, bringing the kaleidoscope of forms inside his head, and tried to distract himself by remembering last night's telephone call from Andy. Navel Lint was hot, he'd said, and the buzz in Los Angeles was very strong. Andy and Kayla had been taken to dinner at a restaurant in Beverly Hills and seen Edith Bunker eating in a booth directly opposite theirs. Some kind of fish dish, Andy thought. The producer loved Kayla's voice and presence, Andy's lyrics, the band's chemistry. Sam thought the last time he'd heard Andy sound so excited was when he'd won the Portland Public School invitational mile, upsetting the three co-favorites in the race with a three-hundred-meter finishing kick.

When Sam opened his eyes, his vision was still disturbed. He got up and headed for the bathroom. Hell, a guy could take a shower with a hole in his sight. Really, when you thought about it, could do almost anything, maybe even fly a helicopter. That'll be the day. Anyway, the hole would probably be gone by the time he had to be at Cascade-Kennedy.

4.

Tracy woke up so full of energy she thought she would burst if she couldn't get rid of some. Her head roared with it, like the inside of a conch shell. She felt as though she'd been levitating all night and was surprised to see the impression of her head on the pillow or body on the sheets.

What to do, what do to?

She knew what Wally would suggest if she woke him and said that she needed to burn off some energy. *What say I plug into some of it, sweetie pie?* But all that would accomplish, in the sixteen seconds it took for him to finish, was to send Wally back to sleep and make Tracy even more irritable.

What to do, what to do?

She tiptoed from the room and immediately dropped to the hallway floor, where she did thirty-five pushups. Silently. Good start. Then she went into the bathroom, locked the door, lay on the rug, hooked her feet under the washing machine and did thirty-five noisy sit-ups. Now we're getting somewhere. She carefully opened the bathroom door, jumped up to catch herself on the lintel and did a few chin-ups before dropping softly to the carpeted floor and closing the door again. Next she pulled off her nightgown, stepped back to view herself in the full-length mirror behind the door and did a set of twisting stretches, a dozen back arches, some windmills with her arms. Rose up on her toes a few times and held herself there. She was beginning to breathe hard.

Tracy liked the way she looked again. Her weight was the same as always, but she was firm again, toning up. Her neck was long and solid, with a couple of nice veins showing now that she was a bit more pumped up. After a couple of kids, she knew her breasts were fuller and softer than they ought to be on a woman her age, in her shape. But she was OK with them. Hardly mattered, though. Wally treated them like the fine-tuning knobs on his stereo anyway.

She put on yesterday's sweats, which were in a heap by the hamper, and walked into the hallway. No sound from the kids' room, so maybe she could sneak down to the basement and run in place for a while, or do a few reps with the free weights that her dad had given her back when she was competing in racquetball. Couldn't go out and run in case someone woke up and God forbid Wally might have to do something for them.

In the basement, Tracy began running in place. Hey, maybe a trampoline would be nice down here. Nah, probably crack her head open on the ceiling, which Wally wouldn't like because it might wake him up. Lordy, it would be nice to play racquetball competitively again. She watched herself in the mirror against the basement wall, but without real concentration, content just to see her legs working like this, her arms pumping, her face relaxed. It sure was amazing, this Zomalovir miracle. *Look at me! Just look at me!*

5.

It was ninety-two degrees in the Research Department, and Sam sat as far from the radiators as possible. He had stripped down to his 1986 Portland Marathon tee-shirt and a pair of nylon running shorts. He dragged an old wooden rocker across the room and turned it toward the east windows to watch Mount Hood hover above the river on a cushion of haze. His vision was normal again. Maybe it was the drug.

Tracy found a matching rocker near the television and carried it over beside him. She found an empty wastebasket to set upside-down in front of the rocker for a hassock, and a rickety steel table on wheels to hold her thermos of hot water and sack of Gala apples. Her movements were sharp and precise, their energy causing all the other subjects in the room to stare as she settled next to Sam and began lurching back and forth like a child on a hobbyhorse.

He reached over and rested his arm on the arm of her chair, slowing it till they settled into a rhythm together, rocking in silence. They stared at the mountain like a couple on the eve of their golden anniversary, each lost in thought.

Earlier in the morning, Kate McCabe had called the Research Department's administrator to leave a message for Sam and Tracy. She was running late, there had been changes in the study protocol, and she had some things to arrange before coming over to tell them about it. The message posted for them on the bulletin board suggested that they wait with a cup of hot tea and—a touch of typical McCabe whimsy—enjoy the November silence. Right, silence on the wild frontier of biomedical research. She said if their blood pressure was less than 100 over 70 when she arrived, she would give them gold stars.

No way. Not only was the heat on high, so was the volume. Sam could swear there had to be a second television hidden somewhere, a machine hooked into a stereo sound system and tuned to a sitcom rerun with a horrible laugh track. There was also a steady moan coming from one of the adjacent rooms, the screak of rubber soles as the nurses hustled down the hallway, a background hiss of radiator steam, and a whine from a cranky machine near the reception desk, something designed to drive dogs mad. Great for the blood pressure.

Homer and Vi were back today, still radioactive, still working on Matisse's *Harmony in Red*. Several other people had fiddled with the puzzle during the last week, but it remained only half-finished. When Sam had walked into the room, Homer looked up and winked at him, saying in hushed tones, "We're both under three hundred," before returning to the puzzle. Vi patted his hand. She must have given Homer one hell of a lecture last time. Or spiked his oat bran with valium. The old man was positively taciturn this morning.

Two women, different from the ones last week, were ensconced before the television with catheters jutting from their arms. They stared, rapt, as *The Galloping Gourmet* demonstrated how tomato paste should be heated until its natural sugars caramelized in order to provide depth in low-fat dishes. Another man with Parkinson's disease was being interviewed in the far corner, his face a mask, hands clasped above his belly as though in prayer, head nodding in agreement with everything the nurse said. In answer to every one of her questions, he repeated the word "rock."

In the corner near Sam and Tracy, an elderly couple stood gazing at the parking lot while discussing their granddaughter's new boyfriend. It was impossible not to overhear them, despite the television and other assorted commotion.

"His name is Bill also," the woman said.

"Bill Olson?"

"Jackson."

"And he's the paving contractor?"

"Painting contractor."

"Right, and she started a cookie business last year, didn't she?"

"A quickie business?"

"Cooking business. Right, right. I knew it was something."

A woman hooked to a portable intravenous drip crisscrossed the room, dragging her medical apparatus with one hand and pulling a rack of handmade running tights with the other. The tights bore wild floral patterns, geometric shapes, and abstract forms in bright, mismatched colors. They were for sale, prices as marked, and the woman wore a leather pouch around her waist in which she collected the proceeds. Her long salt-and-pepper hair was braided, each braid held in place by a thick fluorescent hair-scrunchy, also for sale. She stopped next to Sam and Tracy, halting her IV-holder and rack of tights just behind her like well-trained pets, and looked out with them at Mount Hood for a while.

"They're studying the effect of exercise on insulin levels," she announced, jangling her drip. "I've been here, let's see, twenty-two hours now, with this thing stuck in my arm. That's one thousand three hundred twenty minutes, give or take. Damn these eighteen-gauge needles, you'd think they could do better than that, wouldn't you? Like being stabbed by a javelin. At least my blood sugar's down some, not that they care very much about my clotting problems. Yeah, the stuff kept her blood sugar in line just fine. Too bad it killed her with a stroke. My name's Bree, by the way. Well, Sabrina, but."

Tracy looked away from the window and smiled at the woman. *Don't do it,* Trace, Sam thought. *Don't ask her.*

"What are those?" Tracy asked.

Sam moaned.

"Are you all right?" Bree asked, leaning over to get a better look at him.

"Oh, he's fine. Half-asleep, that's all. We're just sitting here waiting for our infusions." She started to rock harder again. "They were supposed to start at ten, but there's some kind of hold-up. I'm sure you know how it is, right? Just let the white rats sit in their cages. Let them run on their little wheels. No, that's gerbils, oh well. Whatever. We're not really important, are we? I mean *they* don't have two kids coming home at noon today because it's a half-day at preschool and their aunt has an appointment for a perm and there's nobody home to meet them because my husband Wally, of course, he's too busy to take an afternoon off from not working on the day I get an infusion when it coincides with when the kids are home early. It always makes me feel so tired, this drug, so what am I supposed to do, you know what I mean? My name's Tracy. Better known as Patient o10."

Bree pursed her lips and shook her head sadly. "Awful. Believe me, I know, I know." Then she perked up and jangled her drip again.

"Why don't you buy them each a pair of tights! Boy, that'll make the kids happy when you get home, don't you think? Can wear them around the house all afternoon, not a peep out of them, you know? Only eight ninety-nine each, three for twenty-five dollars, but."

Tracy reached behind her chair to finger a pair of tights. "Oh, I couldn't. Thanks anyway, though, they're really neat. Just what I'd need today, come home with twenty-five bucks worth of tights and Wally would kill me, just kill me. Take a knife and put me out of my misery. We're on a very tight budget since I got sick. I couldn't, no way, sorry, thanks."

Bree had looked at Sam for a moment, but he had let his eyes close now and was completely still in the rocker. When Bree moved off toward the blind man who was part of a study on visual dysfunction and depression, Sam leaned back and put his hand on the arm of Tracy's rocker. He kept his eyes closed, but turned his head slightly toward her. "Can I ask you something?" he said.

Patient 002   95

"Sure, Sam. Anything."

"What do you think's going on?"

Tracy rocked harder in her chair, looking out the window. "This makes me feel so dumb, Sam. But I just don't know what you mean. *What's going on?* Kate's late, it's too hot in here, I'm worried about Wally and the kids. Those are going on, is that what you mean?"

"About the protocol, Trace. Kate said it's changing."

"Shoot, it always changes." She stopped rocking and turned to face him, her voice a breathy whisper as though she were sharing a deep confidence. "One minute we don't have to have spinal taps, then suddenly we're curled up on Fong's table with those huge prongs sticking out of our backs and we've got killer headaches for the next three weeks. One minute the study's a year long, then it's nine months, then it's back to a year. Wake up in the morning and it's *Hello, we need a skin test.* If they didn't change something at least once a week, that's when I'd start to worry."

Sam had to smile. He reached over to refill their cups with hot water and watched Tracy resume her rocking. "I just hope that's all it is this time. Another little modification of the rules."

"Stop worrying, Sam. What else could it be? I know, maybe now they want you to undergo a pelvic exam." She rocked back hard, smiling to herself. "Yup, I bet that's exactly what's going on."

6.

Kate McCabe knocked open the doors with her hip and looked around. Her notebooks were stacked under each arm and she wriggled in place to balance them. Her sunglasses, which she'd neglected to remove, had fogged over completely as soon as she entered the room.

"Sam? Tracy? Are you two in here? I can't see shit."

Homer and Vi, working on the maid's white skirt at the edge of their puzzle, were the only ones not staring at Kate. Everyone seemed to shrink from her as though she were the Grim Reaper.

"There you are," Kate said, as the glasses slipped down her nose and she noticed Sam and Kate getting out of their rockers. "Follow me." She bumped the door open wide, then spun around and headed down the hall.

She led them to one of the semi-private patient rooms near the kitchen. Not a good sign, Sam thought. Away from the infusion room, no "Good morning," no "How are my little rats today," just tromping along the corridor and a terse "In here." A separate room.

Kate followed them in, shut the door, and dumped her notebooks on one of the two beds. She motioned them to hop up on the other bed, then stood there rubbing her hips, looking out the window.

Sam and Tracy sat on the bed for a moment like chastened children, with their legs dangling over the edge. No one spoke. Then Kate shook her head and moved the notebooks onto the windowsill, concentrating hard, stacking them in a neat row. She mumbled "What the hell am I doing?" and straightened her shoulders with a deep breath. She turned around and told Sam to switch beds.

"Yoo-hoo, Kate," Tracy said, waving her hand as though cleaning a windshield. "Lovely day, isn't it?"

"Gorgeous. A gem of a day. Just a real sparkler."

"What are we doing in here?" Sam asked.

"Private treatment, my friend. It's your special day."

"I get it," said Tracy. "Just like I told you Sam. Lie down and put your feet in those stirrups."

Kate looked at Tracy, then at Sam, and a smile threatened at the corners of her mouth. But she just shrugged and returned to the notebooks. "Very funny."

"So what's wrong?" Sam asked.

"Wrong?" She came toward them. "Nothing's wrong, I'm just in a hurry. Now roll up your sleeves."

"We're both wearing tee-shirts," Sam said. He reached out for Kate's arm, which at least stopped her from darting back and forth even if it didn't soften her tone.

"What?" She didn't pull away. Instead, she gazed at Sam's face as though hoping to commit it to memory.

"Kate, you're managing to scare both of us a lot more than you probably want to. What are we doing in here? And why are you stalking around like a panther?"

"I'm not stalking, I'm moving purposefully. Because I'm a very busy girl." She backed away from him and began to set up their infusions, laying out her instruments, adjusting the carts that held their solutions. "Look, there's just some things a person's not cut out for, that's all. I should never have gotten into running a research study."

"Just tell us what's happening."

"Look at your arm," Kate said. She prodded the crook of Sam's right elbow, searching for a vein, then felt her way down the underside of his forearm. "You're tattooed with bruises, Sam. Tattooed." She turned his arm over, then dropped it like a ragged sheet and picked up his left. "And this one's even worse. You never listen to me. I told you a thousand times to press down hard on the cotton when I take out the catheter."

Sam held his arms out and studied them. "They're no worse than they were last week."

"Still."

Kate was closed, her eyes hooded, shoulders hunched, voice shut down to a murmur. Sam had seen her like this only once before, when her husband had wrecked their van driving home after a night out with his friends from the construction crew. That dark spell had lasted two whole days and part of a third; now she seemed even lower.

"Come on, Kate, talk to me."

"What's happening is that PER is cutting the study off. All right? What's happening is that after today you're finished. At least for now." She folded her arms under her breasts and sighed as though relieved that it was said. "Which is a good thing, right Sam? No more infusions of salt water, no more treadmill tests or pregnancy tests, no shrinks and bloodwork and physical exams and chest X-rays and forms to fill out. Hell, now you'll have nothing to complain about."

"Finished? What does that mean?"

"Ceased. Scratched. Discharged. Culminated. Wrapped. Words to that effect."

"Who's finished?" Sam asked, his voice growing very soft. "All of us? Some of us?" He looked over at Tracy, who was gazing out the window and rubbing her eyes like a child just waking up.

"What?" Tracy asked.

Kate shrugged. "Nobody knows yet. What we do know is that they gave us exactly forty-eight hours to get all the information from these notebooks on each one of you organized and Fed-Exed to them."

"What are you talking about now?" Sam asked. "I mean exactly, Kate."

"Compiling the data from the books, then sending copies to everyone in the world. That's exactly what I'm talking about."

"That's not what I mean."

Kate nodded. "Phase One is over. That is all I know. No word about Phase Two."

Sam felt as though he'd just been pushed out the open door of an airplane. He swallowed to be sure his throat still worked and said, "How could it be over?"

"I don't know how, but it is. They said they've got enough data and there's no point in continuing the double-blind study."

"So what does that imply?" He patted his chest, then his hip, as if searching for something in his nonexistent pockets. "We all start in on the drug next, right?"

"That's the part we're having trouble nailing down, Sam. We left a lot of questions on PER's answering machine, all of them unanswered as of this moment. But that doesn't automatically spell disaster, you know."

"Kate, can I ask you something?" Tracy said.

Sam and Kate turned to look at her. Tracy's voice was so calm, so unruffled, so unlike her own.

"Sure."

"You did say we get our stuff today, didn't you?"

"Yeah. Everybody gets one more infusion." Kate smiled. "You're right, of course. Take things one day at a time, don't worry about what happens next week till we get through this week." She turned back to Sam. "See, my friend? A little calm, a little common sense."

Sam frowned and looked toward the window.

"Left arms today, I think," Tracy said.

7.

Martin Fong left his office at noon and headed downtown. He hadn't been off the hill at midday for ages. It was as though the Cascade-Kennedy campus were a separate society altogether. Almost everything a person needed was available within a ten minute walk. He was surprised to see so much traffic at noon, so much construction work going on. Whole blocks of buildings had disappeared since he'd last been downtown, replaced by chain-link fences that surrounded deep holes in the ground out of which the superstructure of new office complexes were rising.

He entered Chinatown. Well, some things don't change: he couldn't find a place to park anywhere. All the restaurants were offering dim sum lunch deals, there was a small demonstration going on near the train station, and another construction site had taken away an entire parking lot. A line of homeless people waiting for free lunch at the mission stretched for three blocks. As Fong circled, he tried desperately to keep his thoughts from straying back up the hill to his office, where he knew that patients from the Zomalovir study would already be flocking. His phone was ringing steadily by the time he'd walked out.

What, exactly, did they think he could do for them? When they had been his patients, he'd told them there were no treatments and no cures. When they joined the study, he'd told them there were no guarantees that the drug would work, or that the study would move along as planned. Hadn't he? It wasn't an engineering project, it was medicine, it was a trial, an experiment.

He would return to the office shortly. Of course he would. Everyone's entitled to lunch, even a doctor. But now Fong realized he wasn't really hungry. Not at all. Hell with this. He headed east over the river to spend an idle hour at the classical music shop. It was time he got some new recordings. Looked through the stock. Could use a new set of *The English Suites!* A new *Goldberg Variations.* It was time Fong treated himself to a bit of a spree.

The clerk greeted him like a long-lost cousin. There was Haydn coming through the shop's sound system instead of the customary Pachelbel *Canon* you'd hear everywhere, every airport Fong had ever walked through, every shopping mall and restaurant. All right, so he was crotchety today. Fong stopped and looked up at a poster of Beethoven glowering down at him. Talk about crotchety!

As soon as Kate McCabe had told him about the message from PER, Fong called them. Of course he had. Dialed the number himself and was put on hold for ten minutes. Spoke to a chain of useless voices before being told No, Doctor Rowland was not available today. Nor Doctors Devlin or Holtzman-Bell. Sorry. No, there was only the release that had been read to the site nurses today, nothing else available at this time. No, there was nothing more to say at this time.

Well, fuck you at this time.

He would finish up here at the shop, stop for a quick lunch if he felt hungry enough and then get back to the office. He would see only those patients with scheduled appointments and then he would go home and listen to his new music. He was a human being, just a regular guy like everybody else, wasn't he? Enjoyed cloudy days, the color blue, Bach. Preferred Hungarian goulash to moo shu pork even if he was Chinese. Knew a little virology, a little infectious disease, epidemiology. Just a regular guy. *Get off my back.*

8.

For the first time in more than a year, five days passed without Sam and Tracy seeing each other. He found himself missing her. She called once, at 9:30 Tuesday morning—the time she would normally have picked him up—and they spoke for nearly as long as it would have taken to get their infusions. Tracy was frantic because her symptoms were beginning to return. How was she going to study for the mail carrier's exam when her brain didn't work? She'd had to look up Sam's phone number because her memory was playing tricks on her. She'd put pancake batter in the toaster and tried to clean the downstairs den with a toilet plunger instead of a vacuum. She could not bear the thought of being sick again.

He spent hours each day on the phone. All the subjects in the study called one another daily, updating the latest rumors. There would be legal action, government intervention, television exposés, everything short of military invasion. Embezzlement inside PER, bribes, scandal. The rare voice of sanity came from Jessica's occasional calls. She would be gone a few more days than planned, but looked forward to being with him soon.

In the middle of the next week, Sam tried to reach Tracy, but she didn't return his call. Wally said she'd gone out and he didn't know where she went, which made no sense at all from what Sam knew about their marriage.

That same day, sitting on a stool in his kitchen, Sam went on a telephone rampage. He called Fong's office, but was told the doctor was away at a conference in Pittsburgh and would be back sometime in the middle of next week. He called Cascade-Kennedy's Department of Patient Advocacy to ask what could be done if he felt he'd been treated unethically in a drug trial. The Advocate's assistant thought it was a very good question and recommended a meeting early next year. Sam called Molly Carroll, who seemed to spend all her time on the phone talking to the other members of the group or to people from the other study sites. He couldn't get through. He called PER Pharmaceuticals' headquarters in Seattle, was transferred to their public relations department and left a message asking anyone there to call him back. Finally, he beeped Kate, trying to get some information, any information. It took her three hours to return his call.

"Look, Sam, I don't know any more than I did last week." She placed her hand over the phone and said *two minutes* to someone nearby. "I'll let you know as soon as there's anything."

"This is crazy, Kate. What does Fong say?"

"He's so overworked it's not funny. The AIDS clinic alone is enough to keep him busy twenty hours a day. I'm not sure he's thinking about PER or your study, to tell you the truth. Besides, he's in Pittsburgh."

"All right." Sam took a long, deep breath. "I'll have to get along on rumors. You know about Rhode Island?"

It was Kate's turn to sigh. "Yes, Sam. My husband's from Woonsocket."

"I see you haven't lost your whimsy."

"Sam, I lost that when I was thirteen."

"Kate."

"OK, yes Sam, I heard about Rhode Island. There are people talking about it in Chicago too, and a meeting's scheduled for Thursday in Albuquerque. So what?"

"So what? So I got a call from the attorney, that's so what. A fellow named P. J. Cooper, from Providence, Rhode Island. Cooper wants to know if anyone from Oregon is interested in joining a lawsuit."

"That's crazy."

"It's getting less crazy every day that PER keeps us in the dark. It's almost two weeks now and we're all just dangling here. No word from the drug company or from you guys or anybody. We were promised the drug."

"So you're going to sue?"

"I said I'd get back to him. But tell me this, how come we didn't know about the study being stopped at the other sites till ten days after it happened? How come we were kept out of the loop?"

"Because I was out of the loop too. What did you think?"

"I didn't know what to think." Sam took a sip of tea and tried to shift gears before saying anything more. "Look, there's no way I'm going to join a suit against Fong or against you, all right? And I think I can convince most of the others here, at least for now. Everyone's coming over here on Friday night. But I have to know what the plan is, Kate. PER's got to tell us something so I can talk to the rest of the group on Friday."

"No argument there."

He waited a moment, giving her a chance to say something more. Then said, "So why not call them and ask?"

"Me? Call PER? If they took my call, Sam, do you really think they'd tell me anything? I've talked to my counterparts at the other sites just about every day and no one has any information. When there's a decision, I'm sure PER will let us know and then I'll let you know."

"Yeah, yeah. So what's going on with Tracy? Is she all right? I can't reach her."

"She got another infusion, Sam."

"She what?"

"Two days ago. She was a Responder, no question about that. PER said to keep her on the drug."

"When did they say that?"

"Three days ago."

"I thought you said you'd let me know when you heard something."

"This just applies to Trace. Besides, I thought you knew."

Sam looked at the calendar taped above the phone, but nothing made sense. Kate was doling out information in careful measures. An image took shape in his mind: Kate holding up a small bottle and slowly drawing the medicine from it into a fat syringe. All right, she doesn't know PER's overall plan, but she knows pieces of it, knows what's happening here.

"No one else is getting infusions?"

"No." There was a slight cough. "No one here, at least."

"Oh boy." Only one of the Portland subjects got to continue taking the drug. That meant a lot of people who had been getting it during the study but hadn't responded as dramatically as Tracy had been cut off and would be relapsing. It also meant that Sam, as one of the people on placebo, stood no chance of getting the drug now.

"Sam?"

"What?"

"Good luck with your meeting."

9.

Gary Maxwell arrived at Sam's place the next afternoon, balancing two medium pizzas, two small salads, and two large Sprites in a neat stack. A Portland Trailblazers game from Chicago would be on television soon, and they planned to watch it. He brushed past Sam and headed for the kitchen.

"Hot," Max said.

"Impressive. You've got presents I never knew about."

"This is dinner, for Christ's sake. Six separate containers, but one dinner."

"Huh?"

Max peeked back into the room and said, "Let's start over, OK? Tell me again what you just said."

"Jeez. All I said was you've got gifts I never knew about. Talents, you know?"

"Right. Well, I worked as a busboy when I was a kid. Eleven-years-old, if I remember right. I looked twenty when I was eleven."

"You still do."

"Aren't we in a jolly mood, considering."

Sam sat on the couch and picked up a piece of paper. He trusted his friend's political skills as much as his writing skills. If Max saw anything wrong with the letter he'd say so.

"Something here I want you to look at for me. It's a letter to the drug company that I'd like everyone in the group to sign."

Max came into the living room holding his hands up like a surgeon before scrubbing, grease gleaming in the light. "Lawyers write letters, Sam. Subjects shut up."

"I'm not sure we want a lawyer. Not yet, anyway."

Max shrugged. "OK, a letter might not be a bad move. The company knows a lawyer's out there already, so they might like it if you came to them with something less threatening. A letter, then, but you have to be careful not to give them something they can use with a judge."

"See what you think." Sam held out the letter. "I'll get the dinner set up."

"The hell you will. I don't want to be scraping pizza up off your damn kitchen floor. Just let me finish laying things out. I'll read it while we eat."

After reading the letter twice, Max didn't say anything. He put it down and took two large bites of his pizza.

"Pepperoni, hot chilies, sausage, and onions," he said. "I think two bites of this would kill you, Sam, otherwise I'd offer you some."

"My veggie is fine." Sam licked his fingers. "So are you going to tell me what you think, or do I have to guess?"

"It's fine. Especially for someone with brain damage. I'm just trying to think through what happens when PER reads it. What it gets them to do that they wouldn't do already."

"Give us the drug."

"That's not real likely. Basically what you said is that you all have the same goal in mind—getting a safe and effective drug into the marketplace—and you should all work together. That's good as far as it goes. But from PER's point of view, that's what's happening already. Giving you the drug now, especially for free, doesn't accomplish anything new for them. If they can get away with cutting you off, they'll keep doing it. That's my guess, anyway. I figure they must be in a tight financial spot and are trying to see if they can avoid giving the stuff away."

"Then we sue."

"Yeah, a bunch of disabled, financially strapped, sick people suing a pharmaceutical company. Cost you each more than you can afford, take so long in court that you're all too sick to see it through, and meanwhile they can take their drug to the next phase of study."

"So they're stonewalling us, is that what you're saying?"

"To the max, my friend."

"Then there's nothing we can do but sue."

"Well, maybe you can reason with them. It's worth a try, for sure, and you're letter's fine as far as it goes." Max stopped to finish his slice of pizza and have a drink.

"But," Sam said.

"But I think we need to come up with a back-up plan for when they say *Fuck you, we'll see you in court.* Because I think you know, and I think they know, that only a handful of their subjects around the country are actually going to show up in a court of law someday. Way, way down the road."

"So what do we do, hold a gun to their heads."

"Now you're thinking."

10.

"Hold it down," Sam said, though he knew it was a waste of breath. He stepped into the ragged oval of chairs scattered around his living room, handed the platter of sugar-free cookies to Daphne Warren sitting by the window and went back into the kitchen to heat more water for tea.

It was amazing how much noise a group of sick people could make. Occasionally, a voice that Sam recognized would flash near the surface of the clamor like seaweed within a breaker and be gone before he could make sense of it. Tracy, he gathered, was willing to talk about anything except the study. Molly Carroll, lying on the living room rug with her feet under the coffee table, talked toward the ceiling about nothing but the study, not even to acknowledge greetings or indicate her choice of drink. There was that woman with a shrieking, three-note laugh who lived way out east in Boring, Oregon. Sam had always referred to her as the Boring Woman, without realizing what he was saying, until Tracy had cackled and told him her name was Laurel Blackburn and she was hardly a boring woman. Laurel was on the sofa next to Alice Hardy, who seemed to be losing ten pounds a month during the study. Laurel's incongruous voice was almost a baritone, like her cello in its lower register. Daphne Warren addressed everything she said across the oval to Hannah Lee Price, talking slowly and loudly as though the woman with the lavish clothes and Ph.D. from Stanford in American history could not, in fact, understand English. All fourteen of them were talking at once. Sam considered turning the burner down to simmer, sitting alone at the kitchen table, and waiting a half-hour for everyone to tire out.

He had done his homework, but facts seemed to have little value at this meeting so far. *Facts,* he remembered Vic reciting to him once, *are the enemy of truth.* Sam had a copy of the brief that P. J. Cooper had filed in New York on behalf of the study's subjects. The suit was on a fast-track and Cooper claimed he was trying to hold down costs, so he wasn't going to file it as a class action. The only ones the suit covered would be those who joined in and paid a share of his retainer. Sam had spoken with at least one person at each of the other three sites to get a sense of what the different groups were doing. He had his letter to PER drafted for all of them to sign.

"Sam?" Molly yelled above the hubbub. "What do you think?"

He walked slowly back into the living room carrying a thermos of hot water. "About what?"

"Suing. Do we sue PER or not?"

"It's not that simple."

"Seems pretty straightforward to me," said Laurel Blackburn. "We have a contract. They broke the contract. We can sue for birth. I mean breach."

"Yeah, all it takes is about six thousand bucks to join in," Molly said. She sat up and looked across at Laurel. "You may have that much lying around, but a lot of the rest of us don't." Then she lay back down.

Maybe rephrasing it will help. Sam said, "There's more to it than that." Except for Tracy, they all looked over at him. "Our suing PER is the same thing as our suing Doctor Fong. Technically, he's their agent. Most of you have known him a long time. Do you really want to be taking him to court?"

"It's not personal," Laurel said.

"Where was he when we needed him?" Molly said. "He could've spoken up."

"And done what?" Sam couldn't figure out why he was the only one speaking up for Fong. Surely they weren't all ready to join the suit. Maybe they just wanted to vent their frustration over PER and were using Fong as a convenient target. "There was a protocol he had to follow."

"But he didn't, did he?" Laurel said, punctuating it with her wild, contagious laugh.

"We don't know what happened. That's the point."

Molly sat up again. "I know what happened. Fong sprayed us."

"What are you talking about?"

"You heard me. He betrayed us."

"Betrayed? Don't you think that's a little strong?"

"Not at all. He promised us the drug if we stayed in the study. He said so at that patient meeting we had, when we all signed the consent forms. He promised. We're not getting squat and we're all off our pickle."

"Not all of us," Laurel said.

At that, several nodding heads turned toward Tracy. She added sugar to her tea and stirred it without looking up at them.

"Well," Sam said, "but that isn't what happened. He never *promised* we'd get anything. I have it on tape."

"What?" Several asked at once.

"This is rich," Molly said. "We all heard him."

Sam retrieved his microcassette recorder. "Just listen."

He placed it on the coffee table and pressed Play. Doctor Fong's voice came on, tinny and distant, but quite clear.

"All I can tell you is we're advocating as researchers that those people receiving benefit from this drug should be continued on it and have the cost paid for by the company until it becomes licensed and available. I can't tell you that's what's going to happen, but it's what we're assuming."

Sam shut the machine off and sat back down. There was a moment of silence before Molly said, "Horseshit."

"That's not what I heard," Laurel said.

"But it's what he said." Sam rewound the tape in case they asked to hear it again. "Fong couldn't promise us that PER would do the ethical thing, only that he'd try to advocate for us."

"Well, I for one don't believe he even did that," Molly said. "He should've insisted that those of us who were getting the drug should keep on getting it. So what if we weren't all responding as quickly as Tracy? I'm telling you, it's like someone opened a trap-door under me. The last week, I've just fallen right through the floor and now I'm sicker than before the study began."

"I have a question." This was the first time Hannah Lee Price had spoken since saying hello at the door. She leaned forward.

"I don't know if I can deal with this," Molly said.

"I have a question," Hannah said again.

"There's another thing," Molly said. "What about Kate Mc-Cabe? I think we should be sure she's included."

"Molly, Kate can't sue PER, for God's sake." Sam shook his head. This was getting ridiculous.

"I know that. She works for them too, which is exactly my point. I say we stew her too." She stopped talking. Tears filled her eyes and she quickly shook her head. "Sue her, damnit. I mean sue her. She's been in on everything right from the start."

"And she's also been on our side. Right from the start."

"Kate looks terrible," Tracy said, finally speaking up. "She looks like she's been crying all week. I really think it's getting to her."

"Boo-hoo."

"What about those of us on placebo?" Daphne Warren asked. "We weren't responders because we weren't getting the drug. Instead, we just got sicker. I think we, of all people, should get the drug now."

"That doesn't make any sense," Laurel said. "But it does point to the real issue, which is that everyone should get the drug at this point, just as PER agreed we would when they roped us into this thing."

"I have a question," Hannah said.

Alice Hardy leaned forward and dropped her teacup. It hit the edge of the coffee table and split neatly in half, dousing Molly's thighs and abdomen where she lay there. Molly didn't react at all.

For a moment, nobody moved. Sam watched the tea seep into his rug. He stood again, turned to head into the kitchen for some paper towels, and tripped over his chair, stumbling a few steps until he ended up falling over Daphne Warren's legs.

"I know that dance," Molly said.

Sam sat up. "I'm OK."

Tracy darted past him into the kitchen, returned with towels and began cleaning up the spill. Daphne shifted over to help her and stepped smack on the plate of cookies she'd laid on the floor in front of her chair.

"Look at us," Alice said, covering her face, her deep voice commanding attention. "We're a clown act."

"We can't do anything right," Daphne said.

"Which makes us easy targets for people like PER, or Fong, or Kate McCabe," Molly said.

"I have a question."

They all looked at Hannah. When she was sure no one was about to speak in her place, she smiled and closed her eyes. "Has anyone thought that PER stopped giving the drug because they know there's a problem with it? Maybe it's showing up toxic. Maybe it only helps certain people, or it only helps you for a little while and then you have a relapse. Tell you what, it's at least possible to assume, and it's probably logical too, that they cut us off because the data was beginning to look bad. Are we all sure we really want this drug?"

There was another silence, this one filled, Sam thought, with wonder. Poison! That would be just like PER. Know that Zomalovir is poison and give it to us anyway.

"I'm sure," Molly said. "The only thing I might want half as much as the drug is to stab someone from PER through the heart."

"I'm sure, too," Alice said. "Just look at Tracy."

Daphne was nodding, as was nearly everyone else in the room. They wanted Zomalovir, it seemed, especially since they'd seen how much it helped one of their own.

"Well, I think PER is trouble and so's their drug," Hannah said. She picked up her cup. "Sam, honey, you have any more hot water?"

As he stood up to get it, Laurel sighed and said, "Should we vote?"

"Wait a minute," Sam said. "Some of you have already seen this, but not everybody." Instead of getting hot water, he went over to the stereo speaker where he kept his important items handy and picked up copies of his letter to PER. "There is another option to suing. At least for now."

He handed the copies out, then left to get Hannah her hot water. For two or three minutes, there was blessed silence.

"I can't read this," Molly said when he returned. "I can't make any sense out of it."

"I can," Laurel said. "It's good, Sam. It gets us on record as strongly objecting to their failure to honor the Informed Consent contract, but buys us a little time before we actually have to commit to joining the suit."

"Big deal," Molly said.

There was a long discussion about Sam's letter, and finally he seemed to be accumulating some allies. With Laurel and Alice supporting the idea, the group agreed to sign it. Even Hannah signed, though she made it clear she was doing so out of solidarity with the others, not because she intended to accept the drug if PER offered it. She was through.

There was also a long discussion about whether to vote on joining the suit or to delay voting until PER had a chance to respond to their letter. Eventually, with everyone yawning and having trouble following the discussion, they agreed to wait for two weeks.

With Tracy's help, Sam got the coats and wished them well as they left. Before shutting the door, Laurel turned back to him and said, "Be careful, Sam. If this Cooper fellow knows you have that tape, he'll try to subpoena the thing. It may get Fong off the hook, but I'm not sure it helps PER's case."

11.

Tracy stayed to help him clean up. Sam couldn't remember a time when she'd said so little over a three hour period. In some ways, her silence seemed louder to Sam than her talking. He knew she must feel awkward being the only member of the group still receiving the drug, but he'd never known her to let awkwardness stop her from talking.

When the dishes were stacked in the dishwasher, the spot on the rug dry, and the cookie crumbs swept up, Tracy began putting on her coat. Except for asking where things went, she'd barely spoken to him. Sam stepped closer to help her with the coat and Tracy stopped moving entirely, freezing in place with one arm inside a sleeve and the other reaching behind her. Suddenly she was leaning back against Sam's chest. He realized she was crying. In seconds, the cries became sobs and he thought she might actually collapse. Leading her to the couch, he helped her sit.

"What is it, Tracy?"

It took her a while to gain control. Her fair skin was blotched, the redness oozing down her cheeks to her neck, where it seemed to cascade into her blouse. She looked grief-stricken and kept her eyes down as she spoke.

"I can't stand this, Sam. I feel so guilty for continuing on the drug. But those two weeks when I was off it were hell. I could feel myself slipping right back into the swamp. I want to get better." She finally looked up and found his eyes. "I have to stay on it."

"Of course, Trace," he whispered. "I'm sure everyone understands that."

"No they don't. They hate me for it and they feel like I'm taking their doses. But it doesn't matter. The only thing that matters to me is that if anybody sues PER, or if PER gets pissed off about this letter, they might cut me off again. I don't think I could stand that."

Sam moved over to sit beside Tracy and put his arm around her. She leaned against him again, putting her head on his shoulder. He wrapped his other arm around her too, completing their embrace.

"We won't let that happen," he said. "You'll be their poster girl, Trace. They have to make you better."

She tilted her face slightly, brushing his neck with her lips. "Even I know better than that, Sam."

He felt her kisses moving slowly toward his ear, drifting up a half-inch at a time. Her breath made small whistling noises through her nose. *What's happening?* He thought that these were somehow not kisses directed at him, not meant to arouse or encourage him. At least he hoped not. This was not a path he wanted to go on with her, and he didn't really believe she wanted him to join her either. He sat straighter and moved gently backwards toward the arm of the couch.

"What do you mean?"

She moved away then too, dropping her arms, resting her head against the back of the couch, blinking her eyes as though waking from a trance.

"I mean they don't have to do anything."

Six

1.

Gary Maxwell had been on the phone for five hours and was prepared to stay on the phone for five days if he had to. He was prepared to call in every political favor he was owed, or go so deeply into political debt that it would take two lifetimes to work his way back out.

He wanted to get at PER, and he knew there were two likely ways to do that. He could get at them financially, by finding out who their big investors were and seeing if he could get some pressure applied to them. But Max thought the company was probably on the edge of bankruptcy, so pushing them over wouldn't solve Sam's problem. That meant the most effective way to get at PER was through the FDA.

Max thought anyone who failed to recognize the Food and Drug Administration as a political rather than medical agency was naive. If drugs got approved for sale on the basis of effectiveness and safety alone, drugs to combat AIDS would have been available long ago, and might be priced so that people who weren't in the top tax bracket could afford them. Hell, AIDS finally got on the research agenda because of political action by people who already had HIV. No, the system was political, Max believed, and he had already spoken to three of the state's congressmen, already had calls in to both of the state's U.S. Senators and their chiefs-of-staff. Good thing he had call-waiting.

Meanwhile, Max was worried that even political pressure wouldn't work. He knew that anything political was also subject to financial pressure, and that the wealthiest pharmaceutical companies had the most clout in Congress and with the FDA. He didn't think PER was among those companies, not now, anyway. So he wasn't sure how much attention would be paid to his meddling.

Max was sore from sitting so tensely. He'd switched to a headset an hour ago, even though he didn't like the way it messed up his already messed-up hair, but at least he was able to roam the office while he made his calls. Like a bright law student, he could now recite the salient facts of the case in ninety seconds, knowing he had to be tight with the story if he wanted to hold people's attention on an issue like this. Everyone was sympathetic but no one committed to do anything. They all got around to the same point: campaign contributions. The pharmaceuticals had been generous over the years, and no one intended to irritate them. Still, Max wanted phone calls made to the FDA director, to the head of their clinical field trial operation, and to members of the House Committee that handled the FDA budget. Was that too much to ask?

He'd long been friends with the people who could make those calls. He reminded them they owed him for past services rendered, but he was getting nowhere. Max had no idea the FDA was this well guarded.

He couldn't believe what Sam Kiehl was going through over this little gambit of PER's. For too long he'd watched his best friend wither away in a recliner, losing ground, disappearing. He missed Sam. He missed their workouts and their struggles to master Asian cooking and their long talks. Which was the better candy bar when they were kids, Milky Way or Forever Yours? Which was the better breakfast cereal, Rice Krinkles or Trix? The guy was even too sick to hold an hour's worth of conversation about whether the

Pittsburgh Pirates of the early 1960s or the Brooklyn Dodgers of the early 1950s were the better teams, and that showed you how far he'd fallen.

And Max was worried. He thought that if this drug study really did fall apart, Sam might have nothing left to hope for, and might just give in to this thing. He'd die, or anyway he'd stop living, and Max couldn't bear to think about that. There was this new relationship Sam had with Jessica, which sounded promising to Max, but he knew such things required energy.

Max and Sam had run too many miles together, and watched too many games of basketball, and they'd teamed up to tell too many civic leaders how to manage their duties and save their hides, and had helped each other out of too many sinkholes over money or romance or child-rearing to stop now. Max dialed the office of the chief lobbyist for the Department of Health and Human Services. Even as he dialed he knew that what he was doing was totally beside the point. But he couldn't stop. He knew that what he felt most was flat-out helpless. He'd felt that way since Sam first turned up sick. But at least now his friend had stumbled onto turf that Max thought he understood. Thought he could do something about.

Damn. It was 4:30 back east. The offices were closing.

2.

Sam could not believe the level of noise inside Memorial Coliseum. It was still a half-hour before game time. The place was far from full, but already rock music blared from loudspeakers, people stood in clusters near the court or scuttled among the aisles, thousands of voices merged into a ceaseless babel punctuated by hotdog and peanut and ice cream vendors bellowing out their wares, seats squeaked and clanged, and two dozen basketballs smacked against the floor. It all blended together and penetrated Sam's skin until the sound found its way into his bloodstream and his heart pounded in time to the amalgamated beat.

Sitting back against the hard, slatted seat, Sam didn't know what to watch. The flickering scoreboard kept attracting his attention and he tried to read the messages there but couldn't focus long enough. The players stretching at mid-court or practicing jump shots at either end caught his eye, then the fans waving at friends twenty aisles away, the spandexed Blazer Dancers rehearsing cheerleading routines, uniformed police officers moving around the perimeter, radio announcers conducting pre-game interviews, a beautiful young woman in a black and red Portland Trailblazers warm-up suit with long golden hair in a pony tail hanging through the hole in her black Blazers cap as she moved back and forth a few rows away.

Max had been urging Sam to come along with him to a game all season. But Sam hadn't thought about all the stimuli he would encounter in a place like this. Everything came at him at once, with equal value and claim on his brain, and he couldn't sort it all out. This was why he didn't drive anymore, why he couldn't stand being in crowded shopping malls or electronics stores with their banks of televisions and blasting music systems.

He sat there with his mouth open, feeling the energy seeping out of him. Clutched in one hand was a Polish sausage that Max had gone to buy after first leading Sam to their seats. Grease oozed through the flimsy waxed paper, but Sam had forgotten the sausage was there.

"It tastes better if you actually put it in your mouth," Max said.

Sam didn't move. After a few moments, he turned his head toward Max and blinked. "Did you say something?"

Max pointed to Sam's sausage, then to his mouth. Sam nodded, and took a large bite. He reached down between his feet for the cup of water and knocked it over. Without a word, Max handed him his cup of soda.

"Pretty good seats, huh?" Max asked.

Chewing slowly, watching the court, Sam nodded. Then he angled his head toward Max and said, "How'd you get them? People pass seats like these down through the generations. They never let them go."

"I bought a quarter-share from Lennie Koslow."

That got Sam's attention. Lennie Koslow was the cofounder of CyberSpeke, a software company in Beaverton that developed programs for scanning and converting photographic imagery to digital formats. He was twenty-five, reportedly worth eighteen million and refused to act like a rich man. It would be just like Lennie Koslow to buy only part of a season's ticket, though he could easily have afforded an entire box. With the sausage poised before his mouth, Sam turned in his seat to look at Max and said, "I didn't know you knew Lennie Koslow."

"I know everybody, my man."

"Yeah. But Lennie Koslow?"

"He's a nice kid. A little zealous, maybe. But a nice kid."

"Zealous." Sam took a bite of his sausage. "I like that. Guy rents a fleet of airplanes to buzz downtown Portland when his company goes public, and you call him zealous. I could live for two years on what he got fined for that little stunt."

"First of all, it wasn't a fleet of airplanes, it was two helicopters. Second of all, it worked. Share prices went through the roof."

"Give me a break."

"Eat your dinner."

When warm-ups ended, the Coliseum went suddenly dark. Sam was still licking the mustard off his fingers when the synthesized sound of drum beats and a hundred horns began throbbing from the loudspeaker. Everyone rose from their seats as spotlights flashed and crisscrossed the ceiling.

He could follow the action for most of the first half, though the public address system was driving him nuts. During every timeout, when Sam wanted to snag a few moments of rest like the players were doing, music wailed from the loudspeakers and the crowd was urged to cheer along with a frantic progression of chords. No rest. The Blazer Dancers did their routines, the giant screen hovering above midcourt either showed madcap automobile races that had fans on their feet or flashed slogans welcoming various groups to the game, kids in special uniforms darted onto the court to wipe sweat off the floor with towels. Nothing was still, no matter where he looked.

Sam felt that he could keep up, though. Neither team played well and the game was low-scoring, with the Blazers ahead by eight. Great. As long as it was boring, he could manage. If it got exciting, he'd probably have to leave.

Max turned to see Sam slouching in his seat. He nudged him gently with an elbow and leaned closer. "Can I get you anything? Maybe another drink?"

At that moment, looking into Max's face, Sam at last felt truly overwhelmed. Not by the chaos around him, not by fatigue, but by gratitude for his friend's steady support. At the same time, he was struck by the sudden realization that, no matter how much sicker he had become in the last year, no matter how limited medical science was in treating him, no matter how disappointed he was in what had happened with the study, he still had choices. There were things that he could do for himself, things that people close to him could do. It was like getting doused with a bucket of ice water after a hot and muggy marathon. He might be light-years away from a cure, but he could begin the journey toward healing.

3.

Cascade-Kennedy's Ethics Committee had an office in the basement of the library. The man Sam spoke to said that finding their office shouldn't be difficult, since it was located immediately to the left of the front door. But finding the library itself might be a real problem. The directions were precise to the tenth of a mile, but made no sense to Sam. He wrote them down, read them back and still couldn't imagine where the library might be. Tucked behind a new dental clinic, it was invisible now from the main road. Sam had gone past the library twice a week for six months but had never noticed it.

The committee's Executive Director, Doctor Consuela Perez, had refused to meet with the Zomalovir group officially. It was, she said over and over, premature. Yes, the situation sounded difficult for the subjects. Patients. Yes, it bore further consideration. No, it was not necessarily an outrage against humanity or a violation of civil rights, but yes, she would talk to Doctor Fong. Soon.

After a brief exchange of letters and phone calls, Doctor Perez had found out little more than what she'd learned from Sam originally. At that point, she agreed to a general discussion with a delegation of no more than three subjects. This was, Sam though, like trying to set up a meeting about North Korea at the United Nations.

It took a few days of telephone round-robins for the group to agree on who would comprise its trio of delegates. They agreed the meeting was important and, at first, everyone wanted to attend. Then no one wanted to attend. Tracy was so worried about what might happen that she hung up on Sam. Daphne Warren suggested they all get together and draw straws, but Molly said she was done having her fate decided by random events.

Somehow, they'd gotten it done. Tuesday morning, Laurel Blackburn, chosen for her medical connections, picked up Hannah Lee Price, chosen for her doctorate and her restraint and perhaps her minority status, and then stopped to pick up Sam, selected for his gender, shortly before 9:30. They drove up to the campus and circled the clinic three times before Laurel spotted the library.

"Did you see that?" Hannah asked.

"Yes, after Laurel pointed it out. Looks more like a trailer than a library."

"No, I meant did you see what was standing at the entrance to the library?"

"Give me a break, Hannah. I barely noticed the library."

"Top of the stairs?"

"Nope."

"Off to the right?"

"Sorry."

They parked and Laurel locked the car. "Did I miss something? Are we playing 'Twenty Questions'?"

They walked toward the library and Sam said "Oh my God."

"Good morning, Molly," Hannah said.

"I'm coming in. Don't try to stop me."

"You look cold," Sam said.

"Of course I look cold. It's thirty-four degrees this morning. In the sun."

They stood in front of the door blowing into their hands and looking everywhere but at each other. Hannah had a faint smile on her face. "I'll go to the reading room instead," she said. "I don't mind skipping the meeting."

"Fine," Molly said. "Let's go in before we get pneumonia."

Laurel thrust her hands into her pockets. "That would be convenient for PER."

Sam opened the door and motioned for them all to go in. "No way, Hannah. We all go to see Perez. If she objects, we'll tell her she can bring reinforcements of her own."

Doctor Consuela Perez was waiting for them, seated at the head of a long conference table, warming her hands around a mug of coffee. Sam wondered why the table seemed so scarred and chipped. Maybe things got violent when it came to ethics. Nah, could just be surplus furniture. *Take it easy.*

"Please call me Connie." She seemed tall for a seated person. She smiled, jerked her head left to indicate a tray of beverages and sweet rolls, and leaned toward her phone. She pressed a button and said "Jeremy, bring in another mug, please."

Sam smiled back at her, slowly closing his eyes in thanks. She had a stunning face, round and toffee-colored, with enormous eyes, one dark brown and one pale gray. Sam thought that the dual colors probably explained why her gaze seemed at once sympathetic and shrewd. Then he noticed that she seemed so tall because she was sitting in a wheelchair that was almost too large to fit under the table.

A deep bass boomed from behind him. "I thought there was supposed to be three of you." Sam turned to see Jeremy, whose voice he recognized from the phone. Jeremy was built like a defensive lineman, wore an eye patch, had rings in his ears and nose and through one eyebrow, and looked like an off-duty pirate. He carried a coffee mug dangling by its handle from one vast finger, put it down gently on the tray and left, shutting the door behind him.

Everyone sat except Molly. She planted herself by the far window, looking onto the road, and wrapped her arms around her torso. From where he sat, Sam could see her fingers turning white as they gripped her ribs.

Sam, Hannah, and Laurel looked at each other, then at Doctor Perez, and each coughed as though it had been rehearsed. *Now what?*

"So what can I do for you?"

"What we need," Sam said, and stopped.

"What we need," Hannah said, "is some clarification and some advice."

"We can't get anybody to talk to us," Laurel said, then put her hand to her mouth. "I sounded seven years old just then, didn't I?"

Doctor Perez smiled at Laurel, then took a sip from her mug. "Let's start with clarification, all right? First, I should make clear that the Ethics Committee has a formal procedure for investigating potential problems with research studies, including clinical field trials." She handed three copies of the procedures to Hannah, who was sitting immediately to her left. "As you'll see, there are guidelines for initiating such investigations. The faculty member can request one; the agent contracting with the medical school can request one; or a subcommittee of the Ethics Committee, which I would chair, can request one."

"What about patients?" Laurel said. "How do patients get into the act?"

Doctor Perez smiled. She passed out another paper and said "This is the Informed Consent Document you all signed. When you reread it, you'll see that, well, let's put it this way: you don't get into the act. Your agent, as it's worded here, or we could say your representative in the study, is Doctor Fong."

"But I thought he was the agent of PER, the drug company," Sam said.

"No, he is employed by the Cascade-Kennedy School of Medicine."

"But the study is funded by PER."

"Correct."

"So let me get this straight. Doctor Fong is paid by PER, works for Cascade-Kennedy, but is our agent?"

"That's customary with these things."

There was silence around the table. Sam tried to read the Informed Consent document but gave up.

"So you're saying that the only way the Ethics Committee can get involved with our problem is if Doctor Fong asks you to?"

"Basically. Though I could form a subcommittee to look into your allegations of wrongdoing if I felt it was warranted."

"Please do," Laurel said.

Doctor Perez looked down for a moment. Sam realized his hands had become fists and loosened them.

"As you know, I agreed to this meeting only to discuss general issues, and we've stuck to that so far. I am not prepared to undertake any sort of official consideration of the Zomalovir study. But why don't one of you tell me briefly what you think, exactly, is the nature of the ethics violation here."

Laurel looked at Hannah who looked at Sam who looked at Laurel.

"Sam, you wrote that letter, so maybe you could sum it up easiest," Hannah said. Then she turned toward Doctor Perez and said, "Without meaning any personal offense to you, I must say that this arrangement you refer to as *customary* sounds customary in a place like Mississippi before the Civil Rights Act."

Doctor Perez sighed. Sam wasn't sure he knew how to launch into his summary of the study after a comment like Hannah's. *Well, Ku Klux Klan aside, here's the problem . . .*

"You've read the Informed Consent document," he said. "In a nutshell, they promised all of us the drug for free and they reneged. They said the study would last a year and it didn't. We signed a contract and we honored it." He closed his eyes to block out distractions and tried to think if he'd left anything out. "Not only were these things in writing, Doctor Fong repeated them at the original patient meeting, and he said they were the customary and ethical way to conduct such studies. If we stayed in the study through Phase One, we would all get the drug. We would get it for free."

"I see." Doctor Perez ruffled her papers. "But the Informed Consent document is a bit ambiguous about where Phase One ends and Phase Two begins, and about the timing of continuation. So it is, as I've said, premature to make any claims just now. And I am sure that Doctor Fong never promised what was not written in the Informed Consent document."

"I have the meeting on tape."

Doctor Perez looked at Sam without speaking. The brown eye had taken over and her glare was mesmerizing.

"That," she said, "may or may not matter."

The meeting ended a few moments later, when Jeremy reappeared to say she had to leave for her next meeting. Doctor Perez said she would continue speaking with all the parties involved and keep everyone posted. She appreciated their time and energy in coming up to the campus again. Then she was gone and Sam, Laurel, Hannah, and Molly were on the steps again, freezing.

"Well, that was interesting," Hannah said. "In a purely theoretical way."

"I think it may be time to talk to that lawyer again," Laurel said. "Has PER responded to our letter, Sam?"

He shook his head. "I didn't expect to hear from them yet."

Molly snorted. "Yet?" She was trembling with the cold. "We're pretty easy targets, aren't we?"

"What are you talking about?"

She just shook her head and looked away.

"I know what she means," Hannah said. "After all, we were powerless against the virus, then we were powerless against Fong and PER, and it's clear that we don't have any allies here either. We're alone, folks. You'd think that between the doctors who are supposed to help us and the pharmaceutical companies who are supposed to provide our medicines and the committees who are supposed to protect us, someone would actually be interested in what's happening to us."

"I've got to get home," Laurel said. They walked down the front steps, but Molly stayed where she was. "You need a ride? There's plenty of room in the van."

"No."

"You were pretty quiet back there," Sam said. "Come all the way up here just to sit and listen?"

"I stood." Molly took a tissue from her coat pocket and blew her nose. "You want to know why I bothered to come, right? Well, I just wanted to hear this with my own ears, Sam. Get it straight from the horse's ass."

4.

The next day, Sam crossed the boulevard behind his house and headed for the river. Just a few hundred yards north, there was a small park with a marina and boat launch at its far end. Tracy was sitting on the dock waiting for him with her feet dangling above the water. She wore a down jacket the color of wintry river water, battered old purple sweatpants, and purple mittens with a purple and white ski cap pulled low over her ears. An empty barge working its way upriver had her complete attention, and she didn't hear him coming.

Sam stopped near a drinking fountain to look at her. Small as she was, and so preoccupied, sitting with her head pulled down into the raised collar of her jacket, Tracy looked exactly like a child. He could tell from the way her body moved that she was swinging her legs.

"Hey there," he called.

When she turned, he saw that her face was raw from the wind, her nose red and probably running. She smiled at him and stood.

"I want to show you something," she said.

As he started towards her, Tracy held up a hand to stop him. She unzipped her jacket and dropped it on the dock, revealing a thin purple sweatshirt with a few bleached patches of white. She did a little curtsy, then turned and began running away, moving easily, a wild purple and white iris scooting north toward downtown Portland. As the distance and the backdrop of sailboats seemed to swallow her, Sam could still see the cap with its little ball of purple on top. In a few minutes, she turned and came back toward him, waving and grinning when he applauded as she passed and made her way south toward the edge of the park. When she returned, barely out of breath, she did a few sideways and backwards dance steps, then some moves from the racquetball court accompanied by swings of an imaginary racquet.

"So what did you think of that, Mister?"

"This was a vision. You're in great shape."

They began walking south together. Tracy shifted to his left side so she wouldn't accidentally knock into his cane.

"Sam, I'm ready to reserve a court and play. This is more than I hoped for."

"Let me know when. I intend to show up and cheer till I'm hoarse."

Tracy took his arm and hugged it for a moment. They walked a few yards in silence before she spoke in a voice utterly unlike the one she'd just been using. "Is there any progress with PER?" she asked. "Kate won't tell me anything. She just says be glad I'm still getting the drug and shut up."

"It's good advice, Trace. PER isn't saying anything, as far as I can tell."

"What about the lawsuit?"

"I think that's a big part of the problem. PER is in an adversarial mode now. They see us all as potential enemies, and they've decided to keep us totally uninformed. No response to my letter and I don't expect one. Ethics Committee's not going to be much help either."

She stopped walking, turned, and grabbed his arm. "Sam, I heard something yesterday afternoon up at the clinic, when I was getting my infusion. Kate was talking to one of the research department nurses. You remember Judith? The one who gave us our infusions when Kate was on vacation, the one who took four tries to find your vein? Well, I heard Judith say that Molly Carroll came storming through the clinic earlier in the day yelling at the top of her lungs. She was going to sue them all, from the President of

PER down to the people who cook in the kitchen, and all the girls in the study were going to join her. Is that true, Sam? Is that what's going on?"

"Do I look like one of the girls?"

"But what about the rest of them? Maybe everybody but you is in on it."

"I don't think so." He was getting cold. "Let's go to my place and I'll make us some tea."

"You don't *think* so?"

"I talked to Laurel and Hannah yesterday. Daphne called this morning and she had talked to Alice for two hours before that. Nobody said anything about joining the suit. As far as I can tell, it's not happening. All right?"

Tracy had her head down. Both hands were thrust into the pockets of her coat and she was nodding as she listened to him.

"All right. But you should have heard Judith. She said Molly was threatening to invade Fong's office. That's the word she used. Invade it, and use a scalpel on him, something like that, pay him back for his betrayal. And there was other stuff too, I don't remember it all."

"I don't think Fong has to worry. What else did you overhear?"

"Nothing."

"You know, this is supposed to work both ways, Trace. If you know something, even if it's bad, I want you to tell me."

She nodded some more. "It's nothing, really. Kate was just rambling on about how shabby the whole thing was, how PER is a mess. What's Chapter Eleven, Sam? She kept saying they were thinking about Chapter Eleven. I figured it was about some famous book, maybe something bad happens in Chapter Eleven and I ought to get ready for it."

They were just outside Sam's house. He grabbed Tracy's arm and she pivoted at the base of the stairway. "Can you remember exactly what Kate said about Chapter Eleven?"

"Exactly? I don't know. She said four or five more months and if somebody like Crystal & Myerson or Uptown doesn't buy PER, they'll probably go Chapter Eleven. She said she was just guessing, Sam. What does it mean?"

"If it's true, it explains a lot."

"I don't get it."

"They have big money trouble. At least that's what Kate thinks and it makes sense to me. Either that, or they're just a bunch of bad guys. Was there anything else?"

"Well, I found out what PER's name stands for. Kate thought it was a riot."

"I just thought it was the initials of the guys who put the company together."

"It stands for Physicians for Ethical Research."

5.

After Tracy left, Sam barely made it up the stairs to his bedroom. He threw his clothes on the floor and went to sleep immediately, not even bothering to shut the blinds. By the time he woke up in the late afternoon, it was already dark outside. Snowflakes drifted past the window, nothing dramatic, nothing that would stick.

He went downstairs to fix something for dinner. There was a container of raw vegetables he'd cut up a few mornings ago, when he felt energetic enough, a fresh focaccia, and the rest of a can of chicken barley soup. A feast! It was like the diet he used to follow when he was trying to cut down two or three pounds before a rigorous climb. No use lugging extra weight up the face of a rock.

The phone rang as he was about to stick the bread in the oven. He went to answer it, then hesitated as he thought of all the trouble the phone had brought into his life in the last month. If it was Molly, he'd hang up.

"Hello," he whispered, making his voice sound a little weaker than it really was, just in case.

"Dad? You sound dead."

Sam sat on the stool and assumed his customary phone position, elbow propped on the counter, chin in palm. The only prob-

lem was that he crunched his elbow through the center of the focaccia, scattering crumbs and herbs as the loaf cracked in half.

"Ah shit." He got up and put both halves in the oven.

"I was expecting something more like *how're you doing* or maybe
Merry Christmas, but *ah shit* is all right. At least you sounded more
normal when you said it."

"It's Christmas?"

"Day after tomorrow. But I called today because we've got gigs
both Christmas Eve and Christmas Day and I wasn't sure I'd be
able to call then. So how are you?"

"Better than I thought I'd be at this point."

"That sounds pretty bleak."

"Listen, Andy, there's been a change in the drug study."

"What, you're getting the drug?"

"It went the other way. They stopped the study. The only one
who's getting the drug here is Tracy Marsh. You remember her, she
was my partner."

"I don't understand. When are they starting you up?"

"They haven't said."

In the ensuing silence, Sam could easily conjure up his son's
face. When Andy was lost in thought, his lips pursed as in a kiss
and his eyes practically disappearing while he squinted, brows
merging, ears turning red. It was as though his whole countenance
sealed up, as though everything that might reveal how he felt was
hiding while he worked out his response. Sam struggled not to cry
as he waited for Andy to speak. It was astonishing how much he
missed his son now that Andy was on the road, even though Sam
hadn't seen him very often in the last year.

"I always wondered about this," Andy finally said.

"What do you mean?"

"Ever since this thing started, I wondered what would happen
if they just blew you off."

"Funny thing is, that thought never occurred to me. I never
imagined them doing it. And I'm supposed to be such a wise political animal."

"Something about that consent form you had me read didn't

seem right. I mean, it said what they could do to you if you failed to live up to all their conditions, but it never said what you could do if they welched. It was all one way, like high school."

"Well it's only been a month or so. Things could change. They could just be tabulating their data before moving to the next phase."

"You believe that, Dad?"

Sam laughed. "No."

"There's more, isn't there? Tell me, I'm sitting down."

"I think the company's in danger of going under. They do that, and we're all sunk, because the drug will disappear with them. For a few years anyway."

"So what are we going to do?"

"*We* aren't going to do anything. You and Kayla and Navel Lint are going to continue knocking them dead through California and points east."

"And you?"

Sam tried hard never to mince words with Andy. He'd learned how important that was when they'd talked about Vic, when he tried to explain how she could phase herself out of her son's life. Andy, even as a young boy, could detect when his father wasn't being straight. He might not have been able to figure out what the truth was, but he knew when he was being lied to, or told half-truths.

But as of this moment, Sam didn't know what he was going to do. He wasn't going to sue in order to get the drug. In fact, he was no longer sure he wanted the drug at all. Hannah's doubts gnawed at him, and possibility was growing into probability that PER was either in trouble, and therefore would not be able to maintain patients on the drug long enough to effect a cure, or concealing something about the drug's toxicity or benefit. Maybe it was time to think about getting on with his life and stop trying to find a magic bullet.

"As long as Tracy's getting the drug and it's helping her," Sam said, "I'm not going to do anything." He didn't know that was how he felt until he'd said it.

"That doesn't make sense to me. Shouldn't you at least start taking some of those medicines you took before? The stuff for pain, or those sleeping pills. Or go see that acupuncture guy."

"If I take any drugs, I can't go back into the study if they do open it up."

"That's great, Dad. Just sit there and wait. And suffer. I'm sure that's what you'd tell me to do."

It'd be a lot easier here if the kid wasn't right. "As a matter of fact, I've got an appointment with Eli Moskowitz tomorrow. He helped me a bit before, maybe he can do more for me now. And Jessica's coming back soon. Things are happening."

The conversation drifted away from the study and toward Andy's music. Navel Lint would be leaving Los Angeles in two weeks, just after the new year, and traveling hard. By private bus. Excuse me, private coach. They didn't need any money. It seemed to Sam that this was the first time he'd heard Andy say those words in his entire life.

After the call, Sam assembled his dinner and went into the living room to eat. He put on a tape that Andy had made for him, a dozen Navel Lint songs on each side. Nibbling on slices of green pepper, he leaned back on the couch to listen.

Kayla's voice was big and rousing, consistent with the power of her body. She did the first three songs, then Andy got to sing one. When Sam heard his son's voice, he lurched forward on the couch, put the pepper and wedge of bread down, put his hands to his face and let his emotions go.

It wasn't just missing Andy, or being saddened by the passing of time. It wasn't about a Christmas without family and with no particular plans, no tree, and just a few presents to wrap for Max, who would hate getting something from him, for Tracy and her kids, for Kate and Jessica. It wasn't frustration over the way the study was going either, or anguish over his lost well-being, which he felt he had already mourned extensively. He felt neither depressed nor lonely, not even particularly worried, and he was happy to have spoken with Andy.

If he had to give it a name, he would say this was simply unfocused grief. He was overwhelmed by something that felt to him like pure emotion, something new in his experience, a desolation that for all its enormity felt all right, even appropriate. It seemed like part of a larger pattern of feeling that was revealing its presence to him. In the past, not even joy had seemed this unadulterated.

Sam knew one thing. He couldn't blame this on the drug.

6.

Eli Moskowitz grabbed Sam's hand and smiled. "Sam Kiehl. You are a sight for sore eyes, my friend."

"It's good to see you too, Eli."

Moskowitz rocked back on his heels and rubbed his hands together, still smiling. Somehow, he managed to look both totally focused and utterly distracted at the same time. He appraised Sam, his gaze moving across the face, settling on the eyes, checking the hair, the forehead. He narrowed his right eye as though sizing up a potential composition, perhaps *Still Life With Patient*. Then he nodded. "You're standing straighter. That's a good sign."

"It's just that you're so damn tall I have to bend backwards to see you."

"I'm not tall, Sam. I'm just a little exaggerated. It has to do with a past life, but let's not get into that. Come on inside, I can tell we have some work to do."

In the room, Sam started to take off his shirt but Eli stopped him. "Not so fast. Just come over here a minute, we'll talk first."

Sam climbed onto the table. Eli leaned against the edge of it, folded his arms and crossed his legs at the ankles.

"I've been thinking about what you told me on the phone and there's one thing I need to get straight. If they end up deciding to continue the study, would you go back to it? It's something I need to know up front."

"If I do, Eli, I'm still coming here. Now that I've been in the study, I can't see any reason your treatments would be in conflict."

"That's not why I asked." He waved his hand, swatting away

Sam's comment. "It's just that I want to design a treatment for you long term, something that will work its way through the surface symptoms and get to the source. If you were going to leave again, I'd take a different approach altogether."

"Such as?"

"Such as undoing what they've done to you. Sam, you don't look bad, not half as bad as I thought you'd look. But I can tell that you've been through a great deal for someone in your condition. They took too much energy out of you and didn't put any back."

Sam nodded. He had no idea what Eli was talking about, but he sensed the truth of it. He would have said that PER took more than energy out, took his medical faith perhaps, or the bedrock of hope, whatever had grounded his belief in the polysyllabics and acronyms of contemporary pharmaceutical miracles. He no longer felt sure that his disease, indeed every disease, had a discoverable cure.

"Sam, your mouth's hanging open. So stick out your tongue, all right? Let me have a look." Eli grasped the tip of Sam's tongue and gently pulled it down, then turned it counterclockwise. "Lots of bite marks at the edges, lots of white matter." He let it go. "But where it's pink, it's quite pink, which is a good sign."

Sam pulled his tongue inside and bathed it in saliva till it felt normal enough to permit speech. He shook his head. "This stuff still gives me the willies."

"Of course it does. Now let me take your pulses."

After Eli let go of Sam's wrist, he walked over to a bookcase and took down an ancient tome covered in cracked brown leather. The book fell open to a page that must have been precisely what Eli was looking for because he didn't turn it. He read, looked up at the ceiling, looked back at Sam. "This is very strange," he said.

"Nothing that happens in this office is strange, Eli. That's part of your mystique."

"No, I really mean it. It's clear to me that you're still very sick, that your liver and spleen, your lungs and brain, so many organs are unwell. But underneath, Sam, underneath there's greater balance than you've shown since I've known you. It's quite bizarre, actually."

"I don't understand what you're saying."

"Me either. But there's movement going on, that much is obvious." He shut the book and put it back on the shelf. "Talk to me a little more, Sam. What exactly did they do to you?"

"There was some stress, I suppose."

"Stress, schmess. What went on?"

"Like I told you on the phone, Eli, two doses of salt water a week and lots of procedures. I got worn down, I think. And since they backed out of the deal, I've been having trouble sleeping. Is this the kind of thing you're after?"

"I don't know what I'm after. You have to tell me."

"I can't."

Eli held up a hand and nodded. "It'll come out eventually. Let's do some points now. And I want to give you some herbs to try."

7.

Three nights later, as Sam was dozing in his recliner and listening to Vaughn Williams, the doorbell rang. At first, he thought it was a part of the music that he hadn't noticed before, so he didn't move. Then there was loud, rapid pounding on the door that was impossible to mistake as a percussion interlude. He cranked the chair down and stumbled across the living room, too disoriented to check through the peephole before opening the door.

"I knew you had to be home. Even with the lights out, you couldn't fool me."

Molly Carroll walked past him, threw her wet coat across the arm of his sofa, picked up two throw pillows and lay down on the floor. She used the pillows to prop one leg at the knee and stuck the other leg on top of the coffee table.

Before saying anything, Sam went to the hall closet for a hanger, then got her coat and hung it over the door to dry. He needed the time to finish waking up, let alone think of how to deal with Molly.

"Want something hot to drink?" he finally asked.

She moved her head stiffly from side to side like a robot. "A Dr Pepper, if you've got one, and preferably not hot. It's the only drink I can stand."

"Sorry."

She blinked once, very slowly, and said, "Damn rain." Then she folded her arms across her chest and seemed to fall asleep.

Sam tiptoed toward the kitchen, thinking he'd heat some water for himself and maybe pop a couple of frozen turkey pot pies in the oven in case she hadn't eaten dinner either.

"Hurry back," Molly said with her eyes still shut.

When he returned, she propped her head against the front of the couch and studied the painting hanging directly across from her. It was another landscape by Sam's friend Barry Callendar, smaller than the one in the bedroom but equally striking. An island, heavily treed and with a ragged coastline that seemed shorn out of lush high bluffs, waited in a sea boiling with angry gray and white waves. Clouds, heavily outlined in black, loomed low over the treetops. What saved the painting from gloom, what made it instead an almost joyous scene, were patches of bright color deep within the landscape. Carefully sited and enduring homes, perhaps, or flowers that could thrive in this element. Places of safety and vitality that captured the eye, the heart, the soul. At least that was Sam's feeling, and it explained why he'd hung the painting in the place most people would have put a television.

"What the hell is that?" Molly asked.

"It's called *Hidden Island*." He put a tray on the coffee table and poured them both cups of peppermint tea.

"Never heard of it, myself. Must be back east, right?" She picked up a cup and sipped, apparently forgetting that she only drank Dr Pepper.

"Not exactly. A friend of mine from childhood painted it, and he says it's due south of the superior vena cava."

"I don't know anything about astronomy." Her eyes followed him as he went to the recliner. She waited until he'd settled himself and said, "I'm dying."

"What are you talking about, Molly?"

She sipped, then carefully put her cup back on the tray. "Which word didn't you understand? I'm. Dying."

Sam sighed. "Of what?"

"It's too soon to tell."

"That's what you came over to tell me? You're dying but it's too soon to tell from what?"

"Do you want me to leave?"

"That's not what I mean." He looked at her lying there on his floor and felt unsure of himself. Should he be stern with her, should he try to talk sense and help her see that this obsession with being betrayed was damaging, should he just be quiet and let her talk, should he get down on the floor with her and hold her? "I need a little more information, Molly."

"Day by day, I can feel myself going. What's the word I want? Crumbling, eroding. I'm passing away and I can feel it happening."

"Have you talked to Fong?"

She let out a harsh chortle. "Oh that's a good one. Besides, he'd just tell me to go back to my shrink."

Sam looked at her for a moment before speaking again. "If you're depressed, that's not a bad suggestion."

She sat up and glared at him. "I'm not depressed. I'm not lethargic and I want to get better, Sam. I'm nowhere near depression."

"But you think you're dying."

"I am dying."

They sat in silence for a while. Sam finished his tea and put the cup on the table.

"Do you think I'm ugly, Sam?"

Oh boy, be careful. "I don't Molly. Not at all."

"Do you know that I haven't had sex in nine years? Actually, eight years, ten months, and I think four days. I shouldn't exaggerate."

Sam took a deep breath. "Molly, I . . ."

"I'm not coming on to you, you idiot. I'm lesbian, all right? But sex takes energy. Plus you have to actually have someone in your life, you know?"

"Were you in a relationship before?"

"Before I got sick, or ever before? Sam, look, all I meant was, well, I don't know what the hell I meant. In fact, I don't even know why you started asking me about my damn sex life. That's not what I came here for, so back off, OK?"

"Sorry." He looked at Molly lying there and felt a wave of such sorrow for her, for them all, including himself, that he thought he might scream. Instead, he asked, "Are you hungry?"

"Hungry? What are you talking about."

He couldn't resist: "Which word didn't you understand?"

Molly stood up as though jolted by a charge in the floor. She walked quickly over to the couch, and Sam didn't know if she was going to hit him, sit beside him, or pour him some more tea. She looked behind him and frowned.

"What did you do with my cracker?"

He smiled at her. "Your what?"

"My slicker, damn it. My thingie, my coat. Where is it?"

"Don't go, Molly. I didn't mean to upset you."

"Do I look upset?" She actually looked like a linebacker waiting to crunch him into the ground. "Do I look angry?"

"There's a couple of turkey pot pies in the oven. I thought you might like to eat with me."

"Then why didn't you ask?"

"I did."

"Oh yeah? And where was I when this happened?"

"Could you please sit down? Or lie down, whatever you want, and let's just take it from *are you hungry?*"

"Where's my coat?"

"Over there by the door. I hung it up to dry."

She looked to confirm what he said, nodded and sat down next to him. "I hate turkey pot pie."

Seven

1.

On Thursday morning there were two inches of snow on the ground, glistening in a cold, clear light. By Portland standards, it had been a blizzard. School would have been canceled if classes hadn't already been out for the holidays. Buses shifted to snow routes, city trucks were out spreading gravel on the main roads, and people who didn't have to travel were advised to stay home.

The phone woke Sam at 7:30, and as he turned over in bed he thought the snow was screaming at him. He'd had about two hours of sleep all night. Too damn much going on. He picked up the phone, yawned, and whispered hello.

"Sam, I'm sorry to wake you." It was Tracy Marsh, and she was already in high gear. "I did wake you, didn't I?"

"No, I had to get up to answer the phone."

"Oh, good. I'd feel awful if I woke you just for this, but I didn't know who else to call. Wally's no help, and the kids are still asleep. Not that the kids could do much about this if they were awake. Oh I'm sorry, I'm rambling, aren't I?"

Sam yawned again. "So what's the matter?"

"The snowstorm, that's what"

Sam peeked outside and was nearly blinded by the glare. "There's two inches on the ground."

"I know. It's awful. Do you think the clinic will be open? I'm supposed to get my infusion today, and I don't know whether to go up there or not."

"I'd guess they would be. Why don't you give them a call?"

"I tried. No one's there yet. Do you think that means they're closed?"

"Yes, but it's only 7:30. They're always closed at 7:30."

"Maybe no one can get up the hill, you know?"

"I wouldn't worry. By 9:00 the sun will have melted a lot of it anyway. And doesn't Kate have a four-wheel drive?"

"Right! A Toyota. Why didn't I think of that?"

"Is that it? I mean, you called to ask if I thought the clinic would be open?"

"Of course not, Sam. How would you know, anyway? I called to ask if you'd like to come with me this morning while I got my infusion. We've been missing you there. Me, Kate, the whole crowd. I could pick you up at the usual time."

Offhand, Sam couldn't think of one thing he wanted to do less than spend an hour at the Research Department of Cascade-Kennedy *not* getting an infusion. Well, maybe undergo another spinal tap, or one of those electromyograms, where they stuck sabers into his large muscle groups and jolted them with a charge.

"I don't think so," he said.

"You don't?" She suddenly sounded ready to cry.

"Maybe some other time, OK? I hardly got any sleep last night and I have to go back to bed."

"I'm so sorry, Sam. I mean, I shouldn't have called."

"No, it's all right. Look, why don't you phone me after you're done. Maybe we can get together for a cup of toast. Tea, I mean. A cup of tea."

"No way, Sam. I can't leave Wally with the kids that long."

"Maybe some other time, then."

"Sure. Some other time." Again, she sounded close to tears.

"All right, then." He started to hang up, but heard Tracy speak again. "What?"

"You really think they'll be open?"

2.

When the phone rang again, Sam checked the bedside clock because it seemed as though he'd just gotten to sleep again. It was 9:48. He had.

This time, Tracy was hysterical. All she could say was his name, then she would hiccup and say his name again. He shook his head to clear the fog.

"Tracy, try to take a deep breath, all right?" He wondered if Kate was there, and if she was, why she wasn't helping Tracy get hold of herself. What could it be? he wondered. Oh God, PER had dropped her from the study too. She must have gotten to the clinic and found a note from Kate telling her to wait. Tracy would have thought the snow had delayed her, would have passed the time chatting with other patients, and then Kate had swept in and told her. Damn them all. He really doubted she could survive that.

"Sam," she said again, controlling her breathing. He heard her blow her nose. "Sam."

"Tell me what happened, Tracy."

"It's Molly, Sam. She's dead." Tracy stopped talking. He could hear her gulping air, fighting for control. "She killed herself. Late last night. Her mother found her. This morning. She called Kate and Kate just called here to tell me to go home."

Sam stood up. He cupped his left hand over his ear, shutting everything out except the sound of Tracy's sobs. He took the phone to the end of the bed and sat on the floor, resting his back against the frame. "How did it happen?"

"Pills. Kate said she must have taken her whole month's supply of everything. Sleeping pills, pain pills, that muscle relaxer Fong gave her. Antidepressants. Molly's mother said there were empty bottles all over the bedside table. Oh, and an empty bottle of whiskey. She was on top of the bedspread with her hands folded on her chest. Molly was, not her mother."

Sam tried to remember what Molly said to him a few nights ago, but it was all so disjointed he couldn't recall much. Was there anything he should have noticed? Had she been telling him something? Sam had not thought it too strange that she just showed up like that because she used to call him all the time, at odd hours, when they'd first met. Maybe he should have called yesterday, just to check up on her.

"What?" he said, realizing Tracy had spoken while he was lost in his thoughts.

"I asked, do you think she felt any pain?"

"She didn't, Trace. She just went to sleep." He thought of her finally at ease. It was a difficult image to form.

"It's PER's fault, isn't it?"

"It's nobody's fault." But Sam wasn't certain he believed that. Sure, Molly was unstable, but most people with chronic diseases were unstable from time to time. He remembered Molly was suspicious of the setup from the start. Events over the last month or so had just pushed her over the edge. Tracy was talking again. "What did you say?"

"That I'd better go home. Kate said she'd call me later to set up another time for my infusion."

"Do you want to stop by here first?"

"Yes. But I think I should just go home and relieve Wally."

"OK. Drive carefully. And call me later if you want to talk, or if you hear anything more. I'm not going anywhere today."

3.

The more Sam thought about Molly, the angrier he became. He was furious with her, with himself, with the whole group of subjects in the study for not pulling together more closely. Doctor

Martin Fong and Doctor Consuela Perez and Nurse Kate McCabe. He thought the medical school should have provided immediate support, should have gotten all the subjects together as soon as the study was stopped. Fong was in a peculiar position, split between physician and researcher, working both for the school and for PER as its agent. Sam wondered if Fong's research salary was being paid by PER during the course of the study, while the school paid his clinical salary. Had his income been cut when PER stopped the study? Regardless, Fong should have seen each of them at least once during the last month, if only to check up on their mental health. And surely there were resources at the school, other than the doctor in charge of a study, for supporting volunteers in clinical research. Especially during a crisis. Perez had a clear conflict, even if her position as head of the Ethics Committee implied independence, since she was supposed to police the very institution that paid and promoted her. Sam knew Kate well enough to know she must have tried hard to keep in touch with all the patients, as she had with him. But he also knew that she didn't like Molly—few of them did—and perhaps Kate too had missed something she'd been trained to see.

By noon, everyone knew about Molly. Laurel, Alice, Daphne, Hannah, all shocked, all frightened, and also all worried about what Molly's suicide meant for the future of the study.

Sam's anger gradually shifted. Like a lighthouse beam, it had been sweeping the sky and finally locked onto its true target. PER had treated them all shabbily, of course. Not just in abruptly changing the protocol and cutting off communications, but during the course of the study as well. Pushing them to the point of exhaustion on tests of dubious value, adding and subtracting elements from the protocol, ignoring their complaints about side effects because collecting non-laboratory data on side effects wasn't on their agenda, breaking their own rules and, finally, their own contract.

They had everyone over a barrel, Sam thought. No: off their pickles. *Molly, Molly!* Because the goal was to develop a drug that treats the disease. No single patient's health was more important than that cause. That's what everyone said. Sue them? If they really are in financial jeopardy, does it make sense to push them out of business and stop development of the only promising drug so far? The patients were powerless; the medical school was implicated and defensive; Fong had AIDS patients to treat, people who were much sicker than Sam or Tracy or Molly had been.

Finally, in mid-afternoon, Tracy called again. It didn't seem possible, but she was more upset than when they had spoken that morning. If the day's trend continued, she'd be ready for an institution by sundown. For the first minute of the call, as he listened to her cry, hiccup, and blow her nose, Sam thought he knew what she was going to say. As she quieted down, he spoke for her.

"They dropped you from the study, didn't they?" That started a whole new round of crying. All that surprised him was that they'd waited this long. Maybe they hoped her great response to the drug would improve their data. "As of when?" he asked.

In a moment, she could speak. "Today. I don't even get the stuff I was supposed to get this morning, and it's already mixed."

"What was their reason?"

"Kate said they didn't give one. She thinks they're circling the wagons, whatever that means."

"It means they think they're about to get slaughtered and they're trying to protect themselves. God, if the media got hold of this, it would look very bad for PER. It might push more people into the lawsuit. It might sway a judge and jury, might scare off potential investors. I hadn't thought of this before, but they must be very very scared."

"So am I, Sam. I've never been so scared in all my life. I just know I'm going to fall apart again without the drug."

"Maybe you're not. Maybe you've had it long enough that you won't relapse."

"I doubt it."

"Well, who knows? That was part of the reason the study was done at all, to find out what the drug can do, right? Maybe you'll hold your own."

"I'm so frightened."

"Be positive, Trace. That can only help. And thinking negative can only hurt." She was silent, trying to get herself to believe what he was saying. "Besides," Sam added, "you've got Wally to help you. I'm sure he'll be there for you."

"Think again. He freaked out, Sam. He took the kids and went over to his mother's house. You know what he said to me? He said if I was going to get sick again, he was out of here. Enough was enough. Which was about the only sensible thing he's said to me in the last ten years."

"He took the kids?"

"He'll bring them back in the morning, don't you worry. No way he's going to take care of them himself. His old lady either."

"I'm really shocked."

"Don't be." She blew her nose. "I'm not. The only thing that shocks me is that it took him this long. Looks like PER did me a big favor."

4.

Jessica was back from her trip. He'd been talking to her every few days, waiting to hear that her schedule was easing up, wondering if she'd been joking when she said he had to find another massage therapist.

She hadn't been. But since he hadn't found another therapist, Jessica said she'd come over and work on him one more time. But not for money. They agreed that he would buy her dinner at the café again.

At 4:30, after a full afternoon on the phone, he turned off the ringer and turned on his answering machine. If he hurried, he could still get in an hour of rest in the recliner before Jessica arrived. He certainly needed it. As he lay back and closed his eyes, his stomach turned over. It felt as though he were perched on top of a stopped Ferris wheel, the car tilted backwards slightly, all the lights of the city mystifying in their sudden disorder. He was nauseous and dizzy.

The day had been too full, too fast. Sam sat forward a little, put his hands on his belly and breathed deeply. He felt surrounded by images of Molly and Tracy, of Kate inserting a catheter in the crook of his elbow, Fong playing a sonata. The colors he was seeing were all reds and yellows, the colors of fire, of rage.

Sam tried imagining beautiful, peaceful things. A field of daffodils. No, dahlias. Wait, which ones were the little white things? Poppies? Nah, too bright. Cosmos? *Imagine being lost in the vast whiteness of the cosmos.* Maybe not. He thought of the stillness that comes in the moment before a hard climb begins, the drawing-in, the massing of strength. He shifted to being at rest in the landscape his friend Barry had painted for him.

It wasn't going to work. He was too agitated.

Music, maybe that'll help. Sam got up and put on Grieg's *Lyric Pieces,* something mellow and sweet, but knew at once that it was the wrong sound altogether. Too slow and dreamy, too much space between notes in which he could still think. He had a disc of Celtic music by a singer named Enya which Jessica had recommended, and he tried that. Her haunting melodies, smooth voice, strange instrumentation, and indecipherable lyrics turned out to be just the right thing. In five minutes, Sam was deeply asleep.

He heard Jessica's car door slam and jerked upright. When he got the door open, she was already coming up the stairs, lugging the massage table in front of her, both fists wrapped around the handle, knuckles against her chin. She looked up at him and smiled, and Sam realized he'd neglected to make her tea.

He'd never really thought about how warmly she smiled, though he knew he was always glad to see her. It had been so generous of her to continue working on him, to come here after she had essentially quit the massage business, and now she was coming through for him again. It was nice to be friends, long-term friends, with someone who was about to become your lover. The heavy work of friendship was done first, Sam thought, and all the rest should be light by comparison. And even if he was wrong, it was certainly a new way for him to go about things.

As usual, she arrived looking exhausted after a day of work at the nursery. Even in winter. Soon she'd be working harder still. Her target was to be selling plants out of her own nursery in February.

She put the table down carefully in the living room and paused to catch her breath, leaning her weight on it.

"Listen to this," she said. "A woman comes in today with at least a hundred questions about how to make her yard deer-proof. So we talk, and the whole time her kid is in the other room chatting with one of the parrots, right? With Zeppo, not Zorro, because Zorro probably wouldn't have anything to do with him. Me and the mom do our business, they leave, I go back there to work a little on the plans for the new nursery, and Zeppo greets me with *Fuck you, lady!* Just as clear as could be. Do you believe this? From the mouth of a seven or eight-year-old kid."

"Amazing." Sam noticed that there was high color in Jessica's cheeks, as though she were still annoyed about the parrot, or embarrassed about the language she'd just used. Or maybe she was cold. He wanted to warm her, now and for a long time to come.

"I can't help wondering if the mother knew what her little boy was up to." Jessica's eyes narrowed and she looked at him closely. "You look different, Sam."

"It's been an intense day. I'm real tired."

"Then we'll spend a little extra time on your shoulders and neck." She continued looking at his face. A small smile moved across her face. "I don't know yet what it is. But I have to tell you, to me you're really looking good."

"I am?"

She nodded. "I started noticing it two visits ago. There are some changes going on. I felt them in your body too. You're looser." She began setting up the table. "Or maybe it's softer."

"Gee, thanks."

"No, I mean that in a good way." She cocked her head. "A very good way," she added, reddening again. "It's like your armor is melting."

Without further thought, Sam reached out for her and Jessica moved into his arms. He whispered, "I thought that if I ever told you how beautiful I think you are, how much I love to be with you, you'd never come back."

"Silly man. You've been telling me that for most of the last year. I've watched you evolve. No, I've felt you evolve, if that's the right word. You, and me too. It's been deeply moving to me, Sam."

Their kiss was chaste. Sam was surprised at how soft her lips felt. Then she gently pushed him back toward the couch, and turned back to her table. Watching her set up the massage table, he thought about what she'd said. Things had certainly been getting through to him lately, that was true. He'd figured it was just a phase, a touch of despair over his lost hope in the study. He watched Jessica lock the table's legs in place. She would never let him help with the table or the sheets. He sat and studied her movements, his mind growing calmer.

"Do you mind if we talk for a while?" he said. "Just a few minutes, really, if you can spare the time."

She stopped working and leaned forward, resting her elbows on the table. He thought that she was thinking about her schedule, or her long drive home after finishing the massage and dinner, or maybe how hungry she was or what was on her calendar for tomorrow. Or about having to fend him off until a better time. But she said, gently, "What is it, Sam?"

"I told you what's been going on with that study I'm in?"

Jessica nodded. Her green eyes were steady as they probed his face. He wasn't used to looking at her when they talked. It seemed like ninety percent of their conversations took place while he was lying on his stomach or had his eyes closed. Poised like this, she reminded Sam of the actress Cate Blanchett.

"And I described some of the people in the study with me, didn't I?"

"Yes, I remember that woman who's your partner, and that other one you knew from before the study, the woman you said caused so much trouble all the time. And wasn't there a woman you thought was anorexic?"

He was silent for a moment, unable to trust himself to continue. "Molly, the one I knew from the pilot program last year? She killed herself last night." He looked away from Jessica, out the front windows, over toward the kitchen, up at Barry's painting, then down in his lap and his shoulders began to tremble. "Oh shit."

Jessica came quickly around the massage table, dodged the coffee table and sat next to him. She took his hands in her cool dry ones, and exerted slight pressure until he looked up at her and she saw his eyes focus. "Sam, that's just horrible. What happened?"

"I don't know the whole story. But she came over here uninvited a couple nights ago and didn't seem any weirder than usual. She was upset about the study, and she was making threats against everyone and everything. I thought she was a bit off-the-wall, but I guess that didn't seem especially noteworthy to me." He took his glasses off and laid them on the coffee table. He was still shaking. "I simply wrote it off. I figured she was just being her usual bitchy self."

Jessica went into the bathroom and returned with a box of tissues. She sat back down and handed him one.

"Her mother found her this morning," Sam resumed. "It was no accident, that much is clear."

He shook his head and was silent. Jessica let the silence settle for a while.

"What are you thinking?" she asked.

"Half of me wants to cry and mourn for her, the other half wants to curse and scream at her." He sat back, arms twitching as he emphasized his words. "I don't *know*. I need to *do* something about it. I need to *not* just let this go."

"Relax, Sam. I don't get what's wrong with all that. It makes perfect sense to me that you have conflicting feelings. You've had less than twelve hours to deal with this."

Sam found himself getting lost in Jessica's face as he tried to think about what he needed to do. Do about what? Do to whom? Nothing made any sense. More than anything else, Molly had seemed to want to live. Her behavior, he'd thought, was fueled by the desire to get well and get back into the life she had lost to illness. He didn't know what to say.

"Her funeral's the day after tomorrow." It had just slipped out. Sam didn't know why he brought it up.

Jessica shut her eyes, but kept her head still. She's looking inward, he thought, and she has something there for me. He started to reach for her hands again, but stopped himself. She kept her eyes closed and breathed in very deeply. "What you're feeling, the contradictions, the confusion, that's really familiar to me, Sam."

"What do I do with it?"

"Nothing. Which is everything. Before, you would never have let something like this reach you. Now, it's part of your process, part of healing because, I think, you're learning to face difficult things and grow through them."

"But Molly. I should have known."

"You really think you could have stopped her?"

Sam opened his mouth to reply but found himself with nothing to say. Of course she was right. He couldn't have done anything. He looked at Jessica again, and was back where he'd been a few moments ago, wanting her but not wanting to mix his sadness and confusion over Molly with his desire and hope for Jessica.

Jessica smiled, then leaned over and kissed him. "I know what you're thinking, Sam." When he began to protest, she placed a finger across his lips and said, "I want the same thing. But this doesn't seem like the right moment to begin as lovers, and I'm so happy you see that too."

It was good, he thought, that he couldn't read Jessica's thoughts the way she read his. He wasn't quite ready for that. "How about dinner? We could just walk over to the café now."

"I have a better idea." Jessica stood. "How about that massage. It is what I came here for, you know."

"It is?"

She smiled, stood, and said, "Why else would I lug that table up all those stairs?"

Sam wondered if he could relax during a massage, with desire now so clear between them. That would be a good test of his ability to control his mind.

"Exactly," Jessica said, and walked toward the bathroom to change her clothes.

5.

Molly Carroll's mother looked like a darker, freeze-dried version of her daughter. She wore her black hair in the same short, swept-back style, and Sam could swear that she had on the same pair of earrings that Molly had often worn. She stood beside the casket looking around the room bewildered, as though wondering where everyone she expected to be there had gone.

Sam stood nearby in a loose semicircle with Kate, Tracy, Alice, Laurel, and Hannah. An elderly woman sat in the third row, a neighbor of the Carroll's, and a man who'd introduced himself as Molly's cousin Allen sat in the front. That was all.

A particularly lugubrious selection of organ music was being piped into the small room. The group had shifted its location twice so they could hear one another's whispers. When he'd first walked in, Sam approached Mrs. Carroll, identified himself, and offered his hand. She'd stared down at his floppy, black silk pants and black clogs, frowned and brushed his hand briefly with hers. This, Sam thought, was interesting; he'd often wondered where Molly's bitterness came from. Maybe it was as hereditary as a predisposition to the disease that had overwhelmed her.

When the minister arrived, he too approached Mrs. Carroll and took her hand. Sam noticed she did not give him the once-over before enclosing the hand in both of hers. They spoke for a few minutes, the minister withdrawing an index card and pen from his pocket and jotting down notes.

He began the service with a thirty-second coughing fit. Then said, "I want to open by paraphrasing something the poet Robertson Jeffrey once wrote. He said that strong people lean on death as on a rock." The minister paused, looking around to be sure everyone was paying attention. "Let us think upon that idea for a moment, friends. The idea that death, which the Lord has put at the end of every person's journey here on earth, is something from which we can draw strength rather than weakness. Hope rather than despair. Death solidifies our lives with its weight, and helps mark our path. It is there for us like a boulder is there for the mountaineer needing a handhold. One of life's essential mysteries! Friends, that which seems to destroy us makes us stronger in the end. Yes, as our dear friend Molly knows now, death is our rock in the lonely climb up the mountain of life."

It occurred to Sam that something about this eulogy would have tickled Molly with its perverse logic and empty consolation. He looked over at Tracy sitting next to him and was surprised to find her glaring at him.

"What?" he whispered.

"I have to talk to you. Don't leave right away."

The minister, glancing down at his index card, was speaking about Molly's love of clog dancing, frozen yogurt, and professional football, particularly the Seattle Seahawks.

Football, yes, this too reminded him of one of life's essential mysteries. "As in that great American sport, football, you never know when the hole is going to open up, friends, and let the daylight through. Our Molly, in the daze and haze of her illness, could not see the light. The illness had tackled her roughly and the blow made her mind unclear. How do we explain the terrible choices people sometimes make? How do we deal with our own mystification when a beautiful young woman, a woman who loved life and loved football and had so much to live for cannot go on? Picks up the stone of death and ties it round her own neck. In our Molly's case, the explanation is clear enough: she did not know what she was doing. She was not herself and so God will welcome our Molly as an innocent child is welcomed, will bring her the comfort she could not find amongst us, and eternal rest for which we are grateful."

Sam could not move. He stared at the minister. In his chest and belly, Sam felt the way he felt just before a race began. It always struck him as strange that people yawned as they bounced in place at the starting line, the body seeking to calm itself, to remove itself from the rush of energy being stirred up by the brain as it waited for the sound of the starter's gun. Sam was calm, but also rigidly focused. This man had just done to Molly what she thought PER had done to her, and Fong and Kate and all of them. He had rendered her absurd, extraneous. He ignored what she'd said and done, had not even glimpsed who she was, as he went blindly and dumbly through his ritual procedures.

Outside the funeral home, all six of them, including Kate, huddled in a semicircle at the edge of the parking lot. Molly's body was going to be cremated, and Mrs. Carroll had not wanted them around for that, or anything else connected with her daughter's final rest. They spoke about the minister and his eulogy, none of them wanting to leave just yet. Sam could feel Tracy's urgency as she stood beside him, thrumming with the effort to remain silent. Finally, it was too much for her. She stepped forward and spun around to face them.

"Listen, I have to say something. I suppose it's OK for all of you to hear. Even you, Kate, if you want. Of course, you won't know if you don't want to until you hear it, I guess, so you can stay or go, it doesn't matter to me." Kate smiled and turned to leave. "I didn't mean that the way it sounded Kate. I mean, I'd really like you to stay."

Looking first at Tracy, then slowly at each one of them, Kate came back. "As long as you don't talk about the Seattle Seahawks."

"Will you help me?" Tracy said, addressing them all. "I can't think of anything else to say. I know you're all out of the Zomalo-vir study for now, and I was the only one still on it, but the drug gave me back my life. If I have a relapse, and Wally already said he's leaving me if I do, then I might have to pull a Molly. I just don't know what I would do if I start to get sick again."

"Your husband said that?" Hannah asked.

"Said what?"

"He'd leave you if you suffered a relapse?"

Tracy nodded. Hannah looked quickly around the group, then back at Tracy. Sam was glad they didn't all look at him then, as the only male around.

"Honey, dump that loser and get on with your life."

Tracy waved a hand as though swatting a mosquito beside her ear. "Wally's the father of my kids. They call him Daddy. If they called him Wally, then maybe I could dump him, you know what I mean? I'd rather dump myself."

"So what do you think we can do?" Hannah asked, sighing so deeply it seemed that she was doing it for all of them.

"This may sound crazy, but I have this idea that if we act to-gether, maybe we can shake PER up enough to change their minds.

We're the only site in the study where not even one person joined the lawsuit against them. So I thought maybe we could send someone up there to talk to them, you know? Lay it on the line. We're all you have left, we're trying to be your friends, something like that. *We're helping you, you idiots.* I know it's a lot to ask, but if we said we'd all jump into that lawsuit unless they gave me the drug . . ."

In the silence that followed, Sam wondered how Tracy had summoned the nerve to ask this of them. And now, of all times. A few of these women probably hoped to get the drug themselves, though only Tracy had still been getting it as of yesterday. Obviously, PER couldn't put them all on the drug now. But perhaps they could reinstate Tracy without too much risk.

"I'll go," Sam said.

"What do you mean?" Tracy asked.

"I'll go talk to PER. We can't ask Kate or Fong to do it. If they could, they already would have. We can't all go, and I don't think another delegation would be any more potent than it was with the Ethics Committee. I used to do this sort of thing for a living, talk people into doing something they didn't think they wanted to do, or into spending money they didn't think they had to spend. Since I'm not a lawyer, there wouldn't be that edge to it." He looked around, hoping he hadn't offended anyone by suggesting that he was better equipped than they were to do this. No one seemed annoyed. After all, they'd already tried sending a delegation to work with Doctor Perez and gotten nowhere. "Yeah, I'd like to go."

"Really, Sam?"

"Alice and I can call the others," Hannah said. "I don't imagine they'd mind agreeing to Sam as the Portland group representative." She looked toward Kate. "Do you?"

"I don't think I should say anything."

"See, Kate?" Tracy said. "You should've left."

Kate shook her head. "Daphne Warren could be a problem, if you do this. She might want to get whatever concessions Tracy gets."

"I think I can convince Daphne to wait," Hannah said. "One of us gets it first, then when Tracy is taken care of, the rest can make the same request, if they want. Anything else probably wouldn't work."

"You'd go to Seattle for me?" Tracy asked.

"As soon as PER will see me." Sam turned to Kate. "Do you think they will?"

"Will what?"

"See me."

"They just might, if you ask them right."

Eight

1.

Max drove him to Seattle the following Wednesday. Once Sam had reached the correct person at PER, it hadn't been difficult to set up a meeting.

Emma Cameron was the company's head of public relations, and on the phone she'd sounded pleasant enough. A little young perhaps, and full of jargon, but sharp. After a few minutes of uncertainty, she began to see things quite clearly. Yes, it was best to have all the information available when a group tried to reach a difficult decision. Yes, it might be of benefit for the two of them to spend an hour or so together, just to be sure they both understood all the ramifications of the present situation. To be absolutely sure they agreed on what they could agree on, and agreed to disagree on what they couldn't. Far better one-on-one than for the whole group to show up, certainly. Or even a delegation. And yes, it was a good idea for Sam to meet with Oswald Rowland, PER's president, after he and Emma were through talking. She would set that up. Would Sam care for a tour of the facilities, a chance to see where the drug was fabricated and to learn a little about how it was developed? Good, good. Right after lunch, say 1:00? That was an excellent time, she thought.

When Max said they didn't have to leave Portland until 10:45, 10:30 if they wanted to stop for lunch, Sam had his only moment of panic. He would have said 10:00, the latest, even taking into account Max's Grand Prix driving tactics.

"It's a hundred-eighty miles to Seattle," Sam said. "Maybe two hundred by the time we get to the suburbs."

"That's what I figure, too."

"In two hours fifteen minutes?"

"Well, I'm allowing for traffic. Seattle's a mess since you were there last."

"So why press it?"

"My point exactly."

They left at 10:30, and Sam packed a lunch for them to eat in the car. Max loved playing Mozart operas on the car's stereo when he drove long distances. Today it was *Die Zauberflote*. Every once in a while, he would join in an aria for a few off-key notes, then remember Sam was in the car and shut up again. When Sam handed him a turkey sandwich just before they reached Fife, he could hear Max humming as he chewed, a vastly preferable option.

During the first hour of the trip, they had discussed what Sam would try to accomplish and how he might go about it. Max agreed that it wasn't necessary to come out and say *if you don't give my friend the drug, I'm going to the press, and all fifteen of us are going to sue your asses. Plus, I have a tape you're really not going to like.* Surely PER grasped that if Portland joined the suit, they could no longer argue before a judge that the study's patients weren't united, that a significant number thought they'd been treated fairly. PER wouldn't have agreed to see him if they didn't want to keep Portland out of the suit.

Max thought the key to successful negotiation was the properly dropped bombshell: PER didn't know what Sam really wanted. They probably thought the group was distressed by Molly's suicide, especially Sam, since he was the person coming to see them. They assumed he'd demand that the group be given the drug. Or at least half of them. He should be prepared for PER to imply that if Sam kept a low profile, they might be willing to start him on it, but no one else. Divide and conquer.

Timing was everything in this kind of bargaining. They didn't know that Sam had grown less interested in receiving the drug himself, or that there were a few subjects in Portland who were glad to be done with Zomalovir forever. PER certainly didn't know that he was coming to their offices to argue for Tracy rather than himself, that he feared she might follow Molly's example. Once he told them it was Tracy who must continue to get the drug, he should add that this strategy made a lot of sense for the company too, since she was such a strong responder. The data would look excellent. It would be good if Sam could find out exactly why they had cut her off again. Was it, as he imagined, a defensive action following Molly's suicide? Did they know something about the drug's toxicity, its diminishing effectiveness over time, its limitations? Above all, keep focused, keep cool.

"I wonder if I'm capable of this," Sam said. "I can't remember half the things you just said."

"You are and you will. Good old even Kiehl, back in action. You know how to do this."

"I'll grant that I once knew how to do this sort of thing. But after the tour and the preliminaries with Ms. Cameron, it's entirely possible I could fall asleep on Ozzie's conference table."

"Oswald Rowland, old Ozzie, aka Oz," Max said. "I wonder if they call him *The Wizard* around the office." He changed lanes, then checked his side-view mirrors. "Adrenaline alone should see you through. I may have to carry you back to the car, but you'll do the meeting with no trouble. You won't even recognize yourself."

"That's what I'm afraid of," Sam said.

"This is a good sandwich."

"I wish I had your confidence."

"Just remember, this kind of meeting is probably the one thing you were ever good at."

"Thanks a lot."

"And if you use the wrong words, or mispronounce something, don't worry. The more they underestimate you, the better. We're here. What did I tell you? It's 12:53."

As they turned off the county road onto a wide slab of un-striped asphalt, an opened gate loomed before them with a guard standing at it, barring their way. He took Sam's name and used a phone to verify the appointment. Max dropped him off on a gravel loop near the front door, told Sam he'd be back in two hours and, if the guard didn't let the car back in, to walk out to the gate. He'd wait for him there. Then he sped off, heading into downtown Se-attle for a few meetings of his own.

2.

Sam studied the building before going inside. Ever since ru-mors of the clinical field trial had begun circulating nearly two years ago, he had been trying to picture PER Pharmaceuticals, Inc., and its offices, the miracle factory from which this synthetic drug had emerged. None of his special-effect imaginings had prepared him for a building which looked more like a bank than a medical research facility.

The shell was a splayed, prefabricated gray block pitted with a few long, narrow windows. The roof bled dark stains down to the tops of the windows, and Sam could see that PER had tried repeatedly to patch it, then to paint over the walls. Except for the company logo above the front door, the building had no decora-tive design features, no signage, no style. But the area between the gates and building itself had been nicely landscaped with shrubs and native trees, especially Pacific madrones showing now their smooth winter skins and persistent clusters of orange-red berries. Sam would love to see how this stand looked in July, when the papery bark would be peeling in a kaleidoscope of chartreuse, red, orange, and brown shreds. There were also vine maples, alders, and hemlock, but these seemed stunted, and a few beds of flowers were now bare or covered in mulch. Sam thought it was odd that so much effort had been put into flora and so little into the aesthetics of the building.

The front doors parted and Emma Cameron walked out to meet him. She was the tallest woman Sam had ever seen, at least six feet five inches, and was wearing high heels as if to say *Why not? If I wore pumps would you think I was average size?* Sam wondered what was going on, why lately every woman he stood near seemed to tower over him. Maybe the illness was making him shrink. Or all the salt water they'd shot into his veins.

Emma Cameron's hair was completely gray and pulled back in a braid that hung to her waist. Her thin face was pale and smooth except for a long dimple on the right side, and she carried her hands curled across her palms when she walked. Then she waved and smiled, her eyes a youthful bright blue, and Sam thought she couldn't be more than twenty-five. Premature aging as a hazard of working for the sinister PER? Dressed in a loose gray suit a few shades darker than her hair, the woman must have known how disconcerting she was to meet for the first time. She approached slowly as though giving him several seconds to collect himself.

"You must be Sam Kiehl," she said, extending her hand. "Emma Cameron. I saw you admiring the landscape. You should get a look at it in the spring and summer."

"I was thinking the same thing, Ms. Cameron."

"Please, call me Emma so I'll know who you're talking to. Ms. Cameron? Puh-lease. May I use Sam?"

"Of course. I stopped being Mr. Kiehl shortly after I got sick. Threw away my business suits and wingtips, bought floppy pants in the wildest colors I could find, soft slip-on shoes, and had my ear pierced. Anyway," he turned to look at the madrones, "You were talking about Flowering Time in the Valley of Medical Science. Tell me all this is not thriving on toxic effluents."

"Nothing but rainwater. June, July, August are just incredible around here. Doctor Rowland is so passionate about flowering things. Staff sometimes see him walking in the gardens for hours at a time, taking meetings on the lawn, looking at lab results under the trees, dictating letters beside the rhodies. Sometimes he stays overnight, or flies off in his helicopter at midnight just to enjoy the place longer."

"I was born in Brooklyn, myself," Sam said. "We didn't have Nature there."

Emma's laugh was a little girl's giggle, shocking enough to start Sam laughing as well. Hold on, he told himself, don't get too relaxed here. You've got work to do.

She led him inside the building, then past a reception desk perched in the center of the lobby like a ticket booth. Entering a small chamber behind it and to the right, she picked up a thick manila envelope, tore it open and handed Sam a day-glo orange badge emblazoned with his name. He was glad she didn't squat down to pin it on.

"Let's chat in my office for a while first. Then I'll show you around the facility, if that's all right. You're scheduled with Doctor Rowland at 2:30."

Without waiting for his response, she led him down a narrow hall. It felt to Sam as though they were moving east, directly away from the front entrance and deeper into the building. But with only the faintest of light seeping through the odd windows, he couldn't be sure.

Blocking their way was an older man in the requisite white lab coat, arms on hips, legs firmly parted. His smiling face was angled toward Emma but his pale eyes were focused on Sam. Nearly bald on top, he had long hair gathered behind in a much smaller version of Emma's braid.

"Good afternoon, Doctor Shields." Emma and Sam stopped, since Shields didn't move out of their way. His attention was now totally on Emma. "This is Sam Kiehl," she said. "He's a patient in our Protocol 793a."

"So nice to see you," Shields said. He did not offer Sam his hand, nor look his way.

"Doctor Rowland thought it was an especially fine opportunity for us to get feedback from one of our subjects," Emma said, her voice a controlled monotone.

"It is, as I have suggested, highly irregular for a pharmaceutical company engaged in research through the auspices of several research sites to have anything whatsoever to do with a subject."

"As I remember, Doctor Rowland took note of that during our recent meeting."

Shields finally turned toward Sam. His face was entirely blank, then shifted dramatically into a brilliant smile. Perhaps its suddenness or its enormity caused his skin to flush so deeply.

"Enjoy yourself," Shields said, then hurried past them.

"Enjoy myself?" Sam whispered.

"I hope you'll forgive us for that. Obviously, Doctor Shields does not consider it wise for us to break with established procedures in any way. You can understand. Perhaps this will serve to demonstrate the strength of our commitment to helping patients."

They continued along the hallway. This was not what Sam expected the inside of a pharmaceutical company to look like. He'd envisioned drug cowboys in bubble suits trailing coils of tubing in their wakes, eerie light emanating from under doorways, glassed walls to permit observation, whirring chromatographs, test tubes held at eye level with droppers poised above their openings. All he saw were gray walls with occasional daubs of slate-blue door.

Emma's office was enormous. She had a series of desks arranged in an arch that spanned the room's core, a kind of command center with several computer screens, a telephone that was as large as his microwave at home and festooned with dozens of buttons, a laser printer, photocopier, and fax machine and stack after stack of documents. No personal photographs that he could see, no art on the walls, but two framed diplomas and a pair of certificates showing that Emma Cameron had been named to the All-Pacific Ten Conference basketball team during her junior and senior years at UCLA, and had been a second team All-American as a senior.

"Would you like a cup of coffee, Sam?" She sat in the command center and waved him toward a plush leather armchair. "I've got some made fresh, and there's a plate of sweet rolls too."

"Thanks. But the docs tell me I'm not supposed to drink coffee and I'm not supposed to eat sweets. How about a cup of herbal tea?"

"Oh my." She pressed a button and, without lifting the phone's receiver, said, "Astrid, do we have any herbal tea for Mr. Kiehl?"

"Herbal tea," said a disembodied voice, which Sam thought could either belong to a computer or a person in deep shock.

Then Astrid appeared in the doorway. Heavyset, wearing a bright orange wig, she was young but so wrinkled that Sam thought she must have been exposed too long to cigarette smoke or high winds. At least he hoped that's what explained it. Astrid shrugged her shoulders, held out a cupped hand as though it contained a live grasshopper, and said, "I have one bag of something called Grandma's Tummy Mint, Ms. Cameron. But it was in my drawer when I first took this job last year, so I can't promise it'll be fresh. Besides, there's no boiled water outside of the labs. I could let the hot water faucet in the sink run for a while."

"Never mind," Sam said. "I had enough tea this morning to last me all day."

Smiling at each other, Emma and Sam settled back down in their seats. Finally, the meeting was about to commence. He watched Emma's face undergo a thorough transformation. Both the smile and brightness in her eyes faded, her cheeks went slack, and she seemed to age twenty years before Sam's eyes. This, he thought, was not a good sign.

"Drugs," she began, "originally were extracted from natural substances. To ensure consistent composition, potency, and availability, most are now produced synthetically in laboratories much like ours. Scientists are able to customize drugs almost for any purpose. We don't have to rely on and be limited by copying nature any more."

"I understand that, Emma. It's what makes me so hopeful that PER can help us."

"I'm glad you bring that up," she said. "Physicians for Ethical Research was founded in 1978 by a group of practicing physicians in this region devoted to unlocking the mysteries of the human immune system." She was looking at a spot just to the left of Sam's ear. "It remains a small, independent, privately held biomedical research company whose achievements, particularly in the management of viral disease, are renowned throughout the world. Our studies appear regularly in the peer-reviewed literature. Our work with the Centers for Disease Control, the National Cancer Institute, the National Institute of Allergy and Infectious Diseases, is

exemplary. I think it's safe to say the words *cutting edge* apply here."
She smiled in his general direction.

"I've read a little about the company," Sam said. "A long string
of successes. Which is why I thought we should have this meeting
now, before things got any further out of hand."

Sam watched her lean back in the chair, folding her long arms
behind her head, her elbows jutting out, and thought she looked
like a prisoner about to be frisked. There was still plenty of time.
He listened carefully to figure out where she might be heading.
Her eyes scanned the ceiling as she spoke.

"The process by which a new pharmaceutical product achieves
approval from the Food and Drug Administration is both cumber-
some and unbelievably expensive, Sam. It can easily take a dozen
years and cost hundreds of millions, and that would not be atypi-
cal. The commitment to testing on human subjects is not taken
lightly, as you must be able to imagine."

"I do appreciate that," Sam said, since she had stopped talking
for a moment. He was getting tired, leaking energy in pools he
thought might be visible to the observant. "We all feel fractured
that your company has chosen to devote its resources and itches to
finding a treatment for us." *Fractured? Itches?*

"I'm glad to hear that. The world of biomedical research is so often misconstrued, you know. People tend to think one of two things:
either we are all motivated by base financial considerations foremost,
or that we are inspired geniuses who remain out of touch with humanity. Drug nerds, if you will. Neither, I can assure you, is close
to the truth. Most biomedical researchers that I know are dedicated
men and women driven to helping humanity. That's why I joined this
field in the first place, Sam. Coming out of school with a certain
public acclaim as well as with a degree cum laude, I had dozens of
options, let me assure you." Her gaze shifted back down toward Sam
and she frowned in the direction of his knees. "And I wouldn't stay
in this field if it wasn't filled with dedicated, selfless people intensely
devoted to helping battle some of the worst diseases known to man."

"Which brings us directly to some of our main cornerstones as
a group," Sam interjected. "Concerns, I mean. Our main concerns."

Emma held up one finger, signaling him to wait until she finished her point. She leaned forward again.

"This reminds me of when I was playing basketball at UCLA. You don't mind if I introduce a personal note here, do you Sam? We were such an effective team, I always thought, because of how well everyone worked together. Let me give you an example. Whenever we prepared for a game, the starting team would scrimmage against a team of our own players, substitutes who would pretend to be players from the opposing team. They were so dedicated. Very few of them had any hope of actually playing in a game. Very few of them could dream of playing in the Olympics or hooking up with one of the few professional women's teams after graduating. But they played their hearts out in these scrimmages, Sam. They didn't give up, they didn't complain or meet with the coaches to demand that they have our starting jobs. They challenged us to be better than we were, they inspired us. Do you understand what I mean?"

Sam thought this was a lot like talking to someone with his own disease, except she didn't seem to misuse any words. Nothing she said connected with what his part of the conversation was about. Before he could answer her question, even though he assumed it was rhetorical, Emma's phone rang. She spun her chair around, plucking the receiver from its cradle and turning her back toward him. Sam had been in meetings before with people who had the gift of talking on the phone without being heard by those in the room. Emma was particularly gifted at it. She seemed to disappear entirely, so he looked away, studying her All-American certificate.

"I'm sorry," she said in a few moments. "That was Doctor Rowland's assistant, Charlotte. It seems that the doctor will have to see you at 2:10 instead of 2:30. Something's come up. He needs to leave the office a bit sooner than expected."

"Oh," Sam said, checking his watch. It was 1:35. "When does he leave?"

"2:20, the latest. I am sorry." She stood. "Come, why don't we do that tour now. If there's still more ground to cover after you've seen Doctor Rowland, we can meet again."

Emma came around her command station, picked up a folder

and headed toward the door. Sam looked down to locate his cane, which he'd laid beside the chair, and couldn't help noticing Emma's shoes. They had to be a man's size twelve. He might be able to fit both his feet into one of her shoes.

He followed her down the long hallway again, noticing that names instead of functions were stenciled above the doors. Dr. Devlin, Dr. Kim Jong Sam, Dr. Holtzman-Bell, Dr. Petrie. Not very informative about what was going on inside.

"Over here," Emma said over her shoulder, "we did some pioneering work on mapping chromosome 11. Back when we were looking at sickle cell anemia and porphyria. Doctor Rowland thought Chromosome 11 was going to be a huge breakthrough for us. Still does, but the time frame wasn't persuasive. Like everybody else, we devote most of our energy to AIDS and cancer drugs now."

"Is that how you got to us?"

"We got to you through sheer serendipity, Sam. Your immune profiles are almost the opposite of AIDS. When the drug proved inconclusive in our AIDS trial, we saw the logic of trying it elsewhere. Am I walking too fast for you?"

"No, I was just taking it all in. I guess I have trouble thinking and walking at the same time. Why was the AIDS trial incomprehensible?"

"That wasn't the problem. We just didn't complete the trial. It's a very long and very technical matter," Emma said, continuing to walk. Her stride seemed to be lengthening. "Perhaps this isn't the right time or place for us to get into it."

"Was the drug ineffective? Was it toxic?"

"Neither. It didn't react well to the plastic used by the investigators to contain it on-site." She came to a closed door that blocked further access to the hallway. "Now DNA research is located down that wing," Emma said, pointing to their left. "Sequencing, cloning, replication, all our genetic engineering research. Doesn't have much to do with what you're interested in." She had taken a printed page out of her folder and was studying it. He wondered whether anything she told him on this tour would actually be true, or whether it had been freshly scripted for his benefit. She pointed to her right. "Let's go this way, immunodiagnostics."

"What is that?"

"Oh, exactly what it sounds like. Then we'll continue on to the animal rooms, show you some of the advanced equipment we use, the biohazard stuff, end up at the actual drug labs themselves, where we fabricate."

Fabricate. Make things up. Oh, she's referring to the drug. Sam was getting very confused. He tried to remember what he knew about Zomalovir from the original material Fong had handed out. He knew it was extremely fragile, that much had been made clear. It couldn't be mixed until shortly before being used, arriving at the Clinical Research Department packed in steaming dry ice. What else? A mismatched double-stranded RNA molecule capable of crossing the blood-brain barrier, as Fong had explained it. Sam remembered that because he'd loved the way it sounded. But if Zomalovir was a genetically altered RNA molecule, why had Emma told him genetic engineering research was not something he'd be interested in? That's part of what he was here for. What else could he remember? A Poly-this, Poly-that compound. Antiviral and immunomodulatory.

Suddenly Sam felt that everything around this place could be of vital significance to him, even if at this moment he couldn't imagine how. Perhaps, he thought, I am making some kind of pilgrimage here. PER's headquarters might not exactly conform to the conventional idea of a sacred place, but in many ways it bore the greatest significance for Sam. Seeing exactly where this drug was made was of vital importance. Witnessing it, coming to the very spot, even if he was about to reject the drug for himself. His interest was now no longer generalized, no longer merely curious, and he could feel the difference in his guts. He might no longer want to put the drug in his own veins, but Tracy desperately did, and he was going to see to it that she had the chance.

"Emma," he said as she turned a corner and disappeared. "I need to take a break."

Her head popped back around the corner. "Come on. The bathroom's straight ahead."

"Not that kind of break."

She checked her watch. "Well, we're on a pretty tight leash here, Sam. Doctor Rowland is set for 2:10 now, and we don't want you showing up there feeling all ragged."

"That's why I need a little rest. Is there a lounge nearby?"

She shook her head and led him into a small conference room a few yards down the hall. He hadn't noticed it when they first went by. It was empty, though a portable screen was standing at the front; an overhead projector was perched in the back, and chairs in disarray suggested a recently ended meeting. "OK," Emma said, "we can take a break in here. Sorry I can't offer you any refreshment."

Sam plopped down in the chair at the table's head, leaned back and sighed. "I really want to ask you a few questions before my meeting later."

Emma sat at the opposite end of the table. She rested her chin on a scaffolding of long, interwoven fingers and said, "I'm sure they'll all be answered by our tour and by Doctor Rowland, but go ahead."

"I assume you know the real purpose of my visit?"

Emma nodded slowly. "That poor, misled young woman."

"Who do you mean?"

"The one who killed herself, of course, Patient 004. Who did you think I meant?"

Sam thought about his lengthy strategy discussion with Max this morning. The properly placed bombshell. Well, having listened to Emma Cameron this long, having glimpsed Doctor Shields, and knowing he now had only ten minutes coming up with The Wiz, he could not imagine there being a proper place to drop it. How do you negotiate with people who are neither listening nor talking with you? Easy: you don't. He could walk out, which was not a good option, or he could capitulate, which was not an option. What the hell.

"I thought you meant Tracy Marsh."

"Which one is she?"

Sam withdrew an index card from his pants pocket. "Patient 010."

"Ah," Emma said. "The Significant Responder."

"That would be Tracy Marsh."

"I'm sorry, Sam." She stood and neatly replaced her chair. "I don't understand. I thought you were here either to talk about the group as a whole or about yourself in particular. What does Patient 010 have to do with anything? I mean, she's just one subject."

He stood too. Perhaps that was how real discussions took place around here. "Exactly," Sam said. "And your best demonstration of both efficacy and safety, at least in Portland."

"For scientific purposes, one subject has no importance." Emma came dangerously close to looking at him. "We must demonstrate statistical significance for the FDA and that is not done on an individual basis."

"Is that why you discontinued Tracy?"

"We didn't discontinue her. Protocol 793a ended."

Sam rested his haunch on the table, yearning to sit. "Can I be frank?"

"Please."

He didn't know if she meant *Please do* or *Puh-lease* again. This was no time to back off. "Bullshit," he said.

Emma blinked. She took a step back as though she'd been fouled in the act of shooting. "I beg your pardon?"

"Which word didn't you understand?" *That one's for you, Molly.*

Sitting back down, looking more confused than annoyed, Emma thought for a moment. She now seemed somewhere between the young woman from outside the building and the older woman from inside her private office. Good, Sam thought, perhaps I'll get to see the median Emma Cameron. "Patient 010 was not the only subject discontinued in the last week. All the Significant Responders at each site were discontinued. Phase One is over."

"When will Phase Two begin?"

"That's unclear at this time."

"But we'll all be continued on the drug, correct? That's the Open Label Phase referred to in the Patient Consent Form."

"I don't have the form with me, Sam, and I'm not an attorney. But I believe you're misreading the language of the Consent Form."

"I do have it." He reached into his pocket and drew the form out, unfolding it and offering it to Emma. "And the language is clear.

The drug and everything, quote, required by the research study will be provided or paid for by the sponsoring company, unquote."

"Provided to those involved in the study," Emma said.

"Us."

Emma slowly shook her head. "Now it'll be my turn to be frank. All right, Sam?"

"That's why I drove two hundred miles."

She sat back and he watched her changing again. "It is this company's position that, perhaps through an unfortunate confusion on the part of the lead investigators at each site, the subjects were under the misapprehension that they were entitled to receive the drug upon completion of their participation in the study, and for as long as it took to be approved for use by the FDA, without charge. That is not, nor was it ever, the intention of this company. To do so would be financially infeasible. The drug is only provided to those subjects who are in the study. When your protocol ended, so did your involvement in the study."

"I see. Is that the position you've developed for litigation?" Lookit, Sam thought, she's got me sounding like her.

"It's the company's long-standing position."

"Read this form."

"I reviewed that form before it was disseminated."

"Well, this form, along with the unanimous testimony of all the Portland patients saying we were led to believe our involvement in the study continued beyond the conclusion of Phase One, and a cassette tape I have of our original recruitment meeting in Portland, will in my opinion be very persuasive in court. If things should get that far. And in the media, while matters wait to reach the courts."

"I see." And for a moment, she did seem to see, looking directly at him, playing back in her mind the exact words he'd spoken. Then she sat back. "We really should continue our tour, Sam."

"Is that it?"

"What more do you want me to say?"

He took a deep breath. It was obvious to Sam that this was perhaps the only moment he would get in which to present his deal. She was already standing up again to begin tromping through PER's bleak hallways with him, and he'd bet he was going to get little more than a smile from Doctor Oswald Rowland.

"I want you to say that you can see the wisdom of working with the Portland group, which has been so cooperative and understanding thus far. I want you to say that you appreciate the value of our remaining outside the litigation. The fifteen of us as a group, plus that tape of mine, not joining the legal action against PER. And I want you to say that you believe it would be of great benefit to everyone if Tracy Marsh were allowed to continue receiving the drug until she was well enough to live her life without it."

"Impossible. There were Significant Responders at each site."

"Give it to them all."

"If I'm not mistaken, Sam, that option has already been rejected by the Board."

At that moment, Emma's beeper sounded. She reached toward her hip, where it was looped through her belt and hidden beneath the fabric of her suit jacket.

"Excuse me a moment," she said, darting out of the room.

3.

Sam slumped exhausted in his chair and fought to stay awake. Do not put your head on your arms, Kiehl. He could not decide if he had made a mistake in being so direct with her. He didn't think Emma had been trying to confuse or mislead him. Despite the canned speech at the outset, and her early resistance to actually responding to what he said, he didn't think she was trying to wear him down either. She was telling him PER could not deal, period. Either for legal or financial reasons, but under the cloak of conforming with FDA regulations and established procedures, PER could not give Tracy the drug because it would mean they at least had to give all the Significant Responders the drug. Without quite using the words, Emma had said *Fuck you, we'll see you in court.*

Which brought back clearly something Max had said to him a few days ago. "We need to come up with a back-up plan for when they say *Fuck you, we'll see you in court.*" Sam remembered how that conversation had ended, and he began to see that it might, indeed, be necessary to hold a gun to their heads. Even to pull the trigger.

When Emma returned, Sam stood to meet her. He knew what she would say even before she opened her mouth.

"I'm sorry, Sam. That was Charlotte again. Doctor Rowland is unable to meet with you after all. Something came up that needed his attention immediately. He left the building in a helicopter ten minutes ago."

"I understand," he said. He could pull the old switcheroo too. "And you've certainly been most generous with your own time. Shall we continue through the facilities now?"

Emma smiled. She pivoted neatly on her heels and led him out the door.

"We certainly appreciate your understanding." She seemed enormously relieved to be out of the room and out of the discussion. Now he was behaving in a way she could recognize. "Over here is the animal room," she said. "Right now, we're testing a synthetic version of chemicals found in the bark of the Pacific yew."

When Emma walked Sam out of the building forty minutes later, Max was sitting on the hood of his car looking at the madrones. The day had warmed up enough, especially in the sun where he was sitting, to permit him to remove his jacket.

"Gary Maxwell," Sam said, "this is Emma Cameron, head of Public Reactions here at Physics for Ethical Reference."

"Ah," Max said. "That would explain it."

"Mr. Maxwell." She came over to the car and shook his hand. "I'm afraid we've tired our friend here out. Maybe he can sleep in the car."

"As you no doubt can imagine now, having spent the last two hours with him, I'd much prefer that to listening to him talk."

Emma laughed her little girl's giggle again. She shook hands again, wished them well and walked back into the building. They watched her disappear.

Max and Sam got into the car. Before starting it, Max looked over at him with a look of mock concern on his face.

"I have to tell you I'm relieved," he said.

"What do you mean?"

Max started the car. "For a minute there, I thought they'd compressed you. Which is not exactly what you needed."

"Very funny." Sam reached into his pocket for a pen and notebook. "Now don't talk to me for a while. I have to write some things down or I'll forget more than I already have."

They rode in silence until I-5, until Sam put away his notebook and sighed. Max was accelerating sharply along the on-ramp, then switching two lanes to his left as soon as he reached its end. "So," he said, unable to wait any longer. "Tell me how it went already."

"Let's say we have the classic Good News/Bad News situation."

Max nodded. "Why don't you give me the bad news first. That way we'll end on an up-note. Goddamn this traffic. Why would anyone want to live in Seattle?"

"The bad news is that I never got to see The Wiz, and Emma Cameron said flat-out No to our proposal about Tracy."

"I see." Changing lanes, zipping past a tractor pulling three long trailers, Max waited till things settled down a bit before responding further. "Yet there is good news."

"There is, yes. Tracy is going to get the drug. I'm not sure how much yet, or when, but she's going to get the drug."

"How?"

"We're going to go in and get it for her ourselves."

Nine

1.

Sam spent the next three days in bed. He slept for five or six hours at a time, got up to snack or go to the bathroom, read a page of the newspaper and fall asleep again with the paper across his chest like an extra comforter.

The few dreams he had were cinematic. In one, he was dressed in a stylish silk suit, dark blue and baggy, with a hint of thin gray pinstripe. It was roomy enough to hold the small, rectangular gun he had strapped to his hip precisely where Emma Cameron held her beeper. Special Agent 002. Sam was leaning against a curved mahogany bar located in the far reaches of PER's headquarters. His legs were crossed at the ankles and he had an all-knowing, crooked smile on his face, the very picture of suave continental elegance. *Kiehl. Sam Kiehl.* He ordered a drink from the scantily clad female bartender, who elongated to reveal herself as Emma Cameron.

"What was that?" she asked.

"Carrot juice," he said. "Stirred, not shaken."

In another dream, he was flying. Not in an aircraft, not behind the sticks of a helicopter again, but on his own, although he didn't exactly have wings. Instead, with his arms held tightly to his sides, he was using his hands as flippers to generate speed and to steer himself upside-down above the earth. Farmland, everything in neat grids of green and brown, with here and there a stand of trees to indicate water. Soon, he knew, he would be able to turn himself over and fly face-down, which would be more comfortable, more natural. However, for now he had to stretch his neck backwards and down in order to see below; he resembled a figure in a Marc Chagall painting as he soared over vaguely familiar houses, barns, and silos.

The dreams didn't disturb him at all. They were at least as good as the movies he'd been watching lately on HBO and Showtime, and he awoke with mixed feelings about having failed to see how they ended. In fact, dreaming at all marked a definite change in his sleep pattern. It might even be a good sign. Since first getting sick, he had only rarely achieved dream-level sleep. This was such a common symptom of his illness that doctors were beginning to use it as a criterion for diagnosis. Sam was not sure why he'd had such good sleep since his trip to PER's headquarters, but he hoped it would continue. On the other hand, he hoped the muscle twitches flashing across his back like Christmas tree lights would not continue. Though they didn't hurt, some were powerful enough to make his entire upper body shudder and jerk.

Late in the afternoon of the third day, he showered and ate a full breakfast before listening to the accumulated messages on his answering machine. Nothing earth-shattering. P. J. Cooper, the attorney representing those patients who were suing PER, wanted Sam to call back collect at his earliest convenience. A hearing was scheduled and Cooper had a few questions to run by Sam. Tracy had called three times wanting to know how things had gone with PER. Sam didn't want to speak with her until he'd had a chance to think his plans through a little further, though he felt he couldn't hold her off much longer. Kate had called to see how he was doing. Andy had called to wish him a Happy New Year, as had Jessica. Good Lord, he had slept right through the holiday. Knowing Sam must be exhausted, Hannah, Alice, Laurel, and Daphne had gotten together at Hannah's house to call on a speakerphone so they could all talk to him without making his phone ring four different times. They would appreciate it if he called as soon as he felt well enough.

Returning calls could all wait another twelve hours or so. There was something he wanted to do first. He dressed warmly, throwing on a pair of old red sweatpants from his running days, a hooded gray sweatshirt and his navy-blue down jacket, then set out for the bus stop with a beat-up paperback copy of Oliver Sacks's *The Man Who Mistook His Wife for a Hat* stuffed in its inside pocket. Though the bus trip would take a full hour and he would have to change at the southwest Transit Center, Sam really wanted to see Jessica again before doing anything else. And he wanted to see her in a place that had nothing to do with massage. Talk to her face-to-face, tell her that he was beginning to understand what she had meant when she said he seemed to be changing. Looser, she had said, softer. Transparent. Actually, clearer was the word he was thinking about. Flying on his own and ready to turn over for the clearer view. And what he wanted to see from that perspective was Jessica looking back at him.

Sam arrived at *Foster's Plants* at about 4:45. The side and back yards sprawled for a half-acre with rows of small trees and shrubs. There was a miniature parking lot for red wagons that customers would pull through the yards to load with their selections. He saw a woman walking among the rows of flowering fruit trees and heard the squeaking wheel of her wagon. Near the main door, black plastic pond forms were stacked beside a haphazard arrangement of fountains and waterwheels, all dry and quiet now since it was so near closing time.

He walked inside. Jessica was off in a rear room somewhere, but she heard the bells on the door as he opened it. "Be right there," she called.

He moved into a room in the opposite direction, wanting to be sure she was alone before greeting her. The space was bright and warm, humid as a midwest summer noon. A blue and yellow parrot with long green tailfeathers welcomed him by shrieking *Fuck you, lady!* Its short legs reminded Sam of his own. The other parrot, smaller and gray with a small red tail, ignored Sam and continued to nip at its wing, making odd clicking sounds. When Sam turned away, however, it said as though under its breath "Happy New Year," to which the first parrot responded "Buy lobelias."

The room was like an herbal zoo. Its far wall was lined with shelves containing row after row of herbs in small boxes. As Sam approached, the rich scents reached out for him and he inhaled dizzily. At the east end of the wall, he recognized the cooking herbs, little sprigs of parsley, basil, oregano, savory, mint. There was feathery dill, thick spikes of rosemary, slender stalks of chives. He saw lemon, silver, caraway, and nutmeg thyme, as well as something labeled mother-of-thyme, which Sam thought no home should be without. A whole shelf was devoted to varieties of sage: blue, pineapple, golden, purple. He could not resist rubbing a few leaves between his thumb and forefinger, then sniffing at his fingertips. Jessica had hung a sign above them, printed in careful calligraphy, quoting a tenth century Italian aphorism: "Why should a man die who has sage in his garden?"

The cooking herbs modulated into the medicinal herbs at the other end of the wall, with overlaps in the middle. Sam was particularly interested in seeing and smelling these medicinal herbs. For the last few weeks, he had been taking capsules crammed with a rich assortment of them, brewing strange teas from them, and reading about them in a book he'd bought from Eli. It was good finally to find some in their natural state. He recognized a few names. Ginger root. For nausea, he remembered. Chamomile to help with sleep, echinacea for stimulating the immune system, feverfew for headaches, hyssop as a purgative. There were more hand-lettered signs. She wrote that rue was the herb of grace, lavender the herb of love. St.-John's-wort clears the air of evil spirits and horehound breaks magic spells.

"Pretty, pretty," the larger parrot said. He had a sign on top of his cage identifying him as a military macaw and urging customers not to stick their fingers in his cage.

Returning to the main room, Sam looked around for Jessica but still couldn't locate her. Along the rear wall, near where Sam thought he'd first heard Jessica call, there were a dozen burbling aquariums with their strange lights and brilliantly colored fish. He walked into a rack of books on fish and caught them before they fell into a stack of empty aquariums. Nearby, he saw displays of materials to put inside the aquariums, a pyramid of exotic fish foods and a group of lizard and turtle tanks. The rest of the room was given over to a collection of smaller trees and houseplants. They stood in pots, hung from the ceiling, reached out from shelves. All sizes and shapes, an astonishing assortment of textures and shades of green. Looking around, Sam felt two conflicting urges. He wanted to straighten things into neat rows, and he wanted to wait outside until Jessica closed up the nursery.

"Hello?" Jessica called. She still hadn't spotted him. "Can I help you?"

Sam parted the leaves of a small king palm and said, "Someone had better. I'm going out of my tree."

"Sam!" Her obvious pleasure at seeing him made Sam's heart lurch. He was fairly sure that wasn't a symptom of his illness. "What a sweet surprise. I've been thinking about you." She took two steps toward him, then stopped. Her brows narrowed and she said, "Wait, is everything all right? How did you get here?"

"Yes. Bus."

She looked at him closely, then broke into a wide smile. "Sure," she said, "I'd be glad to."

Sam shook his head. "Ordinarily, I'd probably start finding this mindreading business a little creepy. But I suppose there's another way to look at it. I mean, it saves me from actually having to ask you anything."

"I think it's fun. And no, I don't care where we eat, just as long as we stop by my house for a half-hour or so first. I absolutely must shower and change out of these clothes." She wiped her hands on a towel strung through her belt and walked to the main door. "There's still a customer or two out there. Let me close up, clean the place a bit, do a few things with the computer. It won't take long."

"Anything I can do to help?"

"Would you mind talking to Zorro?"

"Who's he?"

"The quiet one."

"As far as I can tell, they're all quiet. Even the ficus."

"The parrot, Sam. Actually, the mature African gray parrot. They're supposed to be the best imitators of human speech, by the way. But he's in a funk. I think it may be weather, because he's pretty healthy. I can't see anything wrong with his feathers or his eyes, he isn't quivering, he doesn't shift back and forth on his perch like his legs hurt. It's probably just a mood." She pulled open the door and, as the bell rang, said, "See what you can do with him."

Sam went back into the muggy room. The talkative parrot, who must be Zeppo, advised Sam again to buy lobelias, then put a fat Brazil nut in its hooked beak and cracked the shell. Scattered on the floor of its cage was a medley of hard-shelled nuts. He seemed to be saving walnuts for later. Sam approached the quieter, smaller bird. Zorro had the husk of a sunflower seed in one claw, raised it to his mouth, then dropped it as though unwilling to dine in front of Sam.

"Hello," Sam said, bending down to meet Zorro's eyes. "Hello there, handsome."

"Hello," Zorro said. "Goodbye."

Sam didn't think Zorro looked sick either. Those were amazing claws. Feet, whatever. The first and fourth toes were turned backwards, which is how Sam sometimes felt when he tried to walk. Zorro seemed very deft with them. From behind him, Sam heard Zeppo crack another hard shell and looked over to see the bird with half a walnut in his beak, working his thick, muscular tongue carefully, eyeing him. Maybe Zorro just wants some privacy. The big guy can be a bit spooky.

"How's it going?" For a moment, Sam thought it had been Zorro who spoke and he was amazed at the bird's diction. Then Jessica stepped into the room. "Making any progress?"

"I think he just wants to be alone. This one's driving him crazy with bad manners and sarcasm. I say move Zorro in by the fish."

"Oh, they're pals. I couldn't do that." She reached in and rubbed the back of Zorro's head a few times. "Isn't that right, Zorie? By the way,

Sam, don't try that yourself," she said, starting back out of the room. "I just have some things to do on the computer, then we can go."

After a few more minutes of trying to get Zorro to say *Honey, I'm home,* Sam walked out to find Jessica in a small office behind the aquariums. She sat in a high-backed desk chair with her feet drawn up onto the seat and folded lotus-style. She rocked back, studying the screen, and didn't seem to notice his presence. He watched her concentrate on the screen.

"About ten more minutes," she said without moving.

"Now how did you know I was here? I wasn't even breathing."

"Saw your face reflected in the screen."

At least it wasn't all done with divination and ESP. He came up behind her. "What are you working on?"

"Writing a program to track how certain plants do under special conditions. Drought, prolonged sun, artificial light. Right now I'm working on deer. Most of the literature about which plants they won't eat is worthless. My customers are always coming in asking for deer-proof stuff."

"You're writing a program for that? I didn't know you knew so much about Cuisinarts."

She swivelled her chair around in order to study his face. Then she smiled.

"Programming's how I put myself through school."

"I'm impressed."

"I know computers better than I know human bodies."

"Sorry. I don't believe that for a minute."

Still seated, she reached out and grabbed his arms, pulling him closer. Then she wrapped her arms around his waist and, turning her head sideways, rested her cheek against him.

"I liked that," she said.

"What? That I'm impressed with your programming skills?"

"The way your mind works now. It's so different from when I first knew you in your sleek business suits and with your hard little attache case and your hard little body. Computers/Cuisinarts; word processors/food processors. It's very intuitive, I think."

"I said Cuisinarts?"

She nodded against his chest, then leaned back again and looked up at him. "And you probably taught Zorro to say *Polly want a corker*, but I want you to know I don't mind."

2.

Jessica lived in an old farmhouse on three acres at the west edge of the county. It was about a twenty minute drive from the nursery. She spent most of the drive talking about her house, getting Sam ready for it.

"It's not Brooklyn," she said. "And it's not Portland. It's not even Tigard, for that matter, Sam. We're talking seriously rural."

Sam decided not to tell her about the year he had lived in a Missouri farmhouse. This was while he was going to graduate school and living with a young widow named Sylvia Harmon. Sam hated it. All winter, on a chalkboard hanging above their kitchen sink, he kept a running tally of the mice he'd caught in traps overnight. Five times every night, he would wake up when each of the strategically placed traps was sprung. Each morning, he would use a pair of extra-long barbecuing tongs to carry the traps outside and into the neighboring soybean field in order to dispose of the night's gleanings. After that, it had taken him years to be able to look at an Andrew Wyeth painting again.

"The place needs a lot of work," she said. "Of course, I've done a lot of work already and it feels like I've barely begun. It's cozy and comfortable now, but I won't see charming or elegant for another five years at the rate I'm going."

Sounded to Sam like a perfect time for her to sell it. Where he'd grown up, if your place needed repairs you called the building Superintendent. He thought he'd been living on the edge by owning one unit of a new four-unit row house in which nearly everything that could go wrong was still covered under warranty.

Sam learned that except for the two cats Jessica kept for mousing, the koi in a pond near the storage shed, and the occasional snake, skunk, raccoon, or porcupine that wandered through the front yard, she had no animals sharing her life. No parrots, no dogs, and the cats mostly stayed outdoors. She had been alone by choice for years. It gave her deep pleasure to come home to lasting silence.

The final quarter mile of the drive was along gravel that led to the house from a rutted, pot-holed county road. Jessica stopped before turning in, got her mail, threw it onto Sam's lap, and drove on. The house was painted a light gray color she called pussywillow, with lavender accents around the windows and doors, and a lavender swing dangling on the porch. It was set among maple, oak, and Douglas fir at the edge of what must have been the property's original farmland. The house itself was larger than Sam had imagined, rambling casually toward a creek he hadn't noticed from the road, and he could see where a previous owner had added on a few back rooms.

Before going indoors, Jessica walked around the far side of the house to the pond. It was a small, irregular oval that she'd dug and lined herself and surrounded with a rim of flat, stacked stones. She squatted down and the koi swam to greet her and be fed. Sam could see the relaxation sweep over her. Jessica dawdled with the koi, scooped some mossy stuff off the water's edges, then moved languidly across the grass. Throughout, she wore a constant small smile. On the little front porch, she kicked off her shoes before going inside. She didn't even look at her answering machine, which was blinking with messages. Two, Sam counted, even before realizing he was paying attention.

They went directly into the kitchen, stopping only long enough for Jessica to turn on the baseboard heat. He put her mail on the table, where she continued to ignore it. She threw her coat over the back of a chair and poured him a glass of sparkling water.

"There's a very cushy sofa in the living room. Why don't you put on some music and rest while I take a shower and get ready."

The living room, cozy and comfortable as promised, was full of odd objects placed, it seemed to Sam, randomly on whatever surfaces were available. There were feathers, woven baskets filled with weeds of some kind, a stained glass tulip, a Native American drum, enamel boxes and wooden boxes, a cube with photographs, three decks of well-thumbed playing cards. He picked up a long tube which made a sound like rain in the woods when he turned it over. A table was set up for her laptop computer. There were vases of dried flowers, vases of fresh flowers, a bowl with one flower floating in it.

Sam suddenly realized he could hear the shower running. Glad he hadn't put on any music, he sat down on the sofa, resting his head against its back. It was entirely too easy for him to imagine Jessica now, her dark blonde hair plastered to her head, soapy water cascading off her shoulders and breasts. Then, loud and clear, shocking in its joyous power, he heard her begin to sing.

"Chain chain chain! Chain of fools." He heard a clatter, which was probably the sound of her dancing and banging into the shower door. "But I found out, I'm just a link in your chain."

When the singing and then the shower stopped, Sam thought about getting up to look through her bookcase but decided it felt perfect for him to just stay put. He felt mesmerized by the vines and leaves he noticed that she had painted onto the lintel and frame of the vanished living room door. The level of detail in it, the patience, the passion for plant life were almost overwhelming. There was so much about her that Sam didn't know. Finland, for God's sake? Why not Greenland, or the Antarctic, if she wanted a little contrast in her life?

In a few minutes, Jessica walked right into the space where he was gazing. She was wrapped in a thick, white terrycloth robe and carried a hand towel to continue working on her hair, which stuck out wildly. She stopped, leaning against the door frame, watching him as Sam's eyes found hers and stayed there.

After a moment, she raised the towel to her head again and rubbed briskly. Sam came over to her, took the towel, turned Jessica around gently and began drying her hair for her. She leaned back against him. Just as he was wishing he had put music on after all, she began to hum "Chain of Fools." He could feel the sound through her back and his chest wall.

He draped the towel around his neck and, gripping her shoulders, turned Jessica back toward him. She spread her legs slightly as she rested against the wall, which brought her closer to his height, and their lips casually brushed across each other's a few times before they actually kissed. Jessica smelled of Dove soap and coconut shampoo, a wholly different smell from the one he was used to from her.

"Obviously," she said, and at the same moment they nudged one another in opposite directions, Sam angling for the bedroom, Jessica for the sofa. She took his hand and led him back into the living room. She stopped beside the sofa, turned and untied the sash of her robe. Sam slid his hands inside at her waist. They moved along the line of her hips until coming together over her tailbone. He liked the feel of her skin, which was not quite dry yet, and the insistent form of her bones beneath his hands. Maybe this was part of her pleasure as a massage therapist, the very thereness of a body giving itself over to her hands. He pulled her toward him. She emanated heat, whether from the shower, the warmth of the room, or their contact he couldn't tell. As they kissed, he ran his hands up her long, muscular back, then slowly spread them to shift the robe off her shoulders.

Jessica sat on the couch, her neck supported by its back, and Sam knelt in front of her. She closed her eyes as his hands stroked up from her calves to her thighs and lifted her legs until the heels rested on the cushions. He bent to her. After a while, she reached down to touch his hair, then his neck, signaling her urgency. Sam leaned back on his haunches, kissing her thighs and knees before rising to join her on the sofa.

3.

"You're sure this is OK?" Jessica asked.

"Perfect. I'd been hoping all day that I could eat a mushroom and pepper omelette for dinner."

She was wearing the same white robe. Sam had on a pair of

Jessica's baggy Bermuda shorts and a *Foster's Plants* tee-shirt, and he was still too hot. But he was also too hungry and too content to care. It was 10:30. About a half-hour ago, they'd realized how hungry they were and got up to begin scrounging for dinner.

Jessica brought the plates over to the round oak table where Sam sat, and joined him. There were sprigs of fresh thyme across the omelette, and the plate was decorated with a scattering of chanterelles and thick slices of whole wheat toast. She leaned over to kiss him, bent low over her plate to breathe in its smells, folded her legs lotus-style and dug in. Though he was far from symptom-free, Sam thought he hadn't felt this good in nearly three years.

"Dig in," she said. When he did, she added, "I really like to watch you eat."

He took a bite of toast, then leaned back. "And all I want to do is fast."

"Now you tell me." As she raised a forkful of omelette to her mouth, some filling began to ooze out. She sensed it and jerked herself forward so fast the food landed on her plate. Sam admired her reflexes, knowing he'd be wearing that foodslide on his chest and lap. "You need your energy," Jessica continued. "Not that I noticed anything at all wrong with your stamina, but you need to eat, and eat right, to heal."

"You know what I regret? I regret that I couldn't bring the body I had three years ago to bed with you tonight."

"What nonsense. I didn't want the body you had three years ago to be in my bed."

"I just feel so soft."

"Sam, how can I explain this so you'll understand?" she said. "You're not soft in a way that's unpleasant or unmanly or whatever it is you think." She reached her fork over to his plate, picked up a chanterelle and put it in his mouth. "Men can be so muddled about this stuff. A certain kind of strength is good, but a coat of mail is not so good."

"I'm going to need my strength." He tucked a napkin into the neck of the tee-shirt and started eating again. The omelette was delicious.

"Good." She twitched her head back, shaking phantom hair from her eyes. "I was thinking the same thing."

Sam smiled at her. "I was referring to something else altogether."

As they finished their meal, Sam brought Jessica up to date on the drug study and his trip to PER's headquarters. She ate less heartily, the details seeming to weaken her appetite.

"So they're not going to give that woman the drug?" Jessica asked when he had finished the story.

"I'd say not in a million years."

"And she's convinced it was helping her?"

"She is, and I saw it working with my own eyes."

"Are you sure it was the drug that was helping her?"

"Well, PER seemed to be. So did Fong. As far as anyone can be sure about these things, it certainly seemed to be effective in Tracy's case." Jessica nodded. She got up to clear and wash the dishes, but Sam stopped her and began to do it himself, continuing to talk as he worked. "When they stopped it the first time, she relapsed. When they started it again, she improved. I think she's terrified of what happens now."

"What did she say when you told her about your trip?"

"I haven't told her. In fact, I haven't spoken to anybody yet. I wanted to get clear in my head what I intend to do." Sam turned to look into Jessica's eyes, so deeply and nakedly that she could feel herself even more connected to him than when they had been making love. He whispered, "And I needed to see you."

Jessica walked over and put her arms around Sam. "I don't understand. What's there for you to do?"

"I want to go get her a two month's supply of the drug."

"Get it how?"

"Steal it. They practically showed me how to do it while I was at their headquarters. I just have a few details to think through, but I think it's something I can do. Have to do."

"Steal it?"

"Maybe a better phrase would be 'liberate it.'"

Jessica nodded, then shook her head. "Why a two month's supply?"

"If she's relapsing more slowly this time, it must mean that the drug's immune boosting properties are working for her. So if she can have another substantial jolt, it might get her over the top. Two months ought to be more than enough. In theory, and if anything we've been told about Zomalovir is actually true, she should be able to maintain her health without the drug after that."

Jessica was silent for a few moments, concentrating on something just to the left of Sam's head. "Three thoughts come to mind," she said. "One is that I just hope you know that what you're planning to do isn't about your friend Tracy. At least not most of it. Because as long as you know that, you'll be open to the real risks and you might actually get what you're after. Two is that you know stealing this drug would be a felony, not some game of capture-the-flag and not some wartime flashback. Three is how can I help?"

Sam blinked. This woman was full of surprises, all right. He stroked the side of her face. "I don't know yet," he whispered.

"When you do, then." She kissed him. It looked like this time they would actually get to her bedroom. "Just remember this, though, while you work out your plan. Computers rule. For getting information, for thwarting security systems, for all sorts of lovely nastiness. And I may be a lot more dangerous with a computer than you could ever imagine, which is the real reason I'm running a nursery these days."

"You lost me."

"Let's just say I once did some things with a computer that got me in a great deal of trouble."

He leaned back to look at her eyes, which were definitely in a green phase now. "This was before Finland or after?"

"This was before Finland. Immediately before."

4.

Jessica's alarm was set for 5:30. When it went off, she whacked the snooze button and turned back to Sam's arms. He hadn't budged. They'd had about four hours sleep.

It took three rounds of the snooze alarm before she finally

risked shutting the thing off outright. They lay in bed for a few more minutes, Sam's toes reaching no further than Jessica's shins as they cuddled and whispered. Her hair miraculously retained its shape while she slept; Sam's resembled a fright wig. He offered to fix oatmeal for her breakfast while she showered.

"That would be lovely, Sam."

"How do you like it?"

"Cook the raisins in it," she said, throwing off the covers and heading for the bathroom. "Don't just add them at the end. And salt. I don't like oatmeal without salt. Also some cinnamon and a little nutmeg. I prefer it soft, not grainy, so ignore the instructions on the box and put the oatmeal in at the start, not after it boils."

"I wish you'd be more specific." Sam thought he should write this down rather than trust his faulty memory. But he didn't see a pencil nearby. He also thought it was wonderful that she didn't just say *oh, any old way is fine.* "Anything else?" he asked.

"Well, a slice of toast."

"Ok."

"With butter and orange marmalade."

It took Sam a few minutes to locate everything and a few more minutes to figure out how to operate her gas stove. By the time he had everything organized, he could hear that she was finished showering and was blow-drying her hair. This rattled him, but he managed to get the food ready just as Jessica came into the kitchen. When she sat down for breakfast, Sam felt ready for a nap. She kissed him, thanking him for breakfast, and ate every morsel of the food.

She dropped him off at the bus stop near her nursery and promised to come see him later in the week. She knew he had work to do and rest to catch up on. During the bus ride home, Sam never opened his book. Yawning, smiling to himself, he watched the dull urban drive through Tigard and southwest Portland without noticing much detail, focused instead on his time with Jessica.

Though they had known each other a long time, and he'd regularly turned his body over to her care, Sam was amazed by the nature of Jessica's touch on his flesh. Her hands, so familiar to him as a therapist, were vastly different as a lover, elegant and light, but intensely charged. This was a woman who knew how bodies worked. He was also amazed by her joyful openness, her receptivity. He hadn't imagined she'd be so ardent. Or so much like himself in the way she yielded to her passions. It was as though he'd found a deeply kindred spirit, and found her in the most overlooked of places, right within the circle of his closest friends. They had an ease together already, and it was as sweet as it was unexpected.

When the bus stopped at the Transit Center, it filled with commuters heading for downtown Portland. Standing room only. Sam found his thoughts shifting toward PER and the drug study. So far he'd told only two people, Max and Jessica, about what happened in Seattle and about his idea of going to get the drug for Tracy. All right, stealing it, might as well say the word. Liberating it, retrieving it for its rightful use. He'd told them both and they'd neither laughed at him nor tried too hard to dissuade him. Jessica had only reminded him to be clear on what his plan was really about. Helping Tracy, yes, but also, he knew, doing something vital for himself, sick as he was, in responding actively to his disease.

He understood that a raid on PER's headquarters to liberate a two months supply of Zomalovir was actually part of a larger healing plan he was developing. His work with Eli was part of it. His changing relationship with Jessica was part of it. Perhaps the biggest part was the change going on inside, his increasing sense of balance and purpose, his respect for what illness had brought into his life. Oh, and one more thing he was doing it for. Revenge. For himself, but truly for them all.

The bus left him off a short walk from home. As Sam climbed the stairs to the front door, he could hear his telephone ringing. He fought down the urge to race inside and answer it. Letting himself in, he listened as the machine recorded the message.

"Sam?" Tracy said. "Sam, are you all right? I've been calling for days and I'm so worried." He was tempted to pick up the phone but couldn't remember how to override the answering machine. Last time he tried, it had squawked at him so loudly that he couldn't hear for hours. He let Tracy go on. That way, when he called her back she might be a bit less frantic. "Did they kill you? No, of course they didn't. Probably what happened is they told you something so awful you can't face telling me about it. Right? Am I right? Sam, are you there? You can tell me. Whatever it is, it can't be any worse than not knowing what's happening. I hope going up there didn't make you so sick you can't move. That would be another thing on my conscience. Like I haven't already taken enough from you by being the one who got the drug while you . . . Look, here's what I'll do. If I haven't heard from you by noon today I'm going to come over to your place and see what's happening. Sam? Sam? OK, I'll see you soon, one way or the other."

Sam went upstairs to get out of his clothes, then came back down and collapsed in a kitchen chair. There were seven messages, for God's sake, as many as when he used to miss a half-day at work because of meetings. He put a kettle of water on to boil and played them back.

Same basic list. Cooper, Kate, Tracy, Doctor Fong's office asking him to call for an appointment, the Zomalovir group this time with Alice Hardy as the designated caller, then Tracy twice again. Sam poured water into his cup and sat back down at the kitchen table with a pen and several sheets of graph paper. It was time to make some notes, just a little chart of possibilities, a rough draft. Down the left side: what, when, who, how. Then over on the right side: how much.

About a half-hour later, he called Tracy back. Before she could get started, he asked her to come over for lunch. She was so startled that she agreed and hung up without saying anything more.

Sam napped in the recliner until the sound of Tracy's car pulling into his driveway woke him. For an instant, he thought it was time to rush up to the medical school for an infusion. He got up and heard the doorbell at virtually the same time he heard her car door slam. He could just imagine what she looked like, with her eyes wide open and jaws clenched, her arms tensed, her legs slightly crouched. He would bet she was terrifying to behold on the racquetball court in her heyday.

"I'm not even hungry," she said as soon as she was inside.

"That's good, because I didn't fix anything for us to eat. I slept instead."

Tracy walked to the couch, plopped down, opened her purse, took out a wad of tissues, looked up at Sam and began to cry. She lay down on her side, curled up, and really let go.

Sam sat by her, lifting her head onto his lap. He took the tissues from her hand, sorted through them for a clean one, and dabbed at her eyes. There was nothing to say, so he stroked her head, brushing the hair back behind her ear, and told her it was all right.

When she had calmed down a little, he began to talk. She kept her head in his lap, looking toward the big landscape on his wall, and Sam could tell she was listening intently.

"So here's what I want you to do," he said at the end. "I want you to focus on staying as strong as you can over the next few weeks. I want you to come see this alternative doctor I've been seeing, Eli Moskowitz, and do whatever he tells you to do. It'll help keep you from losing ground for a while, I know it will. I want you to keep as fit as you can, too, because when we get inside PER's headquarters I'm going to need you and Max to do all the work. And I want you to study every day."

There was a long silence while she absorbed all that and waited to see if he was finished. Sam watched her staring at the painting, blinking slowly, almost hypnotized.

"Study?" she mumbled.

"That's right. Every day."

She sat up slowly and turned to look at him. She seemed utterly exhausted. "Sam, I think I missed something in there. What am I supposed to be studying?"

"I'll show you in about an hour, after you take me to the bookstore."

Tracy nodded as though now she fully understood. "The bookstore. But what about lunch? I kept you from eating."

"This is a great bookstore. We can buy a sandwich in the back, and eat it while we get what we're after."

She started to smile. For the first time since arriving, she looked into Sam's eyes. "Which is what?"

"Your guide to preparing for the postal carrier examination," he said, standing. "The time has come."

Ten

1.

Sam settled on the couch with the phone nestled in his lap. He had a pot of tea and some Lorna Doones on the coffee table, the blinds open to allow sunlight in, Brahms violin sonatas playing softly, and he was ready to talk.

"Cooper here. And may I say thank you for calling back, Mr. Kiehl."

"Sorry it took so long. I've been out of touch for a few days."

"Well, forgive me for saying so, but I've been dealing with you Zomalovir people for almost two months now and I'm used to you being, shall we say, out of touch."

"Nothing to forgive. We drive me crazy too."

"I'll cut right to the chase, Mr. Kiehl. Are you in or not? Is anyone from Portland in or not? You see, I have a critical hearing coming up and it would be useful for me to know exactly what I'm dealing with. What do I have there in the Rose City?"

"There's been no change. That's why I haven't called you. The group here feels that litigation is not our best route for now."

"You got the documents I sent? The affidavits and briefs?"

"Got them and read them. But our position hasn't changed. In fact, I sense a growing disinclination to talk about PER or the drug."

"Not to put too fine an edge on it, sir: the others need you. Need you badly. Sick people all around the country are looking in your direction for help." Cooper rattled some papers and added, "Plus it's now or never, if you get my drift. The hour is at hand."

"That's what we thought. Which explains why you didn't hear from us again."

"Mr. Kiehl, let me call a spade a spade here. The defendants have thrown up so many roadblocks that they've got the traffic completely stalled. Gridlock, pure and simple. Do you prefer plain English? We're going nowhere. Motions and petitions, depositions. I won't bore you with details. Quite simply, no one is likely to receive this vital medicine for many years to come unless together, we as a team, can force the defendant to provide it as originally promised. What I need, what your fellow subjects in this unfortunate experiment all need, is a bombshell to drop upon the defendant's collective lap."

There it is again, the Bombshell Strategy. Sam knew that the joining of the litigation by the Portland group or the sudden appearance of his tape in evidence had the potential for being such a bombshell. But he didn't want to talk about the tape, didn't want Cooper to think it had enough value to be worth a subpoena. Nor did he want Cooper to know it might actually benefit the defendants, since the tape showed that Fong hadn't promised them the drug. It made PER look like unethical predators, but not like liars. No one else needed to know that.

"There's nothing we can do for you. I'm sorry."

"Ah, that's most unfortunate, sir. There is a certain amount of, shall we say, panic among your compatriots around the country. However, I have gone so far as to speak with a few of the subjects in your area and I find they are all united behind your position. So do me one favor, if you will. In the same spirit with which you all joined the study in the first place, consider joining the litigation now. For the common good of all victims of this dread disease. For the sake of striking back at it and at those who take advantage of its victims. For the sake of the Great American Civil Rights Movement of which this is but a continuation. For the sake of future subjects in any similar drug trial. Yes?"

Sam paused, nearly breathless at the man's audacity. Pretty soon, Cooper would be telling him how therapeutic it would be for them all to join the suit. It can save your life, my good man, so sign on.

In the space created by Sam's silence, Cooper had something to add. He lowered his voice nearly a full octave, toned down its dynamics and confided, "You know, I was reading the beloved American poet James Russell Lowell the other day. What he said is not only deeply provocative, it delivers its message replete with a pun on your very own name, Mr. Kiehl. I believe this is something you were meant to consider, something fate has thrown in your path. Lowell says, and I quote, *There is no better ballast for keeping the mind steady on its keel, and saving it from all risk of crankiness, than business.* Isn't that wonderful, Mr. Kiehl? You see, getting yourself involved in a business such as the one I am pursuing on your behalf does more than just afford the possibility of gaining access to the drug, or appropriate compensation for your injuries, or correcting the imbalance in private-sector economics that provides incentives for companies like PER to behave as they do. Getting involved in something like this steadies the troubled mind. It provides balance in an unsteady time."

Sam leaned forward to reach a Lorna Doone. He could think of no circumstance in which he'd want P. J. Cooper acting as his attorney. "I understand what you're saying. But we have no plans to meet as a group again and I'm not sure there's anything else I can do for you."

"We need you, Mr. Kiehl."

"Just tell me one more thing, and then I have to go. How much would it cost each one of us to join the plaintiffs at this stage?"

"Well, now that's difficult to say, my good man. Difficult indeed. You see, it all depends on how long the matter takes to resolve, what sorts of actions we are required to take, how much assistance I might need and so forth. For now, all I am asking is for a small retainer."

"And that's the $7,500 per person?"

"Correct."

"How high could that amount eventually go?"

"I couldn't say, sir. But of course my fees would be part of any settlement we achieve."

"All right. If there's anything further to tell you from Portland, I'll call."

2.

Three nights later, Sam's team sat around the table in his dining room. It was just past 8:00. They'd pushed empty mugs and a bowl of potato chips off to the side, and were concentrating on a large piece of flip-chart paper spread across the middle of the table. Tracy knelt on a chair and Max sat leaning forward in another chair like a gambler poised to show his hand. Hannah sat on a pillow on the floor, with her back against the refrigerator door. Sam stood with his hip against the rim of the table. Jessica sat back with the fingers of one hand gently stroking Sam's forearm.

Across town, Kate had agreed to make herself available to the group by speaker-phone. She'd also agreed that she didn't want to know what Sam's meeting was about but would be glad to answer any questions he might have. Say at about 8:45.

"That's it?" Max said, looking up from the chart. "That's your whole plan?"

"All right, *plan* may have been a little too strong," Sam said. "All I meant was that I had an idea of what I wanted to accomplish."

"Yeah," Max nodded. "Go to Seattle, get into office, steal drug, come home. This is quite a plan."

"Come on, it's not that bad. You drive me and Tracy up there and back, so that takes care of parts A and D." He pointed to them on the paper, where he'd written the letters in large black blocks. "It's B and C that need a little work."

Max leaned back. "I remember that one article you showed me, where it said people with your illness lost their abstract reasoning powers. They weren't kidding, were they?"

"Look, that's where you and Jessica come in. Vision, concept. Then we all sharpen the details."

"And what's this?" Max asked, pointing to a second flip-chart sheet lying on the floor. "A sketch of your DNA?"

"It's a rough floor plan of the inside of PER's offices."

"Ahh, a floor plan. How could I have been so stupid?"

"I said it was rough. This part here contains the deep freeze where they store their products. Emma Cameron even told me it was where our *agent* is kept." Sam picked up a marker pen and drew a series of circles around the storage room.

"It's almost exactly in the middle of the building," Max said. "Could there be a more difficult location?"

"All we have to do is get past the guard at the gate," Sam said. "Or get over the gate without him knowing about it."

"And get inside," Max said.

"My memory's come back," Tracy said. They all looked at her, unsure what to say. Memory? Was someone talking about memory? Tracy took their silence to mean she should continue. "I can tell when I try the exercises in that postal carrier book we bought, Sam. They give me a bunch of boxes filled with street addresses I'm supposed to memorize, like 4300-4799 Foster and 7200-8199 Riverside? And then all these individual addresses and I have to figure out which box the letter goes in. I get five minutes to sort through eighty-eight addresses, so I have to do seventeen or eighteen a minute." She looked around the table, then said, "I've only tried to memorize three boxes at a time so far. Pretty soon I'll do all five."

"That's great," Sam said.

"Unless I start to relapse again. I can still run a mile. I did one this afternoon over at the high school track, just to be sure. I finished it without having to stop, but I'm quickly getting slower. You know what I mean?"

"Don't worry, Trace, we're going to do this very soon. And you're definitely part of the occupation."

"I am?"

"We're counting on you." Sam reached over to touch Tracy's arm. "A key part of the operation."

"Jessica," Max said, "doesn't listening to them do wonders for your confidence?"

"Extrumatively," Jessica said, nodding.

"Also I'm small," Tracy said. "I can crawl through ducts or little windows, and I'm a lot stronger than I look."

There was a moment's pause while everyone considered this. Then Hannah said "Security."

"That's right," Sam said. "We need to get the keys away from the guard."

"They've probably got a computerized security system," Jessica said. "If you can get *to* the building, I think I can get you inside."

Max looked first at Sam, whose eyes met his, then at Jessica, who smiled at them both.

"You can?" Max said.

"And into the freezer room, I'd imagine," Jessica said. "I've got all I need: a modem, a computer, and a few other little gizmos. So I don't see why not."

"My goodness," Max said.

"Of course," Sam said, "when this is over, Jessica and I may have to move to Finland for a while."

"We could parachute down," Tracy said. "I saw that once in a movie."

"Oh, man, of course," Sam said. "Why didn't I think of this before? Tracy, you're a genius. We come in from above. I still have my license to fly a helicopter."

"You what?" Jessica asked.

"But you can't even drive a car any more," Tracy said.

"True," Max said, "but there would be less traffic where a helicopter goes. And all we have to do is steal one. So we can then steal the drug."

"This is foolishness," Hannah said.

Sam clapped his hands. "There's probably a door up there on the roof for Rowland to use, or at least a heating vent for our small member of the occupation force to wriggle through. Bear with me now. Using her computer magic, Jessica has us covered going in and coming out. My sketches more or less show where to go, once we're inside. Tracy here, let's say with Max to help her, will then liberate the merchandise, hop back aboard and off we go."

"This is foolishness."

"You're not going to believe this," Max said, "but I think I can find us a helicopter we won't have to steal." He was too agitated to stand still. He moved around behind Jessica and said to her, "This comes from knowing everybody." Then he went over to lean against the kitchen sink and address the table from there. "My friend Lennie Koslow would be happy to serve as our copter connection. Next problem."

"Can we put like a silencer on the engine?" Tracy asked.

"Good point," Sam said.

"We don't need it to be quiet," Max said. "Didn't you tell me Mister President Doctor Oswald Rowland, aka The Oz, left the place by helicopter to avoid having a meeting with you?"

"That's what they told me."

"And didn't you say that what's her name, Emma Cameron, told you Rowland sometimes stays late and flies away in his helicopter in the middle of the night?"

"Yeah, but maybe she meant just in the summer, when he enjoys being in his garden."

"My guess is, he comes and goes by helicopter at all hours, all seasons. The guards won't think a thing about a helicopter landing on the roof of the building. Next problem." No one spoke for a moment. Then Max said, "Think about it. What could go wrong?"

At that point, they all started to laugh. Sam said, "Well, I could get us killed, for one."

"Aside from that?"

"We get caught?" Tracy said. She sounded like a young student who didn't know the right answer but had to say something since the teacher had called on her.

"Not with the guard hoodwinked and the security system taken care of."

"And assuming there are no guards inside the building," Sam said.

"Or dogs," Tracy said. "What about dogs?"

"This isn't the movies, guys. One rent-a-cop at the gate, maybe a simple computerized security system at the building. It's just a small company, right? And obviously in financial trouble, probably cutting back expenses wherever they can, like for security and public relations. We're not raiding Merck or Eli Lilly here. I don't think they have a whole lot of corporate espionage to worry about. Besides, if they were good enough to be a target, if they were hot, they wouldn't be in this kind of trouble in the first place."

For a few moments, no one spoke. Sam looked again at the drawing of the lab layout. Max seemed to vibrate in place, glancing out the window and around the room without seeing anything. Tracy shifted in her chair, massaging her legs, looking as though she were getting primed to play a hard set of racquetball. Jessica's eyes were closed and she was smiling. Hannah shook her head.

"Could I mention that this is a crime? A significant one. You could all go to prison."

"Well," Sam said, "it's a chance I'm willing to take. But I don't think it'll come to that."

"Speaking of crimes, I may also have to modify their inventory a little bit," Jessica said. "We don't want them to miss any of the merchandise."

"Jesus," Max said, turning toward her. "Would you like to work for me? A guy I know wants to run for U.S. Senate."

Sam took a slow, deep breath. If he got too worked up, he'd only start to feel sicker. "Tell your friend Lennie we need a single-engine three seater," Sam said. "Piston, not a turbine. Let's see, we'll be carrying some extra weight on the return trip, but we're all pretty small so I don't think that'll matter much. Ask if he can get us a Bell 47, maybe a Schweizer 330. Or I could try one of those little Enstroms, the Shark or the Falcon."

"Would you prefer red or olive?"

"I'll have to brush up," Sam said, ignoring Max. "I mean, I haven't flown in, um, in a number of years.

"So brush up," Max said. "Give your friend Clem Garnett a call, see if he'll let you go up with one of his officers. Or we can just rent you some time."

"Hey! We can study together," Tracy said. "I have to do these exercises for remembering direct addresses. Like Gantry Street sounds like Pantry Street and what do I keep in the pantry?"

Sam nodded at her, but remained lost in his thoughts. "Flying a helicopter is about hand-eye-foot coordination," he said. "That's precisely what this disease takes away."

"And rational thinking, honey," Hannah said. "That sure is *your* problem."

"Here," Max said. He tossed his empty mug across the table to Sam, who caught it by instinct. "I rest my case. You've still got it."

"Yeah, well throw it at me while I'm also trying to stir up a bunch of pancake batter and dance the tango."

"Next problem?" Max said.

Everyone settled into silence again, turning inward. They were actually beginning to picture the thing happening.

"Flashbacks," Sam said. "You and Tracy are going to need them once you're inside, in case the place is dark."

"I carry a flashback with me at all times," Max said.

"And we need to know how to handle the drug," Sam said, "since it's so fragile. If I remember right, the Research Department kept it frozen till a few hours before it was used. I think Emma Cameron told me PER keeps it in a freezer till the last minute and ships it frozen to the various clinics. Tracy, remember how Kate was always saying we couldn't be late for an appointment? They were always in a big rush for the infusions so the stuff didn't go bad after they thawed it out."

"This reminds me of something," Hannah said.

"Dry ice," Max said. "This we can do."

"All right, but let me call Kate now and make sure I haven't missed something."

"Just a minute, let's see what we've got, first." Max picked up the marker pen and stood over Sam's chart. As he spoke, he jotted down notes. "Say we target a week from Thursday, since we don't have much time to waste. OK, here's what we do: I arrange a helicopter, somewhere near Seattle. We drive to wherever the helicopter is located. Sam flies us from there to the roof of PER's office and lands so softly he has to tell us we're down. He stays inside the craft. Jessica has disabled the security system. Tracy and I enter—details to follow—and head straight to the room where the materials are—more details to follow—carrying whatever sort of container we need. We fetch the drug and return to the roof, where Sam is waiting to ferry us out. Sound right? Now we each have some things to follow up on, so we should gather again, same time, same place, in one week."

"This reminds me of something," Hannah said.

"How *do* we get in?" Sam asked.

"My husband," Tracy said.

"We hadn't planned to bring anyone else along."

"We don't have to. Wally taught me everything he knows."

Again, Max and Sam exchanged looks. Max said, "This is quite a crowd you hang out with."

"I'm not following you, Trace."

"Wally's out of work again," Tracy said. When she didn't continue, Sam forced himself not to say anything. Wait, just wait. He knew her well enough by now. Max stood there with his mouth half-opened, staring at Tracy, and Jessica continued smiling. Tracy began again. "I mean, he never went to school or anything, but he's been trained to do a million different things. Welder, surveyor, house painter, electrician, glazier, you know, but he just can't find something he likes enough to stick with. He was good at fixing furnaces. For a while there, before our last baby was born, he ran this storage place off I-205. The kind of place where people rent space to store all their worldly possessions? Well, let me tell you, a person has to learn all sorts of tricks for opening locks and getting into places. I used to help him all the time. He said I was better at it than he was, and quit."

Max was beaming. "I'm beginning to think this is going to be a lot of fun, you know what I mean? Not just a noble undertaking, but a real gas. Who knows what other talents we may uncover before it's all over."

"I just have one more question. What do we do when we get the stuff back?" Tracy said.

Max sighed. "Did I say *Next problem* yet?"

"That's easy, Trace. You either infuse it yourself or get Wally to do it."

"Right, Doctor Doolittle himself."

Jessica took a long breath and rejoined the conversation. "I've actually been thinking about that ever since Sam told me he wanted-ed to go get the stuff," Jessica said. "How do you get the drug into yourself? I think this idea will work, assuming you trust Kate enough. Would she be willing to install one of those in-dwelling catheters in Tracy's arm? My sister had that when she was getting a two-month course of antibiotics. It's no big deal. They insert the thing into a vein, you hardly know it's there. Then all you have to do is pull out one bottle of the drug at a time, get it ready, hook it up, and let it drip."

"I know what this reminds me of," Hannah said.

"I can check when I call Kate," Sam said. "She's waiting to hear from us."

"It reminds me of *The Gang That Couldn't Shoot Straight.* That story didn't end well, and this one isn't going to either."

"One last thing," Tracy said. "I think we need a name. Like The A Team, or The Sickos or something. Don't you?"

"Operation Zomalovir," Max said.

"The Odd Squad," Jessica said.

"Idiots at Large," Sam said.

3.

Hannah Lee Price didn't need any fancy name for it. She knew what was wrong, and had known for the better part of three months, since before the Zomalovir study was halted. But at first the feeling was too vague, too much like a continuation of her lingering illness, and so the gravity of it didn't register.

There was only so much a person could complain about, she remembered thinking. Already had plenty of specific symptoms to talk about, lots of boxes to check on the forms provided by the drug company, and places to point to when Doctor Fong asked her questions. She didn't need to complain about a few more, especially when they were so, well, "unimpressive" was the word she knew the doctors used.

Besides, at her age Hannah figured a little bleeding was nothing to worry about. A little indigestion, some gas, a bit of a belly all of a sudden. It ran in the family, mother and father both, this middle-age spread. It was in the genes, especially the women's genes. They all looked like this, come mid-forties. And who, precisely, was there in her home to mind the way things sounded and smelled and looked?

Then all of a sudden the bones of her pelvis started to ache and Hannah lost weight, ten pounds in two weeks alone. They noticed at church. That was when Hannah began reading the books. It was all so confusing. Her symptoms had been imprecise, and could have been associated with getting Zomalovir, if she was getting Zomalovir, or even with getting the placebo, for that matter. Let alone with aging or early menopause. Cancer she didn't think was a legitimate risk. Nobody in her family had died of cancer, at least as far back as she knew about, her two parents and four grandparents. Died of plenty other things, but not cancer.

Even thinking about cancer showed how far she'd drifted into the zone of hypochondria. Just like that poor Molly Carroll. Hannah hadn't wanted to join the drug study in the first place, hadn't wanted to approach the management of her illness that way, searching for magic, crazy for miracle cures. She wanted, almost immediately, to learn how to live with it instead. Besides, Hannah knew herself well enough to know she would start manifesting all kinds of symptoms as soon as she had to pay undue attention to her body.

After she first got sick, she'd tried to work, then went on disability leave from the college. To keep occupied, she tried to write a little essay about the white male domination of medical research as it pertained to women's illnesses, but her heart wasn't in it. Instead, she stewed.

It turns out her cancer stewed too. She had advanced ovarian cancer, stage IV already. Her mother always said Hannah was advanced in everything that could be measured. The cancer had metastasized to her uterus and lymph nodes and now beyond, perhaps to the lungs. She would know for sure in a week.

And why aren't I surprised? she thought, driving home from the meeting at Sam's house. For six months after she got sick with that other business, she thought she was going to die. She faced up to that. Accepted it and got her affairs in order. So that was good practice, she thought, and now that she knows her death is certain, though from a different cause entirely, she doesn't have so much to do except pray. The oncologist said Hannah was not a candidate for surgery or chemo at this point, lungs or no lungs, and from what Hannah had read, she wouldn't put herself through all that anyway.

No, Hannah didn't need a diagnosis, a label, to know what was wrong inside her. It was just that everything happened so quickly. It was just that she had a lot she still wanted to do.

She didn't want to frighten her friends from the Zomalovir group. But if the drug had triggered her cancer, or had made it grow more swiftly, more deadly, shouldn't they know about that risk? Poor Tracy and Laurel, poor Alice and Daphne. Sam on his mission.

4.

After Max and Tracy left, Jessica helped Sam clean up. When he put the two neatly folded flip-chart pages in the oven, she retrieved them and stored them behind the pantry door. She opened the refrigerator and removed the thermos he had placed inside, rinsed it and set it upside-down in the drainboard.

"You look tired," Jessica said.

He came over to hug her. "The odd thing is, I'm not. I feel drained, and I'm achy everywhere, but it's good anyway. Power to the People! If it didn't sound so New Age, I'd say I felt centered. And I'm really glad you stayed."

"Sam, why didn't I know you were a helicopter pilot? I didn't even know you were in Vietnam."

"It was a long time ago."

"So was Finland, for me. But you know about it."

"Well, I know about some of it. But not what you did that made you have to flee the States."

Jessica looked away, then nodded. "You're right. We're both going slow. But let's not try to build a future by jettisoning the past, all right? We can't ignore *anything* if we want this to have integrity."

He kissed her. "This. I'll be the first to say it: I'm falling in love, Jessica."

"Why don't we let the rest of this wait." She nodded in the direction of the sink, which had a few dirty mugs and bowls stacked in it.

Sam agreed. Holding her hand, he led Jessica upstairs but surprised her by moving toward the bathroom instead of the bedroom and pulling her in there. He removed his shirt and sat on the tub's rim, turning on the taps, adjusting them for warmth. He added bath oil. As the room filled with steam and the oil's soft scent, he turned toward her and lifted off the sweatshirt she was wearing.

"Not quite a Finnish sauna," he whispered, bending to kiss her breasts, "but it should be nice enough."

They helped each other out of the rest of their clothes, enjoying the warmth of the room, and climbed into the tub. It took several attempts for them to arrange their limbs comfortably. Jessica finally settled back, her long legs draped around his hips as Sam leaned back gingerly to avoid the taps. Her glistening knees were out of the water from mid-thigh to mid-shin.

"This won't do," she said, shifting so that her legs were together and stretched alongside him. She turned the tap off with her toes. Then she draped her legs over his thighs and put her heels against the tub wall, her feet and ankles protruding from the water. Sam was now squeezed into the remaining space with most of his body out of the water. "Much better," Jessica said.

"For me too. I prefer being cold."

Sam tried not to stare at her body as she closed her eyes, shrugged her shoulders and sank deeper. It was no use. He picked up the soap, lathered his hands, and began working on her from the feet up, washing carefully around each toe, taking the time to massage the thick tendons behind her heels, her calf, and thigh muscles. The water grew slightly more opaque.

"Mmmmm," she said. "Sam, I have to tell you something. It's really bothering me."

He stopped moving immediately, dropping the soap. She reached down for his hand and put it back on her thigh.

"Not that, dummy. I was thinking about this business of you flying a helicopter."

"I've been thinking about it too," he said, finding the soap again, lathering her shoulders and arms. "Some things are buried so deep in this brain of mine that the virus hasn't gotten them. Listen: *Make all approaches into the wind.* Or how about this one: *Avoid low tail attitude while near the ground.* I hope you've been appreciating my tail attitude here. There's an even better one: *The size of any obstacles within a confined area should dictate type and angle of approach.*" He leaned closer, touching her from beneath the water. "That's what I'm working on now."

"Knowing you, I wouldn't be surprised if you put the gasoline in where the oil is supposed to go."

"I don't forget what goes where. Besides, that's why we'll have the owner take care of the prep work." He kissed her. "Shouldn't you be thinking about something else at this point?"

"All right, but tell me what happens if you accidentally press the wrong button or something? This isn't out of the realm of possibility, in case you haven't noticed. I have these visions of you suddenly firing off a rocket or flipping the whole thing upside-down and landing on one of the blades."

"It's not quite that delicate, you know. But if I don't feel confident enough, we'll scrub the plan. Speaking of which." He fished out the soap and started lathering his hands again.

"Forget the soap." She snuggled her hips downwards a bit further, lifting her legs to drape them over his shoulders so that Sam's hand touched directly where she wanted it to. He moved it in a slow circle. Jessica's fair skin, already mottled by the heat, blended more evenly red. He no longer tried not to stare at her. "It's really too small," she whispered.

Sam looked down at himself the water and shook his head. "Maybe you need to put on your glasses."

"The tub, Sam. The tub's too small." She sat up. "Let me wash you a bit and let's get out of here. You did turn the heat on in your bedroom, didn't you? I like a bedroom to be very warm after my bath."

5.

When Jessica left for work the next morning, Sam lingered in the kitchen waiting for Clem Garnett to call him back. For old-times sake, he thought the state police superintendent might be willing to let him fly with one of the officers. If not, he would have to rent some time from a charter service, and that could be pricey.

Sam opened the pantry and took out a broom. Then he moved a chair from the dining room into the middle of the kitchen, sat down, and laid the broom on the floor to his left. With the bristles behind him, he lined the top of the broomstick up against his foot so that when he leaned over and grabbed it, he felt as though he were sitting in a helicopter cockpit with the collective lever beside him.

With the way his brain now worked, Sam guessed that the collective would be the trickiest flight control for him to operate. The stick not only governed ascent and descent as it was raised or lowered, it also had the throttle control affixed to its top like a motorcycle grip. Raise the stick and forget to add power, or lower the stick and forget to cut power, and they would be in big trouble. While he waited for Clem's call, Sam practiced power on/power off moves, lifting the head of the broom and rotating his knuckles toward his body, then lowering the broom and rotating away. After five minutes, besides growing very tired, he had only killed himself three times.

Sam soon lost himself in the routine. As he worked the broomstick, he began imagining the terrain around PER's headquarters, the flat stretch of road, the trees, the distant ridge of foothills in the moonlight. When the phone rang, his first thought was that it was an alarm signaling imminent crash. He flipped the broomstick sideways with a twist of his wrist and it clattered across the hardwood floor. He jammed his feet against imaginary pedals and nearly fell out of the chair groping with his right hand for the cyclic stick.

When Sam picked up the phone, he had to stop himself from yelling "Mayday." It was Sasha O'Neill, Clem's administrative assistant.

"I'm afraid Superintendent Garnett can't talk to you, Mr. Kiehl."

"Is he out?"

"No, sir. He's right here. He just doesn't want to talk to you on the subject you called about."

"We could talk about the Trailblazers chances in the playoffs."

"The superintendent thinks they'll get their asses kicked in the first round, as usual."

"Well, ask him how he's feeling, then."

"About an hour ago, he told the Governor he felt dandy. He also asked me to remind you of something. It seems you owe us an interim report on the police force's image. Verbal will do, it doesn't have to be in writing. The thing is, he'd like to know how the helicopters we bought have altered that image. So he'd like you to fly with me and Officer Roy Hastings tomorrow morning at 0900 hours. Can you meet us at the Portland airport?"

"I think I can arrange that."

"Superintendent Garnett also wanted me to say that he's glad you're feeling up to doing this, but you shouldn't feel obligated to produce the report immediately. He says to give him a call in a few months because he'll be too busy to talk to you before then anyway. Much too busy."

"Thank the superintendent for the consultant."

"Nice talking to you, Mr. Kiehl."

After he hung up, Sam put his kitchen back in order, then went upstairs. He was already exhausted and it was only 10:00. He was also upset with himself for the ignorant and impulsive way he'd approached Clem. For God's sake, you don't just ask the state police superintendent to let you take a joyride in one of his publicly funded helicopters. What had he been thinking? Everything had to have a cover story. You could do what you wanted, you just had to have a reason that the auditors, the legislature, the media, the public, or a jury could be forced to accept.

He stayed in bed for most of the day. He visualized the flight controls of a helicopter, but as he dozed all the switches were misplaced, hidden, or missing altogether. There were thousands of spinning dials and flickering lights. Sam thought they were probably the reason his head hurt so badly.

At about 3:00, he concluded that this was not a particularly good sign and called Eli Moskowitz. Eli was not in any of his offices, so Sam called him at home.

"House calls I don't make, my friend," he said when Sam explained what was going on. "So how about I meet you at my office near your place, say in an hour?"

"I really appreciate this."

"Don't be silly. It's the least I could do after you send me a client like Tracy Marsh. Suggestible? The woman would treat herself with a chef's knife if I happened to suggest it. Enthusiastic? I have seldom met a person as willing to surrender to Chinese medicine, or as desperate to be healed. She actually asked me if an egg roll would help her."

"And of course you sold her one."

"Sam, I think she'll do all right. She's been holding her own, which is certainly a good sign. At any rate, it's clear that this woman is a true commando."

"Uh oh," Sam said. "Sounds to me like she's been spilling the beans."

"Well, she does talk a lot."

"And she told you about our little plan?"

"My lips are sealed. Only there's one thing you may not have thought of. Nausea. Given your neurological symptoms, your balance problems and so on, I would imagine you and Tracy could have some trouble in flight. Take a small slice of ginger root and hold it between your teeth the whole time. Both of you. Don't swallow it, though."

"You're amazing, Eli."

"One other thing."

"I know. It's a felony and I could go to prison."

"I figured you'd already thought of that. Besides, I'm a child of the sixties myself, and I'm proud of you. No, I want to tell you about something else."

"Tell me. I'm sitting down."

"Part of me thinks you're absolutely crazy. But another part of me, a much bigger part, thinks this is the most healing thing you could do. That is, if you live through it."

"That's just about exactly how I see it, too," Sam said.

"Good. See you in an hour."

6.

That night, as Sam was fumbling around his kitchen trying to prepare dinner, the phone rang. Why wouldn't it ring, he thought, since this was the only half-hour all day when he was actually busy? Intending to turn the front right burner down so that his vegetable stew could simmer, Sam instead turned on the left rear burner, where his empty sauté pan sat, and left the stew boiling when he picked up the phone.

It was Andy. He was in Flagstaff, Arizona, freezing, getting ready to play for the next four nights in a club near the university. His back and neck hurt, Kayla had a cold and sounded like Perry Como. They weren't getting enough rest.

"You've got to be careful," Sam said. He stopped for a brief coughing jag, then continued. "I'm living proof of that. When you just keep pushing, it weakens the immune system and makes you vulnerable to whatever's out there. Plus, you're in a lot of strange, crowded places these days. Take it easy, all right?"

"You sound like what's-his-name, the guy I listen to on the radio in the car every afternoon. The doctor who tells everybody the same thing no matter what they call to complain about."

"It's my job to worry about you, Andy. Always has been. Wait a minute, you called to complain?"

"Sure. After all, I don't really need any money, so why else would I call?"

Sam coughed again and reached for a Kleenex. "There's one more thing, before I forget. I've been hearing that this disease could have a genetic component. That means you have to be extra cautious."

"All right, I'll be careful, Daddy. Now tell me what's going on with the drug study. Have they come around yet?"

Sam explained what had been going on since their last conversation, shortly before Christmas. Andy listened without interrupting. As he finished outlining the plan, Sam looked over at the stove and said, "Oh my God!" He dropped the phone and ran over to turn off both burners. He flicked on the exhaust fan, grabbed a pot holder and moved the empty sauté pan, which was a smoky black mess, then moved the pan containing what was left of his vegetable stew, caked now to the bottom and filling the kitchen with its scorched odor.

When he picked up the phone again, Andy was laughing and calling to Kayla. "Come here, you've got to hear my old man in action."

"Never mind that," Sam said. "I have everything under control."

Andy was still laughing. "So let me get this right. You're going to fly a helicopter with two of your dearest friends aboard and you can't even operate a stove properly?"

"Cooking is harder. Anyway, I've been brushing up. I plan to do some flying east of Portland tomorrow. Listen to the two of us. You sound like the father and I sound like the kid here."

"That's right, now that you're feeble it's my job to worry about you. We had to read a play about this kind of thing in high school. Seriously, Dad, are you really going to do this? You weren't just blowing smoke in my ear?"

"Next week."

"Then I should be home," Andy said. "Definitely. There's got to be some way I can help out."

Sam realized how much he had wanted Andy to offer that. It felt like the missing piece of the plan's puzzle. He very much missed his son's sweet, casual presence, and he took comfort in knowing that Andy still thought of Portland as a place to return to.

"Don't even consider it," Sam said. "You're already overloaded. Besides, there really is nothing for you to do."

"I could come along, you might need some young legs. I mean, suppose someone's working late at the lab. Suppose Max and Tracy have to fight their way out of the building. Come on, this could be your chance for a big payoff on all those karate lessons you bought for me."

"None of that's going to happen. But if it did, we'd just let Tracy talk him to death."

There was a moment's silence while Andy thought about what to do. Sam had to smile. He could easily imagine his son's face, brows pulled together in concentration, eyes narrowed to slits. His tongue would be probing the hole where his lower right wisdom tooth had been.

"I've got it," Andy said. "I could supply the soundtrack. We've got a whole bunch of new songs and there's even one about soaring with the hawks and eagles. You could play it through the headsets and get everybody psyched up."

"Sounds perfect," Sam said. "Precisely what I need. Max and Tracy screaming like red tails while I try to figure out how to land on the roof."

7.

Sasha O'Neill and Officer Roy Hastings were waiting for Sam when he arrived at the hangar the next morning. He wouldn't have recognized Sasha if he hadn't known she'd be there. When Sam had last seen her, Sasha was obese, the same size as her boss, Clem Garnett. Sam had often overheard fellow officers referring to them as the Twin Turbos. As a non-sworn officer, Sasha wasn't required to wear a uniform and had tended toward dark, voluminous suits, adorning herself with outrageous feathered hats. Now she was trim and chicly dressed. As Sam approached, she shielded her eyes from the winter sun, but he could see that she was smiling.

"Good morning, Sam. It's very good to see you again."

He took her proffered hand. "The same. You look wonderful. What did you do, swear off Desmond's cooking? Wait, I know: you took that trip to Russia you were always dreaming about and walked all across the country, eating nothing but beets."

"Diabetes, actually." She squinted at him, studying his face. Her eyes were filled with tenderness, something he'd never seen in them before. "I've learned you can never relax your vigilance with this thing."

"Sasha, I didn't know." It was beginning to dawn on Sam that he was hardly alone in dealing with a life-changing illness. Nearly everywhere he went, there was someone dealing with being sick, or dealing with someone they loved who was sick.

Sasha patted Sam's forearm, then gripped it and steered him over to her left. "Could you please stand over here, out of the sun? I didn't want anyone to know, at least not while I was learning how to eat and take care of myself. Clem was very good about that. He told everyone I'd gone crazy."

"Sounds like Clem."

"Hey, Hastings," Sasha called.

Roy Hastings looked at Sasha from the cockpit of his helicopter. He held up an index finger and smiled at her, wanting to complete the inspection. Sam and Sasha drifted toward him.

Hastings hopped down and moved toward the rear of the craft. Stocky and crew-cut, he moved with the purposeful swagger of a fullback, accustomed to plowing straight ahead when he moved and ignoring any obstacles in his path. In his thick hands, he held a leather folder embossed with the Oregon State Police seal. Surrounding the seal like decorative feathers was a circle of tiny yellow Post-It notes, each one filled with scribbled reminders of things to do. As he proceeded through his routine, Hastings removed another note, folded it in half so that it stuck closed, then crumpled it and put it in his pants pocket. They didn't speak as he concluded the inspection, lifted a finger to his lips, then touched the tail rotor in a kind of final blessing.

The morning was windy, with gusts from the north that rattled the drooping blades of the main rotor. Sam would have preferred calmer conditions for this first flight, but he supposed it was good to deal with wind right away. Besides, Hastings would handle the takeoff, and maybe the landing too, depending on how Sam felt.

"All aboard," Hastings said, climbing in and reaching for his seat belt. He tugged on a pair of leather gloves, settled a hat on his head and removed another Post-It from his folder.

Sasha hopped up and into the seat behind the pilot. When Sam hesitated, shifting his weight from one foot to another, Sasha leaned over to offer him her hand. Their eyes met for a moment before she said, "Right foot first, Cowboy."

After he shut the door and put on his headset, Sasha leaned forward and patted his shoulder. Sam turned partway around to smile at Sasha. Over the last few years, he had grown familiar with the casual kindnesses sick people often shared with one another, the spontaneous sympathy and comprehension. Sasha gave him a thumbs-up sign, then offered him a stick of gum. Sam declined, reaching into his pocket for the slice of ginger root he'd cut for himself before leaving home.

The helicopter swayed back and forth as Hastings started the engine and the blades began turning. Soon the familiar vibration took over the cabin, and Sam tried to relax, leaning back into his seat, watching Hastings check his systems. He had faced the helicopter into the wind, but the gusts and backwash caused some of the exhaust to circulate inside the cabin. Sam knew he was extra-sensitive to all sorts of toxins these days. Fine, another little thing to worry about.

Stay focused, he told himself. This is like riding a bicycle; you don't forget how, but those first few moments can be a little wobbly. Just watch him and let your mind go. Pretend you're flying it. Shadow his moves, but keep your hands and feet to yourself.

Hastings lifted into a hover, held there for a minute as he checked the engines and controls, then lifted into the wind. He was a good, smooth pilot. There was little turbulence as he headed out over the Columbia River and turned east. They gained speed, staying level, and Sam settled back. The land out toward Troutdale was relatively flat, not unlike the area around PER's headquarters, and until they reached the gorge he could easily imagine this was the start of the raid.

After banking south, Hastings flicked on his microphone and asked Sam if he wanted to take control. He sat up straight, flexed his fingers and wrist, rolled his shoulders. He eased his feet forward till they made contact with the pedals, gripped the collective and cyclic sticks and took a deep breath. Looking ahead, he picked out a huge Douglas fir in the distance and, like sighting a gun, lined its tip up with the spire of a church beyond it. Confident he would be able to keep the helicopter moving straight and level, he let out his breath.

"I have control," he said into the microphone.

"You have control," Hastings replied.

Eleven

1.

The lights were off and the sign on the door of *Foster's Plants* said ...CLOSED. But Jessica had left the door unlatched for Sam. At a little past 7:00, he let himself in and locked the door.

"Hello," Zorro said from his side room. "Goodbye."

"Buy lobelias," Zeppo added.

Sam inhaled the nursery's herbal aroma backed by a scent of rich soil. By now, he knew his way across the main room in the dark. Hanging plants brushed across his face, but he didn't knock into anything, didn't trip himself.

In her small office behind the aquariums, Jessica sat cross-legged in her chair, staring at the computer screen. Her knees jutted out through the oval openings under each armrest. Sam could tell she wasn't really seeing what appeared in front of her, a cluster of slashes and peculiar marks, letters that made absolutely no sense to him. Jessica was turned inward with that familiar smile on her face, cheeks pink, eyes half shut, rocking gently back and forth. Her hair was pulled back and clipped. She had a pen gripped between her teeth. A scattering of notes on scrap paper littered the desk, some blue, some pink, some green.

When Jessica heard the door ring open and the parrots greeting him, she had called *in here*, but had said nothing to Sam since then. He'd kissed the top of her head and felt a slight upward movement in acknowledgment. He pulled a chair over, placing himself just behind her right shoulder. When she worked, her left shoulder was hitched much higher than her right, making it seem as if she were about to fall sideways out of the chair. He was in a position to catch her if she did.

From time to time, Jessica murmured a few unintelligible words in the direction of the screen. She was working with a rhythm, every third or fourth forward motion of her chair coinciding with short bursts of typing, the backward motions with a quick scan of new information as it appeared. Aside from the bubbling of the aquariums and an occasional, distant comment from Zorro or Zeppo, the only noise was the sporadic clacking of her keyboard.

Sam noticed a few red and blue boxes stacked between the phone and computer. Cords spiraled out of them to run along the desk top, half leading toward her computer and the other half toward the phone jack. On the floor below the boxes, he saw a troika of empty corn chip bags.

Jessica took the pen from between her teeth and, without looking around at him, said, "I always eat junk food when I'm hacking. Everybody does. Used to be Twinkies and Ding Dongs. Before I left for Finland, I weighed a hundred-seventy pounds."

She reached into her lap and withdrew a couple of chips from the bag stashed there. He listened to her crunching them, then watched her reach without looking for a can of Pepsi standing in the top tray of her correspondence file. She sipped while staring at the screen, then put the can back, also without looking.

Sam touched her shoulder. "Can I ask a question?"

With a flurry of struck keys, the screen changed. A list scrolled by too quickly for Sam to read. Jessica spun her chair around and looked at him closely as though trying to see what his question was before he asked it. She blinked and smiled. "Go ahead."

He nodded in the direction of the phone cords. "Aren't you afraid of the calls being traced?"

"Not really. I went into the server's computer and blitzed the relevant primary commands." She laughed in response to Sam's half-opened mouth. "Relax, my dear. Till I let them, they can't isolate any information about the line I'm using. Even if they could, I've routed the call through enough different places that they'd need an hour to find me. I'd almost forgotten how much fun this was."

"Amazing," Sam said. He pointed behind her at the screen. "What's that?"

She turned back toward the computer. "Emma Cameron's main directory."

Sam left his chair and came to kneel beside her. "You're kidding me."

"It's amazing how little attention PER gives to the security of their files. I was prepared to take a half-hour figuring out her password if I had to, but you know what it was? Ememem. Duh. I was in there in three minutes twelve seconds. Just don't tell Ms. Cameron you know her nickname is Em."

Sam looked over at her. Jessica was studying the screen and didn't seem aware of how astonishing her performance was to him. The woman who had once advised him to consult with spirit-helpers before a race also had this other side. He thought it was best to act as though it was what he had expected. Maybe, if he stayed as nonchalant as Jessica was, he might even be able to fly the helicopter as though it were no big deal. Stick to the business at hand.

"I don't get it," he said. "Why do you need to be in her files? I mean, she's not in charge of security or the deep freeze."

"Of course not. But she is the head of public relations. I figured she ought to have one of the highest levels of computer access in the whole company, so she could get hold of just about any information she needed out of their system." Jessica pointed to the screen with the tip of the pen. "Turns out I was right, too. Look at this. It's like they've removed whatever obstacles came loaded in the operating system. I can use dear Em to get right into the company's security system, into the inventory. If I wanted to, I could write and disseminate a press release announcing that PER was donating its entire stock of Zomalovir to help all the people in America who need it."

"Could you get them to Fed Ex two months worth of the stuff directly to Tracy? That way we won't have to do any of the James Bond stuff."

"I wonder." Jessica picked up the pen and put it back between her teeth. She seemed to be considering his proposal.

"I was kidding."

"That's not what I was wondering about. But it would be nice to stop them from altering anything between now and next week, just in case. You know, suppose she changes her password, or gets fired for treating you like a jerk and they take away her access."

"Surely they'd discover that someone had messed with their computers by then. We can't risk it."

Jessica turned to look at him again. Sam had an eerie feeling he could read her thoughts this time.

"No way," he said.

"What?" she smiled.

"We're not pushing the raid ahead to tomorrow."

"Did I say anything?"

Sam stood and kissed her. "It's getting to the point where neither of us has to speak. Pretty soon, the only things we'll need to say are *higher* and *now* and *mustard, not mayo.*"

"Speaking of which," Jessica said.

"Yes, I'm hungry too." He reached into her lap for a handful of chips. "There's that Japanese place near the movie theater. Or the little Tacqueria across from the bus stop. That is, if you still have an appetite."

She sighed. "Let me take a look for one more thing before I leave our Emma for the night."

"Sure. Maybe there's a combination lock on the door to the roof. That'd be handy."

"I want to see Doctor Rowland's schedule. Just in case he's out of town that night. We don't want the guards to hear a helicopter landing on the roof when everyone knows that Rowland's in Atlanta with the CDC"

"Good idea. See if you can find out something else, too, while you're at it."

"What's that?"

"Whether they have their maintenance records on-line. I'd feel a lot better knowing what kind of copter he has. If he uses one of those six-passenger Aerospatiale AS 350s or something, we're in a lot of trouble."

2.

The next morning, Sam waited for Kate McCabe to meet him for breakfast at the café near his house. Tracy was going to join them later, maybe for a cup of tea, after running some errands. The last time Sam had been at this café was when he'd had his first dinner with Jessica. It seemed like such a long time ago already.

Sam scanned the menu, waiting for Kate to show up. Then he put it down and took a sip of water. He gazed out the window toward the river, thinking about how easily he and Jessica had moved from being friends to being lovers. He wondered why they had waited so long, then realized that nothing could have happened sooner. She hadn't been interested in him like that, not until she had seen him change, and he hadn't changed in the ways that mattered to her until he'd gotten sick. No, that wasn't exactly right. It was only in the last half year or so, he thought, only since he had begun to find a sense of peace within his illness, to locate the places that illness couldn't touch. Looking back, he could identify the gradual differences in their friendship, how he had spoken to her in the minutes while she set up her massage table, how she'd looked at him when he spoke, the things she'd been willing to tell him when he lay beneath her hands with his eyes closed, her voice moving over him like a second pair of hands.

Two nights ago, when she arrived at his house after work, Jessica had been luminous. She was carrying a bag of takeout Thai food and seemed to float up the stairs. When they kissed in the kitchen, she was smiling so broadly their teeth clacked together.

"Sorry I'm late," she said. "But I'm about to make it worth your while."

Sam came back for another, softer kiss. "I like the sound of that."

"Sit down." She led him to the kitchen table, forgetting about the food, and perched next to him on the edge of her chair. She was too excited to sit normally. "Since I didn't have a single customer after about 3:00, I closed early and got everything cleaned up so I could pay a little visit to our friendly drug company this evening. Like I told you, I could ride Emma Cameron's computer right into the security system. You'll never guess what I found."

"That's a safe assumption."

"They put in a new building entry system January first. Card readers, even on the roof!" She leaned back and waited for Sam to react. "Don't you understand? When I shut down the security systems, I can also program the locks to disengage for the entire time you're there, then set them back to normal when you're through. No picking locks, no wasting time. In fact, I already tried and it worked. For sixty seconds. It was a breeze."

Sam was beginning to understand what she meant. "So Tracy doesn't have to bring her tools?"

"Well, she probably should anyway, just in case there's a padlock or something on the freezer. But all you'll have to do to open the doors is turn the knobs."

"You're sure?"

"Each PER employee has a card. Looks like American Express, but with encrypted codes in them that the card readers scan. Everybody has different clearances, but Emma is top level. Anyway, the codes disengage the locks. I go into the computer, control the relay and rewrite the software to disengage all locks, say from 6:00 to 7:00. It's just as if you had Emma's card in your pocket."

As Sam sat in the café remembering the conversation, he kept seeing Jessica's eyes while she spoke. They were gray at first, and enormous as they watched him slowly grasp what she was saying. Then he could actually see them warming toward green, softening as something she saw in his own eyes made her laugh and reach for him.

Sam didn't even see Kate come into the café. She stood next to the table and passed her hand before his eyes like a hypnotist demonstrating her client's trance state.

"Yoo-hoo, Captain Marvel," she said.

Sam jerked backwards, splashing himself with water but catching the glass before it fell. He struggled to get up and greet her, but Kate moved the hand onto his shoulder to keep him seated.

She plopped down opposite him, rested her elbows on the table, and cupped her chin in her hands. It seemed to take her a moment to bring him into focus. She shook her head.

"What?" Sam said.

"I'm very happy that I don't know anything about what you and Tracy are planning. No idea what you guys are up to. What's good here? I'm in the mood for French toast. But if you get to wherever you're planning to go, and start to do whatever you're planning to do, you may find that there are bottles of a certain drug stored in the same freezer with bottles of placebo, all with the number 493 A printed on them. You may find that there's no way to tell the two apart, which is as it should be. That's the whole point in a double-blind, placebo-controlled clinical field trial, isn't it? So how's the sausage in this place? They make it with chicken? Probably has beaks and toes ground up with bones and a little bit of dark meat for color. Do I dare? Where was I, Sam?"

"I never thought of that," Sam said. "PER makes the placebo too? For some reason, I thought you did that yourself, in the lab."

"Oh, right. Then we'd know which was which, and who was getting what, wouldn't we? Of course PER makes it themselves. And I would bet they keep it in identical little bottles in the very same freezer as the drug, but marked with some kind of code that you won't have time to break."

Sam wrote down some notes. Then he said, "The French toast is famous. They soak it in cream overnight or something. And the sausage they grind themselves, from Oregon-grown chickens raised without any chemical additives. All right? So tell me what we do."

"Order French toast and sausage, of course."

"Very funny. I mean on this raid we're not going to make and that you don't know anything about, when we encounter the mixed-up bottles."

"Well, I would imagine you'd have three choices. You can take everything you see, which may be too much to carry and would obviously tip them off. You can take as many bottles as you can manage and hope your luck is good, that you end up with at least half drug. Or you can open one and taste it."

"What good would that do?"

"If it's bitter, it's the drug. If it's salty, or tastes like tap water, it's fake."

"Of course. And then we see what the code on the bottle is, right?"

"Voila." She leaned back in her chair and smiled at him. "Pretty slow service here. I've got to get to work this morning."

"Wait a minute, Kate. How do we taste the stuff if it's frozen solid."

She frowned. "Good point."

"How long does it take to thaw?"

"Normally, we do it very slowly, like I told you over the phone. Gentle heat and slow agitation till all the ice crystals are melted. But you don't need to do it that way in the lab, right? You can waste a bottle just to see what it is. So bring along a heat source, a little butane torch or something. Maybe they've got hot water in the lab. But bring heat just in case."

Sam nodded. "This gets more complicated every time I go through it."

"That's why you go over it and over it ahead of time, isn't it? It's like with emergency nursing procedures. Over and over."

The waiter came to take their order. Kate asked for a Greek omelette, heavy on the feta, and narrowed her eyes at Sam when he laughed. He ordered oatmeal and wheat toast.

"Very noble, Sam. Lots of hearty grains. Meanwhile, you're sick and I'm healthy as a horse. Oh, there's something else I need to tell you."

He found a pen in his coat pocket and moved his napkin into writing position beside his plate.

"Put that away. Jeez, what kind of operative are you, 002? This is purely a social breakfast."

He put his pen away and laid the napkin in his lap. The waiter brought Kate some coffee to which she added sugar and cream. She sipped, then looked out the window.

"How about telling me what you were going to tell me, before we get too much older."

"Patience, my friend. I was just getting organized. All right, here it is: the Albuquerque site is talking about a demonstration. They're thinking of coming up to Seattle and staging a sit-down in front of PER's headquarters."

"When?"

"Need I say?"

"Oh my God." Sam stared at her to be sure she wasn't teasing him. Kate shut her eyes and slowly nodded. "Who'd you talk to? Is there anything we can do to stop them?"

"I talked to my counterpart there, a woman named Lucinda Westcamp. She says the group is split right now, about three-fourths pro and one-fourth con. But it looks like the pros are will-ing to come anyway."

"I don't suppose you could tell this Lucinda Westcamp she needs to stop them. Or at least get them to postpone for a week."

"How can I do that, when I don't know what you're up to in the first place?"

"Shit."

Their food arrived. Sam sat back, his appetite gone, and watched Kate dig into her omelette. "Why did you talk me out of ordering the French toast?" she asked.

"Maybe we can get that attorney, P. J. Cooper, to stop them. For tactical reasons."

"Actually, I think it may have been partly his idea." Kate picked up her spoon to reach across the table and taste Sam's oatmeal. "This isn't bad. Cooked with milk. Eat, Sam."

Gazing over Kate's shoulder, Sam saw Tracy dart across the street and open the café's door. She scanned the small room, found their ta-ble, and was seated beside them before Sam had a chance to greet her.

"Look what the wind blew in," Kate said. She carefully placed a chunk of omelette on a slice of toast. "If you're hungry, Sam's not eating his food."

"Why not?" Tracy asked. "You've got to eat breakfast. It's the most important meal of the day. I always make my kids eat their breakfasts, Sam." She stopped talking to look at him more closely. "What's wrong?"

"Nothing much. Kate just told me the group in Albuquerque plans a demonstration in front of PER's headquarters on the same day we plan to be there. Extra security, lots of people hanging around. That's all."

"Oh, that," Tracy said. She reached over to take a piece of Sam's toast, took a bite, and beamed at him. "Next problem."

"What are you talking about?"

"I took care of Albuquerque. That's why I was late. I thought I could get here in time to keep you guys company all through your meal, but it took a few minutes extra."

Kate had stopped eating now, too. They both were leaning over their plates, heads turned toward Tracy. Kate said, "This thing that I don't know anything about is getting so interesting I just may want to come along for the ride."

"This day is too young for me to feel like this already," Sam said. "Remember, stress is very bad for someone in my condition."

"I talked them out of it."

"Who?"

"Well, Caroline Burke, who's sort of the leader of the Albuquerque group. I've talked to her every week since we started the study. She talks with a woman from the Rhode Island group, who talks to a woman from the Chicago group. We're like this informal committee, you know? Share information, complain, keep each other's spirits up. Caroline was meeting with a couple other women who were all gung-ho. Her brother's wife is a travel agent there in Albuquerque, and she was already working on plane tickets and everything. Good thing I called this morning, huh? They'll wait another two weeks, no sweat."

"Please tell me you didn't let them know about our plan. Trace, half the western United States is going to know about it before we leave Portland."

"Not exactly."

"Not exactly?" Sam leaned back in his chair and sighed. "You told them part of it?"

"I said that we were engaged in some very delicate dealings with PER over a two-months supply of the drug for me, since I was so close to getting better. *Behind the scenes dealings,* I called them. Which is not really a lie, you know. I was careful not to use the word *negotiations* or anything. I also said I would appreciate it if they could hold off for a while, as a special favor to me, so PER wouldn't get upset and call the whole thing off. I told them we would consider joining them in Seattle, but since the Portland group didn't get together very much, we'd need a couple weeks to get ready. It was easy." She beamed again, finished Sam's toast, and said, "Where's my tea?"

Kate continued staring at Tracy. She shook her head, then nodded, looked at Sam for a moment, picked up her fork, and continued eating her omelette.

"Very good," she said. "I especially like the part where you go up and join the protest. There's something quite nineties about that approach."

"I don't think the demonstration will happen now. You know how people are, Kate. Once they lose the momentum, they won't pull it together again. Sick people, in particular. I think it'll just fade away."

Sam felt dazed. He'd sat down lost in romantic reverie, then was faced with two tricky problems that he hadn't foreseen, and had them solved before he could even panic. The message was clear. He had a good team and they were going to be fine. That was the message, he thought, wasn't it? He picked up his spoon, stirred the thickening oatmeal, and began to eat.

3.

"Your blood pressure is good," Doctor Fong said. He removed the cuff and put his stethoscope to Sam's chest. "Breathe in for me, nice and easy."

Fong's office had called again, wanting Sam to come in for an exam. It was highly unusual; doctors didn't summon their patients. Besides, he had always had to call weeks in advance to get in to see Fong and now that the study was on hold, Sam thought he wouldn't be seeing the doctor again for months. He knew something was up. Next week and the little visit to PER's headquarters couldn't get here fast enough.

"Any new pain, Sam?" Fong gently squeezed his shoulders and pressed along the vertebrae that had given Sam pain for years.

"Same old same old. I've been doing all right."

"Any recurrence of the sleep disturbance? I could give you something now if you need it."

Sam didn't want any medications. With acupuncture treatments every other week, along with Eli's regimen of herbs and supplements, Sam was managing well enough. Since he and Jessica had become lovers, he was sleeping better too, at least when he was at her place in the country. Instead of sleeping in two hour chunks, as he had for years, he was sleeping for four or five hours at a time. He still felt sick, felt as though his brain, his essential organs, his scaffolding were still deeply damaged. But he also felt better, less frayed, less divided against himself. It was nothing he could explain to Fong. But no, Sam didn't want anything from the doctor.

But he knew that the doctor wanted something from him. However, whether it was some obstacle inherent in the doctor-patient relationship, or because of personal reserve, or a lack of clarity on Fong's part about what he wanted, Fong seemed unable to ask Sam what he wanted to ask.

Sam leaned back on the examination table, resting his weight on his hands. It was difficult, sometimes, to see doctors as real people, as fellow humans with needs and doubts, capable of worry and confused feelings. Maybe it was because medical education trained them to mask those qualities, or worse, trained those qualities out of many medical students, forcing them to be diagnostic or clinical machines with little to distinguish them from the high-tech equipment their profession had come to rely on more and more. Sam knew cynics who said it was a function of natural selection, that to get into medical school in the first place a student had to be so driven, so narrowly focused that only a certain kind of person could actually make it that far. Sam knew this was nonsense. He'd met too many physicians, before he got sick, who were interesting human beings. Of course, that was before he'd become a full-time patient and before he'd become a medical research subject.

Fong sat on a low stool with his knees tucked under the shelf serving as a desk in the small examination room. He scribbled notes on Sam's chart. There was a dusting of gray in Fong's hair, which was freshly cut and at its least unruly. The collar of his shirt stuck out awkwardly above his coat in back. He was humming a delicate melody as he wrote. Sam wondered if Fong would ever be able to unburden himself, to simply say what he had brought Sam in to hear.

"Marty?"

He had never called him that before. Fong turned around on his stool. He looked up at Sam. "Yes?"

"If the exam is over, there's something I'd like to talk to you about."

"Of course," Fong said, putting down his pen. His face was carefully composed.

Sam had to restrain himself from reaching out to touch him. "I just want you to know that I believe you were honest with us about the drug study from the start. I have a tape of that original meeting we had. You said that you couldn't make any promises about what PER would do. You knew what should happen, but not what would happen, and you made that distinction clear. Well, I played that tape for our group a couple of weeks ago and everyone agreed. You didn't lie to us. None of what's happened is your fault."

Fong looked down. Sam could see his head bobbing and twisting slightly, as though he were navigating a particularly passionate passage in a Beethoven piano sonata.

"I appreciate hearing that, Sam. At meetings like the one we had, particularly with patients who are so desperate for help, one never knows what people actually hear. Or more to the point, one never knows what they might remember later."

"You're aware of the litigation?"

Fong nodded. "The group in Rhode Island, yes. I've been told others have joined."

"Chicago and Albuquerque. No one from here is part of it."

"I see." He looked up at Sam again. "You know, I really am very disappointed in how this whole thing turned out. Mostly because I still believe this drug can be effective. I would not have gotten involved in the study at all if I didn't believe that."

"As a political analyst, I think one thing's clear now. There's much more to a successful clinical field trial than having a good drug. In fact, the drug itself may only be a minority component."

Fong nodded. "Perhaps I shouldn't say this, but of course you're right. I'm a physician, a clinical practitioner and researcher, not an economist, certainly not a politician. I would like to believe that if a drug is safe and effective, it will somehow find its way to market."

"Maybe."

"Meanwhile, I wish I could come up with a way to separate the drug from the company that made it, because I'm convinced it would do some of you a lot of good."

"I was thinking along the same lines, Marty."

Twelve

1.

When the engine caught fire, Sam did everything right. He didn't panic, and he never forgot to keep flying the helicopter. He maintained rotor rpm. He slowly reduced speed. Reaching for the fire extinguisher switch, his hand was steady and he didn't press the switch until he had looked to be sure it was the correct one. Broken fuel line? Broken oil line? Maybe a casing burn-through. It was strange that no warning light had come on before he noticed the fire. What astonished him was how cool it remained inside the cockpit despite the licking of flames. Another peculiar thing was how small Sam suddenly felt, as if the fire were melting his edges within the harness of his seat belt. But he could reach everything he needed to reach, so it didn't seem to matter. Now the lights inside the cockpit were flickering as though they had absorbed the heart of flame, had become fire itself. Still, things were not going badly. He was holding altitude, the tail rotor was working so he could control direction, there was no vibration to speak of. That was strange, now that he noticed it. No vibration, no noise, nothing to indicate the helicopter was actually functioning. He looked to the side and saw nothing unusual. Except that the window was covered in fabric exactly like the window at home in his bedroom. Through it, he could see the upper limbs of the great oak across the street and now the first glimmer of dawn. He turned his head to the other side and saw Jessica looking at him, her sleepy eyes a dense green as they struggled to focus.

"Bad dream?" she whispered, reaching out to stroke his cheek.

2.

Sam had hoped to nap in the car. He'd be that much fresher when it came time to fly. Now he couldn't imagine how he'd been so naive. As Max drove them across the Interstate Bridge in the early afternoon, Sam thought the car might become airborne. Why bother with a helicopter? We could just let Max floor it and soar right over PER's front gates. The guard would never believe his eyes.

"Slow down," he said from the backseat.

"It's *Le nozze de Figaro*. First performed in 1786. You want me to turn it down?"

Sam raised his voice enough to be sure Max heard him. "What I said was slow down. We don't need to get stopped by the cops."

Max looked at him in the rearview mirror and yelled, "Picky, picky. I thought you wanted plenty of time to check out the copter and everything. Get the feel of the beast."

Tracy leaned forward and turned up the heat. Like the others, she was dressed in layers of warm clothing. She even had on new black gloves instead of her day-glo purple mittens, and had borrowed Wally's black ski hat, which was tugged down around her ears. But she was shivering anyway. She checked her watch, then tugged off a glove, reached into her purse, and withdrew several small bottles. She placed them in her lap and announced, "I love the names of these things."

"It's *Le nozze de Figaro*," Max said. "Mozart. You want me to turn it up?"

Tracy leaned forward again, careful of the bottles, and turned the volume down. "If you don't mind, I like it better when music's in English," she said.

Max thought about that one for a moment and said, "I'll try to get that version for you."

"What have you got there?" Sam asked, hoping to get Tracy going on a nice, long riff. He was pretty sure Max would be polite enough not to sing if Tracy was talking.

Turned halfway around in her seat, Tracy held up each bottle in turn. "This one's called Minor Blue Dragon. Eli said that it was for my flu-like symptoms. Can't you just see them? The dragons, I mean. Like these giant miniature lizards in your bloodstream snagging the viruses with their tongues and breathing fire into your heat glands when you're cold."

Sam always admired Tracy's grasp of anatomy. He would enjoy hearing her explain something like hiccups or food poisoning to her kids. Or sex. He'd pay well to be in the audience for that one. Background music in English. "What about their tails?" he asked.

"Right, their tails. They must use them to snap those T-cells into line." She paused for a moment, then added, "They are T-cells, aren't they? I think that's what Doctor Fong called them, the ones we have that are too worked up. Anyway, this stuff here is Astragalus 10, to boost my immune system. It's an herb that grows in thick pointy stalks. They boil up ten of them to make each of these capsules, which is why it smells so strong. And this is Major Four, which I think is a lot louder than Minor Blue Dragon once it actually gets inside you. But it tastes like spoiled milk, so I should probably get some new ones."

She took a spoon out of her purse, opened the last bottle, and shook out a substance that looked precisely like dry sand from the part of a beach where the tide never reaches and the sun beats down all summer long. She tilted her head back, opened her mouth and shoved the spoon as far down as it would go, then yanked it out and tried to swallow. For a moment, it looked to Sam as though she might gag the sand back up. He certainly would. Tracy's face reddened and tears filled her eyes. Worse, he saw that Max was watching her too, his head turned away from the road, his concentration fully focused on her.

"Max, watch the road!"

"Relax," Max said. "You let me drive and I'll let you fly. Boy, this is much better than Mozart for making the time go by fast."

When they reached Olympia, seeing the state Capitol building on their left reminded Max about some research he'd done last week. He leaned toward Tracy in order to open his glove compartment, fished around in it for a moment and withdrew a small pad on which he'd taken notes. Then he flicked the door shut, sat back up and tossed the pad into the back seat.

"Take a gander at this," Max said.

"It's just a bunch of numbers. In technicolor."

"Exactly."

"All right, I'll play along. What does it mean?"

"Red is bad, black is good. At the bottom there, green is the amount I estimate their losses will be over the next three years, if they last three years. Does that help?"

"There's something missing."

"Pray tell."

"A name at the top."

Max turned around and reached for the pad. "Give me that." He held it up over the steering wheel and shook his head. "I'll be damned." He turned around again and handed the pad to Sam, then looked at him in the rearview mirror. "Does the name Physicians for Ethical Research ring a bell?"

"I sure wish you'd look at the road, at least some of the time. At this rate, we're not going to live long enough for me to kill us in the helicopter."

"You shouldn't say that," Tracy said. "Not even joking. It's like reverse visualization, you know?"

"She's right," Max said. "Whatever the woman just said, it's absolutely correct."

"You're telling me this is PER's balance sheet? They're a privately held company. I don't think I'll bother asking how you got it."

"Come on, I know everybody. Even in Washington."

"Since I'm a sick man, why don't you just tell me what this all means rather than waiting for me to figure it out."

"Simple. PER goes belly up, early next year most likely. Unless they find an infusion of capital, if you'll pardon the expression." He looked at Sam in the rearview mirror again. Sam looked away, hoping to discourage eye contact. "They need a buyer. Of course, as their reputation for fiscal, medical, and ethical mismanagement spreads, that could be tricky. I hear they're great pure scientists though."

"So what you're telling me is that this drug will never be available."

"Never say never, Kiehl. But my guess is that it's not likely to be available before we're all old fogeys. So we have no choice, do we? We have to go steal it. Be a shame to let all those years of research go to waste without at least getting one person cured."

Tracy looked at Max, then turned in her seat to smile at Sam. "Cured," she said. "Has a nice sound, doesn't it?"

Within another half-hour, they'd passed SeaTac airport and reached the I-405 exit for Seattle's southeastern suburbs. Traffic was heavy but flowing steadily. Max was forced to keep to the speed limit, but that didn't seem to make him as jumpy as it usually did.

"Also might explain why they cut their study short. While the results still looked promising enough to attract a large pharmaceutical company to buy in."

"No clouds," Tracy said as though to herself.

"Not too much wind," Max said.

"Good visibility," Sam said.

With only a few miles to go, they grew silent as though by mutual consent. Max turned the music off altogether. Daylight was fading, though not quite enough yet for cars to have on their full headlights. As their exit approached, Max pulled into the right lane and slowed.

"Shouldn't be long now," Sam said.

The helicopter had been leased to a friend of Lennie Koslow, a Pakistani electronics genius who'd used some of Lennie's money to start up a software company in Redmond. The copter would be waiting for them at a small grassy airfield near Issaquah, where it would be sitting inconspicuously among three other helicopters, distinguished by being the least beat-up of the quartet. They should look for a sign advertising scenic tours of Mount Rainier.

Sam noticed the wind sock at the same time Tracy saw the sign and Max caught sight of the helicopters themselves. Simultaneously, all three of them said "There it is!"

Max drove slowly past a gas station and nearly deserted restaurant, then along the short gravel road that led to the airfield. Nobody seemed to be around. There were no parked cars; no one was waiting at the field for potential customers. Probably don't get too many drive-up customers in January. Max saw a group of trees at the northern edge of the rutted grass and drove over to it, as far from the helicopters as possible, then shut off the engine.

Without speaking, they got out and went to the trunk. The temperature was in the mid-forties, but each of them felt cold. Tracy opened her backpack and withdrew a belt laden with lock-picking tools, which she buckled around her waist. Then she slipped the backpack on and adjusted its straps. Max opened the trunk. He lifted out an insulated container filled with dry ice, checked for leaks and fiddled with the lid. He went through his jacket pocket to be sure he had the map, then closed the trunk and turned to face Sam and Tracy. They stood there for a few minutes looking across the field at the helicopters, lost in their own thoughts, their breath vaporizing in front of them.

"You ready for this?" Sam asked.

"I don't see why not," Max said. He picked up the container again and led the way.

Tracy surprised them by starting to run toward the helicopters. She circled them at a jog, then slapped the nose of the one resting slightly to the left of the others and began bouncing in place by its tail rotor. Sam recognized what she was doing—warming up—and thought it made good sense. But he was doing something different, moving inward, floating toward a still place at the center of his being, getting calmer and warmer as he imagined himself sitting at the copter's flight controls. He thought of Jessica, who at this moment was probably in her office at the back of the nursery, clacking away on the computer. He easily called up the smell and sound of the place, Zorro and Zeppo calling *Go for it!* in unison from their darkened room, Jessica with her legs folded lotus-style smiling as she began to shut down PER's security systems. He reached the helicopter and stopped, smiling. He took a deep breath, said Jessica's name to himself, then looked up and saw a gleam of light from the setting sun caught in the windshield. It looked as if the helicopter were winking at him.

Max and Tracy settled in their seats as Sam walked around the helicopter and went through his pre-flight inspection. He started at the pilot's door and ended at the pilot's door, moving methodically, using his hands as well as his eyes. Fuel cap screwed on tight, oil level OK in the gearbox, no leaks, no wrenches or screwdrivers lying on the skids, no holes in the tailboom, no obstructions. When he was first flying, back in the early 1970s, Sam used to circle his helicopters twice for each inspection, which drove the people he flew with nuts until he discovered a locked tail rotor that would surely have killed them.

Satisfied, he climbed into the cockpit. Max was studying the map spread across his lap. They had decided together that, in Sam's condition, it would be too difficult for him to fly the helicopter and be responsible for navigating at the same time. He might be able to do it, but the risks of making a mistake with the controls would be much greater. Max had gone over the map with Sam several times, marked it with yellow and pink highlighters, made notes in purple, and folded it in such a way that he could see the entire area they would be passing through with a minimum of confusion.

Tracy, seated behind them, was putting on and taking off her headset, adjusting it, untangling wires. Sam reached his right hand back toward her. She grabbed it with her left, squeezed, and reached her right hand out for Max. He didn't see it and had to be tapped on the arm before tearing himself away from his map and grabbing Tracy's hand. Sam then swivelled in his seat so that he could reach his left hand across to Max's right. They sat there, joined in a circle of hands, eyes shut, and no one said a word.

When Sam pressed the starter switch, he was relieved to hear the engine turn at once. Max and Tracy put their headsets on. When the engine was self-sustaining, Sam released the switch, put his own headset on, and popped a slice of ginger root in his mouth. The fuselage swayed back and forth like a bear waking up, then settled down. A fast vibration swept through the cabin.

Max flicked the switch on his microphone and said, "Are we going to disintegrate or what?"

"Relax."

"What?"

Sam leaned over and removed Max's hand from the microphone switch. "If you ever happen to be done talking, you need to release this switch to hear what anyone else is saying. What I said was relax. Everything's fine. In fact, she sounds positively Mozartian."

"I prefer *Don Giovanni*, myself," Max said. "Better overture."

The sun had now set and in the dim light Sam lifted the copter to a hover and turned it to face the wind. This was the part of the flight he was most worried about, when he had to do so much at once. For someone with his particular mix of neurological symptoms, performing any complex task was difficult. He'd spent hours thinking about whether he would be better off operating the controls instinctively, trusting his years of experience, or to slow himself down and make himself consider every move in detail. Flying a helicopter was a little bit of both, instinct balanced by reason, and he didn't feel fully comfortable with either anymore. Not when the risks were so high. Sam was glad he'd gone to sleep early and gone back to sleep after Jessica had left for work. He felt rested and as sharp as he was likely to feel as long as he was sick. The remainder would just have to take care of itself.

Power gauge looked fine. Temperature and pressure in the green, no warning lights, locks off the tail rotor cyclic. The helicopter seemed to want to turn to the right, but he compensated for that with extra pressure on his left pedal. Ok, keep it simple, he told himself. No fancy moves, nothing you don't have to do. If he had designed an evening for flying, he couldn't have done a better job. A steady, very mild breeze, low humidity, and cool but not close to freezing. Good enough light. He rested his forearm on his thigh and eased the stick forward. The nose dipped. Sam lifted the collective while gently increasing the throttle, pressed a bit with the left pedal, and they were in motion. He picked up speed and altitude. It felt fine. His wrists were nice and loose, he hadn't tried to twist the handle of the cyclic instead of the collective, hadn't pressed the wrong pedal, hadn't shut off the engine when he tried to talk over the mike.

"Next stop, PER headquarters," he said.

3.

Max clicked off the flashlight, flattened the map in his lap, pointed slightly to his right and said, "There it is."

"Already?" Sam checked his speed. He looked over to where Max was pointing, but kept the helicopter heading straight.

"Two o'clock. Triangular pattern of lights with nothing else around it."

Sam slowed and banked a bit. He looked past Max. "Got it."

"I thought it would take us longer to get there," Tracy said.

"This looks very good," Max said. "From up here, the place seems even more isolated than when we drove to it."

"OK, here we go."

Sam wanted to come in smoothly and land in one pass, as though he knew exactly where he was going. If their logic in planning this raid had been correct—and Sam knew this was no time to wonder about that—then he didn't think the guard would be suspicious if they put down without hesitation. It might not look good, however, if they looped around the building a few times, hovered too long, and generally looked as though this was their first airborne visit to the site.

Everything looked fine. The interstate was off to the left, the maze of county roads were about where he thought they would be, and he figured that cluster of lights in the near distance was probably the shopping center they had driven past. Sam was delighted with the way the helicopter responded to his touch, as though they were old lovers deeply familiar with each other despite a few years apart. He felt more confident with each move. They were low enough now to see the ground fairly well.

"Now that's strange," Max said.

"What?"

"Well, the fence is down."

"Down?"

"I don't see the perimeter fence. Maybe they're doing some re-modeling. Or maybe Rowland wants to get things ready for spring planting season."

"Where's the guard?" Tracy asked. "I see where the road turns in, but I don't see anybody there."

"Max?"

"I'll tell you what. Tracy's right." Max fumbled for his flashlight, leaned down to block the light and began poring over the map.

"I don't have much time here," Sam said, his voice steady. Should've been an astronaut, he thought. In that nice, relaxed voice, *Uh, mission control, we have a slight problem. I think we're on Mars instead of the moon.*

"She's right," Max said again. "It'll take us a little longer to get there." He flicked off the light again. "Because this is the wrong building."

Sam had already come to the same conclusion and was powering them back up. He banked left, then gained altitude and speed. The helicopter shuddered a bit, hitting some turbulence, and Sam climbed higher. "Hang on."

Sam struggled to balance things out again, get straight and level. The nose wobbled back and forth like an over-steered boat as he worked the pedals. After a few seconds, he had the unnecessary motion resolved. He eased back on the throttle and took a quick check of his gauges. "Smooth as silk."

"Cool," Tracy said, staring down.

Max looked the same as he had after tripping when he and Sam were running on the trails. But instead of dusting himself off, he adjusted his seat belt and said, "Sorry about that, folks."

"Just a dry run," Sam said. "I needed the practice anyway."

With the end of the flashlight gripped in his mouth, Max re-folded the map. He glanced quickly back and forth from the map to the ground. Sam had a good sense of where they were, at least in relation to the building they'd just buzzed, to downtown Seattle, I-405 and I-90, and Lake Washington. He could see Mercer Island and the floating bridges. He figured they were probably above the outskirts of Bellevue and not too far west of their destination. There was plenty of time to get reoriented. It had been an easy mistake to make.

"I see where we went wrong," Max said after a few moments. "I had trouble telling the yellow lines from the pink with this light. But I know where we are now."

"Of course you do," Sam said. "We're in a helicopter."

"Hey, the flight was getting boring anyhow. I can get us there from here."

Within five minutes, Max said they were getting close. This time Sam flew high over the target area, turned around and flew over it again before doubling back to begin descending. He was less worried now about calling attention to their presence than about another false landing.

Once they saw it, there was no mistaking PER's headquarters and particularly its lavish spread of trees. From above, the madrones formed a neat parallelogram he hadn't perceived from the ground. Looking down through his door, Sam thought he saw a circle drawn on the building's roof, a simple heliport pad that should make the landing relatively easy.

This part of a flight would always astonish him when he looked back on it later. Although hyper-aware of the least shift in engine sound, Sam would never remember a landing as loud or clamorous. Sensitive to every vibration, he recalled them all as one integrated movement, each shimmer having its purpose. Despite so many separate things to think about, a landing seemed the most fluid maneuver of all.

Sam decelerated to his landing approach speed and fixed his attention on the circle that was now easily visible on the roof. Holding a constant fifteen degree descent angle, he maintained his speed and direction as he neared the building. It seemed to open up to him, the facility's sprawling wings spread as if to offer them a warm welcome. Satisfied with his approach, Sam decreased the speed and began his landing flare, doing everything now by feel, keeping his eyes on the circle. He didn't want to shallow out or get too steep; nudging the controls with just a twitch of his fingers, he came into his hover and set the helicopter down precisely where he wanted to.

Max unbuckled his seat belt and turned toward the door. Sam reached for his shoulder, holding Max back as he began to shut down the engine. They had discussed this issue before, too. Sam didn't want to call attention to the temporary nature of their visit by keeping the engine running. Also, even though it would have been nice to lift off the very second Max and Tracy were finished with their part of the mission, Sam thought it was best not to risk having the blades whirring while they were nearby. Everyone had to be patient now.

Tracy leaned forward, eyes wide, breath shallow. Sam thought this must be what she looked like in the middle of a hard game of racquetball, just before she tried a killer serve or rocketed a shot inches over her opponent's shoulder. She passed the dry ice container to Max, then slipped her backpack on. With her eyes focused on something outside the helicopter, perhaps the door into the building, she blew on her hands for warmth and flexed her fingers.

"Nice job, Kiehl," Max said. He exhaled as though he'd been punched in the gut. "I knew you could do it."

"I'll be waiting for you," Sam said.

Max opened the door. "Just try to relax," he said, and slipped out onto the roof.

Tracy clutched at Sam's hand for a moment and squeezed him hard. "Sam."

"I know," he said.

Then Tracy hopped down. Crouched low, though the blades had stopped spinning, she reached for Max's hand and dashed with him to the door. Watching them, Sam thought that as soon as Tracy touched the doorknob they would know if Jessica, back in Tigard, had succeeded in fooling the card reader and disarming the security system. Jessica's confidence filled him, he didn't doubt that she could do what she'd said, but he kept his finger on the starter switch, just in case. Squinting, Sam stared at Tracy as she approached the door. She reached back to touch her toolbelt, then said something to Max, who put down the container, took the flashlight from his pocket and aimed a disk of light at the knob. Tracy turned it. When the door opened, she turned back toward the helicopter and flashed a thumbs-up gesture at Sam before following Max inside the building.

4.

They tip-toed down a short flight of stairs. With his flashlight turned off, Max opened the door at the bottom and looked both ways along the hallway. It was illuminated only by Exit signs spaced evenly along the wall. There was no evidence of activity, no one patrolling the corridors, no late-nighters. He unfolded Sam's rough sketch of the building's layout, flicked the flashlight back on and quickly compared what he saw before deciding to turn right.

After two steps, Tracy gripped his arm and said, "Max, wait!" Though she had whispered, the sound was like an alarm inside Max's brain. He dropped the dry ice container, yanked his arm away from her and spun toward Tracy with his hands raised, the edges of his palms ready to slice through the air. Tracy took a few steps back so that she was parallel with the door again and stood there with her hands on her hips, ignoring Max as though she'd had lots of practice dealing with loony men. She nodded firmly, lost in thought, while he took deep breaths and tried to relax.

"Sorry," he said. "A little tense."

Tracy continued nodding. "We have to go the other way first," she said.

Max took a last gulp of air and moved toward her, holding out

Sam's sketch. "Look, if Sam was even close with this thing, I think the storage room has to be back there."

"Yeah, I think you're right. But Doctor Rowland's office is this way."

"True. But they probably don't keep the deep freeze in the good doctor's office. At least not yet."

"We need to turn on his light."

"His light is not going to do us much good if we have to be over at the other end of the building."

"For the guard, not for us. He might not be suspicious of the helicopter landing, but I was thinking he might get concerned if it didn't seem like Doctor Rowland was really around here afterwards, you know? We turn on his light so it looks like he's working, then turn it off before we go."

Max smiled at her and said, "Very nice touch." He took another look at Sam's sketch. "It should be about a two minute round trip, at most. Let's go." Leaving the dry ice container behind, they headed for Rowland's office, which overlooked the front of the building so that the old man could look out at his gardens.

They made their way back down the hallway after turning on Rowland's light. Max snatched the container as they went by, dreading how heavy it would be after they loaded it with bottles. They both heard the sound at the same time and froze. Max snapped off the flashlight.

"What was that?" Tracy whispered from just behind Max's ear.

"Don't know."

"There's a door open, I think. Right there, just before the hallway bends."

Max saw it too. There didn't seem to be a light on in the room, but he could see in the faint light from an Exit sign that the door was open. Someone was moving around inside, but far back in the room, judging from the faintness of the noise.

"What should we do?" Tracy whispered.

"I'm not sure yet. Whoever it is in there, he's awfully busy." Max held his breath and took a few soft steps toward the room. Tracy stayed with him.

They took a few more steps and stopped again. Max put down the dry ice container. The sound of movement continued from the room. Someone walking around, for sure. And papers being shuffled? The scratching of a pen? It was impossible to tell.

"Maybe we could just sneak past," Max said. "He certainly seems preoccupied."

They were shoulder-to-shoulder next to the door now, backs pressed against the wall. Max peeked around the jamb and as he did, a shriek came from inside the room. Something whizzed past his head and smacked against the corridor wall. Max jerked his head back, stumbling against Tracy, who in turn stumbled against the container.

Before either could speak, the shrieking intensified and another projectile hit the wall in the precise spot as the first one. Max and Tracy backed up a few steps. There was another splat against the wall.

"He's got pretty good aim," Tracy whispered.

"For a monkey," Max said. "In a cage."

They both sank down to the floor and spent a few moments calming themselves. The monkey continued to shriek, but not to throw anything more. From the odor, it was not difficult to figure out what he'd been throwing at them.

"You think the guard can hear him?" Tracy asked.

"Probably. But my guess is he's used to it. I'm sure our friend here does a lot of this. Let's go."

They dashed past the door, hearing the monkey's voice shoot up an octave as his final toss missed them and he began to jump against the bars of his cage. They hurried toward the lab where the deep freeze was housed, not wanting to waste any more time. The noise from the monkey's room followed them.

"It should be the second door past the men's room," Max said. "On the left."

A large handle opened the door. Max dropped the container again and started to move inside, but Tracy grabbed his arm.

"Take it easy. There's probably equipment all over the place."

From the doorway, Max scanned the room with his flashlight. Tracy had been right. The room was littered with tables and stools.

Everywhere they looked there was fancy equipment, much of it in towering stacks. He saw a half dozen computer screens, tubing and wires snaking over every surface, storage racks, cabinets, shelves. Everything seemed laden with glass, breakable with one wrong breath. Hanging from the ceiling was a purplish geodesic dome roughly the size of a soccer ball. It was made of interconnecting plastic forms that resembled small wrenches, and as Max shifted the beam of his flashlight several more floated into view. His beam caught a label: Carbon 60.

"Groovy decor," he said. He moved the light back across the tables.

"The place is a mess," Tracy said. "It's like my sons' room, only theirs smells better."

Max continued probing the space with his light. "We should be in spacesuits," he said. "No telling what we're being exposed to."

"Was that the freezer?"

"Where?"

Tracy took the flashlight and shone it to their immediate left, just behind the door. They walked over to the freezer. Stainless steel, wide as a small yacht, the thing came up to their waists and rumbled from somewhere deep under its middle.

"Let's hope this really is the freezer," Max said. "Otherwise, I don't want to think about what might be inside."

"Locked," Tracy said. She lifted the lock with her index finger and let it slap back down against the freezer's wall. "A Medeco padlock over a hasp."

"Can you open it?"

"In my sleep." Tracy reached quickly to the belt on her hip like a gunfighter and drew out a small probe. She knelt before the freezer. "Give me a steady light."

"Take your time," Max said. "But hurry up."

Tracy worked the probe into the lock's cylinder and got the feel of the pin-tumblers. "I could probably do it with this, but I'd bet anything my old pass key would work. This is a pretty half-assed attempt to keep anybody out. Pardon my French." She unhooked a ring of keys from the belt.

"Wonder why they bothered," Max said, crouched behind her shoulder.

"Maybe for the monkey." She jiggled the key and the shackle sprung open. "Next problem."

When they opened the freezer, vapor poured out as though they had stumbled onto a witch's kettle. The interior was full of bottles laid flat like fine wines and stacked on a series of metal shelves. They waved their hands to clear the air and study the freezer's contents.

"I hope all this doesn't set off the smoke detectors," Max said. "Or maybe Jessica nixed them when she closed down the security system." He reached into the freezer and again Tracy grabbed his arm.

"Your gloves."

He turned to face Tracy and put his arms on her shoulders. "Where would I be without you?" Max said.

"Right here, only with Sam, and your hand stuck to the ice."

He put on her gloves and reached into the freezer, lifting out a bottle. As they'd thought, no drug name was written on the bottle. There was only a label with PER printed across the top and a series of numbers underneath.

"It says 662d," Max said.

"And we want 793a." She stood on her toes to peer into the freezer. "You think there's any order to how they're stored?"

"Let's hope." He reached down two shelves and withdrew a bottle. "415, no letter. Oh boy."

It took a few minutes for them to go through the freezer and locate all the bottles labeled 793a. There were three shelves devoted to them, a good hundred fifty bottles. While Tracy held the flashlight, Max removed twenty and placed them on the nearest table. Together he and Tracy studied the labels and contents carefully. The bottles were too frosted to see the contents clearly, but they didn't think they could detect any significant differences. The labels seemed identical. They couldn't see a code number.

"Time for the taste test?" Tracy asked.

"Unless we want to taste every bottle, we've got to see how they've indicated placebo or drug. Something has to be different from one to the other because they're all stacked together."

"Maybe Kate was wrong, you know? Maybe they only store the drug here, and pack up the fake stuff at the last minute. I mean, it's only salt water, they could do that in the shipping department."

"Wait," Max said. "Look at this." He picked up two bottles and shone the light on the lids. He pointed to a removable plastic dot on their tops.

"One's white, one's blue," Tracy said. "The technicians at each clinic must remove them when they prepare the bottles for infusion, before passing them on to the nurses." She folded her arms across her chest.

"Now it's time for the taste test. Did you bring the propane torch?"

Tracy nodded but didn't take off her backpack. "Maybe we should try something less dramatic first. I mean, in the kitchen you could bust a frozen glass if you took a flame to it."

"Makes sense." Max took one of each kind of bottle over to the sink. He looked into the basin and turned around to face Tracy. "I'm not sure we should use this, though. It's been cleaned and dried already."

"We passed a bathroom two doors down."

Max shone the light on his watch, then nodded. "OK, but we need to hurry." They left their things in the lab room and took the two bottles and the flashlight back down the hall.

Tracy stopped outside the bathroom door. "But it's a men's room," she said.

Max laughed and pushed the door open with his shoulder. "We just broke into the company's office building and you're worried about going into the men's room?"

"Somehow this feels worse."

"You can wait out here, if you'd prefer."

Max went into the room. Tracy waited outside for a few seconds, then opened the door and was nearly blinded by the light. Max kicked the door shut.

"I didn't know the light would be on."

"Well, there's no outside window and I thought I had a closed door behind me." He returned to the sink, where warm water was filling up the basin in which the bottles floated. As the water coming in heated up, he swirled it over the top of the bottles.

"I don't know about this," Tracy said.

"I won't tell anyone you came in here, all right?"

"That's not what I meant. I just don't know if we'll be able to tell for sure about the drug. Suppose we end up stealing a cooler full of salt water?"

Max lifted one of the bottles from the water and held it by its neck directly under the tap. "Good point. Let's wait and see how different the two are. It could be that the white and blue dots don't mean anything, or they could just indicate different batches of the drug. If we're not sure, we'll take as much stuff as we can carry and ask Kate to help us when we get home."

"If she will. I don't know whose side she's on anymore."

"Yours, Trace," Max said. "Yours and Sam's and the rest of you. Even I'm sure of that." He shook the bottle and saw that enough of its contents had melted to allow them to have an ample taste. He handed it to Tracy, held the second bottle under the tap for a minute, shook it, turned off the tap and handed the bottle to Tracy too. "Bottoms up."

Tracy unscrewed the lid with the white dot. She sniffed the contents, then put the lip to her mouth and tilted her head back.

"If you say *nice bouquet*, I'm leaving," Max said.

"It doesn't taste like anything."

"Ok, no problem, try the other one."

Tracy repeated the process. As soon as the liquid entered her mouth, she started to gag. She leaped over to the sink and spit the stuff out.

"Bingo," Max said.

They shut off the light and ran back to the lab. Max sorted through the bottles he'd removed earlier, keeping only those with blue dots, picking out others till he had sixteen. Tracy wrapped each in a sheet of the morning newspaper stashed in her backpack. Together they placed the wrapped bottles in the dry ice container and lined them up top-to-bottom to reduce the jostling.

When they finished, Max shone the light around the room to check for signs of their presence. Nothing seemed obviously out of place in the mayhem of the room.

"Set?" Max asked.

"Set."

They ran back down the hall. Max struggled to keep the container from swaying too much.

"Trace, maybe you could run ahead and shut off Rowland's light. I'll meet you at the door to the roof."

She was there before him, holding the door open. Then she ran ahead of him up the stairs and opened the roof door. She made sure it was shut, ran ahead to the helicopter and yanked open the door.

"Holy shit!" Sam nearly vaulted through his window. He had been fast asleep, slumped in his seat, held upright by his seat belt.

Tracy hopped in and turned to help Max with the container. He lifted and shoved as Tracy grabbed the sides and pulled. They got it settled in back, then plopped into their seats and put on their belts. Picking up their headsets, they leaned back and simultaneously released enormous sighs. Then there was a long moment of silence as Max and Tracy tried to catch their breath and all three of them looked at one another.

Sam, still rattled, examined his friends' sweaty, tired faces. Max was smiling. His lips moved but no words came out. It was clear to Sam that things had gone well. He turned back to congratulate Tracy. Her eyes were closed, her mouth was open as though she were struggling for breath, and she was covered in tears as she cried silently, her small body convulsed by huge sobs.

"Trace, are you OK?" Sam said.

Keeping her eyes squeezed tightly shut, still sobbing, she gave them a thumbs-up sign and began nodding her head. Max reached around and patted her hands where they were clasped in her lap.

"She was amazing," Max said. "Let's get this rig airborne."

Thirteen

1.

Kate McCabe was through. She was done, spent, and that's final. Absolute, settled, no bones about it. Finished. Out of there.

Where did she *ever* get the idea that she belonged in clinical research? This was all Marty's fault. Fong was so gung-ho, always yakking about how he had to help these people get better, talking about *doing* something for once instead of always failing to help. Marty believed this study was his chance to push medicine forward, to discover something important, putting what he knew as a clinician on the line. The beauty of the clinician turned researcher. Kate came along with him gladly.

Fool.

She should have known better. She'd been around too many fired-up, idealistic, do-good docs in her life to allow herself to fall for that line. She felt, honest-to-God, like a medical floozy, an easy lay, here-take-me. A woman who blithely left a fine position in Infectious Diseases, the place she knew she belonged, because some guy whispered magic words in her ear. Research, discovery, risk. She should have protected herself and Marty, both. Protected all of them, all those patients who had been coming up to see them for the last few years with this miserable illness of theirs. But she was slow on the uptake. She let herself get sweet-talked. When Kate thought of the last year, she thought of fat black notebooks bursting with misinformation. Disinformation.

Kate didn't believe Marty knew what the company was up to. They paid his salary and dictated the final form of the protocol, but that wasn't unusual. They had a drug that looked promising. He never suspected a thing.

Sitting on her porch looking out toward the Cascade foothills, Kate remembered feeling wary the first time she saw the forms PER wanted her to use for collecting patient data. There was no space for self-reported symptoms. The company would collect plenty of blood, measure all sorts of signs, do imaging and labs galore, but they were not prepared to find out what their subjects were feeling. They wanted no early warning, nothing in writing about the odd tingle or twitch or rash or fatigue. They wanted what they wanted, and every time Sam showed up for a pregnancy test, every time Molly rattled off a thousand complaints that Kate had no place to record, she felt abused. When she began attaching "Site Administrator's Notes" to the weekly summaries, PER had told her to stop. So she did the next best thing. She compiled notes, ordered a few extra toxicity tests on the bloods and kept a folder of her own. You didn't need higher math to see what was going on.

Kate shuddered and put down her mug. It was over. Well, almost over. She'd already accepted the offer from another hospital and was leaving Cascade-Kennedy altogether. She was going back to patient care, back even to Infectious Diseases, and had given her notice at the school this morning.

So she was finished. One foot out the door, the other foot trailing a month behind, and her heart still stranded somewhere in between. She needed to see her little rats one more time.

2.

Jessica worked on Sam's back and shoulders for forty minutes. Muscle spasms had twisted his neck, causing his head to rotate and tilt at a peculiar angle, like a lid incorrectly screwed on a jar.

"This must be where you held your tension," Jessica said. She pressed her thumbs deep into the muscle and Sam groaned. "It's a bad one."

"But I wasn't tense at all," he said. "I was so calm it was eerie."

"You might be able to convince Max and Tracy of that, but not me. These hands cannot be fooled."

Sam figured his warped neck was simply the outward evidence of how his inner organs had gotten spiraled around themselves. He imagined that the conduits of his nervous and circulatory systems had become as contorted as a double helix, that his liver and spleen had switched locations and were only now finding their ways back, that his brain had gotten pureed by the vibrations of the helicopter. The PER adventure had temporarily spun everything completely out of control. The only flaw with the analogy was that, regardless of his renewed pain, exhaustion, and confusion, on the deepest inner levels he felt wonderful.

He had, however, been virtually bedridden for the last three days. During the first two, he'd slept for sixteen hours each, and his greatest exertion had been talking on the telephone. He'd gone over all the details of the raid with Jessica, and she'd filled him in on her success in tampering with PER's inventory. It turned out that Max and Tracy had gotten out of the building with nine minutes to spare before the security system came back online. Jessica wondered why they'd cut it so close. Sam was impressed by how much time they'd had left to spare. Before hanging up, Sam told her that he'd eaten two slices of rainbow bread for breakfast when he meant cinnamon-raisin bread, and she'd wished him sweet, colorful dreams.

Later in the day, he'd talked to Tracy, encouraging her to begin infusing the drug as soon as possible. She said she'd already spoken with Kate. She and Wally would be getting their first lesson in an hour. Throughout the evening, Laurel Blackburn, Alice Hardy, and Hannah Price had each talked to Tracy and then called to congratulate Sam on the success of their visit to PER's headquarters. He wished fewer people knew about what they'd done but figured the group had a right to share in what was happening with Tracy.

Sam had spent a few hours in his recliner trying to read a book about computer hackers. He thought it might give him a firmer grasp of how Jessica had lived during the years before he knew her. But he couldn't concentrate and ended up sleeping most of the afternoon. He did manage to feed himself breakfast at noon, then napped till four and walked two blocks to the market for enough precooked food to offer Jessica a light dinner.

She arrived after work, eager to see what he looked like in the wake of the raid, and found him standing by the door unable to turn his head up for a kiss. She touched his neck and ran her hand down the middle of his back.

"You look terrible," she said. "Let's work on that torticollis."

"How'd you know I bought pasta for dinner?"

"Torticollis, Sam. It's what's wrong with your neck. Let's work on it right now; dinner can wait."

He tried to shrug. The motion made him wince. "I don't remember hurting my neck. Must be whiplash from Max's driving. We got home from Seattle in about an hour and ten minutes."

Since she didn't have her massage table with her, Jessica suggested that they use Sam's bed instead. He took off his clothes and lay like a curlicue on top of the spread. She knelt next to him and from time to time straddled him as she worked on a particularly tender spot. She spoke in his ear, murmuring in a way she never had when they were merely therapist and client. As the spasm began to ease, Jessica tried to help Sam figure out when he had first noticed the pain.

"In the car on the ride home."

"Can you be more specific?"

"A mile and a half past the Centralia exit."

"What I meant was how the pain manifested itself. Suddenly or gradually? In the neck immediately, or did it radiate from somewhere else?"

Sam shook his head. "I just started to notice an ache. The kind of thing where you want to lean your head back against the car seat and shut your eyes, nothing crippling. It wasn't this bad till yesterday."

"Interesting. You didn't pull a fast getaway from the roof or anything like that? A sudden start or stop?"

Sam started to shake his head, but it barely moved. "Sleek as cream."

"All right. Then tell me how the flight back from PER to the airfield went. Maybe that's the key."

"It was mostly uneventful," Sam said. "Well, there was one little incident that struck me as being outside the normal flight plan, but I don't know if it was enough to redesign a person's neck like this. At the time, I didn't want to mention anything about it. Let's just say I saw something very strange on return trip."

Jessica didn't say anything. She finished her work on his trapezius muscles and bent over to kiss him behind each ear. Sam took that for an *ummm hmmm.*

"Lights," he said. "I saw these multicolored lights flashing and whirling off to the west."

"You mean over Seattle?"

"No, that was the strange part. It was definitely over the water, pretty far out in the Sound."

"A ferry, maybe."

"Not unless ferries can fly."

Jessica lifted his left arm out to the side and dug her fingers into the mass behind his shoulder blade. "There is simply no way," she said, "that you're going to get me to ask if it was a UFO. None at all."

"You can see why I didn't want to say anything to Max and Tracy. They'd been through enough already."

Jessica was silent for a minute. Then she asked, "Do you believe in UFOs, Sam?"

"You mean flying saucers from outer space? Little beings that whisk people away for dark experiments?"

"And artificial insemination."

"I don't, actually. But I'm beginning to believe there's something out there that we don't understand. A force, or forces maybe. Trying to teach us something, or straighten us out before we get more lost than we already are."

"You think that's what the lights were about?"

"I know it wasn't a flying ferry. I know it wasn't an airplane or another copter either. You know what it felt like? It felt like something from inside my own head making itself visible out there."

"Remember that time you told me about seeing a hole in this painting behind me? You said it flashed and burst. It had all sorts of blinking shapes inside." She probed the exact center of his spasming muscle, which seemed to make the same lights explode behind his eyes. "That's probably what happened up there, don't you think?"

Sam didn't answer right away. Part of it was the pain, but part of it was uncertainty about what he wanted to say. "It was an alien experience, I'll tell you that much."

When the massage was done, Sam turned over onto his back to look up at Jessica. She was still straddling his middle. He raised his hands toward her and she caught them, twining her fingers through his, then leaning down to kiss him.

"I like what's happening to us," Sam said, drawing her hands down.

"And what's that?"

"You don't know what *that* is yet?"

She moved her hands. "That I know. I was asking what you thought was happening to us."

"I think we need to be together," Sam said.

Jessica smiled and shut her eyes as though hoping to hide what they might show. "Speak for yourself," she whispered. Then she opened her eyes to see Sam squinting hard, trying to figure out her tone. "I think we already are. For good."

3.

Tracy wore a mud-stained orange sweatsuit that said MARSH above the heart and looked six sizes too large for her. She'd left the green-patterned laces of her green high-top sneakers untied. Sam lay back in his recliner thinking she looked like an eighth grader costumed for the school play as a carrot. She stood next to him, barely able to contain her energy, and pointed at a book she'd laid open in his lap.

"You have to see whether each pair of addresses is alike or different. See here: 405 South Redwing and 450 South Redwing, they're different. The numbers are turned inside-out." She held her watch up to study the second hand. "OK, I'll give you exactly forty-five seconds to try the first ten. Ready, set, go!"

Sam looked down at the pages spread before him. All he could see was a blur of numbers and names.

7391 Alameda St 7391 Alameda St

8104 Stonington Ter 8104 Stonington Trl

3642 McCorkadale Ct 3462 McCorkadale Ct.

His eyes began to drift, then slowly close. Tracy was studying her watch and making a buzzing sound with her lips, totally absorbed, her lithe body quivering in place as she waited beside him. The vivid color of her sweatsuit hurt his eyes. He could see and feel it even with them closed.

"Time's up!" she shrieked.

Sam's arms and legs shot out sideways and the chair jerked back a few more loud notches. "Jeez, Trace. I must have dozed off."

She took the book from him and plopped down on the floor. "Same. Different. Different. Same. Same. Different. It's easy, Sam. I was much faster this morning than last week. Don't you think that's a good sign?"

"You're doing great." He cranked down the footrest, sat up straight, offered a lopsided smile. "But it sounds like you've been around Eli Moskowitz too long. No kidding, you feel better already?"

Tracy pulled up her sleeve to reveal the catheter that Kate had installed for her. She peeled back the adhesive tape holding gauze over the crook of her elbow and showed Sam the small opening that protruded from her vein. In his dazed state, Sam thought it looked like a hollow and headless worm. He got the creeps just looking at it.

"This drug's magic," Tracy said. "I can feel myself getting better by the hour. Wally can hook me up to the stuff and I just lie there watching the soaps while it drips in. But we're going to take this gizmo out tomorrow; it really bothers me and I can't keep it clean with the kids and the cats and all the housework and everything. The kids call my catheter *Mom's cat heater*. Get it? So anyway, Wally's going to have to stick me each time from now on. He says he can do it. I didn't even know he was a paramedic once, before he met me. It was when he was going part-time to Portland Community College trying to become a veterinary tech or something. But he dropped out, of course. Hated dogs. Make a long story short, he says he knows how to stick a needle in a vein. Run a line, he calls it, the big showoff. It's like he's thrilled to have something he can do to help me, now he's sweet as candy corn. I don't know. Maybe that's all it was before? Kate was convinced, though. I mean, about Wally being able to stick me right. Run a line, they call it. So I have to go out and buy some sterile supplies after I leave here, and we're going to try it on Monday for the first time. Wish me luck, Sam."

"Good luck." He left the recliner and sat next to Tracy on the floor. He removed the book from her hands, leafed through it without noticing much, and laid it aside. "I'm curious about something. The drug was frozen solid when we took it from PER. I remember Kate once told me that the technician used a converted '57 Chevy Impala engine block to warm and agitate the stuff when they made it ready for infusing. So how the hell do you get it ready at home?"

"Yeah, she told me that one too, though I'm not sure I really believe her. What Wally does is cook the bottle on top of the stove like Jiffy Pop till there's no more ice crystals left. He warms it slow and shakes the pan the whole time. Then we wrap it in a wet sock while it hangs on the hook. Sure smells strange, but that's probably because we use Wally's ratty old socks from when he used to be a welder. It's fun. He even sits there and watches the soaps with me while the stuff drips in."

Sam was glad to hear the way she was talking about Wally. He was so used to hearing her complain about her husband that he'd never wanted to meet him. Maybe that could change.

"So is Kate taking out the catheter, or does Wally get to try that too?"

"I go over to Kate's house after I pick up the supplies after I leave here after we're through visiting. Whew. Getting better is a full-time job."

Sam nodded. "You're good at it."

"Oh, Sam, I'm so sorry. I shouldn't have said that."

"Don't worry about it. Besides, you're right, it is a full-time job. So is being sick. And there's a point at which it's important to be good at that, too."

4.

Tracy's next appointment with Eli Moskowitz was scheduled for Wednesday afternoon. She'd considered canceling it, since she was using the drug again and wasn't sure it would be compatible with Eli's methods, but Sam convinced her to do both. What Eli offered, he said, would only strengthen her further and keep her open to what the drug could do. And the drug would hasten the balancing that Eli sought.

"You could use some balancing yourself," Tracy had said. "Why not make an appointment right after mine?"

"You see him downtown. I always go to his office here in the neighborhood."

"Oh, like that really makes a difference. You think he's got weaker needles downtown or something?"

So Sam went with her on Wednesday. Tracy picked him up ten minutes before their scheduled appointments, sped downtown, found a parking spot on a part of Broadway where parking is never available, and had them in the waiting room precisely at 2:00. Sam settled into the cracked leather sofa to wait his turn and thought he needed to be a whole lot better before he drove anywhere with Tracy or Max again. Then he fell asleep.

He awoke to Eli crouched in front of him feeling his pulses.

Eli's face was turned toward the receptionist's desk and his eyes were closed as he squeezed Sam's wrist.

"Don't say anything," Eli whispered before Sam could speak.

"How'd you know I was awake?"

"Shah!"

Sam saw Tracy sitting across the room poring over the literature Eli had given her, a small box of pills in one hand and a long sheet of paper covered with miniature writing in the other. She caught his eye and held the paper as though she thought he could read it from where he sat.

"It's in Chinese," she said. "Isn't that adorable?"

"You know what I think, Sam? I think you could use a real detoxification. This is what you're ready for now, and much sooner than I would have guessed too. That's a very good sign. You know about Panchakarma?"

"Oh, sure. The new restaurant that serves curried burritos. It's over on Tenth, isn't it?"

"Very funny. It's an ancient Ayurvedic practice, and just the ticket for you. They dislodge toxins from your cells, which you know you've got plenty of from this disease of yours that's like a toxic spill in the first place, and then they flush them out of the body. Bing-bang-boom, you're cleaned up and you get a chance to start over. Friend of mine runs a clinic in northeast Portland."

"Eli, tell me how they dislodge these toxins. And more to the point, how they flush them out. I especially don't like the sound of that one."

"Oil and heat, basically. You eat what they tell you to for a week ahead of time, then for five days they work on you. Trust me, you'll love it. There's various kinds of hot-oil massages, steam baths, enemas, aroma therapy. Opens you right up."

"You know I can't regulate my body temperature. Hot oil, steam baths. And enemas are one of my special phobias. The whole thing sounds to me like torture, not therapy."

"Come on inside and lie down, Sam. When we're done I'll give you some literature on Panchakarma. Next week, you'll call up begging me to let you try it."

After his session with Eli, Sam and Tracy walked across Broadway for a cup of tea. Sam hadn't been downtown in a long time and hadn't sat in the square since before he got sick. One corner of the square had been built as a small natural amphitheater. There was a plaque embedded in the ground to identify the exact spot on which to stand in order to hear your voice vastly amplified. A whisper became audible ten feet away, normal speech ricocheted back as an oration, but none of it was audible elsewhere on the square.

Hot tea gripped in their hands, Sam and Tracy sat on the rim of the amphitheater watching a group of kids, skateboards held under their arms like schoolbooks, singing together in close harmony. Their sweet voices boomed and echoed through the area. When the kids skated away, Sam got up and stood on the plaque facing Tracy. They were virtually alone there, though soon the square would fill with workers heading home for the night. He took a long sip of the tea, enjoying its warmth, and suddenly found himself talking. It was unplanned, all of it, Andy and Vic, the shock of being sick, how much he missed climbing and running, his fear and pain, his happiness now with Jessica, his pride in Tracy, but once he began he could not stop. Tracy watched him more than she listened, but he could see that she understood everything he needed to say.

5.

During the next week, Sam's health gradually approached the level it was before the raid. His strength returned in waves, washing a flood of well-being over him before retreating, rendering him utterly depleted, leaving—as a kind of stain on the sand—only the memory of what strength had felt like.

He began taking early morning walks along the river again. Several times he set out confidently and walked too far, so that he could not make it home without resting for an hour on the bank. Behind where he sat this morning, in the window of a condo, an elderly couple perched side-by-side on their couch reading the newspaper in the morning light, ignoring the view. Sam watched a crew of scullers pulling south, their eight oars stroking and feathering in unison as they cut through the calm surface of the river. He knew they would not be cold, even though they were running dead center on the water, and he envied them their wind-borne laughter. Soon two wet-suited men on jet skis roared past the scull and looped through one another's wakes. Their racket grated on Sam's nerves, but he forced himself to sit there and listen. The frantic scream seemed to him like the river's hidden current at last being given its voice, a sudden rage bursting the surface calm and then fading as the skiers continued downriver. On the island across from where he sat, Sam saw the evergreens and remembered that great blue herons nested in their tops. It would be lovely to land there, he thought, watching one of the birds labor up out of the shallows and head across the river. When Sam finally managed to get home, he turned off the phone's ringer and spent the afternoon in dreamless sleep.

Throughout the week, his only company had come from Jessica, who stayed with him every other night after work. He didn't feel well enough yet to travel by bus to the nursery, as he had been doing before the raid, so Jessica drove into Portland to see him. She would have come every night, but she was too busy with final preparations for the new facility she'd designed. It would begin operating late next month.

On Thursday night, Sam and Jessica were curled together on his couch after dinner. They planned to watch a video Andy had sent. It contained a gig Navel Lint had done a few weeks ago in Los Angeles, and Andy said he'd added a personal message at the end.

"Did you tell him that you didn't use his music as a soundtrack?"

"He understood. It was all I could do to keep the helicopter aloft. Besides, Tracy and Max chattered so much we wouldn't have been able to listen anyway."

Sam reached for the remote control, but Jessica caught his hand and brought it to her lips. She held it there for a few seconds while looking off toward the window.

"What do you think he'll say?" she asked.

"Probably give an update on the band, wish me well with the raid, tell me to get some rest. Stuff like that."

"I meant about us. What will he say when you tell him about us?"

"He'll be elated. He knows who you are and what you did for me all those years. And he knows our relationship has been changing."

"It might confuse him, you know. He might think there was something going on before, when I was coming over to work on you. It could seem pretty sordid, actually."

Sam hadn't thought of that. Jessica had been such a consummate professional about her massage, and had helped him so much, he just assumed everyone knew there was nothing more to it. At least not in the way she was suggesting now.

"He came over once right in the middle of a massage, remember? Walked right in the front door and almost tripped over the table. He saw what went on. He knows."

"I hope so."

"Besides, he's a pretty innocent kid. I don't think it would ever occur to him that we had something going on before."

He flicked on the video tape. Jessica sprawled out across the couch with her head in Sam's lap and her feet dangling over the arm. The first image to appear on screen was of Andy in a muscle shirt, his body gleaming with sweat, a bandana over his hair, flailing away at his drums. Even Sam could see that he shimmered with sexual energy. In front of him, Kayla in a matching muscle shirt and bandana met his stare and gyrated as she sang Andy's lyrics: *move me through the same old same old/I say take me past the threshold/won't you touch me where I'm pure gold/move me through the same old same old.*

"Yeah," Jessica said, "I can see he's a pretty innocent kid."

They watched the hour-long tape, which ended as it had begun, in the middle of a song. The screen went blank for a moment, then flickered on again to show Andy sitting at the edge of a stage with his feet dangling. He wore an old sweater that Sam remembered buying for him two or three years ago, when Andy had lived in an old southeast Portland house with poor insulation, ineffective heating, and thin windows, and Sam was afraid the boy might freeze to death one night over his canned spaghetti. Holding drumsticks in his hands and tapping steadily against the stage, Andy spoke straight into the camera, with the shy smile that always stopped Sam's heart.

"Hey, Dad. Hope you liked what you saw. Being on the road sucks, but Navel Lint's coming together pretty good and word's getting out. The place was packed last night, as you probably could tell." He looked above the camera and stopped talking, then nodded and raised his voice. "Listen, I want to let you know that I miss you and worry about you. If I'd said some friends of mine were going to borrow a helicopter to break into a drug company's labs, you'd have a cow."

"I like this kid," Jessica said.

The phone rang just as Andy had folded his arms across his chest and lowered his head, gazing up at the camera in a pose that looked precisely like his mother. Jessica reached for the remote control and froze the picture while Sam walked into the kitchen to answer the phone.

"Can I talk to Sam Kiehl please?"

"This is Sam."

"Well, when do you expect him back?"

"I said this *is* Sam. He's back."

"Can I talk to him?"

"Who is this?"

"Wallace Marsh."

Sam didn't recognize the name. "Look, are you trying to sell me something? Because I never accept phone solicitations. Sorry." He started to hang up.

"Hey!" Wally's voice went up a full octave. "Don't hang up."

"What is it then? I'm busy."

"When Sam Kiehl gets back, you could tell him that Tracy is in the hospital, all right?"

"Wally?" Sam paused, putting the name together right, then grasping what he'd heard. "Wally, this is Sam Kiehl. What's going on?"

"Man, why didn't you say so?"

Sam realized that Wally must be upset and frightened. Also that he probably didn't relish the idea of talking to someone that his wife may have confided in all throughout the last year. But still, he was beginning to appreciate why Tracy had been so frustrated with the man.

"What's wrong with Tracy?"

"It's that damn drug you went up and stole. The stuff's pure poison. It's toxic as mine talings, if you ask me."

"Did she have a reaction to her infusion, is that it? Sometimes she used to get real itchy and blotchy after an infusion, but it usually passed. We'd sit and drink some tea, she'd be fine in an hour."

"I know all about the famous tea cure. But this is something else. They think she's going to lose her hand." Wally sneezed so hard into the phone that Sam felt as though he'd gotten drenched in the spray. "Exactly what am I supposed to do with a crippled wife and two screaming kids?"

"Wally, I can be at the hospital in about ten minutes, if that would help. You can go home with the kids. Just tell me what happened, OK?"

"We were giving her the infusion this morning, everything going just fine, then all of a sudden she says it's burning real bad. Her hand turns red and everything. Looks like one of her veins must have moved when I was running the line. We missed. The stuff went right into the tissues instead of her vein."

"Oh, God."

"Well it wasn't my fault! I drew up some blood as soon as the needle was set, so I know we were in her vein to start with. Maybe she moved after that, or maybe the vein just closed up on us. Anyway, she felt a lot of pain so we stopped the infusion about halfway through. Then we kept thinking it's just an allergic reaction, like you said. It'd pass. By afternoon, her whole arm was swole up right to her neck, so we went in to see Fong. Guy's out to lunch, in more ways than one. Gets back at 3:00 and by then her arm's like a damn balloon."

"What did he do, drain it?"

"Yeah, but they think it may be too late. They'll know better in the morning. Tell me something, all right?"

"Sure."

"You see a lot of one-armed postal carriers?"

6.

Tracy's left arm, swathed in bandages, dangled from a series of hooks and wires above her hospital bed. All that was visible were the fingertips, livid with Betadine.

She looked pale and shrunken, barely making an impression within the sheets, as though exposure to the direct toxicity of the drug had eroded her core. Sam understood it was probably because the room and special bed were so large, but he couldn't get over how fragile she seemed.

Wally stood underneath the television mounted high in the corner, putting as much space as possible between his body and Tracy's bed while still remaining inside the room. He had tucked himself back where the walls met and, with his shoulders hunched to fit even more closely into the angle, stared resolutely out the window.

Sam walked over, identified himself and shook Wally's hand. They stood together looking out of the window with Wally refusing to speak. Sam noticed that they were exactly opposite the Research Department. He thought he could see movement inside the windows, then turned away and approached the left side of Tracy's bed.

"It felt like acid, Sam. Not that I ever felt acid inside me or anything, but that's what it must be like. I could feel every single blood corp-suckle floating through my veins and it was like they'd each sprouted feathers with pins at their tips. Drove me crazy. Then, whoosh, all of a sudden I got fevery. I think that must have been when the stuff actually reached my brain."

"What brain?" Wally grumbled. He pushed himself away from

the wall and stalked out of the room, turning right toward the elevator. Neither Sam nor Tracy spoke again until they heard the muted dinging of the elevator's bell and the silence that followed it.

"What does Fong say?"

"He says it's too soon to say anything. Tomorrow is very important. Do you believe he said that? You're telling me tomorrow is important! I mean, I didn't really think I'd see tomorrow there for a while."

"You've got plenty of tomorrows coming, Trace." Sam put his hand on her left shoulder and squeezed gently. "But that's it? He didn't give you a prognosis?"

"That's it for now. Oh, yeah, he did say one other thing: *Where the hell did you get it?* Like I'm really going to tell Doctor Fong, right?"

"Tell me what?" Fong said from the doorway. Neither of them had heard him come in. He approached Tracy's bed, avoiding her arm, and reached for her left hand in greeting. Then he turned and said, "Hello, Sam."

How long had he been there? "Marty."

Fong gently peeled back the bandages over Tracy's injured hand and touched the fingers. Tracy winced. He felt along her forearm, over the elbow, up toward the shoulder. Clearly, there was still tenderness. The arm had been drained, and a pin had been inserted through her middle finger, but there seemed to be little more to do besides wait.

"I wish someone would tell me what's going on here," Fong said. "PER says their records show none of the drug is missing. The clinic hasn't had the drug around since the study was stopped and they never lost any. Kate McCabe has no idea where you could have gotten some." He rewrapped Tracy's hand and, without looking away from it, said, "You wouldn't know anything about this, would you, Sam?"

"Nothing that would be of any use."

"I see." He straightened up, stared at each of them in turn, and said, "By rights, I should have nothing to do with this case. You know that, I assume. But Tracy was my patient before the study began, so I feel a deeper obligation than may be professionally called for here. I would like to know exactly how you got hold of this drug."

Tracy closed her eyes as though shutting out the discussion completely. Sam didn't blame her.

"Forgive me, Marty, but I don't see how that helps you to treat Tracy. The drug she was using didn't come from you or from Cascade-Kennedy. Tracy brought you the bottle so you could see it was the real stuff. From a medical standpoint, it's hard to see how anything else matters."

Fong said nothing. Sam watched the color drain from his face, moving down from his eyes to his cheeks to his neck. If it all collects at the bottom, he thought, the man's feet would be scarlet. Meanwhile, his face looked paler than Tracy's. Without even changing his normal expression, an angry Fong was quite scary to look at.

"Medical standpoint? I would expect you, of all people, to appreciate that there are many other standpoints to consider in any medical issue."

Sam held Fong's gaze. The look that passed between them acknowledged the impasse and reached beyond it. They'd known each other long enough now to accept that the motive was integrity rather than treachery.

"How did you do it?" Fong asked. "I would just like to know, for my own curiosity."

Sam shook his head. "I didn't." Which was, technically, true.

"I did it," Tracy said, her eyes still closed. "All right? I drove to Seattle, borrowed a helicopter, landed on PER's roof, broke into the building, found where they store the drug, figured out how to tell the drug from the placebo, stole two weeks worth of the stuff and flew home. It was easy."

"All right," Fong said. "I don't suppose I need to know the answer in order to attend to your injuries." He started to leave the room, then turned back and addressed Sam. "I really did think we were friends, you know. That we had mutual trust. At the very least, this business makes me look pretty bad around here, and within the research community at large. To say nothing of what it might mean for Tracy."

"No one outside has to know about what happened," Sam said. "Tracy already told the ombudsman, and you had nothing to do with it. She said she got the stuff through the drug underground, just like people get hold of unapproved AIDS drugs. Some chemist in the wilds of northern California duplicates the formula in his secret lab. Happens all the time, Marty. Knowing the truth about how drugs get approved in this country, I don't think anyone doubts the story."

Fong shrugged. "I do."

"I understood the risks," Tracy murmured. "What happened to my arm was just a stupid accident. Just think of it this way: if something like this happened during the study, it would have been much worse for you and the hospital and PER."

"But that's the point," Fong said, turning to go. "It wouldn't have happened during the study because the staff knows how to run a line."

"So does my husband. It was a fluke."

"All right, no need to get worked up." Fong nodded at Sam, patted Tracy again and turned to go.

"Doctor Fong?"

"What is it, Tracy?"

She opened her eyes. They seemed enormous in her sallow, shrunken face. "Please save my hand."

Fourteen

1.

Eli Moskowitz sat beside Hannah Lee Price and saw that the poor woman had declined noticeably in the last ten days. But she said that his needles helped her pain and left her mind a lot clearer than the drugs she'd been taking, so she was glad to have him back.

At first, Eli thought the hospice would resist his intrusion. But whether it was something Sam-the-Negotiating-Wizard had said, or whether they were just more enlightened than Eli had given them credit for being, they welcomed him. This was something else Eli thought he should have been doing sooner. Serve this whole new client group, bring some ease and comfort to the dying. It was good work. Eli had been elated after both visits with Hannah, and now was seeing another hospice client as well. A good sign.

When he finished inserting the needles, Eli tiptoed from Hannah's bedroom and went to wait in her kitchen, where a hospice volunteer had put out a plate of cookies and cup of Postum. Eli was always amazed to find out who volunteered for things like hospice or Meals-on-Wheels or Big Brother programs. Certainly not the stereotypical sixties liberals, refugees from the old days of service to the community, the way he expected. This woman was a painter taking time away from her studio. At the home of his other new hospice client, the volunteer was a local attorney famous for her harsh demeanor at trials and nicknamed "The Piranha."

When Sam Kiehl and Jessica Foster entered the kitchen, Eli simply nodded. Of course. Why not? Sam seemed to be everywhere these days.

"How's Hannah?" Sam asked after they joined him at the table.

Eli shook his head. "Seems like she gets some relief, anyway."

"Will she be all right for a visit after you're done?"

Eli held up his hands and shrugged. "We'll see."

After he finished his Postum and checked his watch, Eli returned to Hannah's bedside. She'd dozed, but seemed alert now, mellow, even happy.

"You have guests," he told her.

Hannah smiled. "Eli, I've lived alone all my adult life. Never did marry, never had the children I always wanted, always so busy getting ahead. Now look, I got so far ahead of where I was going, I'm about to die at forty-four. For a boring spinster, I've lived pretty fast, you know what I mean?" Eli hadn't the vaguest idea, but he nodded. "And here come all these good people into my life. Friends every day, people stopping by, I haven't been so social since I was in junior high school. What do you think about that, hmmm?"

"It's Sam Kiehl and his bride-to-be."

With that, Hannah moved her head back and cackled loudly enough for Sam and Jessica to hear. It was hardly the sort of sound they expected. They looked at each other, shrugged and moved into the room when Eli called them.

"Hey Eli," Sam said, "how come I'm never that happy when you work with me?"

"What's this?" Hannah said, smiling more fully than Sam had ever seen her smile.

Sam looked down into his hands and said, "Lobelias."

"I'm talking about this bride-to-be business Eli mentioned."

Jessica came forward and kissed Hannah, then sat beside her. "That's what we came here to tell you. Leave it to Mr. Discretion over there to spoil the surprise."

Hannah fluttered her fingers at Sam and said, "Get over here, please."

They hugged, heads gently coming together and staying together in a neat triangle in the middle of Hannah's bed. She whispered, "Dear Lord, you do something for me now, hear? You bless these two fine people and bless them well." She swallowed and the room filled with silence. Then Hannah said, "Sam, you couldn't have done one single thing to make me happier, you know that?"

"Or me either," Sam said.

"My point exactly," Hannah said.

2.

"They knew the drug was toxic over the long haul," Max said. "That's the real reason they stopped the study."

"Right. And Doctor Oswald Rowland is the real Kennedy assassin."

"Sam, I'm telling you that PER knew the drug was toxic if you guys took it too long. They wanted to collect the good efficacy data before the lousy toxicity data clicked in."

"But it doesn't make sense. The FDA wouldn't approve the study results without that."

"Of course not. But PER isn't after approval right now, they're after cash. All they wanted was favorable partial results to flash in front of prospective buyers. Then Emma Cameron tells them PER had to stop the study because they were short on money, but look at these results! It's a neat scam: they grab money from hoodwinked investors at the same time that they have a timeout to work on the toxicity problem in the lab. Six, seven months down the road, when the cash is there, they'll start a new round of studies. In the meantime, they go to a lot of medical conferences and publish glorious preliminary findings. Puts pressure on the Feds to let them have another round of studies, gets grassroots support from sickies who've heard the drug works wonders, and leaves only a few pissed-off former guinea pigs to placate. Hell, they could even offer to re-enroll you all in round two."

"You figured this out using sophisticated economic analyses?"

"A guy I know works for the National Institutes of Health in D.C. I ran it by him, just as a hypothetical, no names mentioned. But I didn't need to because it's the only thing that makes sense."

Sam nodded. "You think the doctors at each of the sites realized what was going on?"

"Unless they were too busy or too preoccupied, they ought to at least have a glimmer. Companies do fiscal year projections. I don't think this was a big surprise for them. Somewhere along the line, you'd think the docs had to know."

"That really scares me. I put my life in these people's hands." Sam looked around. "Turn left here."

"Nice neighborhood. Where does she live, on Runway Four?"

"It's a little close to the airport. She says the kids love to sit on the roof and watch the jets land."

"Must be quite restful for her." Max turned into the driveway and pulled as close to Tracy's car as he could. Then he opened his door, leaning out to see if he'd left enough room behind his car for pedestrians to pass by on the sidewalk. "I think a kid could squeeze through. A skinny one."

Tracy was waiting for them in the doorway of her house. She stood half-hidden by the frame, so they couldn't see her arm from the driveway.

"Well," she said, "if it isn't the other half of Idiots at Large."

"Nice to see you too, Wonderwoman," Max said.

"Come on in, guys. I'm letting out all the heat."

They followed her inside. Max handed Tracy a small bouquet of flowers wrapped in newspaper, which he'd hidden behind his back as they approached the house. She looked shocked, holding them away from her body and staring as though she expected them to blow up.

"What are these?"

"Flowers, I think."

She brought them toward her nose and sniffed loudly. "But what kind, freesias? No, wait a minute, I think they're orchards."

"They're get-well flowers. That's all I know. I explained to the woman at the shop about my poor sick friend, and she picked them out."

"Should I put them in water?"

"Only if you want them to live."

Sam had never seen Tracy's house before. She would always come to pick him up at home, since he lived so close to Cascade-Kennedy and didn't drive, and she'd never invited him to her home. As he stood near them listening to her conversation with Max, he thought she must have spent the whole morning tidying up. There were signs that children lived there—a cardboard liquor carton teeming with toys, a shelf stacked haphazardly with children's books, a sawed-off round table with three little chairs placed before a television where they probably ate dinner, a lineup of small galoshes by the front door and parkas on hooks—but not the chaos Sam expected. A chaise longue took up one corner of the living room, with a direct line of sight to the television and a cart on wheels beside it for an endtable.

It was clear that Tracy still could not use her right arm properly. Holding it at a strange angle in front of her pelvis and keeping the fingers curled like a claw, she resembled a cocktail party guest gripping a highball. She led them to a reconditioned sofa and went into the kitchen to find something for the flowers and to prepare tea.

"How's the arm?" Max called after her.

"Fifty percent. The physical therapy really helps, though. They think it can be back to seventy, seventy-five percent in another couple months."

Sam knew that she was lucky not to have lost the arm altogether. The first couple of days were touch-and-go. Then for a week, there had been serious doubt about saving the hand. But she'd healed dramatically. Fong thought her healing might, ironically, have something to do with her hyperactive immune system. So she was fortunate that the course of stolen drugs hadn't fully cured her of the illness when the accident occurred, or else she might have suffered greater damage.

Tracy returned with the flowers arranged in a quart-sized canning jar half filled with water. She put it on the dining room table and went back into the kitchen for the tray of tea. Gripping one end in her left hand and balancing the other end on her right, she knelt to let the tray down onto the table without a clatter. Using her injured hand, she carefully unloaded the pot, mugs, sugar, milk, plate of cookies, and napkins before stashing the tray under the table.

Sam poured tea for each of them in turn. With the appearance of cookies, an ancient cocker spaniel sauntered into the room from its quarters somewhere in the back of the house. Visitors didn't interest him, but food certainly did. He walked in obvious discomfort and with a peculiar gait, pausing as though shifting gears between each step.

"Get out of here, Clutch!" Tracy said.

Without stopping or looking around, the dog simply executed a slow semicircular turn and headed out of the room. They listened to his joints clacking as he made his way back where he came from.

"Has he always been like that?" Max asked.

"Has who been like what?"

"The dog, Tracy. Has he always walked funny or is that some kind of adaptation to an injury?"

"Both."

Max nodded. "I see."

"So," Sam asked after he saw Max fold his arms, "have you given any thought to Jessica's proposal?"

"Oh, that was incredibly sweet of her. I talked to the therapist yesterday, and he thinks I can do it. So does Doctor Fong. Who by the way isn't angry at us at all. He keeps asking how you're doing, when he's going to see you, are you taking good care of yourself. He also said he didn't know I could fly a helicopter. Oh, you know what, he told me the medical school is going to try another drug study. Can you believe that? You'd think they'd learned their lesson. It'll be a different drug, of course. That stuff veterinarians use on horses, and football players use it when their pitching arms get sore. It's made out of initials. You don't happen to know what's it called, do you? If I don't think of it, I'll go absolutely nuts by this afternoon."

"DMSO."

"That's it! He calls it Dimso. I thought that was some kind of Chinese food. Hey, wait, that's probably why he likes it so much, you know? Anyway, what he said was it finds these radicals floating around inside us and eats them for free or something. It was real cute, what he did when he was explaining it. He made his hand look like a mouth the way Shari Lewis does with Lamb Chop, and he went *Chomp chomp*. He must think I'm six years old."

"Yeah, I heard all about what they're doing with DMSO. The stuff's amazing. Approved for use in a hundred other countries, treats all kinds of diseases, helps with pain, but of course it's not approved in the U.S. I'll tell you something: I don't want anything to do with another drug study, that's for sure. Let them get it all approved and ready for sale, prove that it helps and that it's safe, then I'll try it. Maybe. No more experiments, at least not in this country."

"Good for you," Tracy said. "I spoke to Alice and Laurel and most of the others. The only one who's not going to sign up for sure so far is Laurel."

"I wish them the best. It's hard not to say yes to whatever the docs bring along."

Tracy dipped a chocolate chip cookie into her tea and took a bite. "Anyway, back to what we were talking about before: No, I haven't thought about it, not really. But I will soon."

Sam nodded. "All right. There's no rush. It wouldn't start till April anyway, and you obviously have to learn some more about flowers first."

"I remember these kinds of conversations between the two of you," Max said. "They're even starting to make some sense to me."

"Sorry," Sam said. "Jessica wants Tracy to help run her old nursery after she moves over to the new one. Half-time at first, then full-time if she likes the work."

"If I can handle the work, you mean."

"I don't think that's what Jessica means. She's sure you'll be able to do it. But she says it's not to everyone's taste. Working with customers, taking care of all the plants and flowers and trees, moving stuff around. It can be hot, dirty work."

"She said she'd leave me the parrots, though. Isn't that nice of her? Give me someone to talk to all day. I guess she knows what a chatterbox I am."

"Wait a minute," Max said. "Let's go back a step or two here. Last I heard, you were going to be a mail carrier. Don't tell me the hand makes you ineligible. They can't do that."

"Nah, but I changed my mind in the last month. Being at home, working so hard to get my hand and arm back, I figured something out. I want to work with people, sure, but I don't want to be putting my body through what a postal carrier has to go through. I mean, I'd be too tired to play racquetball after walking the streets all day, you know? And what I really want to do when my hand heals is win the Class A tournament at the Y and see if I can go to Nationals. Besides, postal carriers bring too much bad news. I just want to help things grow."

"Of course," Max said. "Nothing could be clearer. It's just too bad you wasted all that time and money on the study guide."

"Actually, it turned out great. Wally started helping me, then when I got hurt he decided to take the test himself and become a mailman. The next one is offered at the downtown Post Office in two weeks. Isn't that something? I think he's finally found a job he'll like. He's going to ace the test. Does all these number-word association tricks, sweeps his eyes across a row of numbers like a robot. He'll probably score a hundred percent and become a Four-Star General Postmaster."

3.

Sam was surprised at how glad it made him feel to take the bus again. It was the first time in a month that he'd felt well enough to travel by himself to Jessica's nursery and spend the night with her at the farmhouse. He liked being with her there, in the silence and isolation of the country, and he slept much more soundly.

She was waiting for him outside the locked front door of the nursery with a sheaf of papers in her hand. As soon as Sam got off the bus, she started walking toward him with a huge smile on her face. He felt the impulse to run toward her with his arms outstretched. It would be like the climax of a 1940s movie, the music soaring as they spun in one another's arms, the camera coming close as their lips met.

"What?" Sam said after they had kissed. "What is it?"

She took his arm and started walking. "Do you get carsick?"

"Once I did. It was on this insanely curving road through the mountains outside of Saratoga, California, and Vic was driving. Why?"

"I want you to read this while I drive us home." She handed him the papers. "But I don't necessarily want you to throw up."

"I'm supposed to read a stack of pink summer sale flyers?"

"Turn them over, Sam. I recycle them for personal use instead of tossing them out."

"'Deep Cleaning for Maximum Health'? What's going on here, you want me to vacuum your house?"

"Be serious. Over lunch, I spent some time online, just doodling around. I downloaded some articles for you."

"I really knocked you off the wagon when I got you involved in the PER caper, didn't I?"

"I found this place where they post all kinds of material about your illness. Research, supplements for sale, support group, a chat room. There was all this literature about alternative medical practice, just the kind of thing I was into when I went to massage school and had my own practice. I think there's something here for you. I just don't know why I didn't think of it myself. They're getting unbelievable results."

"I'm already maxed-out on acupuncture, vitamins, and herbs with Eli."

"This is something different. Just don't laugh at it till you've finished reading all the testimonials, OK? I think it may really help. And not just you. I'd go along and try it too. Support you and get myself ready for the new beginning."

Sam turned to study her face. "What new beginning?"

Jessica chuckled. "I'm opening a nursery, remember?"

After they got into Jessica's car, Sam started leafing through the material she'd downloaded. He couldn't help laughing.

"Hey, I said don't laugh."

"Sorry. I just can't believe this. Panchakarma. Eli was talking about it last time I saw him. He said I'd eventually beg him to let me try it."

"You know about it?"

"Not much. Only that it seems to involve a lot of things I don't think I can handle."

"Like what?"

"Heat. They use hot oils and steam baths. The way my thermostat works these days, I'm afraid it would kill me. And they have you drink clarified butter, which I think someone with my cholesterol problems should probably not do. Plus enemas. I have a thing about enemas."

"You work with these people. If you can't tolerate the level of heat, they adjust it. A little butter for a week isn't going to kill you. And I'll explain how you can change the way you think about enemas. Just read. We'll talk later."

Sam read in silence until they reached Jessica's place. He was delighted to be back there, to see the things she had collected, to smell the essence of her home. Except there was a new smell, garlicky but mild. As he turned to embrace her, Jessica smiled and said, "Vegetable stew in a crockpot. I bought fresh bread too, and made fennel salad this morning, so there's nothing we need to do. Dinner's ready when we are."

"I didn't know you were so domestic."

"I'm not domestic, and don't you forget it. But I thought we might have other things to do besides cook. It's been a long time since we were here."

Sam liked making love with Jessica on her bed, which was narrower and softer than his, and had twice as many pillows. She told him that in the summer they could move the bed outside to sleep, that he would not believe how many stars were visible in the country, and that as long as he didn't mind deer and bats and skunks he would sleep like a baby. He found himself looking forward to that, imagining them together come summer and beyond.

Over dinner, Jessica seemed pensive. She sat across from him and didn't eat with her usual relish.

"What's wrong?"

She swirled a chunk of bread through her stew and looked away from him. "I know what you've been thinking, Sam."

"Of course. I expected that. Does what I'm thinking bother you?"

"It's just that I couldn't really consider living in the city, no matter how much I wanted to be with you. Just being there so much during the last month convinced me of that."

"Then you need re-tuning."

"I don't like the sound of that."

"All I meant was that your clairvoyance is a little off tonight. You missed that I was thinking about how good it would be to live out here."

"You were?"

He nodded. "I think it would be very healing."

"I thought you didn't want to spend more than a night here."

"You're kidding me."

"Actually, I am. You're getting very good at this." She reached across the table for his hand. "You'd really think about coming out here for good?"

"I have, Jessica. And for good. For very good. It's time to get out of the city and it's time to be with you. Feels to me like the right next step."

She closed her eyes, keeping hold of Sam's hands, and took a very long, deep breath. Then she lifted their joined hands to her lips. When she spoke, her voice had deepened to the husky contralto that he loved to hear.

"It never stops, you know."

Sam leaned over and kissed her. "I know."

"I mean the healing. Which I believe is really the search for balance. You don't have to be sick to go after it, Sam, everyone does. Everyone has to, sooner or later, and then never stop. I've loved watching you accept that in yourself."

"You know something? I actually understood what you just said."

"I know you did."

"So you want to think about it?"

"No, Sam. I already have."

"And?"

"If you think there's room here for your awful kitchen table, you're nuts."

4.

"That wasn't so bad, was it?" Jessica asked.

"Oh, no. I'm just sitting here with my hair still slathered in oil and sticking out in seven different directions, my gizzards feel poached, I would pay some serious money to be able to sneeze, and I'm wearing a diaper. Otherwise, it's not so bad."

"Sam, you have to surrender to it if the treatments are going to do any good."

"I surrender, believe me. Just like I did after we took the castor oil last week. No holding back for this dude."

"Well, I feel wonderful. I haven't been this relaxed since my last Finnish sauna. This is great."

It was their last night in Sam's house. Tomorrow, while they were undergoing their final Panchakarma treatment, Max would be spending the day coordinating the movers who would pack up Sam's few remaining goods, load them onto their truck, follow Max out to Jessica's place, and unload them according to the precise instructions she'd left behind. She'd gone over them with Max in such exhaustive detail that he thought another helicopter raid might be simpler. When Sam and Jessica returned from tomorrow's treatment, the move would be complete and Max would even be sitting at the table with a tofu stir-fry to celebrate the occasion. At least that was the theory.

For this final night, there was literally nothing left for Sam and Jessica to do but relax. They had been through four full days of Panchakarma's routine together, four days which had followed a full week of special diet and one memorable day of purgation. Jessica had taken the week off work, letting her brother run the nursery and get used to Tracy, and she was planning to take the next week off as well.

Sam felt softened and emptied by what they were going through at the Panchakarma clinic. He hoped that what was being flushed out of him were indeed the toxins and not his vital energy, because he felt utterly exhausted. This was, as he knew Eli would say, a good sign. Because it was a new kind of exhaustion, nothing like the way his illness made him feel. It was more like the aftermath of a hard ascent on a rough rock or a fast 10K race, the exhaustion of good use.

The Panchakarma massages were nothing like Jessica's massages. Two people worked on him at once, and they didn't knead or probe his muscles. Instead, they set up a rocking motion, moving their hands in coordinated circles to emulate a series of waves meant to loosen whatever was clinging to his insides and channel them toward what they called his Openings of Elimination. Later, as he lay back with his head over the table edge, they dripped hot oil on the middle of his forehead for a long time and collected it as it ran back through his hair. The steady stream was mesmerizing, both soothing and intense. Next came a portable steam bath, a plastic chamber they wrapped around his body and regulated carefully to accommodate his level of heat tolerance. This was meant to help him expel some of the loosened impurities through his flesh, and to relax him further. When the steam bath was done, they had to hoist him from the table like a cadaver, but they were very nice about it. After a period of rest, he was given an enema, then permitted to race through the hallway for the bathroom.

Jessica had been correct. The healing process doesn't stop, even if the vision of a cure remains indistinct. He was on a path, had been for two years, with the drug study as one loop with its own particular terrain and views to explore, Panchakarma as another loop, and surely other loops would soon appear. The point was that he was now on the path with Jessica. She filled him with confidence about the journey.

Jessica shifted her feet so that she and Sam were lying joined like pieces of a jigsaw puzzle on the living room's only cleared surface, his recliner. Their plastic diapers crackled as they moved.

"I realized something today," she said. "Besides its healing powers, what we're doing is like some kind of ancient prenuptial cleansing ritual. Our pasts, our impurities, everything washed away so we can come together fresh."

Sam nuzzled her neck, putting his lips in the exact spot where her pulse beat. His words were lost.

"I couldn't hear you," Jessica said. "But I'd be glad to wait till you were through with the kissing if you want."

"I said I'm lucky they don't require a blood sacrifice too."

"Oh, Sam," Jessica shifted back a few inches to get a better view of his face. "Didn't I tell you about tomorrow?"

Epilogue

It seemed to take forever to get there. By the time Sam and Jessica landed at the airport near Milan, rode the bus to Milano Centrale and the train to Genoa, they had already been traveling for eighteen hours. To reach Monterosso, the small village at the beginning of the Cinque Terre where they'd planned to spend the next three nights, they still had to take another train along the rugged Riviera coast. Sam didn't know if he could make it.

When the first train pulled in, the announcements were all in Italian and delivered too quickly to be distinguished as separate words. The train was pointed in the right direction, though, southeast, so they decided to hop on.

Only Jessica made it. Sam's crammed backpack got caught in the door as it closed, and he couldn't move. He waved his arms, hoping to somehow slip out of the straps, but realized he was helpless.

"I've got a problem," he said in a voice far calmer than he felt.

Two teenaged boys sitting near the door began to laugh and point. Jessica turned, saw Sam's predicament and grabbed his shoulders, trying to pull him into the car. The boys came over and tried to pry the doors apart as the train began moving out of the station, toward the tunnel ahead.

"Maybe this releases the door," Jessica said. She reached for a lever beside the door and pulled. Nothing happened. She yanked it down a few more times, then joined the boys in trying to part the doors. The three of them managed to create enough of a gap for Sam's backpack to pop through and he stumbled inside the car.

They heard the conductor screaming well before he appeared in the space between cars. His arms were flailing in the same way that Sam's had, and for a moment Sam wondered if the conductor, too, was stuck. Then he stomped over to them and began to shriek, his tobacco-stained mouth a blur as the words poured out. He kept pantomiming the pulling of the lever and shaking his head so vigorously that saliva began to fly. It sounded as though he was asking questions, but there was no space provided to insert answers. Not that it would have mattered. Sam leafed through his pocket dictionary, looking for the word for 'sorry.'

"*Mi scusi*," he said. It had no effect.

Throughout the conductor's tirade, Jessica kept repeating the same question in English. "Signore, is this the train to Monterosso?" It wasn't comforting that the man didn't seem to recognize the name. Jessica would wait fifteen seconds, nod and try again.

The conductor left the car, only to return when he'd calmed a bit, still trying to impress on them the gravity of their mistake in pulling the lever. He never seemed to hear Jessica's question about Monterosso.

After the train stopped at Nervi, Bogliascco and Sori, Sam and Jessica realized they'd gotten on a local rather than an express. It could take another hour or more to reach their destination and begin looking for accommodations. Jessica got out her map and guidebook. The next large town, just past the Portofino promontory, would be Rapallo.

"This is truly amazing," Jessica said, looking up from the book. "I always dreamed of spending my honeymoon in Rapallo, and it turns out that Rapallo is practically the next stop on this train. Now isn't that something?"

"Must be destiny," Sam said. He was glad for an excuse to stop trying to figure out how much their millions of lire were worth in dollars. Even if his brain worked right, he wasn't sure he could manage that. "I think we'd be fools not to make your dream come true."

They were struggling into their backpacks as the train pulled into the station. One of the teenaged boys gave Sam a hand with his, then winked at Jessica.

"Why don't you give this lever one last pull before we get off?" Sam asked as the door opened.

"Why don't you just concentrate on getting all the way off this time?"

It's never quiet in Rapallo, Italy. They descended from the station into a mist of noise and turned away from the steep rise of hills behind the town. They thought it would be nicer, and perhaps quieter, to walk straight to the sea. But it was difficult to tell which way to go because the streets all seemed to curve back on themselves.

Jessica stopped a gentleman waiting for a bus and pointed to the left, away from the hills. "The sea?" she asked.

He nodded vigorously.

She turned to Sam and said, "Do you think he understands me?"

Sam pointed behind the man, in the opposite direction. "The sea?"

He nodded again. So he had no idea what they were talking about.

"The water?" she asked, raising her voice slightly. "Could you tell us which way it is?"

"*Si.*" He waved his arms in a slow circle and smiled at them.

Jessica moved her hands like the surf and made a sound like breakers. The man's eyes suddenly widened.

"Ahhh," he said. "*Mare.*" He pointed to the right. "*Si. Il mare.*"

They headed in that direction, walking slowly, shifting their packs after every few steps. Sam's hips were sharply painful whenever he moved, but they hurt worse when he sat, so they kept walking. Unmuffled mopeds raced through the streets. Car horns honked and express trains roared by at insanely frequent intervals. It was impossible to hear *il mare* until they stood at its edge and cupped their ears.

"Is this the way it looked in your dreams?" Sam asked.

"Close enough. I don't remember it sounding quite like this, though. But in my dreams I was in a nice, though cheap, room with a view of the gulf."

At a tourist office, Sam asked the official to recommend a quiet hotel, *un albergo quieto* according to the phrasing he'd assembled from his Berlitz guide. The man simply laughed.

After finding accommodations overlooking a canal not far from the harbor, they unpacked, showered, flopped across the bed and were instantly asleep. Sam dreamt about eating pasta cooked in squid ink, a dish he'd read about in their guide book and wanted to taste. The trouble was, with each bite his nose was transforming into a squid's beak and his hands were branching into tentacles.

When they woke, it was getting dark and, if anything, there seemed to be more mopeds on the street. Sam sat at the desk with a pen and hotel stationery trying to calculate what time it was in Oregon while Jessica did some stretching exercises to loosen up her shoulder and back muscles. The constant snarl outside was making it difficult for her to relax.

"So what time is it?" Jessica asked from the floor.

He crumbled the paper. "According to my calculations, it's time to eat."

Without their packs, they felt able to walk again. Along the Via Mazzini, they passed a sixth-century cathedral and a leper house whose walls were covered in medieval frescoes, then looped back toward the beach. Whenever they passed a restaurant, they studied the menu posted outside, Sam flipping through his dictionary trying to decipher the offerings and Jessica using her currency converter to estimate prices. On one of the side streets, they saw a men's shop with a corner of its window display entirely devoted to hand-carved canes.

"Oh, Sam, we have to go inside."

"I am hungry enough to try one as an appetizer. That black one looks well-done."

Inside, the shop smelled mostly of leather and oil. There were no customers, but two ancient proprietors stood behind the counters murmuring to each other.

"*Buono sera,*" the one closest to them said.

Jessica smiled. Sam whipped out his dictionary again and turned to the section on greetings and introductions. "*Bene.*" Then he flipped another page and, trying not to sound desperate, said "*Parla Inglese?*"

The proprietors both shook their heads. "*Mi dispiace,*" the first one said.

Sam turned some more pages, but the book was organized only from English to Italian. He knew Jessica would have loved for him to lose the thing altogether, but having it on hand gave him a kind of hope. He put the book away and hefted his old cane, nicked and peeling all along its shaft, with its twice-broken handle shiny from the oils of his palm. He pointed to it, then to the canes stacked in an umbrella stand beside a swim-suited mannequin.

Everybody smiled and assembled in front of the umbrella stand. The proprietor removed a cane similar to the one Sam was using, very dark brown, thick and untapered from handle to tip. Jessica shook her head and reached for another one, her hand finding it at the same moment as Sam's.

"It's beautiful," she said.

"I know. And long enough for me to use when I go back to pole vaulting."

"Look at how this polished knob fits your hand. Oh, Sam, it's so elegant."

"And gnarled as my legs. I love it."

"We should get it. Something to mark the new phase of your healing process."

"It ought to help more than a year's worth of the placebo ever did."

"*Quanto?*" Jessica asked the proprietor. It was the fourth Italian word she'd wanted to learn, after *Prego, Presto* and *Pronto.*

The price was acceptable. Sam wanted to ask what kind of wood it was made of and started to reach for his dictionary. Then he looked at Jessica, smiled and turned to face the proprietor. He raised his eyebrows, cocked his head, lifted the cane and pointed at it. "WHAT?"

The proprietors looked at one another. They shrugged and the first man gave a slightly lowered price.

"Very good, Sam."

Sam reached for the proprietor's hand. The man took it and began to shake with him, but Sam tugged gently and led him to the doorway. He pointed outside at a tree, then at the cane again, back and forth with his eyebrows raised until the man smiled.

"Ahhh," he said. "Hazel."

Then Sam held the new cane next to his old one to demonstrate that he wanted it cut to size. The second proprietor seemed to be in charge of this part. He took the two canes and disappeared behind a curtain. They could hear him sawing.

When Sam and Jessica left the store, they agreed to try the restaurant they had found earlier, on the block overlooking the water. She carried his old cane. As Sam walked along the sidewalk, Jessica tried to match his gait, using the cane, gimping beside him, swinging her free arm the same way Sam swung his. Their laughter filled the narrow street, making the crowd of tourists and shopkeepers stare at them, then join in as they headed toward the sea.

Patient 002